Mystillion

Redsands Book 1

By
IA Mullin

Mystillion—Redsands Book 1—by I.A. Mullin

Published by Avio Publishing, LLC
PO Box 293, Eaton CO 80615

Edited by Mark Graham of Mark Graham Communications, Denver Colorado.
Proofread and cover design by Deanna Estes of Lotus Design, Fort Collins Colorado.
Cover illustration by Kathy Bornhoft.

ISBN-13 978-1-946023-00-1 paperback
ISBN-13 978-1-946023-01-8 kindle
ISBN-13 978-1-946023-02-5 ebook

Check out magewood.com or @authorIAMullin on facebook for new releases and additional content from IA Mullin.

Mystillion is dedicated to all those individuals who have inspired me over the years. Whether you knew it or not.
Thank you.

Contents

Redsands

CASHAINS
TANZAMELL
PRICINLIA
Castant Estates
Clain Estates
King Carloth's Castle
COANDOR
LENTIER
Draukshar
Abdshar
Reine's Crossing
Eastridge
Lotal Estates
Camp
Kenhol Estates
Mira's Plateau
Maefair
Glancenar
The Beach
Pandensy
Quway Estates
Ruberic Estates
Versith
Inclond Estates
Roana Estates
Herinsford
Pavlatach
Doquib Estates
Bram's Fen
Flaznek Estates
West Cove
Grudent
Arndt Estates
Mystillion
Ranat Estates
Map of Redsands
Kingdom Border
Province Border
Main Road
Secondary Road
Path
Western Sea
Southern Tip
Turmult Gulf
N
0
100
miles
Bandit Camp
GREAT MOUNTAINS

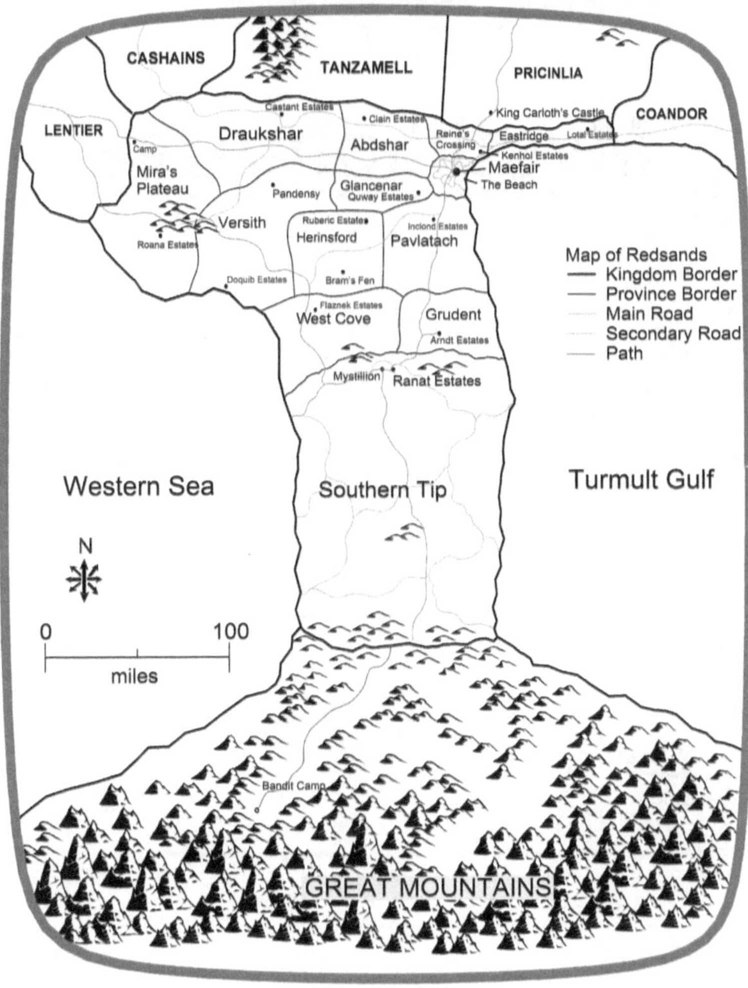

Mystillion Area

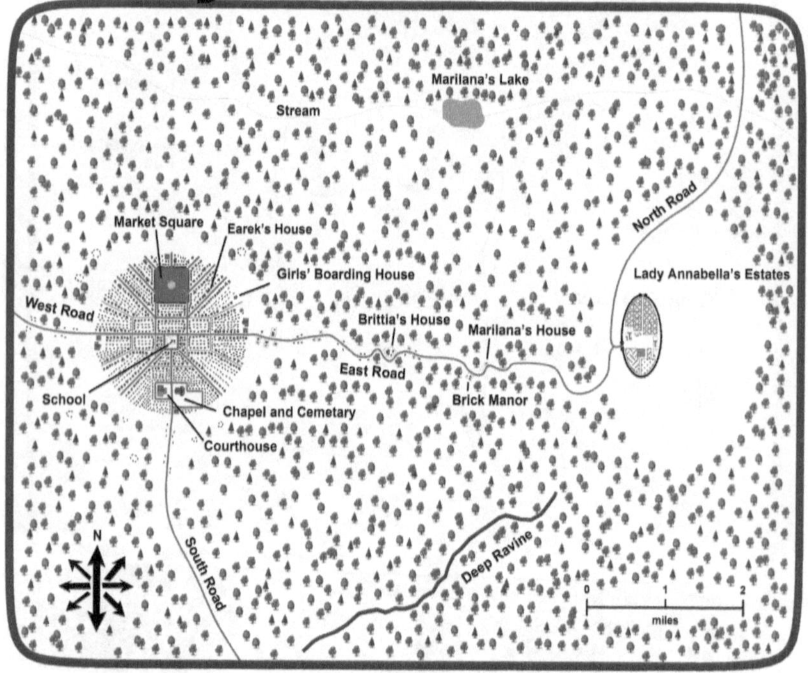

Lady Annabella's Estates

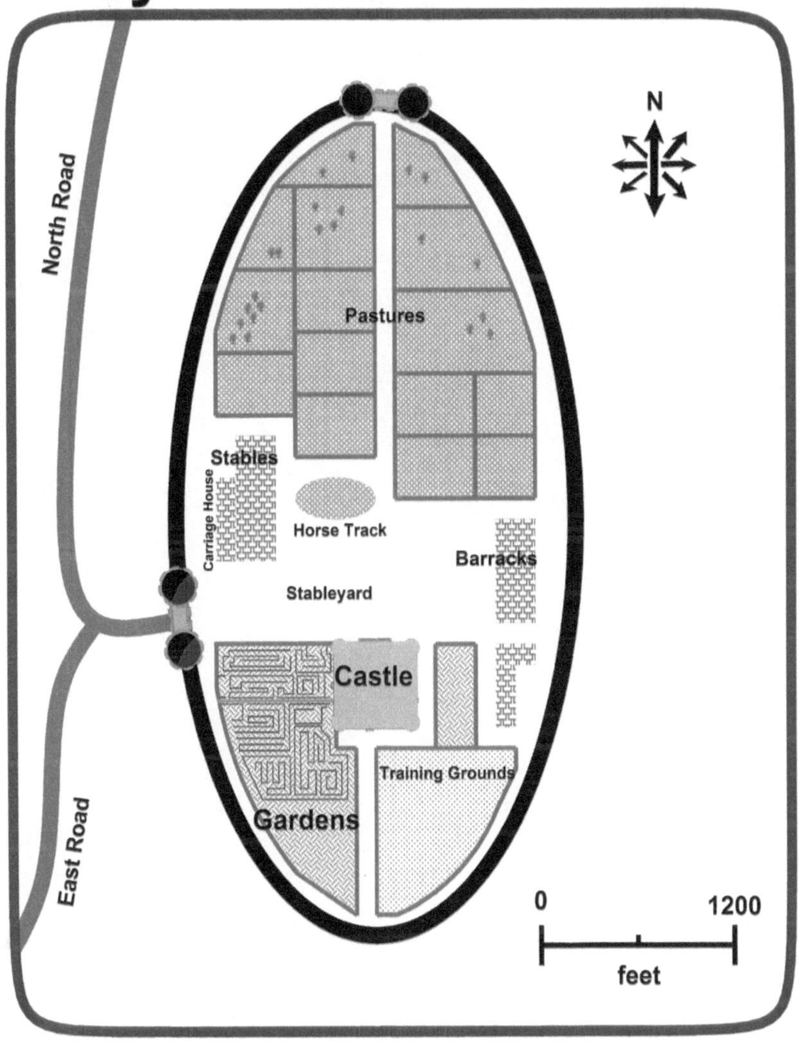

1

"When the world was young, the land that we live on changed suddenly," Mistress Rose told her class. "The temperature dropped, snow covered everything, and storms raged. It was a difficult time with little food. The birds flew away. The reptiles and amphibians froze. Many of the mammals also perished in the harsh conditions. It is theorized that individual animals, lost and weak, found their way into the sea caves along the coasts. There they huddled together for warmth, carnivores and herbivores both, and began to coexist in the same shelter. The lions are believed to have started adopting the other animals into their prides, protecting the herbivores and gathering food for all. The mixed prides began to flourish and adapt. They learned to use tools and build structures. They developed a common language. As time went on, the climate began to warm again and the animals learned to cultivate food. They developed the ability to draw pictures, some of which have been found on the sea cave walls. Their use of tools evolved as their bodies evolved. Their culture became more sophisticated and developed into a civilization.

"At some point, it is thought that two lands collided, and the collision pushed up the Great Mountains of the south," continued the slender horse teacher.

"Not that the land can actually move," scoffed Brittia just loud enough to be heard by those around her.

The girls and boys snickered behind their paws and hooves. Marilana, sitting several rows behind Brittia, pretended not to have heard. She continued to stare out the window, wishing she were out in the forest hunting bandits, and hearing just enough of Mistress Rose's lecture to answer any question her teacher might throw at her.

"Slowly, animals began to cross the mountains. These new animals had not adapted like our ancestors. Our ancestors termed them 'Wild' animals and termed their own adapted culture the 'Ruling' animals. Like we see today, there were physical differences between the Ruling and Wild animals. For example, the Ruling animals were closer in stature to each other. The larger animals, like horses and bears, were smaller than their Wild counterparts, and the smaller animals, like lynx and weasels, were larger. The Ruling animals' diets were no longer divided as carnivore and herbivore. All were omnivores. The Ruling animals lived many years longer and did not walk on all four feet. They stood upright on their hind legs and had developed fore-paws or fore-hooves that could use tools effectively.

"But the biggest differences between the Ruling and Wild animals were their culture and their habits. Just as we do today, our ancestors farmed and cooked food, wore clothing, built buildings, created art, and had both written and oral language. The Ruling animals tried to teach the Wild animals their culture and language, but the Wild animals' brains had not evolved like the Ruling animals' and they could not change their nature so quickly. The Ruling animals, instead, developed ways to tame and use some of the Wild animals. For example, just like today, they used Wild horses to ride or harness, Wild cattle and goats were milked to make dairy products, and Wild sheep were raised for wool.

"The climate continued to change over the centuries. The snow and ice continued to recede toward the north and south. The prides were no longer constrained to the coasts and expanded inland. Our own kingdom, Redsands, was formed as part of Great Queen Maebala's empire and was inherited by her youngest son. His descendants, including our own beloved King Rylan, have ruled over our ancestors ever since. The Redsands capital of Maefair was Queen Maebala's own palace and capital."

Mistress Rose paused. Marilana caught her teacher's scowl from the corner of her eye, but continued to watch a merchant wagon and guards rumble past beyond the schoolyard fence.

"For all of you who are listening, the topography of our kingdom allowed our ancestors to thrive. Redsands is an isthmus bound east and west mostly by ocean, and south by the Great Mountains. The north, northern east, and northern west borders are shared by five other kingdoms and are well defended. We live in the Southern Tip, the southernmost province of Redsands and the only one to border the Wild lands of the Great Mountains and beyond."

She moved among her students, making eye contact: a leopard in one row, a stag in another; a gazelle in yet another. She said, "Now this is important, class. Because of the Great Mountains, the Southern Tip experiences mild summers and cold snowy winters. If someone were to travel north, they would notice that the climate remains mild along the coasts and that the Northern provinces experience hot humid summers and mild winters. The economy of Redsands is as diverse as its climate. Here in the Southern Tip, we depend on revenue from crop and livestock farming, timber, mining, and crafts resulting from those resources. Each county of the Southern Tip has specialized production according to the topography and weather patterns of the area. Here in Mystillion county we rely mostly on the craftsmen residing in the town of the same name. Over the next few fifnights we will study the production of each county and discuss how that production influences the hierarchy of power in the Southern Tip.

"Marilana!" snapped Mistress Rose suddenly. "Describe the hierarchy of power as it stands currently in the Southern Tip."

Marilana broke her gaze from the windows and calmly looked to the slender horse standing at the front of the classroom. Many of the other students snickered behind their paws. Brittia turned a triumphant sneer on Marilana.

"Yes, Mistress." Marilana cleared her throat.

"A general caste hierarchy is as follows: peasant, low-class merchant, mid-class merchant, high-class merchant, landed-gentry, noble, high-noble, great-noble, royal. For example," Marilana recited flatly. "The peasant farmer raises sheep to produce wool. The wool is traded to a low-class merchant spinster who spins the wool into thread. The thread is traded to a mid-class merchant weaver who weaves the thread into cloth. The cloth is then traded to a high-class textile merchant who buys and sells the cloth with other merchants, such as the tailor for making clothing.

"We live in the county and town of Mystillion, adjacent to the estates of Lady Annabella Ranat, Great Lady of the Southern Tip, who rules over us directly and all the Southern Tip in the name of King Rylan Mercurer of Redsands, descendant of Great Queen Maebala. Lady Annabella receives a portion of the sale at each step of the economic chain as tax. In return, she protects us and enforces the laws by which we live. King Rylan likewise receives a tax from Lady Annabella and so the work of a simple peasant influences the whole hierarchy of power all the way to the royalty."

"Thank you, Marilana, for that more than adequate response," acknowledged Mistress Rose. "And since you have spent most of the morning daydreaming, you will remain after class to discuss your punishment."

"Yes, Mistress Rose," Marilana sighed.

Brittia gloated at Marilana before turning back to face the front of the class. Marilana glared at the back of Brittia's head. She would have loved to give Brittia a piece of her mind, but that would have gotten her into even more trouble and made no difference. Brittia was the petite lynx daughter of the richest high-class merchant in Mystillion and niece of the school's headmistress. She was a snob. Her father headed the Merchant Council of Mystillion, the highest rank in the county under Lady Annabella. The other counties all had their ranks of nobles, but Mystillion was Lady Annabella's domain. Brittia used her father's position and power to whatever advantage she could. She outranked every other student in the school and loved to order everyone around. If she did not get her way, she ran to her aunt, and no one liked to be summoned to the headmistress' office.

Marilana sighed, reminding herself that Headmistress Ceta would cane her for affronting her betters. The orphaned lion daughter of peasant scholars was the lowest of peasants. Her parents had left her as a small child to pursue their studies beyond the southern border. The Wild lands beyond the border were dangerous, populated by bandits and outlaws, and her parents had not wanted to risk her life. Instead, they requested Lady Annabella act as her warden. Everyone assumed her parents had died in the south. Growing up in service to Lady Annabella was a blessing in disguise. It had been hard learning to do whatever chores were called for in the castle and the stables. The servants treated her well, and everyone helped to raise her. Yet she was not one of them. She was Lady Annabella's ward. A peasant with no real family or rank. She was different.

She had lived in Lady Annabella's castle until she had proven she could provide for herself and continue to fulfill her responsibilities. She now lived in her parents' former home alone. Her responsibilities were no burden. Marilana had continued to serve as one of Lady Annabella's servants and Lady Annabella directed her to complete additional studies outside of school so that she would reflect honorably on Lady Annabella's reputation. Marilana loved learning and enjoyed the extra studies. She was happy with her place as Lady Annabella's ward and did not seek any special treatment or favors.

Marilana had learned quickly that Lady Annabella ruled alone. Lady Annabella had never married and had no children. Someday soon she would have to choose her successor from the youths of the Southern Tip. Few of the Southern Tip nobles had children eligible to inherit Lady Annabella's title. Most had already come of age and inherited their own family names and titles. The rest were too young. The county of Mystillion had no nobles other than Lady Annabella, and the merchants all worked closely with the Lady's estates. It had long been suspected that Lady Annabella would choose one of the youths of Mystillion to become her heir. Brittia, of course, expected to be chosen since she was the highest-ranking youth in Mystillion and viewed everyone else as a mere obstacle to gaining her nobility.

It was no surprise therefore that the personal attention afforded to Marilana greatly angered Brittia. She did everything she could to humiliate and harass Marilana, and the headmistress willingly aided Brittia's efforts. Brittia was officially ranked at the top of the class, even though Marilana had beaten her on every grade. The headmistress simply had Marilana's grades stricken from the school record stating that it should teach Marilana some humility, after all peasants should not strive to be better than merchants. Brittia also had a spotless behavior record while Marilana was called to the headmistress' office at least twice a fifnight, usually for trumped up offences. As most of the students fawned over Brittia, praising her lavishly, they in turn avoided Marilana. Only the other peasants showed Marilana any friendship, and Brittia couldn't have cared less about them.

Marilana shook her thoughts free of the gloomy ruminations of her life as a knock sounded on the classroom door. A shadow moved on the other side of the frosted glass. A moment later, the headmistress entered. A young lion dressed in blue pants and a green shirt cut in high-class merchant style followed.

"Students, this is Marquiese," announced Headmistress Ceta politely. "His family has just moved into Mystillion and he will be joining your class. Please make him feel welcome."

Marilana was surprised by the courtesy the headmistress had shown. This new merchant must rank high for Ceta to be so polite. Very few lions lived in the Southern Tip. Marilana had been the only one in the school for several years. She watched Marquiese scan the room, analyzing each student in turn. She thought she saw intelligence in his eyes when he looked at her. He stood at his ease, almost like Lady Annabella's soldiers did when off duty, confident and ready. Yet this one seemed somehow more dangerous. She narrowed her eyes suspiciously when he hesitated slightly before putting his left paw casually in his pocket, almost as if he had been intending on resting his paw on something by his belt that wasn't there. A sword hilt perhaps? She was reminded again of a soldier at rest.

"How nice." Mistress Rose smiled warmly at her new student. "Welcome to our class Marquiese. Would someone like to partner with our new student for a few days and help him learn his way around?"

Marilana rolled her eyes as Brittia swayed to her feet.

"It would be my pleasure, Mistress Rose," Brittia said sweetly.

"Thank you, Brittia. Everyone please make sure you write down your history homework before going lunch," Mistress Rose said as the bell sounded for lunch. "Marilana, please wait by my desk, if you would."

Marilana watched Brittia take the new boy by his arm and lead him out of the room. When they were gone, she drew a deep sigh and walked to the teacher's desk. She waited patiently as Mistress Rose cleared the chalk board. She had always marveled at how efficiently her teacher used her hooves.

Mistress Rose slipped her hoof out of the leather strap of the eraser, and into the leather chalk holder. She slid the holder over the corner of the desk and, placing one hoof on each side of the chalk pulled the stub from the holder. She hooked the wide metal drawer handle to pull open the drawer.

"Marilana, what can I do to make you at least appear to pay attention? You know what will happen if the headmistress sees you staring off into space," Rose asked quietly as she used both hooves together to pull a new piece of chalk from the drawer. "I was your tutor for Lady Annabella long enough to know you have already learned today's lesson, but I cannot prevent Ceta from punishing you if she sees you misbehaving. You have to try to follow her rules."

"I get caned enough to know I can't stop her," Marilana replied darkly, watching Mistress Rose carefully push the new chalk stick into the stiff leather holder. "At least if I get caned for daydreaming I know she is not making up some story to cover up her support of Brittia's lies."

"I'm sorry, Marilana. I do what I can, but I'm not very influential with the headmistress." Mistress Rose sighed pushing the drawer closed.

"Please do not make yourself a target on my behalf," Marilana said seriously. "I would rather take the punishments than to have you lose your position here at the school."

"Thank you for your kindness, Marilana," Mistress Rose smiled, and searched Marilana's eyes. "I will make my report to Lady Annabella and try to limit your punishments as much as I can. Now go to lunch."

"Yes, Mistress Rose."

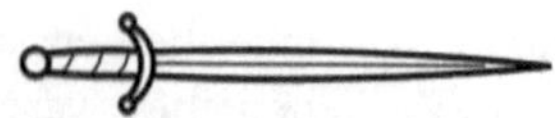

The day was warm and bright. It had rained the day before, but the ground was dry. The autumn flowers were in bloom all over the countryside and throughout the town. Marquiese watched the lioness from his new class as she crossed the schoolyard and joined a group of peasant girls sitting on the grass. The yellows and reds of the schoolyard accented her golden fur and highlighted the contrast to the light blue sundress she wore. He wondered who she was. She had been the only one in the class to inspect him as he was inspecting everyone else. She had seemed to view him as if he were a potential threat.

"Who's that?" he asked Brittia.

"Oh, that. That's just Marilana," Brittia stated dully. "Don't worry about her."

"Is she a merchant daughter?"

"She's a nobody, a peasant. Come along with me and I'll introduce you to some of the other—"

"No, I want to meet her," he said and headed in Marilana's direction.

"But . . . I'm not going over there!" Brittia stomped her foot.

He stopped and looked at her. "I never said you had to," he said and continued on toward Marilana and her friends.

He started to listen to what they were saying as he approached.

". . . and I couldn't believe the gossip she was prattling on about. Honestly, she's so stupid. She even said so herself, she . . . ." The girl's words trailed off when she looked up and met his eyes. She quickly dropped her gaze to the grass. The others looked around at him quickly, and then as one turned their eyes down.

"I hope I'm not interrupting," Marquiese said, smiling at the group. "I just wanted to introduce myself. I'm Marquiese. Brittia has been showing me around."

Unlike the flirtatious merchant daughters he had met, these peasant girls fidgeted nervously and kept their eyes averted. Marilana casually scanned the fence line before turning to study him. Unlike the others, she met his eyes boldly with cold analysis. After a moment, she swept a paw in the direction of her companions.

"Let me introduce you. This is Elza, Jenra, Natly, and Dera," she said simply. "I'm Marilana."

"It's a pleasure. I'm—"

He got no further. Brittia was striding their way and calling, "Marquiese, it's almost time for class. Are you coming?"

"Until next time," Marquiese said to Marilana and her friends as Brittia took his paw and led him away.

"Why in the world would you want to meet her anyway?" the lynx complained. "She's only a peasant."

"Well, she is the only lioness I've seen here," Marquiese shrugged easily.

"Boys," Brittia sighed exasperatedly. "Don't you ever think of anything outside your beds? Can't you see a girl without imagining chasing her tail? You know everyone keeps their tails hidden, not just girls. Its tradition."

"Brittia!" Marquiese gasped slightly. "Speaking of tails is bordering on rudeness."

"Oh, relax," Brittia giggled. "I only wanted to see what you would say."

Marilana watched Marquiese walk away. She had seen pride in his eyes and confusion. The girls' silence had clearly not been what he had expected.

"Marilana! Why did you tell him our names?" Natly squeaked,

"You need not fear him," Marilana replied thoughtfully. "I think he honestly just wanted to introduce himself. I will keep an eye on him, if you wish, but now we need to hurry or we'll be late to class."

*

After the last bell ended the school day, Marilana reported to the headmistress' office. Headmistress Ceta grunted and opened her safe. Marilana removed her bow, quiver, and dagger from the safe. She belted on her dagger and quiver, tightened her satchel across her back, strung her bow, and left the schoolhouse without a word.

"It's about time you showed up," Brittia said snidely. "Honestly, you're so lazy. You know I have better things to do this evening than stand around waiting for you."

"I'm sure your time will be much better spent gazing into your mirror and hoping for a thought to appear," Marilana replied sarcastically.

"Well at least I have something worthwhile to gaze at. All you have are daydreams."

Brittia spun on her heel and a group of older youths gathered around her. They led the way down the road with a group of younger children trailing after Marilana. Yet as confident as the youths acted, they were careful to keep Marilana within sight at all times. At the edge of town, Marilana nocked an arrow to her bow. She scanned the road for tracks and carefully watched the forest around them. House to house Marilana escorted the others, she would nod her head, and one child after another would hurry to the safety of their family.

When they reached Brittia's house, Marilana nodded curtly to the merchant guard waiting there. Brittia walked nonchalantly off the road. After a few more houses, Marquiese was the last of the older group. Marilana looked at him critically. He was slightly shorter than she was, but had a confident air that made him seem taller than he was.

"May I walk with you?" he asked quietly.

"You may, but don't get in my way," she replied coldly returning her attention to the forest.

"You're their escort, aren't you?"

"Some of the merchant families rely on me to protect their children on the walk to and from school. Most of them don't have enough guards to spare. Lady Annabella secured a deal with the merchants and Headmistress Ceta."

"I was warned about bandits kidnapping children for ransom and was told that there would be an escort. Brittia said you were just a peasant, but I can see from your clothing that you are a noble ward. She also didn't mention your skills with a bow."

"I'm not surprised Brittia neglected your education," she said still watching the forest. "I'm the orphaned peasant ward of Lady Annabella, but I'm also a bandit hunter. A very skilled bandit hunter."

"You hunt bandits?" he said skeptically.

"If you've never heard of The Ghost, then I suggest your father ask the other merchants about me. You'll not get a good answer from Brittia and her followers."

"I would rather hear the truth of the matter from you," he said simply.

"Well then, you'll have to settle for disappointment, because I have better things to do than tell you my personal history," she growled softly.

"Why are there no peasant children living along this road?" he asked changing the topic.

"Why are you interested?"

"I have heard that there is a large peasant population here in the Southern Tip, but the only peasants in our class are your four friends. And they were clearly afraid of me. What have I done to cause so much mistrust?"

"You really don't know?" she asked studying his face seriously.

"I grew up in Maefair. I had a private tutor. I have not had direct dealings with peasants before," he said quietly. "I just do not understand what I have done to cause them to fear me."

"You are from the Royal City?"

"Yes. My merchant father was a high-class merchant of low rank. He wanted to move some place where we could live a simpler life. Here he stands as high as the leader of the Merchant Council. It may turn out to be a good place to settle."

Marilana silently scanned some tracks on the road, and then kept walking. Only two of the younger children were left following them.

"It's not something you have done," Marilana said seriously. "It's something you could do because of your rank."

"What do you mean?" he asked suspiciously.

"You are the son of a high ranking high-class merchant. By law, you can do whatever you want to do to individuals of a lower caste, and they cannot stop you," she said darkly. "If you look at the younger classes at the school, you will see a lot of peasant children, both boys and girls. They learn the basics of reading, writing, and arithmetic. By age eight, almost all the boys stop attending school because they are needed on the farm. By age ten, most of the girls have stopped as well. The only girls allowed to continue are the unattractive ones who want to become scholars. By age fourteen, even those will have stopped attending school with the merchant children for fear of attracting unwanted attention. Many of the peasant children live at the boarding houses during the school year and are afraid of being caught outside their protective walls."

"I know about the privileges of rank, but I would never act in such a despicable manner," Marquiese said firmly.

"The peasants are not going to sit and wait to see if you're honorable or not. That would be an invitation for abuse. It is better to hide than to sit in the open and get hurt for sport."

"Why did you introduce your friends to me then?" he asked puzzled.

"I did not see lust in your eyes," she said, glancing at him. "But be forewarned. I will guard them against you if you try anything."

"So you do not fear me?"

"As a peasant, it is illegal for me to use force to defend myself against you. But as a bandit hunter, I can protect those girls with non-lethal force. If you want me, you have to go through Lady Annabella. I am her ward," she replied simply. "Also you would have to catch me, and that would not be easy."

Marilana nodded as they passed another house, and one of the younger children hurried off the road. The last of the children was a young lioness that Marilana had never seen before. The girl hurried to join them. She smiled timidly at Marilana while Marquiese laid his arm protectively across her shoulders.

"Your sister?" Marilana asked as they reached the large manor house on the south side of the road.

"Her name is Lida," Marquiese replied easily.

Marilana stopped and frowned darkly at the old brick house and the bustle of activity inside the surrounding high brick wall. She watched Lida run to the open gate where a mature lioness and a merchant guard waited.

"You are living here?" Marilana asked warily.

"My merchant father obtained it. It's been empty for several years apparently and most people seem to have some superstition about the place." Marquiese shrugged. "I did not expect you to believe in haunts, however."

"I don't believe in superstitions," Marilana replied with dark intensity. "But I know the truth of what happened here, and I will give you fair warning. The last family who lived here was slain by bandits. It is true that those bandits paid for their crimes, but this house is too isolated to have much protection. Do not let your guard down!"

"Marquiese, come on!" Lida called anxiously.

Marquiese studied Marilana thoughtfully.

"I hope you have a good night, Marilana," he said and turned away.

Marilana slipped silently into the forest opposite the house.

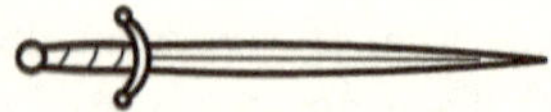

Marquiese looked back from the gate, but Marilana was gone. Surprised, he walked back out on the road and looked both ways. He could not see her. He looked down at the road and spotted her tracks leading into the forest opposite the house. He studied the forest for a moment, but could see no motion or any indication that someone was there. Frowning he turned back to the merchant guard at the gate. The guard was one of a dozen who had traveled with them from Maefair. He did not entirely trust the merchant guards, but they had not caused any problems along the road. He motioned for his merchant mother to lead Lida on into the house.

"Have you heard anything about a bandit hunter called The Ghost?" Marquiese asked the antelope merchant guard when he got back to the gate.

The antelope frowned and studied the forest where Marilana had disappeared.

"I have heard from reliable sources, that she is a young lioness and very skilled," he replied quietly. "I did not think she was that young, but none of the rumors agree on her age. I have heard from less reliable sources that she always gets her target and is considered the deadliest archer and best tracker in the Southern Tip. The rumors I don't believe claim she can't die, can turn into a tree or a bird, or is really an avenging spirit."

"What do you think now?" Marquiese asked indicating the forest.

"I think those less reliable sources knew what they were talking about," he admitted. "I watched her walk off the road, but once she entered the forest, I felt like I was watching for something that wasn't there. I doubt I could find her tracks beyond the underbrush. Chilled my blood to be honest."

"I didn't hear her leave the road," Marquiese said. "I think she was honest with me, though."

"Bandit hunters are a strange lot," the guard said shaking his head. "You can't tell what they are going to do, and they keep a lot of secrets. But you can trust what they say."

"She told me that the last family to live here was murdered by bandits and not to let my guard down," Marquiese said seriously.

"I hadn't heard that, but I can believe it. This place gives me the creeps," the antelope glanced at the house and shook his head. "Just be glad your father hired enough guards to protect this place day and night and accompany him to market."

2

Marilana slipped silently through the trees and approached her small four-room house from the back. The house sat in the middle of a square garden surrounded by a low stonewall. It was the furthest house from Mystillion and was well hidden from the manor house where Marquiese and his family lived.

She paused at the edge of the trees and studied her house. She could see the body of an intruder lying on the front path in a pool of blood. Her traps had served their purpose. Good.

She scouted the area around the house and found the tracks she knew would be there. Bandits. Marilana vaulted the back wall and stepped around a series of traps armed throughout her garden. She quietly entered the house by the back door and searched the interior. No one had made it past the garden.

She unstrung her bow, disarmed a trio of crossbows aimed through the arrow slits around the front door, and then pushed it open. She worked her way to the corpse, disarming the traps along the way. She dragged the dead leopard out the gate, careful not to snag her skirt on the crossbow bolt protruding from his chest. She deposited the body at the side of the road just outside her garden wall. Then she made her way back to her house, resetting the snares, trip lines, and various triggers of the traps along her way. The sun was dropping behind the trees so she lit a lantern and set it on the kitchen table. She laid out her school things and settled down to her homework.

After an hour, Marilana heard the sounds of horses on the road. She glanced up at the clock on the cabinet and smiled; the patrol was right on time. The clock was a beautiful piece of carved dark wood with a small round golden face set between two rearing horses. It was a luxury that peasants could not afford. It had been a gift to her from Lady Annabella when she moved into the house. She had been nine at the time. It had been a test of sorts to see if she could cope with living alone before swearing the oaths of a bandit hunter. That was three years ago. She was almost thirteen now and had been hunting bandits and working for Lady Annabella ever since.

She stroked the clock lovingly before going to the door and peered out one of the arrow slits. Six horsemen wearing Southern Tip uniforms waited on the road.

"Marilana? Are you there?" called the coyote guardsman.

Marilana smiled grimly, they knew not to approach the gate without her. She opened the door and stood on the threshold. Two of the men had dismounted and were lifting the corpse onto one of the horses.

"I'm here, Captain Branth. Sorry about the baggage," she called.

"You alright?" Captain Branth replied.

"Yes, I'm fine."

"It's almost time for you to be at the castle. Do you want a ride?"

"No, thank you, Captain. I'll be on my way momentarily."

"Alright. See you there." He signaled his patrol and they headed down the road.

Marilana locked the door, armed the crossbows, and blew out the lantern. She armed herself, strung her bow, and wrapped a light cloak around her shoulders. She slipped out the back, crossed the garden, and hopped the wall. She entered the trees silently and made her way cautiously to Lady Annabella's estates. She emerged from the trees and trotted down the road to a pair of large iron-strapped wooden gates. Guardsmen on the stone battlements called down to the gate guards, and a small foot gate opened. Marilana slipped through the gate and crossed the stableyard to the wide stone steps leading to Lady Annabella's castle, greeting servants and soldiers as they went about their work. She paused on the bottom step as the main gate was opened behind her. She turned and smiled as the mounted patrol rode through the gate. She waved in return of Captain Branth's half salute to her, and then hurried up the steps. Beyond the main doors, Marilana gave her cloak and weapons to a waiting servant.

"She is expecting you in the library," the young tigress said.

"Thank you, Taslin," Marilana said and hurried down the hall to the library.

Inside, Madam Bila, the wizened old puma librarian, nodded to her. Marilana smiled in return and hurried to a well-lit table positioned in the middle of the room. She stopped a pace away from the chair where Lady Annabella sat taking notes. Marilana watched the older lioness patiently.

"Mistress Rose stopped in a while ago and reported on your behavior today," Lady Annabella said without looking up.

"Yes, My Lady," Marilana replied quietly, her heart sinking from the disappointment in Lady Annabella's voice.

"She said you have a problem with daydreaming."

"Yes, My Lady."

"Marilana, Headmistress Ceta is a hard woman, and I will not stop her from punishing you." Lady Annabella sanded her notes and looked up sternly. "What is more, I expect you to pay attention. You cannot afford to let yourself be distracted. I know you can divide your attention to multiple tasks, but you cannot look like you are focused elsewhere, no matter what your situation. You must control what others see. You are my ward, and your behavior reflects on me."

"Forgive me, Lady Annabella, I was wrong to let my attention waver," Marilana replied.

"You have a lot to study tonight. You should get started," Lady Annabella said more gently. She pointed a polished claw at a book sitting on the table and the empty chair awaiting her.

Marilana perched on the chair. The book was dedicated to the history of law, and she opened it to her marker. She worked diligently for several hours, reading and taking notes.

Finally, Lady Annabella set down her pen and sighed. "Come, Marilana. Join me for some supper."

Marilana marked her place and followed Lady Annabella upstairs to her private study. When Lady Annabella had finished her meal and sat sipping her tea, Marilana decided to ask the question she had been pondering for some minutes.

"Lady Annabella, have you met the merchant who moved into the old manor house down the road from my home?"

"Merchant Colbran is a trader in precious ores," Lady Annabella replied, studying Marilana. "He and his wife paid their respects to me this morning and gave me a beautifully crafted silver ring set with brilliantly cut emeralds. He and Merchant Sleater will share rank for a few years until the Merchant Council can determine who will lead the Council or until Merchant Colbran moves on. He is not sure if Mystillion will be a good location for his ore trade. I did warn him about the bandit threat, and he hired a large contingent of guards to protect his wares and his family."

"I'm sure Brittia will be horrified to learn that her father is no longer the only top merchant," Marilana smiled with amusement.

"Actually, she will probably be quite pleased," Lady Annabella said calmly. "From what I have been told, Merchant Colbran has a handsome son a couple of months younger than you. If Brittia could win the son's favor and wed him, that would join the two most powerful merchant families in Mystillion and increase Brittia's wealth and power. I am sure she would love that."

"She would rather be named your heiress," Marilana grimaced.

"That is not her decision, and if she does not start acting with maturity, she will not even be considered," Lady Annabella said levelly. "Why are you suddenly so interested in this particular merchant? You did not ask about the other three who arrived recently."

"That was several months ago, and none of them are high-class merchants. This one could change the balance of power in Mystillion," Marilana said thoughtfully.

"Mistress Rose said you met the son today," Lady Annabella said shrewdly.

"He introduced himself to the peasant girls."

"Do you think he will be a problem?"

"No, not unless he chooses to explore his new found power." Marilana shook her head. "I talked with him on the way home. He seemed ignorant of the threat he posed to the girls. I had to explain it to him, and he seemed honestly surprised that he was seen in such a light."

"Was he interested in you?" Lady Annabella asked pointedly.

"I don't think so. At least not beyond simple curiosity. He has an air of confidence and pride. He easily defied Brittia, yet kept her happy too. I think he is accustomed to wielding power among his equals. It seems that it's just peasants who have him confused."

"Really? A handsome young lion, just about your age. From Maefair and accustomed to power? I wonder . . . what is his name?"

"Marquiese," Marilana said cautiously. "Why do you ask?"

"Just curious," Lady Annabella said thoughtfully.

Marilana knew better, but she also knew not to question Lady Annabella further. They sat in thoughtful silence for a while before Lady Annabella dismissed her, and she made her way home alone through the dark forest.

Once there, Marilana froze amidst the trees and watched her house carefully. She could just barely make out the shadow moving behind the windows of her dark kitchen. Slowly and silently, Marilana scouted around her house. None of the traps had been tripped, and she had found no tracks. Carefully, she worked her way to the door and tested the latch. It was locked, just as she had left it. Alert to every sound, Marilana unlocked the door and entered the blackness inside. She closed the door and slid her paw up along the frame; the crossbows had been disarmed.

"Child? Are you here?" Marilana called softly.

"Yes, Sissy, I'm in the kitchen getting something to eat," came the soft reply.

Marilana relaxed and hung her cloak on one of the pegs by the door. She placed her weapons in one of the cupboards in the main room, then washed her paws and face in the basin before going into the kitchen. She lit the lantern on the table and turned to face the young, slender deer. They shared a smile and a warm hug.

"I'm glad to see you, Child," Marilana said. "You have been in the forest for several fifnights and I was beginning to wonder. Is everything alright?"

"Oh, yes, the forest is pleasant enough. The bandits are easy to track, and things have been fairly quiet lately," Child said. Then her tone turned serious, and she pinned Marilana with her eyes. "Sissy, someone has moved into the brick house."

"I know, Child. They are a merchant family with a son my age and a daughter younger than you. Both Lady Annabella and I warned them of the bandit threat. They hired a lot of guards, and I am also keeping an eye on the area as best I can."

"I will as well," Child said, nodding seriously. "As long as they don't hurt you."

"I don't think they will." Marilana smiled gently. "Are you staying in tonight or going back out?"

"I would rather sleep out in the forest. Thank you for the food. I will see you again soon."

Marilana watched as the doe strapped on her weapons belts with their varieties of knives, slung her quiver across her back, and strung her bow. They hugged again and then Child slipped out the back door. Marilana secured the locks and armed the crossbows.

Marilana was glad to see Child. She worried about the girl staying out in the forest, but knew that solitude was much better for her than being around other creatures. Marilana couldn't help shivering as she remembered that day three years ago when she entered the ransacked brick house and pulled Zara—that was Child's given name—out from under her dead sister. The fawn had been there for hours, pinned by an arrow in her arm, the same arrow that had taken her sister's life. Zara had been six years old at the time and had not been the same since. These days she only responded to Child, having taken the term of endearment Marilana had first called her as her name. Though Child was mostly recovered, she still lapsed into a severe panic in the company of too many other creatures, especially males.

These days, Child devoted her life to the art of bandit hunting; it was her sole purpose. Marilana had taught her everything she could, and Child was now almost as skilled as her teacher.

Marilana remembered with pride all the times she took Child on the hunt this last summer. They worked well as a team, using specific bird calls to communicate from a distance. After Child had seen the reality of what she had been learning, she asked Marilana to make her a bandit hunter. Marilana had taken her to the one local magistrate that she trusted, and Child had bravely sworn the Bandit Hunter Oaths, oaths she took very seriously.

She sighed sadly for Child's lost innocence, and her own too, she admitted darkly. Marilana exchanged all her crossbows, unstrung and oiled the ones that had been set all day as well as her multiple bows and weapons, performed her nightly stretching exercises, and fell quickly asleep after climbing into bed.

3

The next morning Marilana found Marquiese and his sister waiting for her by the road. She nodded to the merchant guard and continued down the road.

"Good morning," Marquiese said, his sister holding his paw tightly. "Lida, you should say good morning to our escort. It is the polite thing to do."

"Good morning," Lida squeaked nervously.

"Good morning, Lida," Marilana replied sternly.

The little lioness watched her with wide-eyed wonder, peeking around Marquiese. Marilana watched her curiously from the corner of her eye as she scanned the road and forest. Lida tugged on Marquiese's arm and he bent to her so she could whisper in his ear. Laughing he straightened back up. Marilana realized he was also watching the forest and the road. He did not watch with fear or apprehension like most merchant children, but was alert and cautious.

"You can tell her yourself," Marquiese said to the little lioness. "She will not hurt you."

"I . . . I think you're pretty," Lida stammered quietly.

Marilana looked at the girl with surprise and hesitated unsure how to respond.

"Thank you, Lida. That is a nice thing to say," she finally replied quietly.

Marquiese smirked slightly as he looked toward the forest, but did not say anything.

"So then, why are you so mean?" Lida asked, emboldened by Marilana's gentle response.

Marilana missed a step and felt as if she had just swallowed a snowball.

"What makes you say that?"

"The other children say you kill people who make you mad. They say you never have anything nice to say. I did not think you could be pretty and still be so mean."

Marilana sighed sadly and looked down at her bow for a moment. This girl knew nothing about her. She had only been to school in Mystillion for one day and Brittia's lies had already turned negative thoughts toward Marilana. She took a deep breath and returned her attention to the road and forest; after all, she had a job to do.

"I do what I can to protect the children of the Southern Tip," was how Marilana explained it.

She glanced at Marquiese and realized he was studying her with an expressionless mask. She met his look with a glare and then turned away.

"Sometimes, Lida," Marquiese said gently, "a person has to hurt other creatures to stop them from hurting others in turn. Marilana is not being mean when she hunts bandits. The bandits are the ones who want to hurt us and Marilana stops them."

Lida was confused. "But if she protects us, why don't the other children like her? They all said Marilana was mean and told me to stay away from her. They said I could get into trouble if I got too close to her or talked to her."

"I was also told to stay away from her. And that she is dangerous," Marquiese replied. "I chose to find out for myself and not to take their word for truth. I do not think she is someone to be afraid off. I think she is someone who will help us if we need help."

The cold ball in Marilana's gut melted slightly as she listened to Marquiese.

"But why doesn't she say nice things to the other children?" Lida asked.

"Sometimes it can be hard to say nice things to people who don't like you," Marquiese replied.

Marilana stopped walking and studied Marquiese's sad eyes for a moment. He was hiding something. His words had come from a deeper understanding, as if he had also been in a position where he had to do his duty even though others didn't like him for it. Then she knelt down and looked Lida straight in the eye.

"Marquiese is right. It's hard to be nice to people who aren't nice in return," she said quietly. "I need you to understand that I am here to protect you. When I tell you to do something, like hide or be quiet, I need you to do it right away. I take your safety very seriously. I also want you to know that if you ever need help, you can ask me. I will do whatever I can. Alright?"

Lida nodded seriously.

"Good girl." Marilana smiled warmly and touched her cheek. "Now we need to hurry so we make it to school on time."

"I think that was the first time I ever saw you smile," Marquiese said to Marilana after Lida joined the first of the younger children. "You should do it more often."

Marilana watched him as he joined their classmates. He talked easily and smiled frequently, but he also kept an eye on the forest and road. Marilana wondered what training he'd had; also what his purpose was in speaking to her so freely.

*

Marilana was not surprised when Headmistress Ceta pulled her out of class mid-morning. Her crime was fraternizing above her station, and she had been forced to endure five strikes of the cane across the back of her legs.

On the way home, she growled when Marquiese joined her. He had waited until they were alone, but Marilana was in no mood for his company.

"Where is Lida?" she asked coldly.

"With my merchant father at the market. He said he had something to discuss with us both, but I told him I needed to get home to do my homework."

"I think I know what he wanted to discuss. Fraternizing with peasants. Do yourself and your sister a favor and stay away from me."

"What happened this morning with the headmistress?"

"It doesn't concern you."

"Judging by the warning Brittia issued to me at lunch, I have every reason to believe it does. She told me that bad things happen to anyone who talks to you," he persisted. "So? What happened?"

"I received five strikes of the cane for fraternizing above my station. Does that make you happy?" Marilana snapped.

"No, it doesn't. I can speak to whomever I want to speak with, and they have no cause to punish you for it. Besides that, you are Lady Annabella's ward; there is no one in Mystillion above your station."

"That might be true elsewhere. But here in Mystillion, I'm just the orphan of scholars."

"I cannot believe Lady Annabella stands for this abuse," he said heatedly.

"She limits the scope of my punishments, but I must live with the people around me. If they are in positions of authority, I have to accept that authority or move elsewhere. I will not leave my home just because a bunch of merchants treat me as what I am, the lowest of peasants."

"They are not treating you according to your caste. They are treating you like a criminal," he said with disgust. "How can you defend them?"

"It's not that I like it! You just don't understand. Look at the math. Four out of five days per fifnight, six fifnights per month, and ten out of thirteen months per year for the past eight years, I have attended this school. That's 1,920 days of my life. During that time, I have been punished for some misbehavior at least twice a fifnight. Headmistress Ceta's job is to correct the misbehavior of her students. If I were given an exception from the rules, she would not be respected by the community, and they would find someone to replace her."

"But she is abusing her power over you! For any of the rest of the students, she may be a fair headmistress. With you, she over steps the bounds of her position while Brittia is pampered."

"And that is reason enough for you to stay away from me," Marilana said firmly. "Brittia can make sure that your family is not welcome in Mystillion. Your father and hers may be of equal rank, but your family is new, and hers has been in power for several generations. The other merchants have deep respect for her father. She can cause problems for you. I have been dealing with this situation for most of my life. If you stir up the community, it could become a much larger issue. This is between me and Brittia. Listen to your father and stay out of it!"

Marquiese looked away in frustration and took several deep breaths. Finally, he looked back at her with that expressionless mask she had seen before.

"I hope you have a good night, Marilana. I will see you in the morning."

She watched him walk to his gate and stamped her foot with frustration. She had not been so incensed over a single conversation in years. She stormed off into the forest and entered her house through the back door. She fumed as she changed her clothes and was still fuming as she headed off to Lady Annabella's castle. She was scheduled to work in the stables that evening, which always gave her plenty of time to think.

Tonight, every ounce of her rumination went toward Marquiese and why he should be so concerned for her welfare.

What does it matter to him how I am treated? He is a merchant. He should not care that I'm kept in my place by whatever means. He should be more interested in keeping Brittia happy and trying to make friends with the other merchant children. None of them have ever cared;

they back Brittia without a second thought. He's probably just trying to gain influence with Lady Annabella because I'm her ward. He'll soon learn that I have no influence with her or anyone.

Her anger cooled the longer she thought about the situation and the more she put her energy to cleaning the stable. By the time she had finished and returned home, she was calm again knowing everything would be back to normal in a few fifnights.

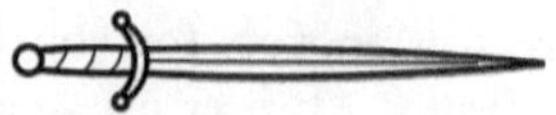

Marquiese leaned against the schoolhouse wall, his paws shoved deep in his pockets, and studied Marilana as she sat on the front step reading a book. Brittia had left him here so that she could speak with the headmistress. He had thought about Marilana's punishments all fifnight. He had stayed away from her whenever there had been witnesses, he tried to tell Brittia that he had forced his company on Marilana, he even had Lida promise not to tell anyone that they talked to her, but it had not changed anything. Headmistress Ceta had caned Marilana twice more, and Brittia had dismissed his explanation with batted lashes and a promise that she was much better company than any orphan. He refused to let the situation continue. There had to be a solution that allowed him to speak with Marilana without getting her in trouble. He wasn't quite sure what it was about Marilana that had snared his thoughts so firmly, but he wanted to learn more about her. The only way to learn the truth about her seemed to be from her own lips. Everything else he and his family had heard seemed filled with rumors.

"I wouldn't, if I were you," said a low voice right behind him.

Marquiese spun around in surprise and came face to face with a black-furred leopard.

"Wouldn't what?" Marquiese replied evasively.

"You were thinking of talking to Marilana again, weren't you?" The leopard grinned. "I'm Earek, second son of

Merchant Yulan. I've been waiting for Brittia to leave you alone all fifnight."

"Not many people can sneak up on me like that," Marquiese said suspiciously.

"I can sneak up on almost anyone as long as I'm on stone or grass, though Marilana remains an exception. She somehow always knows. Most of the other boys have tried to sneak up on her as well, just as a prank. Most of the time she just gets up and walks away, but twice she let me get right up behind her and then spun around and took my feet out from under me."

"You must not like her very much after that," Marquiese grunted glancing back at the step and seeing that Marilana had slipped away.

Earek shrugged. "I didn't much like having the wind knocked out of me, but I can't hold it against her. I was the one trying to sneak up on her."

"So do you talk to her much?"

Earek laughed. "Marilana is out of bounds for socializing. Brittia has made that perfectly clear. Pranks, yes, because it amuses her. But any other kind of interest is not allowed."

"Do you let Brittia dictate everything in your life?"

"I try very hard not to. I rank second in our class behind Brittia and you, but only until I come of age at seventeen. As a second son, I will only keep a merchant rank if I marry a merchant heiress. Brittia has let me know for many years now that she will marry me unless someone better comes along. Like you, for instance."

Earek shrugged. "Some actions, however, have consequences that even I try to avoid. Speaking with Marilana for anything more than a homework assignment, well, let's just say I'd be lucky to walk away from Brittia as a peasant and still be allowed to live in the Southern Tip. Brittia's family has power here in Mystillion, and if Brittia gets her wish, she will be named Lady Annabella's heiress. I have to be careful how mad I make her. We all do."

"What about Lady Annabella? Doesn't she interfere with Brittia's plans?"

"Of course she does. Brittia wants to make a good impression, so she and her family always do as Lady Annabella dictates. They may slip through every loop hole that they can and push every advantage they can find, but they are law abiding," said Earek. He gave Marquiese a nudge. "Come on, I'll introduce you to the guys."

They approached a husky black bear and a sleek silver fox, and Earek made the introductions. "Marquiese, this is Klay and Caton. They are both first sons. Klay's father is a low high-class blacksmith. Caton's mother is a high mid-class glass blower."

"Nice to meet you both," Marquiese said, smiling easily. "So how does this work? Because Earek is the son of a high ranking merchant, do you follow his lead and do as he wishes the way all of Brittia's followers do?"

"We're friends," Klay growled from deep in his thick bear chest. "We compromise and figure out ways to agree on our actions. We are not sycophants like Brittia's girls. We are offering you the chance to join us as an equal."

"I appreciate your offer," Marquiese replied seriously.

"We have a leather ball. Have you ever played wall ball?" asked Caton, bouncing a brown leather ball on his paw.

"I haven't. But I think I would like to learn."

"It's quite simple," Earek smiled. "One of us throws the ball at the wall. Then we try to catch the ball off the bounce. If you get hit by the ball without catching it, you're out. If you catch it, you throw it and try to get someone else out."

It may have sounded simple, but Marquiese found the game harder than he expected. The other three merchant sons had lots of practice at the game and were able to bounce the ball with spin on it that made it harder to predict the bounce and harder to catch. They had been playing for a while when Marquiese spotted Marilana walking past them. She was still reading her book and seemed oblivious to their presence.

Caton also saw her and smiled mischievously.

"Hey, Klay," Caton called, nodding his head in Marilana's direction.

Klay looked around and smiled. He threw the ball hard against the wall, and it sped straight at Marilana. Marquiese was on the verge of calling out a warning, but it proved unnecessary. Marilana's paw was suddenly stretched out beside her, and she caught the ball with a loud smack. Marquiese froze in surprise. He had not seen Marilana move her paw, hadn't seen her look up or flinch. How had she done that?

Marilana looked away from her book casually and glanced at each of them in turn.

"Is this yours?" she asked, fixing her gaze innocently on Klay.

"Hey, Caton, I heard that Marilana doesn't kill her prey with her arrows," Klay said with a smirk.

"Really? What does she do?" Caton asked, playing along.

"I heard she runs around the forest without any clothes on and the bandits die of shock."

Earek and Caton laughed uproariously at the joke, but Marquiese frowned with disapproval. Marilana, however, smiled and bounced the ball in her paw.

"If that were true, you could take on entire armies without wearing a stitch," Marilana replied easily.

Earek and Caton laughed even harder at the scorned look on Klay's face. Then they saw Marilana cock her arm. All three boys stopped laughing and bolted in different directions. Marilana threw the ball sideways. It hit the wall with tremendous force, bounced, and smacked hard into Klay's arm.

"At least I hit my targets," Marilana said with a slight smile.

Marquiese's smirk widened as Marilana walked away and Klay was left rubbing his arm.

"What was that all about?" Marquiese asked after Earek had retrieved the ball.

"Just a bit of fun," Klay shrugged. "Marilana has a sharp tongue, but I think the ball hurt more this time. I never can hit her, no matter how distracted she seems to be. She's smarter and faster than any of us."

"We've all tried. None of us has ever hit her, but she usually manages to hit one of us," laughed Earek. "Come on, let's play some more."

"What's your fascination with Marilana anyway?" Caton asked Marquiese as they started up their game again.

"Well, if you haven't noticed, there aren't a lot of lions around here," Marquiese said, shrugging.

"You're not thinking about chasing her tail, are you?" asked Earek as he caught the ball. "That would land you in a lot of trouble. Not just with Brittia, but with Lady Annabella too. No one is allowed to lay with Marilana without Lady Annabella's approval. Our Lady takes Marilana's protection and honor very seriously."

They were all watching Marquise, waiting for his answer.

"I'm not one to chase tail. That's too vulgar for me," Marquiese said. He shrugged again. "She's just the oddest girl I've ever met. And being the only other lion in the class, I'm curious about her."

The three boys exchanged a skeptical look, but went back to playing the game. Marquiese wondered about these boys. When he had suggested to Brittia that his interest in Marilana was simply physical attraction, she acted as if he had confirmed her suspicions about him and that he was acting just like every other boy. These three friends, however, may have gotten a laugh at Marilana's expense, but that was as far as they seemed willing to go.

"Marquiese!"

Marquiese was jarred from his thoughts by an angry voice that could only belong to one person. He turned to meet

Brittia's furious look and was rewarded with a sharp pain as the ball exploded against his shoulder. He winced, but only for a moment.

"Brittia! There you are! I was worried that you were not coming back," Marquiese said, trying his best smile.

"I told you to wait for me. Why didn't you?" Brittia pouted.

"Oh, lighten up, Brittia," Earek said, stepping up next to Marquiese. "Did you really expect Marquiese to stand around for half the lunch break doing nothing? You've had him to yourself for three and a half days. He's tired of talking fashion. He needs to have some time with the guys, and I'm sure he no longer needs your guidance to get around school. You've done your job, now let him find his own place among us."

"You don't want my company?" Brittia asked, her eyes sad and her chin quivering dramatically.

"Of course I want your company," Marquiese said soothingly. "I will never forget your efforts this fifnight to help me feel at home here. You are a gem, and I will always greet your presence with a smile. But Earek is correct. I need some time to get to know the guys too. We're playing a game; you're welcome to join us."

"Oh, no, thank you. I don't like that game." Brittia continued to pout. "I was hoping you would tell me more about the fashions of the city."

"You know, I think the new dress patterns are arriving this afternoon," Earek said thoughtfully. "I work in the shop every Restday. I would be pleased to show the patterns to you if you came by tomorrow. Marquiese would be welcome to come with you."

"Oh, Earek! What a lovely thought." Brittia smiled. "Marquiese, will you come with me to Merchant Yulan's tailor shop tomorrow, please?"

"I will ask my merchant father," Marquiese promised.

"I will wait all day for you." Brittia smiled and walked away.

"I'm not sure whether to thank you or hurt you," Marquiese muttered to Earek.

"We have started to loosen her clutches a little," Earek said, laughing. "Now all you have to do is show up tomorrow, and she will surely be willing to leave you on your own. Well, part of the time anyway. Of course you could ruin that plan by continuing to show too much interest in Marilana."

"I think I'm starting to have a plan to appease Brittia and satisfy my curiosity," Marquiese said thoughtfully.

"It's your skin," Earek warned as the bell sounded.

They reached the doors of the school house at the exact moment Brittia and Marilana did. Brittia tried to snatch the book from Marilana's paw, but without success.

"What are you reading?" Brittia sneered. "Something to help with that motley appearance of yours? I hate to tell you this, but you would need a whole new face!"

Brittia's friends laughed and tried blocking Marilana from entering the school.

"It's a good thing the world doesn't revolve around looks, Brittia," Marilana retorted coldly. "If it did, you would be buried at the bottom of a mountain so no one would have to get anywhere near you."

"At least I offer value to society. You're just a worthless peasant," Brittia snarled. "Go back to your book, Worm, and get out of my way."

Marilana's lip curled angrily as Brittia and the rest of the students pushed past her and flowed into the school. Marquiese watched this interaction and tried hard to keep his own anger under control. He had dealt with plenty of individuals as arrogant as Brittia. He had never liked them. He had been trained to treat everyone with courtesy no matter their station, no matter their situation. His opinion of Brittia continued to plummet. He cringed at the prospect of spending time with her, but he knew he would have to as long as he lived in Mystillion. He vowed to speak to Marilana and let her know he did not approve of the insults she had received.

Marilana saw Marquiese slow his pace ahead of her and sighed. The last of the children, a young, rambunctious deer, ran for his house, and Marilana continued on. Marquiese fell in step with her and cleared his throat nervously. *What does he want this time?* Marilana wondered.

"Brittia's words at lunch were discourteous and rude," Marquiese stated bluntly.

"Yeah, well, Brittia is an arrogant fool without an original thought in her head," Marilana growled, her fur bristling.

"I also want to say I did not approve of what Klay said today," Marquiese added carefully.

"You had Lida meet your father in the market after school so that you could say that?" Marilana scoffed. "Klay was just joking. He and Caton work hard to try to get past my guard. Today was a pretty feeble attempt."

"I thought you would have been mad. How is it different when they say mean things verses when Brittia or her followers say it?" asked Marquiese, clearly confused.

"Brittia starts rumors to try and hurt or discredit me. She uses her position to get her way. She is cruel to everyone, even her followers. She means what she says in the worst way. Earek, Klay, and Caton battle wits with me, but I don't think they do it to hurt me. Haven't you ever bantered with friends to have a laugh? It keeps my thoughts fast and my tongue sharp," Marilana replied.

"They aren't your friends. So why do you think they do it?" Marquiese asked curiously.

"I don't know really. But sometimes I wonder if they don't do it to let me know what rumors Brittia has spread about me. Like what Klay said today. It was pretty weak for him, but it was also not one I had heard before. It sounded more like something Brittia would say," Marilana mused.

"Still, it was not nice. And he tried to hit you with the ball."

"Everyone tries to hit me with things: balls, snowballs, rocks, sticks. They never have yet. Those three are just more persistent than the rest."

"Why doesn't that bother you?"

"It keeps me in practice. Helps me perfect my skills. So I made the choice to accept the challenge. Why should I let everything other people think and do bother me? I would be stuck in a life of misery. Bantering with those boys and exchanging blows with them is a bright spot. They risk Brittia's disfavor to interact with me in some manner. Why should that bother me?" Marilana stopped and faced Marquiese, searching his eyes. "Why does it bother you?"

"I just felt it was wrong." Marquiese shrugged uncomfortably. "Everyone treats you so poorly, yet you're a noble ward. You should be highest among them, not the bottom."

"Thank you for feeling it was wrong, but maybe after you've been here a while you'll understand the order of things in Mystillion. As things stand now, you need to stop being concerned for me and take care of your own standings. If you keep going this way, Brittia will take action against your family," Marilana warned. "It is your choice to protect your family,"

"I won't settle for that," Marquiese said, fervently shaking his head and turning away.

"Why not? Why are you insisting on changing my life?" Marilana asked angrily.

"I will not have my actions dictated to me by that pampered, self-centered lynx."

"So that's it, is it? It's not about right and wrong. It's not about justice or abuse. It's about controlling the game, controlling politics. Very well. Play your game with Brittia, but leave me out of it. I am not her pawn. I will not be yours."

"Marilana, no. That's not what I meant," Marquiese stated, but by then Marilana was already hurrying down the road, her feet barely touching the ground.

She paused in front of the brick manor until Marquiese caught up; then she nodded to the merchant guard at the gate, turned, and ran into the forest before Marquiese could stop her.

4

Restday was an exercise in frustration for Marquiese. He kept thinking about what Marilana had said about not being his pawn. The entire conversation had gone wrong. He had expected her to be mad at Klay and she wasn't. In fact, she had good reason not to be mad. Instead, Marquiese was viewing the exchange with his own biases instead of keeping an open mind. He needed time to think. Instead, he had to do his homework, help Lida with hers, and then spend the entire afternoon discussing dresses with Brittia.

Earek had been right about that, however. After what seemed like endless hours, Brittia finally seemed satisfied. She went off to her father's shop and left Marquiese to find his own way home.

"I told you it would work," Earek remarked as Marquiese stood in the middle of the empty tailor's shop.

"Right. Now she doesn't seem to care if I exist or not," Marquiese said bitterly.

"Oh, she still cares. She'll let you know every time you stray too far. I know. Other merchant sons have caught her eye over the years, but she still keeps me close. I'm what she calls her 'back up husband' in case things don't work out elsewhere. All I have to do is show interest in another girl and suddenly she is bribing and threatening, doing anything she can to make sure I know I'm still hers." Earek waved a paw in the air. "Rather annoying really. And if I don't marry her, I have no idea what I will do. To be free of her completely is a foreign concept. Even just asking Marilana for help on my homework would be nice. You know, she gets the highest marks in the class. Then Brittia has the headmistress strike her marks from the books just because Brittia can't stand the embarrassment of having a peasant out do her."

"It seems the 'simple life' my merchant father sought really isn't so simple," Marquiese mused. "But that gives me an idea. Thanks, Earek. I owe you. See you tomorrow."

"Owe me for what?" Earek called, but by then Marquiese was out the door and hurrying through the market to his merchant father's small shop. He settled down at a worktable in the back room with parchment and ink. First, he had a letter to write. Then he had to convince his merchant family to agree to his plan.

Marilana sighed with resignation the first morning of the new school fifnight as Marquiese and Lida fell in step with her.

"Good morning, Marilana," Marquiese greeted her pleasantly.

"Good morning, Marilana," Lida echoed quietly.

"Good morning," Marilana replied without looking at them.

The three lions walked on in silence until Lida went off to be with the first of the younger children joining their entourage.

"I spoke with my merchant father last night, and he sent a letter to Lady Annabella," Marquiese said when everyone was out of earshot. "I think now that we shall resolve the issue of the punishment that comes from associating with each other."

"I told you to stay out of it and to keep your distance from me," Marilana growled.

"Yes, and I said I will talk with whom I wish, and Brittia cannot stop me."

*

It came as no surprise to Marilana when the headmistress called her out of class at mid-morning. Marilana sighed. *Now what?* She walked past Brittia and ignored her malicious smile. She glanced at Marquiese and saw his expectant grin.

Marilana followed Headmistress Ceta to her office and stopped with surprise when she found Lady Annabella waiting inside. Headmistress Ceta rounded her desk and curtseyed to the Great Lady.

"Marilana, I have been informed by Headmistress Ceta that you have been seen fraternizing above your station. I have come to set the record straight," Lady Annabella said, focusing not on Marilana, but on Ceta.

Headmistress Ceta swallowed nervously and then gave another curtsey. She said, "I assure you, Lady Annabella, I have punished Marilana only for her misguided assertion."

"You punished her for something that was not of her doing," Lady Annabella said curtly. "You know as well as anyone that Marilana is forbidden from hindering a member of a higher caste in anything that does not threaten someone else's life. I received a letter from Merchant Colbran last night stating that his son was distressed by Marilana's punishments. He informed me that his son approached Marilana and spoke with her about their homework. His son did not intend for Marilana to get into trouble for his assertiveness. He said he would like my permission for Marilana to tutor his son in mathematics."

"But surely someone else would be better suited to tutoring Marquiese than Marilana," the headmistress hastened to say.

"I disagree. Marilana has the highest marks in the class and tutoring would not interfere with her duties. The other students would not have the time to devote to such an endeavor. I have informed Merchant Colbran that Marilana will serve as his son's tutor in whatever subjects he might need."

"As you wish, Lady Annabella." The headmistress mixed a grimace with another curtsey. "I shall inform Mistress Rose and document the agreement."

"Good." Lady Annabella turned to Marilana. "Marilana, I have accepted this agreement, and you will work hard to act as a proper tutor. You shall work with Merchant Colbran's son every afternoon until his homework is completed, and then you will report to my estates to perform your regular duties. Is that understood?"

"Yes, Lady Annabella." Marilana curtseyed with resignation.

*

"Well, servant, let's be on our way," Brittia sneered as Marilana emerged from the school with her weapons. "We know you have important duties to attend to, and you shouldn't be late."

The group of merchant youths all laughed and gathered around Brittia and Marquiese. They set off down the East Road and strolled leisurely to the edge of town. Marilana gritted her teeth in annoyance. She would never abandon her duty, but some days she felt pushed to her limits.

She watched as Marquiese chatted animatedly with Brittia and the group of youths walking in front of her. When they reached Merchant Sleater's manor house, Brittia smiled maliciously at her and went inside.

When all the children were safely home, Marquiese took his place at Marilana's side and said in a most triumphant voice, "So, what do you think of my solution?"

"Solution? More like a plan to make things worse. I will serve as your tutor, but do not expect me to be happy about it."

"I thought you would be pleased." Marquiese was puzzled. "Earek said that you always get the highest marks in the class, but they never get recorded because of your rivalry with Brittia. This gives you a way to prove that you are the top of the class, while at the same time you cannot be punished again because I talk to you."

"But you went above Brittia to do so," Marilana growled, her amber eyes flaring. "You got Lady Annabella to intervene.

Now, apparently, the others think I'm being forced to serve you. That is something no one else has ever accomplished."

"You serve as our escort twice a day. How is this any different?"

"I serve Lady Annabella, not any one school child," she stated flatly. "Now I serve your pleasure every day until your homework is done, and I still have all my regular duties to perform as well. Thank you for your wonderful 'solution.'"

"I did not mean to give you extra work, and it was not my intention to make it appear that you serve me." Marquiese sighed. "Sometimes the unintended consequences can be more damaging than the situation you proposed to solve."

Marilana stopped in surprise and studied him suspiciously. "Where did you learn that phrase?" she asked quietly.

"Oh, that." He frowned thoughtfully for a moment. "I think my former tutor taught it to me. It is a useful lesson to remember."

He turned and walked on. Marilana followed, not fully believe his casual attitude. Lady Annabella had taught her that phrase almost word for word, and she had never heard anyone else say it. She had the feeling once again that he was hiding something and was now sure it was true.

When they reached the old manor house, Lida waved goodbye, but Marquiese remained on the road waiting expectantly.

"Where do you intend to do our homework?" Marilana asked suspiciously.

"Lady Annabella's letter indicated that you would welcome me to your home. Did she not mention it to you?"

"My home is not suitable."

"I guess I don't understand the problem." Marquiese pulled a letter out of his satchel. "Here is Lady Annabella's letter. Read it yourself."

Marilana took the letter and stared at Lady Annabella's familiar writing.

Merchant Colbran:

Thank you for asking about a tutor for your son. Marilana would be a good choice. I will see to making the arrangements with Headmistress Ceta. Marilana's home would be a secure location for the tutoring, which can take place every afternoon when Marilana is at school.

Sincerely,

Lady Annabella Ranat

"She is right that it is a secure location," Marilana admitted. "You have to promise that you will accept my rules, however."

"Your rules?"

"Lady Annabella mentioned that the tutoring would only happen if I am at school. You must respect that part of the agreement," Marilana said seriously.

"I assumed that meant she did not want you to be bothered if you were sick and missed school."

"I'm a bandit hunter and I serve Lady Annabella," Marilana explained carefully. "Sometimes I miss school because I'm on the hunt, or because Lady Annabella requires some service from me. On those days you cannot come to my house. No one comes to my house without me being there."

"I don't understand." Marquiese frowned. "You make it sound dangerous to visit you."

"It is dangerous. I have made enemies of the bandits; they fear and hate me for my proficiency as a bandit hunter," Marilana said seriously. "You must obey my instructions without question. You must trust me in this."

Marquiese studied her for a moment. Finally he nodded in agreement.

"Good. Then follow me as best as you can."

Marquiese was not sure that trusting Marilana was the smartest risk he had ever taken. She was the most unusual girl he had ever met, yet she was Lady Annabella's ward and the Lady herself had said Marilana's home was secure.

He was amazed at the speed and dexterity that Marilana demonstrated as she moved through the trees and underbrush. Even in a dress, she was able to move quickly yet carefully, making hardly a sound and leaving nary a mark on the ground. She kept her arrow nocked in her bow the whole time and watched the forest around them without so much as breaking stride. Marquiese was hard pressed to keep up with her.

He glanced up for one instance trying to get his bearings and a stick cracked loudly under his boot. They both froze, his breathing the only sound. After a moment of silence, Marilana scanned every inch of the forest and then turned a harsh glare on him.

When she was satisfied that Marquiese's stumble had aroused no unwanted attention, they pressed on.

Just as Marquiese was wondering how much further her house could possibly be, Marilana stopped and motioned to him. He moved forward and peered cautiously around her. He was surprised to recognize the East Road just beyond the trees. For all the travel through the trees, they were not far from his house. He studied the small tidy stone cottage with a tile roof sitting in its own square garden. It was a beautiful, homey place surrounded with life, and he wondered if Marilana did all the work in the garden herself. He could make out roses and chrysanthemums, vegetables and fruits, and a large neat herb patch by the back door. Then he frowned. There, in the middle of the front path, was a leather boot pinned to the ground by a crossbow bolt.

He was just about to say something when Marilana grabbed his wrist. She placed a claw to her lips and signaled for him to wait. Marquiese nodded nervously.

Marilana crouched low and slipped away with surprising speed. Marquiese saw her hop over the back wall and dance to the back door. With her bow drawn, she slipped inside the house. After a moment she reappeared. He watched curiously as she stooped several times walking carefully to the back wall where she had entered. She scanned the forest again, and finally motioned to him. Marquiese made his way cautiously down the hill. He climbed over the wall carefully and followed her to the house.

"Wait here and do not touch anything," she said as she went back out into the garden.

He watched from just inside the door as she worked her way through the garden, again stooping multiple times along the way. When she finally reentered the house, she closed the door and locked it. As his eyes adjusted to the dim light, he noticed the mounted crossbows and the arrow slits on either side of the back entrance. He swallowed nervously as he followed Marilana further into the interior.

"Stay here," she said pushing through the front door.

He watched her stepping lightly from spot to spot until she reached to the boot. She carefully removed the crossbow bolt, closed the gate, and did something he again could not quite see. He eyed the crossbows mounted likewise around this door and noticed one of them had been triggered.

When she was back inside, she closed and locked the door behind her.

"What was that all about?" he asked nervously.

"I live here by myself." She gave him the boot. "And I have dangerous enemies."

Marquiese realized that both the boot and bolt were stained with blood. When he looked up, Marilana was carefully reloading the crossbow.

"Traps," he said with sudden understanding. "Your entire garden is full of traps."

"I have lived here alone since I was nine, and I frequently find much more than a bloody boot on my front path."

"Four years and the bandits still try to get into your house?"

"They feel that the prize would be worth it." She shrugged. "I have hunted and killed thirty bandits in the last three years not counting the ones I have killed during raids and skirmishes; they don't like me much. Bandit groups are usually five or six men strong. When they first started trying to get in my house, the whole group would try, and they all paid for it. Now it is usually just one or two who think they have figured it out. I change the traps around so the bandits cannot determine their locations."

He watched her walk casually into the next room. *Thirty,* he thought. *She has hunted and killed thirty full-grown creatures and acts as if there is nothing special in the accomplishment. Plus more she has not even bothered to count.*

Lantern light flared in the next room, and Marquiese examined his surroundings. The main room was tidy and clean. A comfortable chair sat next to the fireplace along with a pile of books and a basket of mending. Peering down the short hallway to the back door, he could see two other doors. One stood open allowing him to see a chamber pot and washbasin. He assumed the closed door opposite the washroom led to her bedroom. The wall next to the front door was taken up by two large cabinets, but Marquiese did not dare open them. Instead, he followed Marilana into what was a very clean kitchen with a large wash basin and a fire crackling in the fireplace.

He smiled at the large pots and utensils hanging on hooks, the herbs and vegetables sitting around in baskets, and the lamp sitting on the scrubbed wooden table with four chairs around it. The house had a comfortable, lived-in feel.

Marilana turned to him as he entered the kitchen and studied him nervously. He realized that under her gruff exterior she was still just a peasant girl and was worried about his intentions.

"I was very impressed with your skills in the forest. It is no wonder you have hunted so many bandits," he said, trying to break the tension between them.

"Lady Annabella's Captain-General began training me when I was six and first expressed my desire to become a bandit hunter. Since then I have honed my skills, ambushing bandits as often as needed and turning in their heads," she said grimly. "You showed quite a bit of skill in the forest as well."

"Do you have many visitors?" he asked, looking at some of the smaller items in the kitchen.

"Lady Annabella visits me once a month except in winter," she replied honestly.

Marquiese pointed to Marilana's clock. "This is a beautiful piece."

"A gift from Lady Annabella," she said simply.

"You have several items that I would not expect to find in a peasant home," he said casually.

"Lady Annabella gives me gifts when she feels I need something to help serve her better."

"Lady Annabella seems to think highly of you, if she gives you such nice gifts."

"She is a generous Lady and has been very kind to me."

"How long have you been her ward?"

"I was three when my parents left me to go beyond the southern border to pursue their research."

"Ten years," he mused thoughtfully. "Why did you decide to become a bandit hunter if you were already Lady Annabella's ward?"

"Let's just do our homework," Marilana said, suddenly cold.

Marquiese looked at her with surprise. She glared at him and held her dagger hilt tightly, ready to draw it at any moment.

"Of course," he said, realizing he had struck a nerve. He sat down at the table and pulled his school things out of his satchel.

He saw Marilana close her eyes and draw several calming breaths. Then she joined him.

When their homework was finished, Marilana escorted him quickly along the East Road around the bend to his house before hurrying off to Lady Annabella's estate. As he watched her disappear into the trees, he admitted to himself that he had not learned much about her. Solving the mystery surrounding her was going to take a lot more time.

5

Marquiese had enjoyed his first month in the Southern Tip. He had been worried about going to a school with other children. He had wondered if he would fit in. To his amazement, the merchant children accepted him without a second thought. After learning more about the expected relationship between the merchants and the peasants, he had no more embarrassing moments with them either. The peasant creatures still watched him warily, but they no longer tried to hide when he looked their way.

He also found the curriculum in the school to be challenging, but enjoyable. The best part was the new friends he'd made. He had worried that he might not be able to relax while harboring so many secrets, but he had found that everyone had some kind of secret to keep.

Earek had quickly become the best of Marquiese's new friends. Both of Earek's brothers had the normal yellow coloration and black spots like their parents, but Earek was one of the rare black leopards. Marquiese admired Earek's attitude toward this. He neither flaunted it nor got mad about it. Instead, he used it. It gave him a definite edge when sneaking up on people, and he loved nothing more than surprising the other kids.

Earek was also much more relaxed about Marquiese's endless questions about the school, town, and Marilana. The leopard was just not as concerned about what the other students would say about him, including Brittia. Like he said, "The worst thing she can do to me is to marry me."

Then there was Marilana. She was still a puzzle to him. He could clearly see that she had a close relationship with Lady Annabella. However, she always insisted that she was nothing more than an orphan and a bandit hunter. He also had come to the conclusion that she held her secrets as close as he did his and was a master at turning conversations to safer topics. Marquiese worried about getting too close to Marilana and having someone from Lady Annabella's estates recognize him, but her intelligence and skills intrigued him. Not to mention her tutelage. At first this had just been a front to be able to talk to her without causing trouble. As it turned out, she had helped him catch up on topics he had not previously studied. In many ways, Marilana reminded Marquiese of his former tutor. Both were wells of knowledge who made him think rather than just giving him the answers.

"Earek, how often does Marilana miss school?" Marquiese asked as they sat together outside in the schoolyard after lunch.

Marquiese had been surprised that morning when a mounted patrol had escorted them to school instead of Marilana. Lida had been scared something had happened, but one of the guardsmen said it was not the first time Marilana had missed school and not to worry too much.

"I'd say once a month or so. Sometimes more often. Less in the winter and spring," Earek replied easily.

"Does she usually miss one day at a time or several days?"

"It varies. From what I know, Lady Annabella doesn't like for her to miss too much school, but she is also the one who sends her out to hunt. Marilana, of course, acts like nothing happened, but we all know she probably just killed someone."

"I can understand how that could make someone uncomfortable," Marquiese said darkly.

"Brittia uses it to keep the younger kids away from Marilana. She tells them Marilana is mean and hurts people who talk to her."

"Lida said as much the first day we were here. I explained to her that Marilana protects us from the mean people.

Marilana is actually quite gentle with Lida and Lida likes her a lot."

"Yeah, the younger children seem to be naturally drawn to her during times of trouble." Earek smiled. "She exudes a feeling of confidence that is calming; even I've noticed that I feel calmer when I know she is dealing with the bandit threats."

"Do the bandits threaten the town?" asked Marquiese, frowning now.

"Sometimes they raid the outskirts and surrounding area. They steal what they can grab on the run, including kids and women. And they'll cut down any man who gets in their way."

They sat in silence for a while. Marquiese wondered if he was as safe as he thought he was at this school.

Earek jumped up suddenly. "Looks like the bandits are raiding today. Come on."

Marquiese followed Earek across the school yard and saw Marilana was running down one of the side streets. She was wearing a dress of dark green divided for riding and her grey cloak streamed out behind her. The merchants who saw her running for the school grabbed their wares and hurriedly closed their shops. Within minutes the street was almost empty.

Headmistress Ceta hurried out of the school just as Marilana reached the fence.

"Marilana, what's the trouble?" Marquiese heard her call.

"A large contingent of bandits has been spotted southwest of town. Lady Annabella sent her troops out to counter them. Lock down the school and keep the students inside until you get word from Lady Annabella," Marilana said hurriedly. She paused only a moment before continuing to race along the street to the west.

"You two," the headmistress barked at Marquiese and Earek. "Help me get everyone inside the school. Run!"

Marquiese and Earek turned and ran across the schoolyard yelling for everyone to get inside. As the last of the students raced inside, Marquiese saw groups of merchants' guards taking up positions around the school. When he was inside, Headmistress Ceta gathered everyone in the eating hall and stationed the teachers at the entrances. Lida spotted Marquiese and ran to him.

"Marquiese, I'm scared," she whimpered and wrapped her thin arms around his waist.

"I know, Lida," he said soothingly. "I'm scared too."

"Really?" Lida looked up with tears in her eyes.

"We are in a dangerous situation," Marquiese said seriously, "and I would be lying if I said that I wasn't a little scared. Remember, though, fear is inside us and we are bigger than anything inside us. We can push aside our fear and think calmly. If we can think clearly, we can find a solution to any situation."

"It's hard to push aside my fear," Lida said.

"I know. It takes practice, and you are young yet." Marquiese stroked her head.

"I wish Marilana was here to protect us," Lida said tearfully.

"She is out there protecting us," Marquiese assured her. "I know she will do everything she can to stop the bad men from reaching the school."

Lida buried her face in his shirt and held tight to him. He looked up at Earek. Earek nodded in appreciation for Marquiese's attitude and words.

"Well put," he said as his brothers Adrek and Jarek made their way over to them.

"I wish I were out there facing the bandits rather than being stuck in here," Jarek said quietly. "I feel like I'm waiting for my own execution."

"Jarek!" snapped Adrek, the oldest of the three. "Keep your opinions to yourself and don't say things like that around others. You know Father doesn't like you talking that way."

"I can say what I want. I want to be a soldier and as soon as I'm old enough I will be. Father and Mother can grumble all they like, but neither they nor you will stop me."

"This is not the place for that argument," Earek interjected. "If you want to become a soldier, you'd better start thinking like one. A soldier's duty is to protect others. You would do well to guard your tongue and protect the children around you."

"You're right, Earek," Jarek nodded. "Now is not the time for harsh words of frustration, but for soothing words of hope."

"Those are wise words," Marquiese noted softly.

"You two should not encourage him," Adrek snapped. "He should be thinking of a merchant future not of becoming a soldier."

"What kind of future do I have as a merchant?" Jarek asked in return. "I'm a third son, I have no inheritance. I have to marry a merchant daughter to even keep my rank. And in case you haven't noticed, there aren't as many girls around as there are boys. At least if I become a soldier, I can gain my own honor."

"Protecting peasants against bandits who are effectively peasants themselves." Adrek sneered. "I don't see that as honorable. I say let them fight each other and stay out of it."

"That's the difference between us, Adrek," Jarek said coldly. "You think only of money, while I respect the lives that work hard to get you that money."

"Enough, both of you," Earek interrupted. "This is not the time to bicker. Save your arguing for closed doors. Small ears don't need to hear it."

"You are right, Earek," Adrek said, pompously glancing down at Lida. "We will have plenty of time to continue this discussion when we get home."

Adrek walked off to join some of his classmates. Jarek approached several of the teachers, talking to each seriously.

"Your brothers are a cheerful pair," Marquiese remarked sarcastically.

"They bicker more when they're nervous. Jarek's right though, he doesn't have much of a future as a merchant."

"I think he would make a fine soldier," Marquiese said watching Jarek walk around the room. "Soldiers are well respected most places and from what I have heard, Lady Annabella's men are some of the best trained."

"I agree. But my parents don't see it that way. Like Adrek, they don't see the bandits as that big of a threat to merchants. Of course we have our house in town and can afford to hire enough guards to protect my father's tailor shop," Earek said, shaking his head.

"But don't let the high-class merchants mislead you. The bandit threat is very real. You saw how quickly the street emptied when the people saw Marilana in her bandit hunter clothes. No one wants to lose their wares, or their lives, to a bandit raid."

Marilana perched carefully in the tree with an arrow nocked to her bow. She had gone out early that morning on her daily patrol armed with her short sword in addition to her normal bow and dagger. Normally, she would have finished her patrol and reported to Lady Annabella's estate for sparring practice, but not today. She had been scouting the forest west of the South Road when she had heard the sharp trill. She made her way carefully toward the sound, and that's when she saw the bandit scout, a sleek orange and black tiger, slipping from tree to tree staying in the shadows. Carefully drawing her bow, Marilana shot the tiger in the neck, dropping him like puppet without strings.

Moments later, Child arrived on the scene, and together they hid the body and removed any signs of their presence.

"I've been following a bandit raiding group of about sixty men, some mounted and some on foot," Child had told her. "They are angling toward the farmlands on the southwest of Mystillion."

"This is not good news," Marilana had said. "Continue tracking them. I'll make my way as carefully and quickly as I can to the East Road and report what you've seen."

Marilana had reached the road just as Captain Branth was returning on horseback from his own morning patrol. She swung up behind him on his saddle and they had galloped flat out to Lady Annabella's estate. The guards on the wall saw them and sounded the alarm.

Lady Annabella and Captain-General Zariff met them at the castle steps, and Marilana immediately informed them of the situation. Lady Annabella then sent her back out to scout south of the estate. Marilana spent two hours scouting the forests and found two bandit scouts attempting to prevent anyone from discovering the tracks of the raiders. She struck fast and didn't bother to hide the bodies since they probably would not be found until after the raid. She then followed the raiders' tracks and quickly found them turning north toward the West Road.

Marilana hurried back and met Captain-General Zariff at the rally point. After hearing her report and equipping her with two full quivers, Zariff sent Marilana into town to sound the warning.

Now, from her current position in the forest west of town, she could see a portion of the meadow surrounding the town and a long stretch of the West Road.

She wished once again that Mystillion had better defenses. Its buildings sprawled from its center in an orderly network of streets like a spider's web. The school was placed almost exactly in the center with several blocks of merchant shops between it and the market square to the north and the Chapel of the Goddess and the courthouse to the south. While the layout made expansion easy and kept the town orderly, it also made the town easy for raids and difficult to defend without a wall. She could see the town guardsmen and a number of merchant guards hunkered down behind the barricades on the main road and larger side streets. Archers had been stationed on several of the taller rooftops. Everyone was tense, waiting for the impending attack.

Just then, the slightest movement from the forest floor caught Marilana's attention. She saw a bandit creeping toward the underbrush at the edge of the meadow. He appeared to be alone, so Marilana drew her bow and released an arrow. Even before the arrow had impaled the bandit squarely in the back, Marilana was already nocking her bow with a second arrow. She spotted a second bandit, this a burly black bear, a moment later as he tried to ease back behind a tree. She aimed and released, her arrow striking the bandit dead center of his left eye. The bear went down in a heap, but the sound of twigs breaking drew several more bandits into her view. She released four more arrows in quick succession, but gritted her teeth in annoyance as the fourth man managed a warning cry an instant before her arrow found its mark in his neck.

The rest of the bandits broke from cover at the sound. Yells rang out all along the meadow as men charged toward the smaller streets, the ones without barricades. Marilana loosed arrow after arrow dropping tigers, deer, bears, and many others as they emerged from the cover of the trees. The archers on the roof tops opposite her began raining arrows across the short expanse of grass. Guardsmen drew back from the barricades and ran further into town, making for the cross streets and smaller lanes in an attempt to cut off the bandits' advance into the town.

Marilana paused with her next arrow as a rumbling sound began to build on the road. Turning on her perch, she grimaced as a group of ten mounted bandits rounded the turn in the road and galloped straight toward the main barricade. With the defenders spread too thin, the horses would be able to jump the barricade and race through the town. Marilana drew her bow and released her arrow. The lead horse cried out in pain as her arrow pierced its chest. It stumbled and fell.

Three of the horses running behind it crashed into their leader and the sickening snaps of their breaking bones echoed among the growing tumult. The horses screamed in pain and thrashed about. One of the bandits was crushed beneath their weight, while the other three were thrown off the road. The six bandits remaining, managed to guide their horses around their downed comrades, and continued toward town. Marilana picked off three more in a matter of seconds just as Captain-General Zariff and his mounted troops emerged from the north. The bandits on foot sent up a signal shout and began retreating into the forest. Captain-General Zariff and his horsemen set out in pursuit of the three mounted bandits racing south along the meadow.

Marilana stood guard as the soldiers routed the last of the bandits. Then she watched as members of the town garrison cautiously entered the meadow and began to check the bodies. Marilana slid quietly from her perch. She crouched on the forest floor for a long moment and scanned the area. Seeing no movement, she raised the hood of her cloak and began silently tracking the retreating bandits who had turned south.

It was mid-afternoon when she finally found where Captain-General Zariff had called a halt to his pursuit. She searched the area carefully and found several sets of boot prints that turned east in pursuit of the soldiers. She was still tracking the boot prints when she saw two spotted leopards emerging out of the trees several paces to her right. She froze.

"I'm telling you I saw something," one of them grumbled. "It was dark and low, but it didn't move like a Wild animal."

"It was probably just a shadow," the other growled. "I don't see anything; let's get back to the others."

Marilana followed the two men carefully. They walked to a thick bunch of bramble bushes, and moved aside a cut section. Marilana paused and watched. After a moment, she heard low voices.

"Not a bad haul considering the raid was so badly fouled up," a deep voice said.

"I think it was the best idea you ever had, to hide inside the town before the others attacked and grab what we could on the way out. The others had huge losses. Still not sure what caused the town folk to scramble that way before the raid even started," another voice said.

"It doesn't matter. As long as we get into town ahead of each raid, we can make a good living off what we can grab in the confusion," said a third voice.

"I think we need to move," grumbled a voice that sounded like one of the leopards Marilana had followed. "Whatever it is I saw may still be around, and it's making my fur stand on end."

"We should wait for dark, then we can slip away easier," said the deep voice.

Marilana eased back away from the bramble wall and slid behind some thicker bushes. She moved to a large tree at the edge of the brambles, nimbly grabbed a branch, and swung up to the perch. She paused there listening, then climbed quietly to a higher branch. From her new position, she could see down into the bramble thicket. Five bandits sat waiting, examining the loot they had stolen during the raid. One of them, a large, knurly badger, wore a sturdy suit of molded leather armor and a metal helmet. He sat with his back to her. Marilana grimaced; he would be harder to shoot unless he turned around. Marilana raised her bow and began to draw when a horse snorted close by. She paused and looked toward the sound. The five men heard it too and dropped the loot to lay paws to weapons. Silence reigned for a long moment. Off to Marilana's right, a group of riding horses moved slowly toward the thicket. Two lanky weasels were mounted and each had four more horses tied to their saddles. Marilana gritted her teeth when she saw that two of the saddles bore the mark of Lady Annabella's garrison.

The riders cautiously approached the thicket.

"Vax, you there?" called one of the weasels softly. "I got some horses."

"Nort, you about got yourself killed riding up that way," the badger with the deep voice spoke.

"Sorry, Vax. Just thought I saw something a moment ago and didn't want to raise a ruckus," Nort said.

"See, I told you I saw something," grumbled one of the leopards. "Now can we get out of here?"

"Did you see what way it went?" asked Vax alert.

"I don't even know what it was," Nort replied. "I thought I saw something, but when I tried to get a better look, it was gone like smoke."

"Weapons out and ready, boys, we may have a Ghost nearby," Vax said quietly.

The other men looked about nervously, but no one moved. Marilana smiled grimly. She drew her bow and aimed at the weasel next to Nort. She released her first arrow, in the blink of an eye drew a second, and used it to fell the one called Nort. Both weasels hit the ground. The bandits inside the brambles scrambled to get out of the thicket. Marilana's arrows took four of the five, leaving only the badger called Vax. He growled and turned in a circle inside the thicket.

"You must be out of arrows, Ghosty," he called dangerously, "or I'd already be dead. Time to come out and play, girly."

Marilana drew her dagger. She knew it would not pierce his armor and so threw it into the brambles on the other side of the thicket. Vax spun with his sword and lashed out quickly, striking the brush frantically where the dagger had smashed noisily into the dense stems. Marilana swung from the limb and landed lightly at Vax's rear. She drew her short sword and parried as Vax swung around with a growl. He hacked at her viciously, but she slid past his attacks, easily blocking them with her own blade. With every lunge, his armor creaked, and Marilana danced lightly to the side. She spun her sword in her paw and slid the point through the gap in his hardened armor under his arm.

Vax cried out. He stumbled forward into the brambles, thrashing as blood spurted from the wound. Marilana stepped back and waited until he stilled before checking to make sure he was dead. She cleaned her blade on his pant leg and checked the other men in the thicket. Assured that they were all dead, she retrieved her dagger and gathered the pile of loot into one of the men's satchels. She slung the loot bag over her shoulder before leaving the corpses.

Marilana left the thicket cautiously and made her way to the horses. The two that belonged to Lady Annabella's garrison whinnied softly as she approached and nuzzled her happily; she scratched their ears in return. The other horses relaxed as well when they saw this. Marilana rubbed each in turn and checked them for wounds. Then tethered them together, mounted the lead horse, and led them all carefully back to Mystillion.

She entered the town via the South Road where the town guards waved her past. The merchants were displaying their wares again, and crowds milled about exchanging gossip. Many of them acknowledged her with curt nods. She led the horses to the courthouse and was pleased to see Captain Branth and a clerk taking damages from a group of merchants and peasants. He smiled with relief as she dismounted and tied the horses. He looked into the satchel and his eyes widened with surprise.

"I found a group hiding from the soldiers with a hoard of loot. From what I overheard, they had come into town ahead of the raid and stole what they could during the confusion," she told him quietly.

"This group will be very pleased to have their possessions returned to them," he smiled. "Lady Annabella sent orders for you to escort the children home and then continue to patrol the area until you feel confident that the threat is ended for the night."

"Thank you, Captain," Marilana said and hurried away.

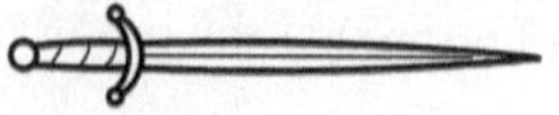

They had been locked in the eating hall for many hours, and Marquiese was relieved when Headmistress Ceta finally sent them all home. Marquiese smiled when he saw Marilana. Lida ran to her and gave her a hug.

"We have to hurry," she said to the children.

They started down the road at a hurried clip, and Marquiese noticed that Marilana was armed with a short sword as well as her dagger and bow. He also saw that the skirt of her dress was splattered with dark spots he knew must be blood.

"What's been going on?" he asked, keeping a careful watch on the forest.

"There was a lot of killing today. Bandit raid. I cannot study with you tonight. I must continue to patrol," Marilana replied quietly.

"Thank you for protecting us," he said simply.

Marilana glanced at him with a slight frown before he turned and hurried Lida passed the merchant guards and inside the house. He wondered how many more men Marilana had now killed to protect people who did not like her.

6

Marilana hadn't wanted the soldiers to escort the children back to their homes, so she had been glad she was back in time to do so. Lida had come to trust her and even like her, and Marilana had to admit that she had grown accustomed to walking to and from school with Marquiese. Sometimes they argued about some event or some homework topic, but usually she walked without saying a word, diligently watching the road and listening to the stories he told. He talked of people he had seen, places he had visited, fabulous parties, and exuberant celebrations held in the city. She said nothing of the pleasure she felt when he told his stories for fear he would say no more about his past.

After a few fifnights, she had found his intelligence to be a match for her own and, instead of arguing, they started happily debating the details of their homework. Marilana was pleased to find that he was a quick learner and easily picked up on any information he may have had missed before coming to the Southern Tip. At other times, she was amazed at how much more he knew about topics that his former tutor had apparently covered in great depth. True, she still felt uncomfortable at times when they were alone in her house. She did not understand his motives for spending time with her and felt sure he was hiding something about his past. So far she had not been inclined to ask him about his secrets. After all, she had her own secrets to keep.

Marilana did not study with Marquiese for three days after the bandit raid. She had spent the last two days of the fifnight hunting bandits and scouting for Lady Annabella's troops. Then, on Restday, she had spent the day at Lady Annabella's estate working in the stables and catching up on her own studies. Marquiese had seemed relieved when she had met him the morning of the first day of school for the fifnight as usual. He had not talked much, but had continued to walk with her even after their schoolmates had been gathered. Brittia had shot him dark looks the whole way to school. He had done the same thing on the way home, returning Brittia's glare with bright smiles and letting Marilana worry about his intentions.

Now, they sat at her table working quietly on the day's homework.

Marilana glanced up from her homework and found Marquiese watching her. He gave her a small smile and went back to his own book. She looked at the next problem in her book and wrote out the solution on her parchment. After a few more problems, she got the feeling that she was being watched again and looked up. She sat back in her chair and met his green eyes with a slight frown.

"What?"

"They trust you," he said slowly. "I was not sure at first because of how strong your rivalry with Brittia is, but the bandit raid confirmed it. They work hard to act like they do not like you and they try to cover it over with disdain for your actions. But when it comes to something important, they trust you with their lives."

Marilana's frown deepened. "What are you talking about? Who trusts me with their lives?"

"Our classmates, the merchants, everyone in Mystillion," he said watching her closely. "All of them trust you with their lives. I thought it was strange that they humiliated you in little ways, punished you for minor infractions, and acted like you were the dirt under their shoes, but also let you escort their children to and from school four days a fifnight. I thought there had to be something else going on."

"Lady Annabella made the agreement," Marilana said simply. "They trust Lady Annabella."

"Maybe at first," he said shaking his head. "But I saw the headmistress take your warning about the bandit raid and act on it immediately. She did not hesitate for an instant."

"She did the first time it happened, some years ago, and spent a fifnight in Lady Annabella's stockade for it. Lady Annabella was furious. Ignoring my warning nearly cost several merchants' lives. Headmistress Ceta had escorted me to the market square to find someone who could validate my story just as the bandits made their raid. I managed to shoot three of the bandits which caused the others to fall back and let the merchants get away. After Lady Annabella was done with her, the headmistress never disregarded my warnings again."

"I am willing to bet that Headmistress Ceta's mind was changed less by Lady Annabella's anger than by your actions in the market square."

"Perhaps, but it took Lady Annabella's anger to change the headmistress' mind about letting me bring my weapons into the school," Marilana countered.

"I can believe that." Marquiese nodded. "My merchant father tried to arrange for me to carry a dagger to and from school, but Headmistress Ceta refused. She said that only in specific circumstances would she allow a student to bring a weapon into the school. Yet you are rumored to be one of the most dangerous people in the Southern Tip, with or without weapons, and the merchants let you attend school with their children."

"I would never harm those children."

"I know that," Marquiese said calmly. "My point is that they all know it too. They trust you with their children, they trust you with their lives, and they rest easier knowing that you are protecting them."

"You may be right. But they will never admit it, and they will never stop treating me like the peasant I am."

"Last fifnight they treated you like the bandit hunter you are, and Earek told me he has noticed your mere presence tends to calm people's fears."

"Earek is good at reading people, and he is honest," Marilana admitted. "Klay, Caton, and Earek are the only merchant sons who remain mostly neutral between Brittia and me."

She watched him thoughtfully for a moment.

"What is it that you want from me?" she finally asked. "Why do you take pleasure in angering Brittia by walking with me and spending time with me?"

He chuckled a little and twisted his pen in his paw.

"Honestly, I have never met anyone like you, and I just want to know more about you, solve the mystery you present. As for angering Brittia, she has been ruling the school for so long that everyone seems to assume she will always get what she wants. I am just mixing things up a bit."

"Dabbling in the balance of power is dangerous," Marilana warned.

"The politics here are incredibly simple compared to what I dabbled in back in Maefair. Even the merchant match-making is very superficial here. I find it refreshing to play these simple games with Brittia. She thinks she is highly skilled at it, but she barely knows the first thing about politics."

"Is that why you walked with me instead of her today? Am I just a strange pawn in your games?"

"No. You are no one's pawn. That much I have figured out. I can manipulate Brittia by my actions, and she can manipulate the other students, even Earek, but you remain outside her control. That is why she dislikes you so much. You are free to act as you will. Even Lady Annabella exerts very little control over your actions. I can see her paw subtly guiding you at times, but most of the time you make your own choices. I walked with you because I wanted to. I have found that I trust you."

"Do you trust me enough to tell me your secret?" Marilana asked shrewdly.

Marquiese's attitude morphed from calm to aggressive in an instant. He sprang to his feet and reached for a hilt that wasn't at his belt. "What do you know?" he demanded harshly.

Weaponless, Marquiese took up a fighting stance, and Marilana merely raised her paws and remained calmly in her chair.

"I did not mean to startle you. I don't know anything."

"How did you know I have a secret?" Marquiese demanded.

"You are not the only one who can read people. You have been careful to avoid talking about your personal past, and Lady Annabella was interested to learn your name upon your arrival. Two plus two."

"What has Lady Annabella told you?"

"Nothing. Honestly, Lady Annabella avoids talking about you at all if she can."

Marquiese relaxed a little when he heard this.

"I am not the only one keeping secrets," he accused her.

"No, you're not. But I do not trust you enough to tell you my secrets. And I would be more worried about your intentions if you had easily told me yours."

"I trust you to protect me," he said after a moment of thought. "And I will trust you to keep the fact that I have a secret past to yourself."

"And so I shall," Marilana replied quietly.

"I will say this much," Marquiese said. "My secret is dangerous, and I take guarding it very seriously. I will not hesitate to kill to protect it."

Marilana raised her eyebrows slightly. "Is that so? And how deadly of a fighter are you?"

Marquiese let out a sigh and dropped his fighting stance.

"I have been trained in many forms of combat since I was a child," he replied. "I have not had to kill, although I have defeated many challengers in combats of arms."

"Taking a life is not easy," Marilana said calmly. "I am glad you hesitated to attack when you did. But remember, hesitation can get you killed. On the flip side, knowing when to hesitate is better than striking a killing blow first. The dead cannot answer questions."

"That is exactly what my combat instructor told me." Marquiese smiled.

"Maybe you would like to join me at Lady Annabella's for sparring practice some time?"

"No," he said quickly. "I cannot risk going to Lady Annabella's estates. You already said Lady Annabella is suspicious of me."

"As you wish," she replied simply wondering why Lady Annabella knew a merchant son, but not his parents.

Marquiese studied her for a moment. He said, "You did not look to defend yourself when I threatened you. Would you have just let me kill you?"

"It is against the law for me to stop a member of a higher caste," Marilana said levelly. "But I saw your hesitation and attempted to placate your fear rather than push you toward action. I don't have a death wish, even if the rumors claim I do. Actually, I have never been pushed far enough to find out if I could restrain myself if someone of a higher caste tried to kill me. I try never to be in that kind of position. Until a moment ago, I was not sure how far I trusted you. Now I know I trust you to keep your honorable ways."

Marquiese stared into Marilana's eyes for a long moment, and Marilana wondered what was perplexing him. "We need to finish our homework," he said quietly. "You still have duties to perform tonight."

"Yes," Marilana sighed. "I do not keep many secrets from Lady Annabella, but I will say nothing of our mishap tonight."

"Why would you do that for me?"

"I don't know exactly," Marilana said thoughtfully. "You are proud without being pompous or exerting your power. You were concerned with my punishment for talking to you. You seem to respect Lady Annabella even though you don't want to get close to her. You are skilled in combat, yet gentle with those around you. You have not pushed your advantage on me even though we are alone and you have had ample opportunity. Lady Annabella has suspicions about you, and yet suggested that you and I study here alone together."

"I suppose those are all points in my favor," he mused.

"I also trusted my first impression of you that very first day at school. You did not have lust in your eyes, and later you were truly surprised that the peasants were afraid of you just because of your rank and caste. My instinct is to trust you."

"Thank you, Marilana," he said seriously. "Your honesty and trust mean more to me than you realize."

<h1 style="text-align:center">7</h1>

It was Restday of the last fifnight of fall. Marquiese stood on a low stool in Merchant Yulan's tailor shop while under-tailors made final adjustments to his new winter clothes.

When Earek had overridden Marquiese's objections and investigated his wardrobe two weeks before, he had declared that Marquiese and his family would freeze to death unless they got some proper winter clothes.

"The winters in Maefair are nothing like the winters here," the tailor's son had said. "We have storms that can bring several feet of snow in a matter of hours, and that snow sometimes lasts all winter."

Marquiese had been sufficiently astonished and had spoken with his merchant father about getting some new clothes made. Merchant Colbran had readily agreed, and now, here he was, thinking about Marilana as he stood waiting for the last adjustments to be made. Their encounter nearly nine fifnights ago had left him surprisingly relieved. Her analysis of their confrontation had been well-reasoned and shrewd. The part that meant the most to him, however, had been her honesty. She had not been afraid of him nor had she tried to play down the seriousness of the situation. He wondered if he would ever be able to tell her the truth. For now, he realized he thought of her as a friend and hoped that she considered him one too.

Though she was as diligent as ever in escorting the kids to and from school, and constantly alert to sounds outside her house when they were studying, she also seemed more relaxed when they were together. He now felt as if they had crossed an impasse and reached a new level of understanding. This made Marquiese surprisingly happy.

"Alright, Marquiese, you can get down now," one of the under-tailors said.

He stepped down from the stool and walked over to the counter. Earek sat on the other side frowning at his history book.

"What's the problem?" Marquiese asked. "You usually do great with history."

"This makes no sense to me," Earek said quietly. "I have no idea why the Battle of Raven Wood was fought. I can't find the answer anywhere in our class texts."

"I had trouble with that one too."

"So, how did you find the answer?"

"Marilana referenced a book from the school library yesterday." Marquiese smiled. "When I asked Mistress Rose about the answer not being in the class book, she said that was the whole point of the assignment. She wants us to start looking into other resources and learn to cross reference information."

"Drat!" Earek sighed. "As if I don't have enough work to do as it is; now I have to find time to go to the library. If this is going to become a common part of our homework, I'm not sure how I'm going to get all my work done."

"You could study with me every day after school," Marquiese offered.

"With you and Marilana?" Earek asked with complete surprise. "She is going to give me the answers?"

"No." Marquiese laughed. "Marilana doesn't give answers. She makes me work them out myself. But if I need help, she is very good at giving guidance. I bet she would let you study with us if you need some help."

"I don't know." Earek hesitated. "I don't want to make Brittia mad; she can make life troublesome. It's alright for you; you rank higher than I do."

"You just have to say I invited you to study with me. I'll fix it with Lady Annabella and you can walk with me after school," Marquiese insisted.

"Well, alright, I'll talk to my father. I could use some help. My scores haven't been as high as my father would like."

Marilana glared at Marquiese as she approached him the next morning, and Marquiese gave her a surprised look in return.

"Lady Annabella informed me yesterday that Earek will be joining our study sessions," she growled at him. "I don't like it. I don't like that you assumed you could invite anyone you wanted to come to my house. I don't like that you went over my head so that I have no say in the matter."

"Marilana, I . . ." Marquiese hesitated, "I didn't think about it. I just thought it would be a help to Earek. I did not think you would mind."

Marilana sniffed and stomped off. Marquiese and Lida hurried to catch up.

"You should have asked Marilana's permission first," chided Lida.

"You're right, Lida," Marquiese agreed, looking down at her. "I made a mistake, and now I have to find a way to make it right again."

"Mother says it never hurts to start with an apology."

"You are correct." Marquiese smiled. "An apology is a good place to start."

Marilana glanced at them, but kept walking.

"Marilana, I'm sorry," Marquiese said sincerely. "I should have talked to you about it first before suggesting it to Earek, and I should have let you discuss it with Lady Annabella if you agreed to help him."

"I'm sorry too." Marilana sighed and slowed her pace a bit. "I should not have acted so harshly. I don't really mind tutoring Earek if he needs help. He is an honest individual and I know his father works him hard. I'm just on edge right now. Lady Annabella left yesterday, and I worry when she is traveling."

"Of course, I had not thought about that," Marquiese mused. "She is off to the annual tournament in Maefair, is she not?"

"How would you know that?" Marilana asked suspiciously.

Marquiese shrugged. "Lots of nobles attend the tournament, and I cannot remember a time Lady Annabella was not present. The people of Maefair love the tournament. All fifnight the city celebrates with grand parties, dancing in the streets, and musicians on every corner. You remember, don't you, Lida?"

"I remember," Lida laughed. "We use to sit on the step and watch the nobles' carriages pass by. We practiced recognizing the livery and crest of each group of soldiers and then would mark the map to count how many nobles had arrived. I loved the dancing, but Mother would never let me stay up late for the parties."

"That sounds exciting." Marilana smiled wistfully.

"Maybe someday you can visit the Royal City during the tournament fifnight and see it for yourself," Marquiese suggested lightly.

"Perhaps when I have finished school I will be allowed to serve Lady Annabella on her travels and see some of the sights you have seen." Marilana sighed. "Meanwhile, we need to get to school and study hard. Let's hurry."

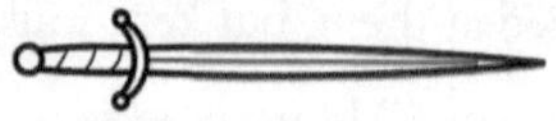

Later that afternoon, two lions and a black leopard moved through the forest in the direction of Marilana's cottage. Marquiese shook his head as Earek stumbled again. Marilana sighed and turned to them.

"Stay here and wait for a moment. I'll be right back," Marilana whispered. She passed Marquiese her dagger. "Keep a look out."

Marilana sprang away. They heard barely a sound as she moved deeper into the forest. When she returned, she said, "There are no bandits in the area this time, but next time we may not be so lucky." She turned an eye on Earek. "If you are going to study with us, you are going to have to learn to move more quietly in the forest. I thought with all your stealth, you would not be so bothersome."

"I have never had to sneak through the forest before," Earek complained.

"It is not so different than what you do in town. You just need to watch where you are placing your feet. The ground here is uneven; there are trip hazards and sound makers everywhere. Watch. And do as I do."

She turned, lifted her skirt so Earek could see her well-made soft leather boots as she placed her feet carefully on rocks and firm ground, avoiding beds of pine needles and grassy areas where traps could be disguised. Earek picked up the trick quickly, and, after a few minutes, Marilana led them back to the road and to her front gate.

Marquiese was accustomed to approaching Marilana's house from various directions. She never used the same route, which precluded anyone from determining a pattern to her movements.

At the gate, she turned and faced Earek grimly.

"This is my house and you will agree to my rules as Marquiese has," she said sternly. "You will do as I say inside my home; if I tell you to hide, you hide. You will never approach my home without me or you will risk death. Are my rules understood?"

"Yes, they are," Earek replied nervously.

"Wait here."

Marquiese scanned the road and forest as Marilana entered her garden and disarmed the front path and the front door. "Alright, stay on the path and go into the house. Do not touch anything," Marilana said.

Earek followed Marquiese into the house and then stood nervously in the middle of the front room, watching as Marilana rearmed the traps.

"You're so calm," Earek whispered to Marquiese.

"I've been doing this for three months now. I am used to the routine, although I never let my guard down," Marquiese replied calmly.

Marilana checked the crossbows at the front door, and then turned to walk past them. Marquiese flipped the dagger end over end, caught it by its point, and held it out. Marilana took the hilt with her right paw and rolled it casually across her claws, then flipped it up in the air, caught it again by the hilt, and slid it into its sheath. She gave Marquiese a mischievous smirk and then walked into the kitchen. Marquiese started to follow, but Earek grabbed his arm.

"Does she usually give you her dagger, and show off that way?" Earek whispered nervously.

"No," mused Marquiese, "that was actually a first."

"Now what?" he whispered.

"Now we do our homework," Marquiese said seriously. "No matter what the rumors say about Marilana and me, she is my tutor, nothing more."

"Good. I did not want to believe the rumors."

Marquiese led the way into the kitchen and was surprised to find Marilana washing vegetables. Her homework was spread out on the table, and she glanced over her shoulder at them.

"You'll have to excuse me for a few minutes. I need to get some stew cooking," Marilana said calmly. "Please have a seat and start on your homework. If you have questions, just ask."

Marquiese and Earek spread their homework out on the table, but they were more interested in watching Marilana as she smoothly and quickly chopped vegetables on her cutting board. Then she scraped them into the kettle, added water from a pitcher, and hung the kettle on the hook over the fire.

Feeling their eyes on her, she turned slowly around, leaned against the counter, and crossed her arms. "What? Haven't either of you seen a lioness cook before?"

"I help with kitchen chores every third night," Earek said quietly. "But I can't chop vegetables the way you do."

"I have never seen anyone manipulate a knife like that," Marquiese agreed. "You hardly seemed to need the cutting board."

"Oh, I don't actually need the board, but it's faster if I use it," Marilana said a bit sarcastically. A slight pink color bloomed through the thin fur on her face and she quickly turned away.

Marquiese and Earek exchanged a surprised look. Had Marilana actually blushed? This was a first for both of them.

"I do not think I have ever seen you cook before," Marquiese said curiously.

"You haven't. But Lady Annabella is not in the Southern Tip, so I will not eat at the castle tonight," Marilana said composedly taking her seat.

"You eat at the castle?" Earek asked, totally surprised. "I never knew that."

"I think there is much you don't know," Marilana retorted sarcastically. "Of course I eat meals at the castle. All the servants do. The stable staff eats in the barracks, the castle staff eats in the servant dining hall, and I eat wherever I'm working on any given day."

"Wait! Does that mean you eat with Lady Annabella when you are studying with her?"

"If she asks me to dine with her, of course I do," Marilana said casually. "I am her ward. I do as she requests."

"I bet Brittia doesn't know that; she would be furious to learn that little tidbit of information," Earek chuckled.

"But she will not learn of it," Marilana said coldly. "What I do outside school is not her concern, and neither of you will inform her of anything I happen to say or do. I am trusting you both to keep our conversations to yourselves."

"Of course, Marilana," Marquiese said, smiling easily. "We do not want to give Brittia any more ammunition to use against you than she already has."

"You have agreed to help me, and I will not use this time to gather information for her," Earek said seriously. "That would not be fair to you."

"Thank you both."

"So let me get this straight," Marquiese said after a moment. "You work in the castle, you work in the stables, you study with Lady Annabella, you have sparring practice, you scout, you track, you hunt bandits, and you go to school."

"Don't forget tutoring the two of you, training several of Lady Annabella's horses, and tending to my own house and garden," Marilana added with a touch of sarcasm.

"Do you ever sleep?"

"Of course I sleep. Just not as much as everyone seems to think necessary."

They all laughed, and then turned to their homework. They worked quietly, discussing the occasional problem while moving from math to history.

Marquiese was glad Earek had relaxed. In the beginning, he had been worried about bringing Earek into the sessions. After all, it had taken months for Marilana to relax with him, so to bring another merchant son into her house could well have caused problems. Marilana, however, regarded Earek with familiarity. After all, they had known each other for years.

They were nearing the end of their history assignment when the sound of horses caused Marilana to look up. Marquiese glanced at the clock and decided it must be the afternoon patrol, there had been no body for the patrol to haul away, so he was surprised when Marilana stood and left the kitchen. Marquiese tensed when the horses slowed and stopped in front of the house.

"Is something wrong," Earek whispered.

"I don't know," Marquiese replied cautiously.

Then they heard a man's voice call, "Marilana, are you there?"

"I'm here, Captain Branth," Marilana replied through the open door.

"And your visitors?"

"Both are here and working diligently on their homework," she assured him.

"Alright. Lady Annabella wants us to stop and check on you every day while she is away."

"Thank you, Captain, I appreciate the concern," Marilana said lightly.

"Will you be coming to the castle tonight?"

"No, not tonight. I will see you in the morning."

"Alright. See you tomorrow." The door closed and the sound of pounding hooves signaled the departure of the patrol.

Marquiese gave Marilana a questioning look as she came back into the kitchen, and she seemed to anticipate his question.

"Lady Annabella worries about me," Marilana shrugged.

"The Captain seemed rather concerned," Marquiese noted.

Marilana laughed lightly. "Some of the soldiers feel I need their protection. Others think I need reprimanding. In Captain Branth's case, one of his daughters is my friend Dera. They live on the northern outskirts of town, and he is glad to check in on me since I help keep watch on his family."

"You know the soldiers well then?" asked Earek curiously.

"I know Lady Annabella's soldiers and staff better than most of the children at school," Marilana replied casually. "I lived at the castle with them until I was nine."

"I . . . well . . . ," Earek hesitated.

"Speak freely," she said to him.

"Would you be willing to make an introduction? I shouldn't be asking, but I would feel better if I knew it were a soldier you said could be trusted."

"For Jarek?" Marilana asked gently.

Earek looked up, surprised. "How did you know?"

"Jarek has been telling anyone who will listen about his plans to become a soldier," Marilana replied. "He won't talk to me directly any more than the other younger children, well, except Lida, but he has made sure to talk loud enough that I couldn't possibly miss the conversation. He will make a good soldier when he has trained a while."

"My parents don't want him to become a soldier, and so they will not make an introduction for him," Earek said sadly. "I know he will run away when he turns twelve, and I worry what will happen to him. I would feel a lot better if I knew he was with someone he could trust and that I knew would help him."

"I understand. And Captain Branth would be a good choice. He is in charge of Lady Annabella's Home Guard. They patrol the county and protect Mystillion. The town garrison is part of his charge. I would be happy to introduce Jarek to Captain Branth when he is ready. You don't need to tell anyone. I will watch for Jarek when the time is close."

"Thank you, Marilana. You know, I never believed half the rumors Brittia started about you," Earek said honestly. "I am glad to learn the truth. You have a kind heart."

"Thank you, Earek." Marilana bowed her head slightly, and they returned once again to their homework.

After another quarter hour, Marquiese closed his book, but before beginning the next assignment, he looked across the table at Marilana.

"Everyone has said that the bandits don't attack as much in winter and spring," he mused. "I can understand that travel in snow and mud is more difficult, but I was just thinking about your traps. Do they work as well in the snow? Aren't they more visible without the vegetation of late spring and summer?"

"Very good, Marquiese," Marilana said as if lecturing a pupil. "You have seen several potential problems. Once you see the problems, you can find a way to counter them. Some of my traps don't work as well in the snow, but other traps do. The crossbows, for example. I also have traps that cannot be seen even if the ground is bare. Most use a fast acting poison. It is a terrible death, one that most bandits fear. I don't like to use it, but it is effective, especially as a deterrent. Also, many of the bandits that ambush travelers in summer and fall are farmers from beyond the southern border who have fallen on hard times. They have families to take care of through the winter, and crops to plant in the spring.

"The mountains and valleys south of the border are good land for crops and livestock, but the weather is unpredictable. Late snows, hail storms, mud slides, heavy rains, and fires can destroy crops, and so some of the farmers turn bandit or tracker for the rest of the year. Very few are willing to brave the winter blizzards though. Like you said, travel in the snow and mud is difficult, and it makes it easier to track their movements. So most only attack at more opportune times in the summer and fall."

"But how do you know what it is like beyond the southern border?"

"When I hunt, I go where the bandits are. I have made many trips beyond the southern border, and I have seen the conditions in which they live. I also know that many of the families beyond the border have relatives inside the border. Trade beyond the border is prohibited, but the families get supplies from their relatives who do the trading for them."

"Do you mean to say that you have killed farmers with families?" Earek asked quietly.

"I do not hunt innocents," Marilana said, shaking her head. "The bandits that I hunt are those who have built up their reputations by violence. The ones that pride themselves on how many children they have caught and tortured to death, how much ransom they have gotten without having to return the captives alive, or the ones that ransack homes and steal everything of value after killing the inhabitants. But I will kill anyone who threatens the people of the Southern Tip, just as Lady Annabella's soldiers do. The farmers know the risks of turning bandit, and the ones who have families and don't want to die, don't take the risks."

"Do I hear you passing judgment on them?"

"Hardly. But, in battle, I act as a soldier. I do what I have to do to protect my life and those of my comrades. I follow orders. As a bandit hunter, I act on the judgments of our magistrates. As a bandit hunter, I bear witness and arrest anyone caught in the act of breaking the law. I can defend others' lives with force if necessary, but I try to only kill in accordance with proper sentencing of crimes committed."

"I don't know if you've heard, but Brittia claims that when she is named Lady Annabella's heir, she plans to send the army south of the border to eradicate the bandit threat," Earek said quietly.

"Does she know about the families living there?" Marquiese asked.

"She does, but she doesn't care. She says that those families have chosen to aid the bandits, and so deserve the same fate."

"She is a fool." Marilana shook her head.

"You don't think she has a point?" Marquiese asked. "You just said the farmers turn to banditry when times are tough."

"First, she is a fool to claim the families made a choice to live there. Most of those people are descendants from people banished there many generations ago. They are living the only life they know. They turn to banditry because trade is not allowed across the border. If there were a better way for them to get the things they need to survive, they would not prey upon the people of the Southern Tip. Second, sending good and decent men to slaughter women and children is a good way to turn your people against you. The people will rise up against her if pushed past their tolerance. Brittia doesn't see the opinion of the lower castes to be important and could cause rebellion because she ignores their protests. Third, using the army to chase bandits through the mountains is beyond foolish. The bandits know those mountains better than the soldiers; they know where to hide, where to set up ambushes, and where to let the soldiers ride over cliffs to their deaths. She would send her army to their deaths in a fruitless campaign for little gain."

"You seem to have put a lot of thought into the matter," Marquiese noted. "So you would do things differently if you were named Lady Annabella's heir?"

"I am the orphaned daughter of peasant scholars. I will never be named Lady Annabella's heir. Lady Annabella and I have discussed the bandit problem because I have traveled there to hunt bandits. Lady Annabella respects my opinion and analyses of the things I have seen," Marilana said with finality. "Now we need to finish our homework before it gets too late. The weather is turning."

Marquiese glanced at Earek as Marilana turned back to her books. Earek wore a thoughtful expression, but shrugged in response to Marquiese's questioning look. They both turned back to their homework. It took them another hour to finish their homework, and then Marilana added some herbs to her stew while Marquiese and Earek gathered their school things together.

"I know history is not your favorite," Marquiese was saying to Earek, "but back home in Maefair, my friends and I used to pretend we were the great generals from the histories and we would try to figure out different tactics for the battles we were studying. If we were back at Raven Wood, how would you have attacked?"

"I don't know." Earek shrugged. "I've never paid much attention to military tactics. I would probably just charge in, like the bandits do when they raid."

"A simple tactic," Marilana said as she swung her heavy cloak around her shoulders. "And not all that bad given the location."

"How do you mean?" Marquiese asked as they followed her out the front door into the dark.

Marilana reset her traps, and they started down the road before she replied. "The forest of Raven Wood is a perfect site for an ambush. A broad sweeping charge is a common tactic when there is a possible ambush on the road ahead, just like the general did in the real battle. But it is not what I would do."

"What would you do?"

"To attack Raven Wood, I would split my force into two groups riding east and west of the road and then turn inward and catch the ambush between the two."

"A classic pincer attack." Marquiese nodded. "It would have been very successful against the ambush that took place there. So then what would you do to defend?"

"Ah, well that would be more involved." Marilana smiled coldly. "Raven Wood is a perfect site for an ambush, so I would not set a full ambush."

"You wouldn't?"

"No, a smart attacker would expect an ambush and attack accordingly, like the pincer attack I just mentioned. No, I would set a small group in the middle of Raven Wood, a token force to make it look like an ambush. Then I would set a force on the north end of the forest as the enemy marched in from the south. I would send my main force through the gully that runs west and south of Raven Wood. Once the attackers had engaged the token ambush in the midst of the forest, my main force would swing up onto the road behind the attackers. The two large groups would then crush the attackers in the middle."

"That would work well. As long as the attack came from the south like the real battle." Marquiese nodded thoughtfully. "I had not considered the gully."

"How do you two know what would work and what wouldn't?" asked Earek, his leopard brow creased with great curiosity.

Marquiese realized he had said too much and may have been giving too much away about his past and tried backtracking. "It was just something I used to do with my friends, discussing the different tactics. Sometimes a higher ranking soldier would come to my father's shop, and he would talk to us about the tactics we discussed. It was fun to think about," Marquiese said lightly.

Marilana glanced his way and then said, "I am a scout for Lady Annabella. Men's lives depend on the information I provide. That information is more valuable if I see that certain tactics would work better than others. I am their eyes in the field, so to speak. I have studied historical battles with Lady Annabella's Captain-General, and it has helped me be a better scout and bandit hunter."

"How do you two learn so much from so many places?" Eared asked amazed.

Marilana and Marquiese both chuckled slightly.

"We listen and remember," Marilana replied.

That seemed to satisfy Earek, and they continued in silence until they reached Marquiese house.

"Why don't I walk with you and Earek into town?" he offered.

"No," Marilana said firmly, "it will be safer and faster if you go inside and let me escort Earek home." Marilana pointed toward the sky. "The winter snows are here. By tomorrow, there could well be a foot of snow on the ground. I want to get

Earek home quickly so I can make it home before too much snow falls."

"She's right. We need to hurry," Earek said.

"Alright. Have a good night, both of you," Marquiese said reluctantly.

He watched Marilana and Earek hurry toward town. He nodded to the merchant guard and headed to the house. Just as he reached the door, something brushed his face, and he looked up. Small snowflakes were drifting gently down from the starless sky.

Marilana and Earek lifted their hoods as tiny snowflakes started drifting down around them.

"You trust Marquiese a great deal, don't you?" Earek commented as they moved quickly down the road. "You gave him your dagger, and you did not even flinch when he and I entered your kitchen."

"You are an honorable person, Earek. I have never had cause to fear you. He is just as honorable. Over these last few months, he has shown me courtesy and kindness."

"You are not worried that he is just trying to gain your trust so that he can catch you with your guard down? That's what Brittia expects him to do."

"She does not know him the way I have come to know him," Marilana replied. "Would you do something like that? Gain a girl's trust just to betray her?"

"No, I would not," Earek shook his head, "but that is what that merchant son did a few years ago."

"Yes he did," Marilana said darkly, "and he had to settle for merchant daughters, because I would not let him close to me or the peasant girls."

"I always wondered why he didn't try his charm on the peasant girls," Earek chuckled. "Now that I think about it, I remember you were always watching him and it made him nervous."

"I was not sorry to see him move away," Marilana admitted.

"What will you do if someone asks Lady Annabella for permission to court you?"

"Why do you want to know? Are you thinking about asking?" Marilana said sarcastically.

"No, it is just something I have always wondered about. I know I have to try to win the favor of a merchant daughter to keep my rank. I know some of the peasant girls catch the eye of merchant sons and raise their rank. You are in a unique position as Lady Annabella's ward. It is not up to you who she accepts."

"Lady Annabella lets me make most of my own choices. I am confident that if I did not wish to marry someone, she would not force me to."

"You realize that she could marry you to someone of any rank," Earek persisted. "She is a Great Lady, and, as her ward, she could use your marriage to strengthen ties to other nobles."

"Nobles?" Marilana laughed mirthlessly. "You think nobles would be interested in marrying a peasant girl? No, Earek, she will not try something as drastic as that. She does not act in such desperate gestures."

"Perhaps not, but marriage to a merchant would not be out of the picture."

"What merchant would want to marry a bandit hunter?"

"Say what you will to deny it, but you have gained the trust of a highly eligible merchant son who does not have to marry well to keep his wealth and rank."

Marilana glanced at him thoughtfully, but said nothing as they hurried on. The snow was beginning to cover the road by the time they reached Earek's house in town. He turned to her when she stopped at the gate.

"Marilana, we have never been friends, but neither have we been enemies. Thank you for tutoring me. I think I will learn a lot more from you and Marquiese than just our homework." Earek smiled at her. "Will you be alright going all the way back to your house? You could stay here for the night if need be."

"You are kind to offer, and you are kind to trust me so easily, but I don't think I would be welcome in your house," Marilana said, watching the woman standing on the top step.

"Perhaps not. Mother looks like she's ready to skin me alive already. She is not happy that Father allowed me to study with you. She thinks the other merchants will think badly of me. We will see what time brings."

"Have a good night, Earek," she said with a slight bow.

"Good night, Marilana," Earek said and turned to the house.

Marilana gave Earek's mother a slight bow as Earek walked up the path, but she offered no such gesture in reply.

Marilana hurried to the end of the street and entered the forest at an easy lope. The snow was not yet covering the ground under the trees, and she made good time returning home.

She carefully covered her tracks through the garden to her back door, and entered the warm house. She was not surprised to find Child's winter cloak hanging on a peg by the back door. She hung up her cloak, took off her boots and washed up before going into the kitchen. Child turned from the kettle with two steaming bowls of stew. She set them on the table, and they shared a warm hug.

"There were two of them tonight," Child said worriedly.

"Yes, and there will be two of them on most nights until something changes," Marilana said gently.

"Did they hurt you? *Will* they hurt you?" Child asked.

"No, Child, these two will not hurt me. They are honorable, and I am helping them with their studies," Marilana smiled. "How are you? Are you feeling well? It has been cold at night this last fifnight."

"I am well, but I would like to sleep in tonight where it is warm, if you don't mind." Child smiled.

"Of course. Let us stoke the fire and eat something warm," Marilana said sitting down and picking up a spoon.

Marilana tramped up the road the next morning through a foot and a half of snow. Marquiese watched her coming and smiled. She carried her bow with arrow nocked as usual; her dagger hilt glinted just inside her heavy wool cloak.

"Good morning, Marilana," his breath misted in the air as he greeted her.

"Good morning, Marquiese," she replied with a glance at his wardrobe and grinned. "You look warm; it was very cold last night."

"I am." He nodded. "I'm glad Earek convinced me to buy some heavy winter clothes. I'm glad to see you made it home all right last night."

"I made good time. I was warm by the fire when the snow started to get thick," she answered. "Where is Lida this morning?"

"Lida rode into town with my merchant father. He had some early business to attend to and he wanted Lida to accompany him so that she could get the final fitting on her formal dress. She is looking forward to the parties this winter. She also wanted me to tell you she missed seeing you and walking with you this morning." He fell into step with her.

"I'm glad she got to ride into town, this snow is hard to walk through, and she is not used to the cold," Marilana said, smiling gently.

"Was this a bad storm?"

"A typical storm," Marilana explained. "If the wind had picked up, it could have turned very nasty. A heavy blizzard can catch people unprepared. Creatures all across the Southern Tip have frozen to death or gotten lost in blizzards. The best thing to do when the wind picks up is to find the nearest shelter and stay put. Swirling snow can easily disorientate you and lead you off track. If you get lost, you could be lost for days. Worse, you could fall into a ravine or a lake. If that happens, you will most likely die."

"That's a cheerful prospect," Marquiese muttered.

"It's the truth," Marilana said honestly. "I would rather you know the grim truth than think you could make it home and die trying."

"Have you ever gotten caught in the snow?" Marquiese asked curiously.

"Yes. A sudden blizzard came up while I was tracking bandits two years ago," Marilana replied bitterly. "I took shelter in a ravine. I managed to cut some pine branches and tie them together into a rough lean-to. It was a cold and very dark night. I did not sleep for fear of freezing. When the sun finally came up, the storm was over and I was able to dig my way out of the snow. I got my bearings and headed toward Lady Annabella's castle. I had only gone a few hundred paces when I found the bandits. They had tried to take shelter in a thicket of trees and froze to death. Every one of them. I was lucky that night. Since then, I pay more attention to the weather, and don't push as hard to catch bandits if the weather could turn bad. Lady Annabella chided me for months after that storm. 'Better safe than dead,' she says."

"You took a big risk last night," Marquiese said darkly.

"Not really," Marilana replied. "I know every inch of these forests and every possible place to hide. I can make the distance from the town to my house in only a few minutes if I'm traveling alone. It takes at least four times as long when I'm escorting the children."

"That's why it was safer for everyone that I stayed at my house instead of taking Earek all the way to his house," Marquiese surmised.

"If you had accompanied me, we would have been cold and tired by the time we reached your house again. I'm more use to the cold and snow; you could have suffered frostbite or gotten sick from the exposure. I was not willing to risk your health on a simple errand."

"Did you have any problems with Earek?" Marquiese asked quietly.

"Of course not. He has never been the type to push an advantage on a girl. However his mother was not very happy when he arrived home. He said she was not pleased that he was associating with me."

"No, she is not a woman to take kindly to anything she thinks will lessen her husband's reputation."

"Your dabbling in the local politics is causing changes," Marilana said quietly. "If you push Brittia's anger too far or cause someone to lose honor, there could be far reaching repercussions."

"I certainly expect so. Your sleepy little town needs a good stirring up, if you ask me." Marilana gave him a worried look, and Marquiese laughed. "Don't worry, I won't go too far."

They were trudging past Brittia's house, but she was not there, and only a pawful of other children had joined them so far. Marquiese studied the children following them and recognized that they were all from low or mid-class merchant families.

"I wonder where everyone is today?" Marquiese said.

Marilana pointed to the wagon tracks. "Lida was not the only one to get a ride into town," she said simply. "The walk is difficult and cold in the snow."

They finally reached the school and found Brittia still outside chatting with her friends. She shot them a dark look as they reached the school yard.

"I'll see you later," Marilana said to Marquiese under her breath. Then she crossed the yard to the front door.

"It's a good thing you're so strong, Marilana," Brittia called to her. "Walking all the time is such hard work, and I'm sure Lady Annabella wouldn't want you to fall down on the job. Maybe someday someone will offer to give you a ride, but it won't be me."

Brittia's group snickered their appreciation of this less-than-clever comment.

"I wouldn't expect you to understand the value of walking, since you have no experience with hard work," Marilana retorted before entering the school.

Brittia's friends exchanged confused looks and Brittia dismissed the exchange with a casual flip of her paw. Marquiese restrained his smile and leaned against the fence next to Earek.

"So?" he asked. "Did you have to stay up all night doing chores?"

"No," Earek sighed. "Other than my mother's icy attitude, my night was quiet. My father told me I am not to talk to Marilana at school, however. He stressed the point that I am studying with *you* and she is *your* tutor. He said studying with you was as close as I am to get to her, and that I am not to be seen fraternizing with her. And from now on, one of my father's guards will wait at your house to escort me home from our study sessions."

"That will spare Marilana the time. She has enough other duties," Marquiese said casually.

"I was hoping that studying with you would help me escape Brittia's clutches, but her mother and my mother had a chat last night, and it is not to be. You may be Brittia's top choice as a suitor, but she is not about to let me slip away as her backup," Earek said with frustration.

"Give it time, Earek," Marquiese said quietly. "Brittia may decide neither of us will make good husbands."

"That would be a blessing for us and a terrible twist of fate for some other poor sap." Earek chuckled, and Marquiese smiled his agreement.

8

Marquiese stretched, and Earek yawned. They both leaned back from Marilana's table.

"Finally, our last homework assignment before the New Year," Marquiese said. "One more day of school, and then two fifnights off. I'll be glad to have a break. Three storms this month alone. I haven't seen more than a half a day of bare earth in six fifnights. Good thing there are only two and a quarter months left till spring. I'm not sure I'll ever get used to all this snow."

"You've been complaining about the snow for fifnights," Earek chuckled. "I'm not sure I'll be able to put up with your complaining for the rest of the season let alone year after year."

"Marilana are you ready for Brittia's New Year's party at school tomorrow?" Marquiese asked as Marilana came in with an armload of snow-covered wood for the wood box.

"Brittia's party is just for merchant children. I am not going to force my presence on her and ruin my own day," she replied.

"Brittia said it was for the whole school."

"She always does," Earek said. "But Headmistress Ceta always dismisses the peasants after announcements. And if they try and stay, they get a personal escort to the door. And if a merchant asks a peasant to stay for a dance, they both get escorted out."

"The more I learn about Brittia the less I like her," Marquiese muttered.

"Don't worry, I don't want to stay for her party anyway," Marilana said easily. "Lady Annabella's staff always has a party, and I have attended it every year since I was three. This year will make ten years running, and I don't want to miss it. Lady Annabella is still in Maefair, but Chamberlain Vikal always makes sure the staff has a good time."

"That definitely sounds like more fun than Brittia's party," Earek said, smiling.

"Is Jarek going to the party? How has he been holding up since his birthday?" Marquiese asked more quietly.

"He is going, but he's not happy, and everyone's tense. My father has ordered a guard to follow Jarek everywhere he goes. Now Jarek regrets waiting for his birthday. I don't know how long this can go on. The guards don't like enforcing the house arrest. Jarek tried to get them to teach him their skills, and they liked that idea. They started to teach him how to use a cudgel, but when my father found out, he threatened to fire all the guards. The only time Jarek is not under guard is at school, and the headmistress makes sure he's not alone even for a minute. I think he will try something desperate if the situation is not resolved soon. I have tried talking to my parents, but that just results in a lecture about my proper place as a merchant."

"Something will have to change," Marquiese said reassuringly. "The guards will not continue on this way for too much longer."

"Time will tell," Marilana said. "Try to be patient, Earek. Your unease will not help your brother."

Marquiese narrowed his eyes suspiciously as he watched Marilana working around her kitchen. He wondered what she knew or suspected that she was not telling them.

*

The next day, Marquiese rode into town with Lida in their merchant father's wagon. This, his merchant parents argued, was an important day, and they would not hear of him walking in his formal clothes.

Everyone gathered in the school's eating hall. All were dressed in formal winter clothes and looked splendid, all except Jarek who leaned moodily against the wall only paces from where Marquiese stood relaxing with Earek, Klay, and Caton. Brittia was, of course, acting the hostess and showing off in a scarlet gown.

The peasants kids were all gathered at the other end of the hall. They all wore their best clothes, some of which was threadbare or fit poorly. It didn't matter; they chatted happily together and seemed to Marquiese to be having a grand time.

A line of merchant children entered from the main doors and caught Marquiese's attention. These were the kids Marilana normally escorted to school, and he smiled at her as she brought up the rear. Her dress was simple dark green wool. On her head, she wore a circlet of green adorned with silver ribbon. Marquiese reached up and touched the brim of his dark blue top hat when she looked at him. She gave him a slight nod and then passed her homework into Mistress Rose's waiting hooves.

Just then, Brittia moved to intercept Marilana, and the room went quiet with anticipation. The teachers, for their part, pretended not to notice.

"What's this?" Marquiese said, exchanging a dark look with Earek.

Brittia greeted Marilana warmly and took a firm hold of her arm. Marilana didn't resist. She allowed Brittia to lead her toward her circle of grinning friends. Marilana held a polite smile, but Marquiese could see she was suspicious of Brittia's intentions.

Marilana spoke politely to the merchant daughters even as some of the merchant sons moved to join the group. Brittia did not release Marilana for a couple of minutes, holding her in the middle of the group as the others crowded in around them. Marquiese could not see what was going on, but wanted more than anything to put a stop to it. The chatter he overheard was all about dresses and girl talk, but he could tell it was a front for something. He started to step forward, but Earek touched his arm in warning. Marquiese took a deep breath and eased back, replacing his scowl with a look of indifference. Earek was right. He could not interfere without dishonoring Brittia, and the ripple effect of that could be costly.

Just then Headmistress Ceta called for everyone's attention. The group of merchants' children surrounding Marilana shifted quickly, and Brittia gleefully gave Marilana a hard shove. Marilana seemed to trip; she started to fall backward. Merchant children stepped quickly out of the way and began laughing. Brittia, however, was too close and Marilana, apparently by accident, grabbed Brittia's arm for support. Together, they toppled to the floor. Brittia's scream caught everyone's attention. The merchant children were no longer laughing, shock now masking their faces.

Headmistress Ceta hurried to the scene. "What is it? What happened?"

"I'm so sorry, Brittia," Marilana said, sounding horrified. She got to her feet and helped Brittia up as well. "I have no idea why I lost my balance."

"Are you alright, Brittia?" Headmistress Ceta cried.

"I think so, Aunt Ceta," Brittia said, straightening her dress and hat. "No thanks to this clumsy ox."

"Marilana, I should have known," Headmistress Ceta growled. "If I weren't so busy today, I would cane you."

"Perhaps, you can punish me after the break when you are less busy," Marilana suggested timidly.

"What foolishness!" Headmistress Ceta shook her head. "I'm sure you will have earned your fair share of other punishments by then. You will, however, leave today as soon as I finish my announcements."

"As you say, Headmistress." Marilana curtseyed.

Headmistress Ceta led Brittia huffily to the front of the room and the other merchant children followed, glaring at Marilana as they passed her. Marilana turned and winked at Marquiese, then walked on her toes to the nearest chair. Marquiese could see that she had allowed someone to tie her bootlaces together while Brittia supposedly distracted her. He chuckled softly, realizing she had fallen for the sole purpose of pulling Brittia down with her.

Marilana quickly fixed the laces on her boots and then waited rather indifferently while Headmistress Ceta announced her various awards for student achievements. To no one's surprise, Brittia was named the top student in Mistress Rose's class.

When the headmistress finished, she dismissed the peasants, but Marquiese was pleasantly surprised to see that there was no mass exodus. Instead, the peasant creatures chatted among themselves and slowly moved toward the exits.

Several of older merchant sons joined his little group, chatting happily. They began a discussion about the annual tournament in Maefair. They had just learned the results of the tournament from six fifnights ago and said that a Master Enton Castant had won. Marquiese was careful to say only that he had watched several tournaments, and discussed some of the knights he had seen compete. When he looked for Marilana, she was already gone. He glanced at Earek and frowned. Earek was frowning darkly and scanning the room. Earek shook his head slightly when he noticed Marquiese's curious look. Marquiese continued with the discussion for a while before the other boys moved off to get some food. Earek leaned close and whispered so that Marquiese could just hear him over the musicians that had begun to play.

"Jarek slipped out with the peasants," Earek said to him simply, his dismay complete.

"Hello, Jarek," Marilana said walking toward the figure moving carefully through the trees.

"Marilana!" Jarek spun around. "You startled me. I was just . . . ."

"Just what?"

"Nothing," he said glumly.

"If you keep walking in that direction," she said, pointing deep into the forest with amusement, "you will run into a deep ravine that you cannot cross for many miles. You will not make a good soldier if you die while trying to run away."

"You might have found me, but I will not go back to my parents. You cannot make me," Jarek said defiantly.

"I have no intention of forcing you to do anything you don't want to do," Marilana replied seriously. "I heard your intentions to run away and suspected you would try to slip away today. Your parents did not think you would willingly miss the party, so they let their guard down during the chaos. And since I would rather not let you die out here in the cold and snow, I waited for you."

"How did you know I would come this way?"

"Your father has the roads watched, and your house is too close to the edge of town for you to risk slipping out north of the East Road. Because of the cold, I assumed you would be heading toward Lady Annabella's castle in a fairly direct route, so that meant you would try to slip out south of the East Road." Marilana smiled.

"So what are you going to do?" he asked dejectedly. "Lead me in circles until I give up or freeze to death?"

"Actually I was thinking about leading you to Lady Annabella's castle and introducing you to Captain Branth, who is in charge of the Home Guard and Mystillion town garrison," Marilana said lightly. "So you can follow me or you can try your own luck. The choice is yours."

"Thanks, Marilana." Jarek sighed with relief. "I think I've miss judged you all these years."

"Don't worry about it." Marilana lead the way through the trees. "Brittia has the rank to back her words, and you never had reason to seek the truth."

"That's true, but Earek has always told me not to believe everything I hear. I should have listened to him."

"Yes, you should have," Marilana said simply. "Your brother is honest and level headed."

"So the rumors are not true? The ones about you seducing Marquiese?"

"Jarek, you are going to a place where people like me, protect my honor, and trust me," Marilana said levelly. "You'd do well to treat any rumors about me as false unless one of the Captains confirms it. I have never seduced anyone. I have never lain with any male."

"So you don't kill bandits by seducing them and then poisoning them?" he asked curiously. "I kind of liked that rumor."

Marilana laughed. "I kill bandits with poisoned traps, bow and arrow, crossbow, sword, dagger, and club, if you want to know."

"What about the rumors that you cheat on all your tests and that's how you get high scores, and why the headmistress strikes all your scores from the record book?"

"If I were to cheat, I would not get as high of scores as the ones I get by studying hard. Brittia spreads that rumor because she doesn't like admitting that I'm smarter than she is. Your brother and Marquiese study with me for a reason. Also, while my scores are stricken from the school records, Lady Annabella keeps close records of all of them."

"Why would she do that?"

"I am her ward, and she wants to make sure I am reflecting well on her reputation."

"What about the rumor that the soldiers at the castle fondle the maids?" he asked with a grimace of disgust.

"My, you've heard them all, haven't you?" Marilana said darkly. "No, Lady Annabella's guardsmen are sworn to treat all women of any caste with respect and courtesy."

"Good! I want to protect people. I do not want to be stuck with men who disgust me," he said brightening.

"Lady Annabella's soldiers are well trained and honorable. I think you will do well with them."

"Will I get to see you at the castle often?" he asked hesitantly.

"I am at the castle every morning, and nearly every evening as well. Why do you ask?"

"I was wondering if you would tell me how Earek is doing."

"I will. Earek was worried about you, too," Marilana said gently. "He was relieved when I told him I would introduce you to Captain Branth. I had been watching you anyway, but I found Earek's concern for your wellbeing encouraging. Your concern for him is also a good indicator of your character. And when Lady Annabella returns to the Southern Tip, she will speak to your parents to settle the issue of your running away. After that matter is settled, I will make sure you and Earek can have time to visit each other."

"You would do that for me?" he asked surprised.

"I would do that for anyone, but especially for Earek. He has shown me kindness this last month, and for that I will do what I can for him," Marilana replied seriously.

"Earek is right. You have changed recently. I never used to see you smile or talk so easily. I like these changes. After all, it is easier to trust a lioness who doesn't growl and scowl all the time."

"And it is easier to smile with people who are actually nice," Marilana said. "Though I am not sure how much I have actually changed. It is only in Mystillion that I have to deal with people who listen to Brittia's rumors. After you have spent some time at the castle, you will see the larger picture."

"You're saying the merchants outside Mystillion don't hear these rumors?"

"I'm sure they do, but they don't have reason to believe them. Brittia's influence doesn't extend beyond the county. Those people know me as Lady Annabella's ward or Marilana the Ghost. Either way, they treat me with respect and courtesy."

"I've heard most people fear The Ghost, don't they?"

Marilana didn't answer.

"So why do you stay if you are treated better outside Mystillion?"

"I have my reasons," Marilana said leading the way out of the trees and toward the castle.

The guardsmen on the wall spotted them and called down to the guard at the gate. The foot gate opened, and they were let in.

"Who did you bring with you, Marilana?" asked the grey wolf gate guard.

"This is Jarek. He would like to meet Captain Branth."

"Well, you're in luck. He just returned and is probably still in the stables."

"Thank you, Shaub," Marilana said leading Jarek toward the stables.

Many of the horses whinnied as they walked past, and Marilana obliged them by giving each a pat on the nose. When they saw Captain Branth talking with a small group of soldiers outside the tack room, they waited. Captain Branth noticed them moments later and dismissed the guardsmen. He gave his saddle to one of the stable staff and stepped over to them.

"Marilana. Good to see you," he said.

"Likewise, Captain Branth."

"And who is this?" Branth asked, eyeing Jarek.

"This is Jarek, Merchant Yulan's third son. He ran away from home today intent on becoming a soldier. He turned twelve last fifnight. Jarek, this is Captain Branth," Marilana said calmly.

"So you want to be a soldier, and your parents don't think it appropriate," Captain Branth said, nodding. "Very well, you can stay in the new recruits barracks until Lady Annabella makes the final decision to accept you or not. Come on, I'll get you settled in." Then he turned to Marilana. "Thank you, Marilana. Dera said you had some business to attend to before coming to the party. She is waiting for you inside."

"Thank you, Captain."

Marilana nodded to Jarek and walked back through the stable, patting noses as she passed.

She crossed the stableyard and walked along the path to the side entrance. Once inside the castle, she descended to the servant quarters in the lower level and the small room that had been her home since she was three. She hung her cloak, bow, and quiver on the pegs by the door and washed her paws and face in the basin. She brushed her dress and made sure her circlet and dagger were secured. Then she left the room and made her way to the servants' dining hall. Chamberlain Vikal, an elder antelope, smiled when he saw her coming.

"Marilana, my dear. Welcome to the New Year's celebration. For ten years I have had the pleasure of your attendance and watched you grow. I hope you will enjoy yourself."

"Thank you, Chamberlain Vikal. I will try." Marilana smiled and joined the party.

"Marilana! There you are! I was wondering how much longer you would be. Come on, let's get something to eat. It's nearly lunch time," Dera said.

Smiling, Marilana accompanied the slender coyote to the tables laden with food. They filled their plates. Dera laughed and chatted, and together they roamed the room talking to the other servants and their families. The staff and guardsmen visited the dining hall between shifts and families came and went throughout the day. Dera left with Madam Bila in the afternoon to go to her apprentice studies in the library. Marilana thought Dera would make an excellent librarian in a few years and be able to replace Madam Bila when she finally retired.

Marilana watched some of the more adventurous creatures dance a simple waltz. When that song ended, the musicians struck up a fast jig and the dancers picked up the pace, laughing and challenging one another to keep up. Onlookers laughed and clapped in time to the music, but Marilana kept to the back of the crowd. It was true that Lady Annabella had insisted that Marilana learn formal dancing and that she was quite good at it, but she also knew that none of males present were brave enough to ask her. She was, after all, Lady Annabella's ward and the infamous Ghost.

She excused herself late in the afternoon, retrieved her cloak, and went back to the stables. There she got a lead rope from the tack room and waved at the stable master. She greeted the sleek white mare known as Snow with a good ear scratching and a crust of bread before tossing a blanket over her back, clipping the lead rope to the halter, and leading the horse out of the stable. They went down the lane and out to the large empty pasture where Lady Annabella's white stallion, Storm, usually ran. The white mare lifted her head and sniffed the air for a moment before nudging Marilana's shoulder with her nose.

"I miss him too, Snow," Marilana said to the mare. "Your son and Lady Annabella will be back in a few more fifnights. In the meantime, we will have to keep each other company."

Marilana let the mare off the lead rope and watched her amble about in the snow-covered pasture. She thought about the conversation she had just shared with Jarek and the party she had just attended. She had told Jarek that she felt more welcome here at the castle than she did in town, and it was true that the staff treated her well. However, she was still an outsider. For ten years she had lived among these people, yet there was still a distance she could not bridge. She was one of the castle staff, yet she was so much more than that. She was one of the stable staff, yet they did not see her as one of them. She had befriended many of the peasant girls, but even they were uneasy with her at times. She was, as Earek had suggested, in a unique position. She was a servant, an orphan, a scholar, and a bandit hunter. She was also Lady Annabella's ward. No matter what the group, she was never fully accepted. How could she be, wearing so many hats?

Marilana sighed as the snow-white horse pressed her head into Marilana's chest, and she absently scratched the mare's ears. According to Jarek, Marilana had changed, yet she could not see any difference in how people treated her. Marquiese was the only one of her schoolmates who seemed indifferent to her position and saw only her. It was true that because of Marquiese, Lida and Earek had also begun to welcome Marilana's presence and to enjoy her company, but that hardly represented a strong turnaround. To most, she was still a lioness to be feared and avoided.

Marilana wondered what it would have been like if her parents had not left her. She would have had a family. She would have learned about herbs and healing. She would have become a respected and welcome member of the community. She would not have been in the woods when the bandits came and took away her innocence.

But they did leave me. The bandits did find me. And now I have chosen a path to protect others. She scolded herself. I don't need a family. The rigors of my duty are more easily accomplished on my own.

Slightly sad yet determined, Marilana took Snow back to the stable, rubbed her down, and said good night to the stable master. She retrieved her bow and quiver and headed out to patrol before retiring for the night. Child was off in the forest somewhere, so Marilana spent the night in dark solitude.

9

“Marilana, are you there?” Marquiese called from the road outside the gate.

Marilana opened the front door looking worried. Marquiese had not seen her during the past two fifnights. He hoped she had enjoyed the New Year break. He had not expected to see her or Earek until school started the next day and had been surprised when Earek had come to him this morning asking for his company on a visit to Marilana. As pleased as he was to see Earek and have an excuse to visit Marilana, he was also worried about what could have driven Earek to want to come to her house unexpectedly.

“Marquiese, Earek, what’s the matter?” Marilana asked quickly from her door.

“School is starting again tomorrow, and we need some help on our holiday homework,” he replied levelly. “Can we come in?”

Marquiese knew she would understand that something was going on. They hadn’t been given any holiday homework. Sure enough Marilana looked pointedly at the two merchant guards that had accompanied them.

“We’ll meet you back at the manor when we’re done,” Marquiese told the men.

“I was told to accompany the lad everywhere,” one bear said gruffly.

“I promise I am not going to run away, and I will meet you back at Marquiese’s house,” Earek said with exasperation.

"I will take responsibility for him, and I will accompany him to the brick manor," Marilana said coldly. "On my honor as Bandit Hunter."

"So be it." The guard glared at Earek for a moment. "We will be waiting."

The two turned without another word and began walking back up the road. Marilana watched the bears until they disappeared around the bend. Then she scanned the forest, disarmed her traps and let Marquiese and Earek enter. Earek immediately started pacing the main room moodily while Marquiese leaned against the wall next to the door watching with his arms crossed. Marilana closed the door and studied them both for a moment. She raised her eyebrows and indicated the long sword hanging at Marquiese's hip. It moved as he shifted and he adjusted easily, as if it was a part of his own body, and he suspected she could tell he had been wearing a sword for a long time.

"You were not escorting us," he said quietly, touching the hilt. "And I don't trust even a half dozen merchant guards with my safety."

"It looks natural on you," she commented levelly. "So? Now that you're here, what's going on?"

"Earek's father placed him under constant guard this morning."

"As his escort mentioned," Marilana said. "This is the first Restday since Lady Annabella returned from Maefair. I know she took Jarek to face his parents earlier this morning. I don't know what occurred, but judging by Earek's brooding, it did not go as well as it could have."

They watched Earek pace in silence for a while. Finally, he collapsed in the chair next to the fireplace and put his head in his paws. Marquiese did not move as he watched Marilana step forward to kneel in front of the chair and gingerly place her paw on Earek's shoulder.

"Why don't you tell us what's wrong. Perhaps we can help?"

Earek lifted his head and studied Marilana's face for a moment.

"I apologize for intruding, but I needed some place where I felt comfortable enough to think for a while. I doubt that you can do anything to help though," he said dejectedly.

"I'm glad you feel comfortable enough in my home to come here to think," Marilana said gently. "We are concerned for you. Please tell us what happened."

"As you said, Lady Annabella brought Jarek home this morning," Earek explained with a sigh. "She explained to my parents Jarek's desire to become a soldier and told them that he had passed the initial trials. She said she would be happy to accept him into her guards, but she wanted the family to resolve the issues that drove him to run away. My father said he would not permit his son to become a lowly soldier. Lady Annabella then reminded him about the honor Jarek could bring to the family as one of her soldiers. She talked about how he could raise his rank with hard work and dedication. That he could possibly become an officer and hold authority equal to a high-class merchant."

"And?"

"And my parents flat refused to give their approval," Earek said. "Naturally, Jarek told them he would just run away again."

"What did Lady Annabella say to that?" Marquiese wanted to know.

"She called it all foolishness and ordered my parents to find a resolution to the problem. My parents . . . ," Earek faltered. After a moment, he drew a deep breath and tried again. "My parents' answer was to disown Jarek."

"They disowned him!" Marquiese exclaimed shocked.

Earek looked sadly from Marquiese to Marilana. "He is no longer a member of my family."

Marquiese growled slightly and started pacing. Marilana reached out to Earek again and spoke in a most gentle voice. "I know it hurts to have your brother treated this way, but you have not truly lost your brother. He is safe and alive. He is living the life he wants to live, and that is a good thing. I made a promise to Jarek when I escorted him to Lady Annabella's castle that, no matter what happened, I would make sure you and he were allowed to visit each other."

"I don't understand. Why would you make such a promise?" Earek could hardly believe his ears.

"I would try to help anyone in need, but especially for you and Marquiese," she said, hesitating slightly. "You are my friends. I would do everything in my ability to bring you happiness."

Marquiese stopped pacing and gazed wonderingly down at Marilana. She did not look up at him, and even though she blushed, she met Earek's look of open surprise. He was speechless, hearing such a thing coming from the mouth of this fierce, independent lioness.

"I have already spoken with Lady Annabella, and she has agreed that you should be allowed to visit Jarek when both your duties and his allow," Marilana said. "I will help coordinate this for you both."

"Marilana, I don't know what to say," Earek said. "I did not expect this."

"Well, I am not just an escort and tutor, you know," Marilana replied sarcastically. She gave Earek's shoulder a slight shove.

"No, you're not." Earek laughed with relief. "I used to think of you as a rock, hard and cold, yet constant. I have learned that you are extremely intelligent and kindhearted, a protector of people, and a stalwart friend. Thank you."

"Even stones can have a heart," Marilana said quietly.

Earek smiled at Marilana and she replied with a squeeze to his arm and a smile of her own. Marquiese watched her rise to her feet with a fluid grace he had not really appreciated before. Only then did he realize that her dress was Hunter green and divided for riding.

"You're wearing hunter garb. Is The Ghost on the hunt?" he asked darkly.

She did not look at him. Instead, she turned away and retrieved a satchel from the hallway.

"No, but I will be missing school for a couple of days," she said, opening the door on one of the room's large cabinets.

He and Earek exchanged concerned frowns and then moved to stand behind her and look into the cabinet they had never seen opened. The cabinet was full of little drawers and shelves lined with bottles of various shapes and sizes. A large mortar and pestle sat on a little shelf. Marilana lifted a panel and slid it into place, creating a small worktable. Marquiese and Earek watched as she began removing dried leaves from the various drawers and packaging each into small linen bags. She then placed the bags carefully in her satchel.

"You have almost as many herbs as Mother Kalan, the herb woman in Mystillion," said Earek, his surprise genuine.

"Before I became a bandit hunter, I wanted to be an herb dealer," Marilana said, her tone reserved. "My parents dabbled in herbs, and I've always loved the smells they make. Lady Annabella encouraged my interest, and Mother Kalan taught me some basic herb lore when I was five. I would have apprenticed with her, if I had not decided to pursue bandit hunting instead. Mother Kalan would not teach me after that. She will tend to anyone, but she does not hold with violent professions. Lady Annabella's head healer, Healer Magus, trained me in the ways of modern healing and blood medicines. And I have continued to learn herb lore from the many books in Lady Annabella's library. I also found books explaining the old ways of healing, and learned many of those as well."

"It sounds as if you could be a healer even now."

"If I wanted to, yes. I use the herb lore and the old ways of healing to stay healthy and tend to my own injuries when I'm on the hunt."

"What's in this compartment?" Marquiese asked, indicating a locked compartment at the top of the cabinet.

"Those are the poisonous herbs that I use for my traps," Marilana said seriously. "I keep them separate from the others and under lock and key just in case."

"You mentioned the old ways of healing. What are those?" Marquiese asked curiously.

"Many of the first healers studied the cause and effects of the energies flowing through the body. Also how such things as meditation, hypnosis, and trances can influence how a person's body heals," Marilana explained.

"Oh, come on," Earek said. "Those old stories are just superstitious nonsense. Children's stories. Like the Hungdie. All nonsense." He threw his arms in the air and laughed.

Marilana spun around and fixed them both with a furious glare.

"Do not be flippant about what you don't understand," she hissed. "I will not listen to it."

"You told me before that you do not believe in superstitions." Marquiese frowned and shook his head. "Aren't those old stories just myths told to frighten children or teach them a lesson?"

"Did you never stop to wonder where those stories came from?" Marilana growled dangerously. "Well I did. I have learned the old ways of healing, I know the truth of them. And I have learned that every story has some origin in truth, even the Hungdie."

"You cannot be serious," said Earek. "You really believe in people who worship pain and suffering?"

"I choose to discount nothing. I have read accounts that mention the techniques of the Hungdie in reference to the old ways of healing." Marilana turned away from them again. "I have reason to believe that they existed, though perhaps not exactly as your parents portrayed them."

Earek looked at Marquiese to support his argument, but he merely shrugged. What difference did it make if Marilana believed something most other people dismissed as myths? After all, she wasn't going around raving about it, and she didn't seem to let such beliefs direct her actions.

"So if you're not going hunting, where are you going?" he said, skillfully changing the subject.

Marilana closed the cabinet and hung the satchel on the wall peg again. She walked into her bedroom. Marquiese glanced through the door and was surprised to see a comfortable looking bed and four large wardrobes. Three of them were beautifully carved and oiled while the fourth was plain pine. Looking closer, he also noticed that the three had keyholes and were presumably locked.

"My friend Natly, one of the peasant girls in our class, asked me to escort her home," Marilana explained, removing a heavy cloak of mottled gray wool from the pine wardrobe. "She has been staying at the school's boarding house because her family lives in the far west part of the county, and it takes a full day and a half of travel to reach Mystillion."

"That makes sense. But why didn't she make the trip during the New Year's break?" Marquiese asked curiously.

Marilana ushered them back into the main room and closed the bedroom door.

"Natly just received a letter from her father yesterday. Her betrothed turned seventeen last fifnight. He is coming to her father's farm tomorrow. They will be married as soon as Natly arrives. Then they will leave the next day to return to his farm on the western coast of the Southern Tip."

"I thought most peasants married someone they grew up with. Is that not true?"

"In most cases. But Natly and her family are jaguarundi; there are no others in Mystillion County or the surrounding counties. Her family searched long and hard to find a boy close to her age whose family would accept the marriage," Marilana said as she tidied a few items around the room.

"Why go through all the effort to find another jaguarundi when there are so many eligible boys here in Mystillion?" Marquiese asked.

"To have fertile offspring," Marilana stated bluntly. "It's a simple matter for merchants and higher castes to adopt children, and so you do not have to think about whether your mate will bear you offspring who can in turn produce their own children, but peasants don't have that luxury. Peasants have no one below them to adopt from or who would be willing to bear their children. Peasants must bear their own children and so must find a suitable mate. Natly has been betrothed for eight years and has only met the boy twice. As you can well imagine, she is nervous. She asked me to escort her home so she would have a friend to help her through what will probably be a difficult time."

Marquiese felt his face flush with embarrassment. The answer was so obvious, and yet he had missed it. He was just glad Marilana was not looking at him.

"Speaking of that, there are not that many lions in the Southern Tip," Earek mused. He was watching Marquiese, but his question was directed at Marilana. "What will you do to find a mate?"

Marilana only hesitated for a moment.

"I probably won't marry unless Lady Annabella insists," Marilana said casually. "You two in contrast will probably have to adopt. I'm sure there are plenty of merchant daughters who would want to marry either of you, Brittia included. In fact, she has her adoptions all planned out. She plans to adopt a lynx girl as her eldest and a leopard boy as a second. She calls the leopard her backup boy. She is insistent that no matter who her husband is, her son will be a leopard in honor of her favorite backup suitor. Though she won't raise him to be so darn honorable."

Marilana turned and smiled at Earek. He, in turn, was lost for a comeback and merely shrugged. "You win that one," he said, laughing.

"My former tutor used to say wit is best practiced carefully among friends and used sparingly against enemies; it can be sharper than a razor, and more devastating than fire," Marquiese said with a smile.

Marilana smiled at him and then turned away to walk into the kitchen. She returned a moment later carrying a pack and bedroll. She added the herb bag to the pack and set it on the floor. She turned to the second cabinet in the main room and opened the door. Marquiese was not surprised to find it full of weapons. She pulled out her short sword, quiver, and a belt of throwing knives all of which she belted on with her dagger around her waist. She picked up her pack and secured it on her back, before swinging her heavy cloak over her shoulders and the pack. It gave her a strange humped appearance, but Marquiese had seen many travelers along the roads from Maefair arrayed similarly, if maybe not so heavily armed.

"I'm sorry to rush," she said "but I must collect Natly and get under way."

She strung her bow, led them out, locked the door, and armed her traps on the way out. They started down the road toward Mystillion.

"So will you have to sleep outside tonight?" Marquiese asked in a low voice.

"There's a place with good shelter that I'm planning to reach before night fall," Marilana said. "It's not the first time Natly and I have made this trip. I'm only a little sad that it will be the last."

"Then you do not plan to see her again."

"It's unlikely." Marilana sighed. "It is also unlikely that I will ever see Elza or Jenra again either, once school is over this year. They will go home to the distant reaches of Mystillion County and probably find husbands soon after. Dera is the only one of my four friends that lives here in Mystillion. The good news is that I will probably see her a lot since she is apprenticing to become Lady Annabella's librarian, but my own future is uncertain. I don't know what will come after this year."

"You know, you could write to them," Marquiese suggested.

"I could. But parchment is unfortunately an expensive luxury for peasants," Marilana said. "And besides, I'm not very good at finding time to write frivolous letters. I doubt Elza and Jenra would be very interested in my excursions chasing bandits, so I wouldn't have much to write about. I may be able to stop by and see them if I happen to travel past their homes, but their husbands may not like having a bandit hunter just show up unannounced."

They walked on in silence for a while, and then Marilana said, "By the way, I wanted to let you both know that Lady Annabella has requested that I do some hostess training. She will be eating dinner at my house one night a month starting this fifnight. You can still come to my house after school to study that day if you want, but we will only have about an hour before I must escort you home."

"Thank you for telling us," Marquiese said as they approached his house. "We will make sure to plan accordingly."

A merchant guard was waiting impatiently for Earek when they arrived, and he said, "We must hurry. Your father is waiting."

"Safe journey, Marilana. I look forward to seeing you when you return," Earek said as he and his guard turned and hurried down the road.

Marquiese watched until they disappeared around the bend, and then studied Marilana intently.

"Did you mean what you said about Earek and I being your friends?"

Marilana returned his look seriously. "Yes, of course. I did a lot of thinking over the break, and I realized that I missed your company, the company of friends. I hope you don't think I'm overstepping my bounds, but I hope you can consider me a friend too."

He looked into her earnest amber eyes and smiled. "I do. I do indeed consider you my friend."

"Thank you. By the way, Lady Annabella invited you to join us for dinner this coming fifnight. She seems to think that you can be of some use in helping me practice my etiquette. But I told her you had other obligations. I wanted to let you know."

"Thank you for doing that. I am not ready to meet Lady Annabella face to face just yet," he replied smoothly.

"So you said." Marilana grinned. "I need to get under way. I will see you in a couple of days."

"May The Goddess bless your journey, my friend," Marquiese said.

Marilana gave him an amused smile and then turned and ran easily down the road. As Marquiese watched her go, he was surprised to realize how disappointed he was that he would not be joining Marilana's etiquette lesson with Lady Annabella. This, however, was a thought he knew was too dangerous to be entertaining, and he quickly pushed it away.

10

Natly's betrothed had been uncomfortable about a bandit hunter attending their wedding, so Marilana watched the simple ceremony from a hidden vantage point before starting on her return to Mystillion. Natly had said she was glad to have been Marilana's friend, and that she would miss her. Marilana did not let her anger at the boy show, it was not the first time she had encountered such superstitions, but she had wanted to be there for Natly. Instead of letting her anger build, she chose to forgive the boy and remember Natly's wedding as a good event. She had few enough good events in her life, she could not let grudges and anger control her. Remembering her new friends, she felt the need to return as quickly as possible to her escort duties at school and did not stop at night. She made it back to her house by the evening of the third day of the fifnight.

She got a good night's sleep and attended school as usual the next day having only missed two days of school.

After that, the days fell easily into a comfortable rhythm. Lady Annabella's first dinner visit went well, although she was disappointed that Marquiese had not accepted her invitation to join them. The storms of winter came and went, school carried on, and Marilana did her chores and maintained her studies.

Winter gradually eased into spring. The snows finally melted away and new green growth covered the countryside. Marilana expanded her patrols, knowing the bandits would become increasingly active this time of year. Child disappeared for fifnights at a time ranging far and wide across the Southern Tip, and Marilana rarely saw her.

Marquiese and Earek continued to study with Marilana almost every day. Earek's father eventually relented and no longer required Earek to be under constant guard. This made it easier for Marilana to arrange Earek's periodic visits with Jarek in Lady Annabella's barracks. Doing so, however, required Marilana to leave Marquiese alone at her house. At first, she worried doing so, but Marquiese promised not to snoop and to diligently work on his homework while he awaited their return. He was, by all evidence, true to his word, and Marilana never found anything disturbed.

As the spring mud disappeared, Marilana began to teach Marquiese and Earek little tricks of tracking as they made their way to and from her house. They were getting good at following her lead. With the changing of the seasons, she knew the risk of bandit activity was increasing, and so she warned them to always be on guard.

The warm spring air was full of bird song as she lead Earek and Marquiese through the trees southeast of the brick manor house when she heard something rustling in the underbrush. She immediately thrust her paw out to her side, and Marquiese and Earek both froze. Then they slowly sank low to the ground, just as she had taught them.

Marilana gripped her bow and listened intently. She heard voices.

"I'm telling you I saw something moving over there," came a whisper from behind a thick patch of brush.

"I don't see nothing," growled a second voice.

"You startled whatever it is and now it's hiding," replied the first voice.

Marilana slowly turned her head and peeked at Marquiese and Earek. They looked at her with wide-eyed concern. Marilana held up her paw, telling them to stay frozen. Suddenly, she burst forward in a sprint. She zigzagged through the trees and bounded off rocks. She hurtled a tangle of underbrush and ducked low branches. She recognized her mistake just before she heard the twang of an arrow being loosed. Two trees grew close together in her path with thick underbrush on either side. She gritted her teeth and used a tree trunk to propel her high in the air. A stinging pain pierced her left arm, but she ignored it. She dove forward and rolled through the brush. She came to a dead stop, lay completely still, and listened intently.

Marquiese could not believe what Marilana had just done. He knew she was trying to draw the men away from him and Earek, but he still could not believe it. He sat frozen in shock. He couldn't think. Through the branches of the undergrowth next to him, he could just make out the shadowy shapes of the two men stalking through some nearby bushes.

"I told you there was something there," whispered the first voice, the low growl of a black bear.

"Did you kill it?" the second asked, his the voice of a coyote.

"I know I hit it. I'm a dead shot at close range. Sounded like it fell on the other side of those trees, but I can't be sure it's dead."

"What was it, do you think? Moved like a deer."

"I don't know, couldn't see it clearly," was the bear's reply.

"Should we check it out? Might be someone we could ransom. Might only be wounded, then we could have some fun too," said the coyote hopefully.

"Wait! Let's check and see if it was trying to draw us away from some other prey," replied the first voice.

Bandits. Marquiese's thoughts ground into motion. They were coming. Marilana had told them to stay put, but she was probably wounded, perhaps even dead. She had taught them that many creatures failed to see what was right in front of them, but this did not seem a good time to test the theory. Marquiese turned his head and met Earek's panicked eyes. He didn't know what to do. He was a strong fighter, but this was real. He had never before faced opponents who intended to kill him and his companions outright. In that moment, he realized he wasn't prepared for the situation. He didn't know how to save them both, but he would try. The men were getting closer. Marquiese could see the top of a raised bow on the other side of the bushes. He tensed his muscles preparing to spring on his attackers should they be found. His heart was hammering so hard, he felt sure the men would hear it.

Marquiese heard two wet *thuds*, and then nearly jumped off the ground as the bear with the bow toppled over right in front of him. Earek stifled a cry, and Marquiese turned to see a pair of eyes staring back at him. He scrambled back and realized the coyote was hanging upside down over the bushes.

Marquiese pressed back against a tree. He looked closer and realized two dark pools were spreading underneath both the bear and the coyote. He swallowed hard and slowed his breathing. Just then, something fell from the tree above them and landed softly on the ground. Marquiese heaved a sigh of relief as he recognized Marilana in the dim light, her bow at the ready. He watched her scanning the forest. Finally, she knelt down and carefully laid her bow on the ground.

She pulled a length of dark cloth from her belt pouch and wrapped it around her arm. She tied it off, then quickly scanned the forest again. She picked up her bow again and put a claw to her lips. Then she motioned for them to follow her.

It took them a half an hour to reach the safety of Marilana's kitchen. Marilana had led them around slowly and cautiously before bringing them to the road and her front gate. She had quickly disarmed the traps, ushered them inside, and reset the traps. Earek and Marquiese now sat quietly in the kitchen, lost in their own thoughts, listening to Marilana grinding something in the front room. Marquiese looked up when Marilana entered the kitchen and set a small bowl of powder on the table. Marquiese frowned at the bowl, but remained silent.

"I'm sorry," Marilana said quietly, breaking the silence. "Are you both alright?

"I will be fine," Marquiese replied. "Just a little shaken."

"How can you be fine?" Earek said angrily. "We were nearly captured by bandits and just saw two men die. To top it off, I thought Marilana was dead. Of course I'm not fine."

"It's natural to feel that way, Earek," Marilana said almost matter-of-factly. "You were scared. You were facing frightening possibilities. You may well have died."

Marquiese marveled at how calm Marilana was as she brought a bowl of water, a clean rag, and a strip of cloth to the table. Marilana added clean water to the bowl of powder.

She looked at the leopard and said, "It is natural to feel anger, despair, relief, and even a bit of shame after such an encounter. Seeing death for the first time is not easy. Seeing a violent death like that can drive some people insane."

"How can you be so matter-of-fact," Earek growled as Marilana mixed the powder and water into a thick paste.

Marilana sighed and laid down her spoon. She clasped her paws in her lap and fixed Earek with a sad look. Marquiese was surprised to see pain and a hint of tears in Marilana's eyes.

"I first saw death when I was five, Earek. It was violent, malicious, and cruel. It was caused by one of the worst bandits to ever prey upon the people of the Southern Tip," she said quietly. "It took months for me to recover. Just thinking about it brings it all back as if it happened yesterday. That pain will never completely go away. If you want to sit quietly and think about it you can. If you want to talk about what you're feeling, I will gladly listen. I want you to know you are not alone. You have friends who know what you're going through, and that care about you."

"You killed those two without a second thought," Earek said.

"Would you rather I had let them kill you and Marquiese?" Marilana said simply.

"No," Earek said, shaking his head. "No. I just ... doesn't it bother you?"

"I have killed too many creatures. I do not like to take a life, but I also refuse to let innocent people die if I can prevent it. I have made the choice to protect others. Your life and Marquiese's life are infinitely more important to me than those of a bear and coyote who have chosen to kill for fun or profit. I will kill as many men as I have to in order to protect my people."

"I'm sorry." Earek sighed and slumped back in his chair. He stared down at his paws. "I know what you are saying is the truth. I just need time to think about everything that happened and sort out my feelings. It all happened so fast."

"There is no shame in what you are feeling. I was frightened too."

"What you did was incredibly dangerous," Marquiese said quietly. "Why did you try to draw them away like that? I mean, I know why. You were trying to protect us. But it was still dangerous."

"It definitely wasn't the smartest choice I've ever made," Marilana said pulling out her belt knife. "I couldn't see where they were and didn't have a clear shot. I had to move, but they were too close. I could have waited for them to get closer, but then I would have had to take them on with my dagger. And I didn't want them to see you two. Give a bandit the choice of a fight or a hostage, and they will almost all choose the hostage. I couldn't give them the chance."

Marquiese met Earek's guarded look and then they watched Marilana slide her knife under the dark fabric strip she had tied around her arm. She carefully twisted the knife and cut the strip off. Marquiese frowned as Marilana twisted her arm around and used her knife to widen a hole in her sleeve. Marilana then dipped the rag in the clean water and gently dabbed at her arm. Marquiese gaped at the red color spreading through the water in the bowl.

"It looks bad," he said unnecessarily.

Marilana graced him with a look of slight amusement. Earek rolled his eyes. "Not too obvious, Marquiese."

"What I mean to say is that this is it, the mistake you made." He indicated her wound. "That you got hurt."

"Not exactly," Marilana replied, applying the paste to the wound. "I got hurt as a result of my mistake. My mistake was the direction I chose to attack. It was not a good one. Had that bear been a poor bowman, I would have been fine. But he was not. He was a good shot and he chose that point of ambush because there were limited ways through the surrounding thickets. I was lucky. I could have ended up with more than just a scratch."

"You call that a scratch?"

"A deep scratch then. But at least I didn't have to remove an arrow from my arm, or one from yours," Marilana said lightly.

She reached for the strip of clean cloth, but Marquiese laid his paw on it first. "Let me," he said.

Marilana regarded him for a moment before nodding. Marquiese then took the strip and gently threaded the cloth under the fabric of her sleeve and around her arm. He worked carefully, wrapping the wound several times before tying it off. Marilana tested the bandage and nodded her approval.

"That was expertly done, thank you."

"My father has always believed in learning basic survival skills." Marquiese shrugged. "He says you can never know when you might need to bandage a wound or treat a mild headache."

"Good advice," Marilana agreed.

"Well, I hate to interrupt, but I suppose that we should still do our homework," suggested Earek.

"Very true. Life goes on, and tomorrow will bring a new day," Marquiese said lightly.

When they were done with their homework, Marilana escorted them back to the brick house that Marquiese and his family called home. Earek may still have been a bit shell-shocked from the incident in the forest, but he seemed much more in control as he waved goodbye and started down the lane with his merchant guard.

"He'll be alright. He is strong of body and mind," Marilana said, watching them for a moment.

"What you said helped him," Marquiese commented softly. "It helped me too. Thank you."

"You're welcome."

"And what you said about experiencing death for first time, seeing it with your own eyes. That is part of why you chose to become a bandit hunter, isn't it."

Marilana looked away. A pained look etched her face. "Yes, it is, but only in part." She answered so softly that Marquiese nearly missed it. "Goodnight, Marquiese. I'll see you tomorrow."

She started to walk away, but Marquiese reached out and gently touched her arm.

"Marilana, when you went through those trees, and everything was suddenly so quiet, so still . . . ." He paused, searching for the right words, "I . . . I was so afraid . . . for you. Yes, I was afraid for Earek and myself as well, but all I could think was that you had fallen. All I could think was that I . . . I didn't want you to be dead."

Marilana turned her head slightly, taking in every word, but did not look at him.

"Thank you, my friend," she replied, and then wheeled away and ran off into the night.

Marquiese sighed, watching as she disappeared into the woods like a phantom. He stared at the emptiness and could not decide what he was feeling. But whatever his emotions, he was convinced that the exchange had not gone as well as it should have, and he chastised himself for not expressing himself better. The annoying responsible part of his thoughts chastised him for making such strong bonds with individuals he would have to leave behind.

11

Marilana focused on her many duties over the next few fifnights, busying herself from well before dawn until late into the night. Earek seemed like his old self again following the incident in the woods, though perhaps, Marilana thought, slightly more mature. Marquiese, she decided, had been similarly affected. She was not sure what she felt about his concern for her that day or what he had said about not wanting her to be dead. It made her happy, to be sure, though he did not seem to treat her any differently. She wondered if he had just said it to be nice or as an attempt to reconcile his own emotions. In either case, Marilana had plenty of other things to occupy her time. For one, Lady Annabella's next hostess lesson was quickly approaching.

Lady Annabella's visits were both enjoyable and stressful. Marilana would prepare a simple if well-thought-out dinner while Earek and Marquiese worked on their homework. After an hour, she would escort them as quickly as possible back to the brick manor belonging to Marquiese's family and return to finish setting up.

Lady Annabella was testing Marilana's skills of etiquette, cooking, hosting, needlework, and the cleanliness of her house. All skills Lady Annabella insisted Marilana would need to know if she ever married. Lady Annabella herself was more than proficient in each of those skills even though she had never married, and, as a great-noble, had never had to cook or clean. She liked to say: "Life is unpredictable, and it is your own fault if you starve to death because you never learned to cook your own meals."

After their last lesson, Marilana could see that Lady Annabella was becoming frustrated by Marquiese's less-than-imaginative excuses to avoid her invitation. Marilana worried that Marquiese's resistance would push Lady Annabella too far, and that she would take the matter to the next level.

As Lady Annabella's fifth monthly visit drew near, Marilana grew apprehensive. The end of the school year was fast approaching. They were studying hard for their final exams. Moreover, an increasing number of bandits had begun to cross the border as the end of spring approached.

On the day of Lady Annabella's visit, Earek told Marilana that his father had received a large order of clothes the day before and needed his son to assist in the tailoring.

"So I will not be able to study with you tonight. Sorry about the late notice," he said.

The change in routine put Marilana on edge.

"Perhaps, it would be better if you did not come to my house to study today," she told Marquiese. "Lady Annabella is a cunning opponent, and she could use this opportunity to catch you without Earek around."

"I respect her skills," Marquiese answered lightly, "but I doubt she will know about Earek. How could she? Besides, I need your help on our math homework. Do you mind?"

"Alright," Marilana relented. "But only for an hour."

They left Lida at the brick manor and continued on to Marilana's house. Marilana set to work preparing a meal for Lady Annabella while Marquiese struggled with the math assignment. Barely half an hour later, they heard the sounds of horses approaching on the road. Marquiese glanced at the clock, but it was too early for Lady Annabella's arrival, so he continued to work on one last problem. Marilana went to the door, looked out the arrow slits, and gasped when she saw Lady Annabella dismounting Storm and the swift movement of her guardsmen as they moved to encircle the house.

Marilana felt momentarily torn. What should she do? She had promised to help Marquiese keep his secret, and yet she was sworn to obey Lady Annabella. In the end, she chose duty over friendship and opened the door without warning Marquiese. She quickly disarmed the traps along the path, and

Lady Annabella walked past her into the house. Marilana acknowledged Captain-General Zariff with a brief nod and followed their lady inside. She was relieving Lady Annabella of her cloak when they heard a sound coming from the kitchen. A moment later, Marquiese appeared in the doorway. He stood straight and tall, facing Lady Annabella with a grim expression.

"So here you are," Lady Annabella said quietly meeting Marquiese's stare. They held that pose for what seemed an eternity to Marilana, and then Lady Annabella said to her, "Light the lantern, if you would, Marilana. Marquiese will be joining us for dinner tonight."

"Yes, My Lady." Marilana bobbed a quick curtsey and used a coal from the fireplace to light the lantern. She hung it from the center rafter and then hurried into the kitchen without looking at Marquise. She closed the kitchen door and took two calming breaths. She then set to work finishing the dinner she had planned and setting the table for a party of three.

*

An hour later, Marilana nearly jumped out of her skin when the kitchen door opened, and her two guests entered. She had been careful not to listen to the soft murmur of voices emanating from the next room and breathed a sigh of relief when she saw they were both smiling and relaxed.

"Marilana, is dinner ready?" Lady Annabella asked.

"Yes, My Lady."

"Very well. Go change. Then we shall practice your etiquette."

Marilana blushed slightly, but did not argue. She went to her bedroom and closed the door behind her. Settling her breathing once again, she retrieved a key from under her bed and unlocked one of the carved wardrobes. She removed a fine light green gown and changed from her simple gray dress. When she was finished, she took a calming breath and walked back to the kitchen. She glanced at Marquiese's surprised expression, and then turned away to attend to her duties as hostess, hiding her furious blushing.

Marquiese assisted Lady Annabella with her chair and took the seat next to her. Marilana served her guests first and then herself. Then she sat in her chair opposite Lady Annabella and waited. Lady Annabella studied her for a moment, smiled, and then picked up her fork. Marilana and Marquiese followed her lead and began to eat. Lady Annabella watched them both with a critical eye, then said, "Marquiese, please explain to us the importance of names and titles and what they mean."

"As you wish, Lady Annabella," Marquiese replied with a slight bow of his head. He laid his fork down and rested his paws in his lap.

Marilana watched him, wondering at the perfect manners he demonstrated with a member of the nobility and how Lady Annabella knew of his skills.

"Names and titles are of the utmost importance when treating people with respect," he began. "Addressing someone by their title portrays respect for their caste. Adding their name portrays a feeling of formality. A peasant or merchant who does not have a family name is addressed simply using their name. If you wish to honor them, you may call them Miss, Madam, or Master. If they are in positions of authority, they would be addressed as Master or Mistress. To address them with formality, you may address them as their caste, Peasant or Merchant.

"In the rare case that a peasant or merchant has a family name, they can be addressed by full name or title and family name to impart respect. Addressing by title and full name is the most formal. Knights of the Realm can be any caste, and so addressing a knight as Sir is always proper. If you know the knight's first name or if they have a family name, they could be addressed as Sir followed by their name. When addressing nobility, the rules become more complex."

He paused, a thoughtful look on his face, and said, "Lady Annabella, might I use your neighbors, the Arndt family, for purposes of illustration?"

"That would be fine," Lady Annabella agreed.

"Very well. Lord Arndt is head of the Arndt Family. He would be addressed by a person of lesser rank as Lord Arndt. He would be addressed by his equals in a casual setting as Lord Arndt, Arndt, or simply by his first name, Armen. In a formal setting, he would be addressed as Lord Arndt or Lord Armen Arndt. Lord Arndt's wife would be addressed by a person of lesser rank as Lady Arndt or Lady Frena. She would be addressed by her equals in a casual setting as Lady Arndt, Lady Frena, or simply Frena. In a formal setting, she would be addressed as Lady Frena Arndt. Likewise, our own Lady Annabella is formally named Lady Annabella Ranat."

Lady Annabella gave him a small nod and he continued the lesson.

"Their oldest son and heir would be addressed by a person of lesser rank as Master Arndt. He would be addressed by his equals in a casual setting as Master Arndt, Arndt, or Frederick. In a formal setting, he would be addressed as Master Arndt or Master Frederick Arndt. Master Arndt is also a Knight of the Realm, and so it would be appropriate to address him as Sir Arndt when he is practicing or competing in trials of arms. If the family heir had been a girl, she would have been addressed by a person of lesser rank or by an equal in a casual setting as Lady followed by her first name. In a formal setting, she would have been addressed as Lady, her first name, Arndt.

"Lord Arndt's second son would be addressed by a person of lesser rank as Master Warhaim. He would be addressed by his equals in a casual setting as Master Warhaim or simply Warhaim. In a formal setting, he would be addressed as Master Warhaim Arndt. The same would be true of any other non-heir sons. Lord Arndt's third child is his only daughter and she would be addressed the same as any non-heir daughter. She would be addressed by a person of lesser rank or by an equal in a casual setting as Mistress Graita. In a formal setting she would be addressed as Mistress Graita Arndt."

"Thank you, Marquiese," Lady Annabella said, glancing at Marilana. "These rules apply for all nobility from landed-gentry to great-nobles. Peasants and merchants who possess family names pass their name solely to their heir and never any other children of the family. A new heir can be named if something happens to the previous heir, but many times the named peasant and merchant families come to bitter ends and the name is lost. Nobles pass their family name to their children within guidelines. The noble heir inherits the family name. If two heirs, or two non-heirs, marry, they take the family name of the higher ranking individual. Non-heirs who marry the heir of another family take on their married family name.

"When a noble heir marries a higher ranking heir, the inheritance of the lower heir is passed to the family's second heir. For example, if Master Frederick Arndt were to marry into another family and take on a new family name, Master Warhaim would become the heir of the Arndt Family and would become the new Master Arndt."

She paused, looked at Marilana with a critical eye, and said, "Posture, Marilana."

Marilana straightened her back and lifted her chin by a degree.

Lady Annabella nodded her approval and then continued, "The rules change again when addressing royalty. Royals pass their family name to all their children and so are addressed by a person of a lesser rank or an equal by their title and first name or by a proper honorific. They may be addressed by first name only by their request or by another royal in an intimate setting. The royal family name is used for ceremonial purposes or in the most formal settings. We address the King as King Rylan, Majesty, or Sire. In ceremony, he is Rylan Mercurer, King of Redsands. A Prince or Princess would be addressed as Highness.

"When a royal child marries, they retain the royal family name for their own use, but it is not inherited by their children. The children of such a marriage would inherit the family name of their other parent. If both parents were royals, but neither inherited the rule of a kingdom, a new family name would be issued to the children for their inheritance. The royal heir, also called the Crown heir, of course keeps the royal name and passes it to all their children.

"Honorifics can also be used to address nobles and royals. A person may use the honorific of my lord or my lady for any individual, noble or royal, to whom fealty is given, or by a noble granting respect to an equal. Likewise, a royal may use the honorific to show respect to a noble."

Lady Annabella paused as Marilana refilled their tea and then served them a simple fruit desert prepared from the bounty of her own garden. When Marilana was seated again, Lady Annabella fixed her with an intense look.

"I know you may not think that you will ever have need of this knowledge, but I want you to learn it well. Do you understand what we have explained?"

"Yes, My Lady." Marilana nodded. "Names and titles are determined by position, rank, and inheritance. Are there any differences for adopted family members?"

"No, adopted family members are given a family rank just like blood members, and they are addressed accordingly," answered Lady Annabella. "Disowned individuals, of course, lose the right to their family name and lose any rank they might have had when they come of age or that was theirs since coming of age."

"How would a royal be addressed when competing with the Knights of the Realm?" Marilana asked curiously.

"An insightful question. A royal can be granted Knighthood; however, addressing a royal as Sir would be disrespectful since royalty are never equal with members of the lower castes. A peasant, merchant, or low noble can be raised in rank by the grant of Knighthood, so knights are treated the same as upper nobility. Royals are always higher. When a Prince competes with the Knights of the Realm, he is granting the other knights the opportunity to compete against him without retribution. No matter if the Prince wins or loses, he owes the knights nothing and the knights have gained honor by competing. The Prince is always addressed as Prince or Highness."

The three of them lapsed into a less-than-comfortable silence and finished eating. When they were done, Marilana said, "Is there anything I can provide you?"

"No, nothing," Marquiese said. "Thank you."

"Nor I," Lady Annabella said. She came to feet, and Marquiese and Marilana did the same. They followed her into the main room.

"You did well this evening, Marilana," Lady Annabella said. "You need more practice, but that is why we are having these dinners. I expect to continue these practice sessions during the summer months, as long as your Bandit Hunting allows, and throughout the school year."

"The school year? You mean next school year?" The confusion in Marilana's voice was obvious.

"Yes, I would like for you to continue to attend school with the merchant youths," Lady Annabella replied. "The next three years are Finishing School for the merchants. You have come a long way on your own, but I would like you to continue with the merchant youths. This will allow you to practice your etiquette, dance, and formal interactions on a continuing basis. They will also begin learning the laws governing the merchant caste's trade and councils. It will not hurt you to learn the ways of merchants."

"But, My Lady, I am merely a peasant. It would be presumptuous," Marilana protested.

"It is my will," Lady Annabella stated firmly.

"Yes, My Lady," Marilana said, acquiescing in a subdued tone.

Lady Annabella eyed Marilana a moment more before turning her attention to Marquiese. "Thank you for joining us tonight. I would like you to join us for future dinners as well."

"I would like that, Lady Annabella. Thank you," he agreed.

"I would also like for you to join Marilana every morning for sparring practice," she said maintaining her firm stare.

"You need to maintain your skills, and that is much better accomplished with a partner and a teacher. She will come get you from the brick manor every morning after her patrol, and you will accompany her to my estates. You will return home and clean up before attending school or going on about your day."

"I . . . ," Marquiese dropped his eyes. He finally said, "I would like that. You are probably correct. My practice routine could be much improved."

"Good," said Lady Annabella briskly. "I shall inform your merchant family, and I will see both of you tomorrow morning for sparring practice."

Then she vouchsafed Marilana a serious look, saying, "Marilana, there is one more thing that needs to be said. Marquiese is the keeper of a dangerous secret. The secret itself is not as important as keeping its holder safe. You know he has a secret, and you know how to keep secrets. I expect you to help him keep his secret and to protect him at all costs. Do you understand?"

"Yes, My Lady. I will do my best."

Lady Annabella nodded and then swept out the door. Marilana followed her down the path to the road where her guardsmen and horses were waiting. Storm nuzzled Marilana while Lady Annabella mounted. Marilana scratched his ears and then stepped back. She watched as Lady Annabella and her escorts rode east down the road, then reset her traps and went back inside.

She closed the door and nervously turned to face Marquiese. He sat in the chair by the low fire with his head in his paws. Marilana decided to let him be alone for a while and quietly went back into the kitchen. She cleaned up the dinnerware and put her kitchen back to rights. When she could find nothing else to do, she took a deep breath and went back into the main room.

Marquiese still sat in the chair, but he looked up at her when she entered the room. Marilana met his eyes, saw the anger there, and waited for him to speak. When he didn't, she decided to break the silence. "I hope you can forgive me."

"Forgive you for what?" he asked, frowning, his anger melting away.

"I did not know Lady Annabella was coming early, but I also did not give you any warning that she was here. I could have tried to slip you out the back door when I heard the horses, but it would not have done any good. Lady Annabella's guards were already taking their positions when I checked the door. I am sorry."

"Don't be sorry," he chuckled. "You warned me not to underestimate Lady Annabella, and you were right. It is my fault for choosing to come here when you suggested otherwise. It was only a matter of time before she caught me anyway. It was better that she caught me here rather than somewhere else. At least your house provided more privacy. No, if anyone should be sorry, it is I. I should not have asked you to help me avoid your warden. You owe her your loyalty, and it was wrong of me to place you in such a position. Can you forgive me?"

"There is nothing to forgive. I understand what it takes to keep secrets. You did what you thought necessary. I would have done the same." Then she changed the subject. "I want to thank you for helping me with my etiquette lessons. I can see that you have had considerable training, and I am glad that you have agreed to help me practice."

"It is my pleasure. You have tutored me. It is only right that I should help you in return."

They lapsed into silence once again. Marilana tried not to fidget as she waited for him to voice his thoughts.

"So that is one of your secrets," he said finally, indicating her dress. "Are all three of the locked wardrobes in your bedroom full of formal gowns?"

"They are not mine to keep," Marilana explained, blushing slightly. "Lady Annabella insists that I have formal gowns to wear when the occasion warrants it. She has all of my clothes made by her personal seamstress. But they are not mine to keep. Neither are the wardrobes."

"You seem embarrassed to wear them. Are you?"

"I wear them because I am Lady Annabella's ward. But the truth of the matter is, I am a peasant. Attractive peasants must hide their looks so that they do not attract unwanted attention. I should not be wearing such nice clothes," she said in a near whisper.

"So you feel guilty that the other peasants don't have the privilege to wear such nice gowns? Is that right?" he persisted.

"No. I feel guilty that they do not have the protection I have against men of higher castes. I wear these gowns in Lady Annabella's presence, and no one thinks anything of it. If I were to wear this gown and walk down the street, it would not take long before some merchant or bandit decided to take me somewhere private. Or tried to. In other counties or towns, there would also be plenty of Lords who would want to invite me in for some so-called 'entertainment.' I have my skills to escape such an encounter, and I have Lady Annabella's protection to use as a deterrent. Any other peasant girl would have nothing to protect her from the predation of such creatures. Even peasant men have appetites that they indulge in, and many times the girl is not a willing participant. Occasionally, it is the other way around; a higher caste woman taking advantage of a lower caste male. But not often, and a male is usually willing to risk any legal problems for the chance, in any case."

She met Marquiese's eyes for a long moment before he turned away from her gaze.

"I understand," he said quietly looking at his paws. "And that is also why you did not intend to continue school next year. You do not want to draw attention to the fact that even though you are a peasant, you are also privileged beyond the rights of your caste."

"Yes," she replied simply.

He looked back up and met her eyes. She was no longer nervous and watched him calmly, wondering what he was thinking.

"Let me change. Then I will escort you home," she said, starting toward her bedroom.

"Marilana," he said suddenly. She paused and looked back at him. "Do you not like wearing such fancy gowns?"

Marilana blushed. "They are both more comfortable and more restricting than my normal dresses," she replied carefully.

"That was not what I asked. But I think your blushing answered my question. You do look nice in that gown and dinner was very good," he said seriously.

She smiled at him briefly and then went to change, stomping dutifully on the pleasure his comment had kindled.

12

Marquiese covered a yawn behind his paw as he watched Marilana approach the brick manor dressed in her hunter garb. It was an hour before dawn, and he had not slept well. He had sat in his dark room and thought about the previous evening's dinner, relieved to have finally been confronted by Lady Annabella. It had gone far better than he might have expected.

He needed to determine his next course of action and had finally decided to do as Lady Annabella wished. He would trust her to protect his secret while he took up sparring practice at her estates. She was a valuable source of information, and a strong link to the world outside Mystillion. She had told him that if he ever needed help not to hesitate to call on her. She also advised him to stay close to Marilana. She was firm in her opinion that Marilana could protect him, and, if necessary, get him to a safe location if the situation warranted such action.

Marilana shook her head and grinned when she saw Marquiese yawn again, but then noted his long sword with a nod of approbation.

"Good. You have your sword. You will need it. But you should have done less thinking last night and more sleeping. You will need your thoughts to be clear," she said, clearly reading his mind. "Come. We have a lot to do before school today."

She turned and walked briskly down the road. Marquiese hurried to keep up, saying, "Why were you coming from the west?"

"I just finished my patrol. I have been up for an hour already," she replied ruefully.

"See anything this morning?"

"Nothing. So far it looks like a quiet day," she said, but her eyes never left the forest.

They hurried along the road and soon came to Lady Annabella's castle. Marquiese took a deep breath and followed Marilana to the gate. The foot gate opened as they approached and the guard, a grim faced horse with a white blaze, let them enter.

Marquiese saw a craggy old lion and a middle-aged, weathered cheetah watching them as they crossed the courtyard. Marilana stopped and bowed slightly.

"Captain-General Zariff. Trainer Hosten. Allow me to introduce you to Merchant Colbran's son, Marquiese," Marilana said politely.

Marquiese gave them a slight bow and met their eyes calmly. Trainer Hosten nodded his head curtly. Captain-General Zariff studied him critically then turned his gaze on Marilana. Marilana met Zariff's eyes with calm determination, and Marquiese watched this silent contest of wills with great interest.

Eventually, Marilana blinked and dropped her eyes, sighing. "One day," she said "One day."

"Yes, but not today." Zariff smiled slightly and held out his paw. "Weapons."

Marilana gave him her bow, quiver, short sword, and dagger.

"Why don't you go work the horses and exercise Storm before reporting to the practice yard," Zariff said calmly. "Marquiese, you will come with me so I can get a feel for your skills."

"Might as well call the stallion and spend some time with him first," Trainer Hosten said as he and Marilana started across the courtyard. "He's missed you."

Marquiese could see that Marilana responded to these words with unexpected glee, and then, to his surprise, she let out a shrill whistle.

"You should watch this," Zariff said to Marquiese with a chuckle.

Suddenly, a magnificent white stallion charged up the lane from the pastures and galloped up to the rail, whinnying loudly, and thrusting his head playfully in Marilana's direction. She scratched the horse's ears lovingly and talked to him as if she did so every day.

"Isn't that Lady Annabella's horse?" Marquiese asked in amazement. "The one they call Storm?"

"The one and only," Zariff said with a satisfying nod. "Other than Lady Annabella, only Marilana can manage him. You will have to ask her about him sometime. They have quite the relationship."

They watched Marilana brush and saddle Storm. Then she bridled him and vaulted into the saddle. As frisky as Storm appeared, he responded immediately to Marilana's touch. She began his workout first with a trot, then eased to a canter, and finally opened up to a full gallop.

"That is a one of the finest horses I have ever seen, and Marilana is a terrific rider," Marquiese commented.

"One of the best I know." Zariff chuckled. "Come on, lad. We have work to do."

Marquiese turned away from the track and followed Zariff back across the courtyard to the practice yard. A shaft of yellow light was just beginning to crest above the horizon, but the yard was already full of soldiers practicing with their swords, staves, cudgels, bows, and crossbows. Marquiese spotted Earek's brother Jarek among those practicing staves. The arms master saluted Zariff with fist to heart and then blew a short blast on his horn. All practice ceased. The men gathered their equipment. Marquiese watched with confusion as the practice field suddenly emptied.

"What's going on?" he asked with a frown.

"Marilana practices alone," Zariff replied easily. "I have been training her since she was little, and I decided long ago that she should not have a bunch of men gawking at her. Since you will be joining Marilana in the mornings, and I will be training you both, our sessions will be private as well."

Marquiese was relieved to hear this. He didn't want to make excuses for his performance or try to hide his abilities.

Zariff unstrung Marilana's bow and placed it with her other weapons on a nearby rack. Then he walked out to the middle of the yard and turned to face Marquiese with a serious expression.

"Let me see your blade," the lion said, holding out his paw.

Marquiese pulled his sword from its sheath and held it out to Zariff. The lion took it, tested its weight and balance, and examined it for quality and wear.

"Good," said Zariff. "High quality, decent weight and balance. It's obviously seen some hard use, but it is still in good condition. Let me see your sword forms."

Marquiese took back his sword and began to move through the forms. Zariff kept at him for nearly an hour working with the sword, staff, and bow. Finally, the lion seemed satisfied and had Marquiese select a practice sword.

"You are well skilled in arms, but you need to get more practice. I'm going to set up some archery targets for Marilana," Zariff said. "When she comes, she will not look at the yard. When I give the signal she will turn and loose arrows at the targets. When she is down to her last two arrows, I want you to attack her from her left."

"That would not be fair," Marquiese protested.

"You're correct," Zariff nodded. "That's why I'll be attacking at the same time from the right."

Marquiese stared at Zariff in disbelief as the lion walked away. Marquiese watched as Zariff moved obstacles around the practice yard and placed targets in random, highly concealed locations. Marquiese remembered Marilana's reputation as a deadly fighter and decided not to argue with his instructions; after all, he was curious to find out how well she could manipulate her sword and aim her bow.

A short time later, Marilana walked around the corner of the castle and into the practice yard. She was accompanied by Lady Annabella. They seemed to be having a serious discussion. Marilana bowed her head before continuing toward the armor stand and gathering her weapons. She kept her face turned away so she would not see the targets until it was time. Marquiese watched her pick up the practice sword and test it. Satisfied, she belted on her quiver and slid the practice sword through a loop on her belt. Then she strung her bow and stepped further into the yard. She glanced first at Marquiese and then at Zariff. Marquiese was startled by the look in her eyes. Her gaze was both piercing and unsettling. She seemed to be looking at him while at the same time looking through him.

"Now," Zariff called.

Marquiese was amazed by how fast Marilana moved. She spun as she drew her first arrow and released it while she was still moving. She drew the next arrow smoothly and released before the first arrow struck its target. Marquiese stopped watching the targets and focused on Marilana. He had a job to do. He paced slowly and quietly to Marilana's left, staying out of her line of sight. Zariff moved to her right, doing the same.

In a matter of seconds, Marilana's arrows were nearly spent. She drew her second to last arrow as Marquiese began his approach. She released, drew her last arrow, and released again. Marquiese closed the distance between them with as much speed as he could muster, preparing his sword for a downward strike.

Marilana dropped low and spun so fast he hardly had time to realize what was happening. She swept his feet out from under him, and he crashed to the ground. She spun again and kicked his sword across the yard. As she finished her turn, she blocked Zariff's strike with her own sword. Marquiese rolled to his feet. While Zariff and Marilana fought in circles around the yard, he darted toward his practice sword.

Marquiese picked up his sword and launched a rear attack. Marilana seemed to vanish even as his sword arced forward. Instead of striking Marilana, his sword collided with Zariff's. His surprise was mirrored on Zariff's face, but only for a breath. By then, Marilana had launched a counterattack. She struck Marquiese's out-stretched elbow, causing him to drop his sword. In the same motion, she swept Zariff's feet out from under him. Zariff crashed to the ground and rolled instantly to the side. Marquiese ducked and sprang away from Marilana's back arm swing. Marquiese realized Marilana was smiling grimly as she stood her ground. Looking at the ground by her feet, he realized that both his practice sword and Zariff's were under Marilana's guard. Zariff raised his paws in surrender and called a halt.

"There is no point in us getting bruised trying to retrieve our swords," the lion said and stretched his back. "I'm getting too old for this kind of thing."

Marilana picked up the swords and gave them back, her eyes gleaming mischievously. Zariff took his sword and backed away.

"You two can spar for awhile and spare me more bruises than I already have," Zariff said.

Marilana faced Marquiese with intense focus, and Marquiese took up his ready stance. This time Marquiese did not rush in. He circled, and Marilana circled with him. He focused on her every move. He watched the way she stepped and how she reacted to his movements. He feinted forward, and she stood her ground without flinching. He lunged to her left, and she slipped away to her right. He stalked forward a pace, and she angled away. He sprang to his right and made a back arm swing at her shoulder. She slipped back away and his swing met nothing. Suddenly, she attacked his newly exposed front. He pulled back and barely parried her attack with a downward block. Immediately, she attacked again, pressing him hard, striking fast, jabbing, swinging, striking, and lunging. She struck his hip as he blocked too slowly. He backed away, but she made three strikes in fast succession hitting his lower leg, upper arm, and finally his sword paw. Her next swing knocked the practice sword out of his slackened grip, and the session ended.

"That's enough for today," Zariff called.

Marquiese stood panting with his paws on his knees. He straightened and looked at Marilana; she was also breathing hard, but stood straight and smiled at him. She turned to face him and bowed. Smiling, he returned her bow of respect. He turned to locate his practice sword and caught sight of the targets Zariff had set up. Marilana's arrows had struck each and every target in dead center. He could not help but be impressed. He knew he could not have done as well. He retrieved his practice sword and placed it in a rack next to a dozen others.

"Marquiese, come over here for a moment please," Zariff called to him. When he glanced in the Captain-General's direction, he saw Marilana doing a series of stretches he had never seen before. "I'd like you to learn these stretches. I normally do not require the practice, but you are more skilled than many and it will do you good."

"Keeping your muscles and joints limber can make the difference between winning and losing," Marilana said seriously. "Doing these stretches before and after strenuous activity, as well as every morning and night, will keep you from getting stiff and sore. They also increase flexibility and fluidity."

"She has proven their worth," Zariff said proudly. "You should learn them too."

Marquiese nodded and followed Marilana's instructions. He could feel the tension in his muscles lessening. Marilana smiled encouragingly at him and Zariff nodded his approval.

"You both did well this morning. I expect you here tomorrow at the same time. Be ready to spar," Zariff said. "Now you better hurry so you can clean up before school."

Zariff walked over and joined Lady Annabella. She had watched the entire practice from a distance, and Marquiese wondered what she had thought.

He pushed the thought away, belted on his sword, and he and Marilana hurried to the gate and on down the road.

"I want to compliment you on your skills," Marquiese said, finding it easy to keep up after nine and a half months of walking with her. "I was not sure what to expect, and now I know I have a lot of room for improvement with both bow and sword."

"You actually did very well," Marilana said. "It has been a while since anyone other than Zariff has been able to hold their own against me. Zariff is not as young as he used to be. I think it will be good for him to have someone else for me to spar with. I have been taking it easy on him for some time, but don't tell him that."

"You care a lot about him," Marquiese noted.

"He is as close to a father as I have. He has been teaching me and training me in combat and battle tactics since I was six. He and Lady Annabella are my family, even if it is not an official family."

"Lady Annabella may well adopt you someday," Marquiese commented.

"No. Great-nobles do not adopt peasants."

"You are her ward. There is no reason why she should not adopt you and name you her heiress."

"She took pity on me as a three-year-old orphan, and now she puts up with me." Marilana shook her head firmly. "I have experiences in my past that are not acceptable for a noble. No, she will not accept the lowest of the low into her noble family."

Marquiese sighed, but did not push the issue farther. They had reached his house, and he watched as Marilana hurried back the way they had come. As she disappeared into the forest, he wondered what could have happened in her past that Marilana now refused to see the possibility of becoming Lady Annabella's heir.

13

After school a fifnight later, Marquiese walked with Earek, Brittia, and the number of other schoolmates down the East Road. He struggled to keep a polite smile on his face as Brittia went on and on about the dress she was going to be wearing tomorrow, the last day of the school year.

"Marquiese, I'm so looking forward to tomorrow, aren't you?" Brittia said, as they reached her house. "You will stand next to me while we watch the exhibition ball, won't you?"

"Yes, Brittia, I will certainly watch the ball with you," Marquiese answered, forcing a smile. "Until tomorrow then. Goodnight."

Brittia batted her lashes at him, waved, and walked through the gate to the manor her family called home.

"Oh, Marquiese, you are so lucky," chatted Estala, a quirky young gazelle and another of his classmates. "Brittia gets to stand next to the headmistress on a raised platform. It's the best view of the dancers." Then she turned to Wahlan, a deer who walked with them every day. "You're dancing this year, aren't you, Wahlan?"

"Yes," Wahlan said, sighing. "Three years of finishing school and it all comes down to this one day, the Dance of the Seasons. It's been hard work. I'll be glad to finally be done with school and be able to work full time."

"What part are you dancing?" Marquiese asked curiously.

"You know the parts of the Dance of the Seasons, Marquiese?" Estala interrupted. "That is amazing! It's reserved for the final year of finishing school. I don't know any of the parts."

"It's not that hard to figure out," Wahlan snorted. "There are only enough people in my class to have three basic parts. Lord Time and Lady Season, of course, are the best dancers out of the high-class merchants, and the rest of us have to fill in the rest of the parts. I've had to learn to be all the different leaves and trees and plants."

"I'm sure it will be amazing to watch," Estala said.

"Sure," Wahlan said listlessly. He glanced over at the black leopard. "Earek, would you do me a favor and tell your father that the next batch of thread is ready."

"No problem, Wahlan." Earek smiled. "Good luck tomorrow."

Wahlan waved and walked toward his house.

"I'm sure the dance is going to be so much fun to watch," Estala said without missing a beat. Marquiese was glad the gazelle's house was next on their route. Some days she talked non-stop, and today was one of those. "I mean, I know there are only seven in the graduating class, but still seven is enough. I mean, you only really need the two main dancers; all the rest are just background. It is such a romantic dance," she plowed on. "The love story of Lord Time and Lady Season. Oh, I can't wait until I get to dance it. Anyway, bye!"

"See you," Marquiese said. He heard Earek sigh as Estala walked away and tried not to laugh.

"I can't believe we were given homework today," a shy young filly named Jasmine said as they rounded the bend. "Did Mistress Rose give you guys homework too?"

"Yes," Earek said heavily. "An essay on the castes of the Southern Tip. We've been working on it all fifnight and it's due tomorrow."

"Yuck! I'm not looking forward to next year if that's the main topic," she replied with disgust.

"It's an important topic. You might enjoy it," Marquiese said.

"I just want to get to Finishing School and learn to dance," the girl said before walking away.

A minute later, Marquiese and Earek waved goodbye to the last of their group, a gray wolf named Enib.

"What is it with Enib? The guy never says a word," mused Marquiese. "Not once all year that I can remember."

"Enib's a low-class merchant. His father travels a lot fixing pots. Like Wahlan, Enib just wants to be done with school so he can work."

"What work does Wahlan do?" asked Marquiese curiously.

"He's a spinster like his mother, and a good one. They supply some of the best thread to my father's shop."

"Seems like you know every merchant family in Mystillion."

"Most of them." Earek shrugged. "My father is the best tailor in town; lots of the other merchants come into the shop. I've been working there since I was six. I've gotten to know a lot of people. Some only come in once a year to have their feast day clothes adjusted. Others, like Brittia, come in constantly."

They slowed and let Lida and Marilana catch up, the elder lioness held an arrow nocked to her bow and her eyes scanning every inch of forest as usual.

"Isn't it exciting, Marquiese," Lida exclaimed. "We get to watch the Dance of the Seasons tomorrow! I have always loved that dance."

"Yes. And it should be interesting to see it performed with only seven dancers," Marquiese commented.

"Only seven?" Lida wrinkled her nose. "But should it not be done with many more than that?"

"Lida, this is a small town. There are not any professional performers here, so the students take on all the parts," Marquiese explained. "The dancers here have put a lot of hard work into this and we need to tell them they have done a good job. Okay?"

"I will. Do not worry," Lida said. She spotted her mother waiting near the manor gate and bolted ahead. "See you later."

"See you," Marquiese called.

The three of them waited until Lida was safely inside, then they plunged into the forest, Marquiese and Earek close on Marilana's heels. It took them very little time to reach Marilana's house. She led them inside and the lion and the leopard set about working on their essays. Marilana started in on her house chores.

"Aren't you finishing your essay?" Earek asked her.

"I finished it yesterday and turned it in this morning." Marilana laughed. "Unlike some I know, I don't leave my work to the last minute."

"Yeah, right." Earek chuckled and continued writing.

Marquiese set down his pen and reread what he had written. It looked good to him.

"Marilana would you read over this and see if you can find any mistakes?" he asked with a smile.

Marilana took the paper and stood behind Earek where she could use the light from the window. Earek paused thoughtfully for a moment and then wrote something down.

"Done," Earek said laying down his pen.

"This is good, Marquiese," Marilana said giving it back to him and picking up Earek's.

"Hey!" Earek exclaimed but did not stop her. "I would have asked, you know."

Marquiese chuckled as he put his books and essay in his satchel.

"So, Marquiese," Earek said, with a mischievous glint in his eye. "Tell me. What are you hiding?"

Marquiese could not have been more startled by the question. He glanced up at Marilana and realized she had her paw on the hilt of her dagger, eyes suddenly cold and hard, studying Earek with a hard intensity. Could Earek possibly know of his secret? Was that possible? Marquiese couldn't imagine how, but he could see that Marilana was thinking the same thing.

"What do you mean, Earek?" Marquiese answered as casually as possible.

"About what you told Lida earlier. That we should tell the dancers from the Dance of the Seasons that they did a good job, even though we have not even seen their performance yet," he said mischievously. Marquiese let out a breath he had not realized he was holding. He saw Marilana's grip on her dagger ease. "So what are you hiding from us small town folk? Have you danced the Dance of the Seasons in Maefair? Perhaps even the part of Lord Time?"

Marquiese shook his head and rolled his eyes. Thank goodness. Earek would never know how close he had come to feeling the deadly force of Marilana's dagger. As a wave of relief rolled over him, he managed to say, "I've seen the Dance of the Seasons performed every spring in Maefair. Always by professionals. But I've never danced it myself."

"Professional dancers must be nice," Earek said sarcastically. He glanced over his shoulder. By now, the tension had gone out of Marilana's posture, the killer instinct abated. "What do you think, Marilana? Would you dance a ditty and sing a song if Marquiese asked you in his sweetest voice?"

"In your dreams perhaps." Marilana said with a flick to Earek's ear and gave him his essay back. "Your essay is fine, but I think you're asking for a thrashing."

"You are in high spirits," Marquiese smiled, "but be careful who you tease, I know Marilana has a staff in her armory cabinet and that she would be willing to spar with you."

"Yes, maybe I could replace some of your energy with bruises," Marilana said barring her teeth.

"That smile of yours is definitely predatory," choked Earek. "I think I will stick to the happy end of the school year feeling instead, thanks."

Marilana chided them as she plucked her quiver from her chair and strung her bow. "Come on you two. Let me get you home. I still have stables to muck tonight."

Marquiese and Earek finished gathering their things and followed Marilana out the door. Marilana reset her traps, and they set off down the road together.

When they had seen Earek on his way, Marilana turned to go.

"Marilana," Marquiese called quickly. "Could I talk with you inside for a moment?"

Marilana glanced fearfully at the house. "I would rather not," she said quietly.

"I can see that. But I must speak with you. Please," he insisted.

"Very well. But not upstairs," she insisted in return.

Marquiese led Marilana past the merchant guards and up the front steps. He opened the door and ushered her in.

"Marquiese, is that you?" Merchant Colbran stepped out of the dining room, and his eyes moved immediately to the lioness. "I'm glad you're home, but we were not expecting visitors."

"I just need a moment alone with Marilana. In the drawing room, if you please."

"Very well. Let us know if you need anything," Merchant Colbran said, still eyeing Marilana suspiciously.

They went into the drawing room, and Marquiese closed the doors behind them. Marilana went straight to the fireplace and stared into the quaking flames. "I think I know what you will ask," she said in a small voice.

"Well then let me say it out loud so you are sure," Marquiese said gently. "Would you have killed Earek if the situation in your house had gone differently? If his question had indeed been about the secret you have pledged to protect?"

Marilana closed her eyes and took a shuddering breath. "I told myself I had to protect you at all costs, as Lady Annabella has ordered me to do, but a small voice in the back of my mind was screaming for me to spare him."

"Could you have done the deed?" Marilana closed her eyes and didn't immediately answer, and only then did Marquiese realize she was trembling.

"Yes, I think I could have. But it would have destroyed my sanity if I had," she said finally. "It would have been like hurting a child; it would have gone against my very nature."

"Would you be able to do it in the future?" he asked softly.

"No," Marilana shook her head and sank down to the floor.

She stared into the flames for a long moment. Marquiese knelt next to her and waited.

"No," Marilana whispered again. "Today, his question took me by surprise, and I was prepared to act. But not again. Even if he somehow fathoms the depth of this secret you harbor. He is my friend."

"Could you kill me, I wonder? If the circumstances called for it?"

"Never," Marilana said bluntly. "Not even if you committed atrocities."

"Really?"

"Well, first of all, I doubt you could commit atrocities, so perhaps that was not an appropriate response. And second, learning that you had indeed done so, well, I probably wouldn't be sane after that."

Marquiese smiled slightly and then brushed Marilana's arm lightly with his paw. She turned her head to look at him. "I thought I knew what you would say, but I needed to hear you say it out loud," he said gently. "And I want you to know I had the same thoughts running through my mind when I first heard Earek's question. But, alas, he is my friend. I do not wish him harm. Ever. And no matter what Earek learns or says in the future, about whatever the subject, he is not to be harmed. Not as long as he is our friend."

Marilana nodded. "I am glad we are in agreement. Now I know I can protect him and, by doing so, protect you." She stood up and hefted her bow. "And now, if you don't mind, I'd like to get out of this house."

"But you don't believe in ghosts," Marquiese said curiously. "You said so yourself."

"No." Marilana shuddered briefly. "I don't need ghosts; I have memories."

14

It had been a full eight fifnights since school had ended. The exhibition ball had been a long day of boring pleasantries, but Marquiese had managed to survive all of Brittia's insinuations and advances. Since then Marquiese had kept busy. He reported to Lady Annabella's estates every morning for sparring practice with Marilana and found himself enjoying it more and more. He was getting better, but he had not realized until his first session with Marilana just how out of practice he was.

Marilana was easily the better combatant, but he was a fast learner. He was getting back into shape and was now better able to hold his own against her. Just this past fifnight, she had shown him a number of different ways to aim his arrows. The advice had proved invaluable, and his accuracy had improved by leaps and bounds.

Captain-General Zariff also had him working on his horsemanship during the summer. Marquiese had always liked riding, and he was glad to be able to get back in the saddle. Marilana had been impressed with his skills, although she had easily out raced him that first day on Storm. Zariff had laughed but said it was not a fair race because Storm was better trained and one of the fastest horses on the estates. Marquiese was curious about Storm—he knew there was some special connection between the horse and Marilana—but he had not yet asked her about it. He thought the topic might be tied too tightly in her past, and he had not found the right time to broach the subject.

When he wasn't training at Lady Annabella's estates, he was attending his merchant father in the Mystillion market. He was careful to keep a low profile in the market, because there were many foreign merchants coming and going and he did not want to draw unnecessary attention to himself. As a merchant son, the lion was expected to be learning his father's business. He had not spent much time in the market during the school year and thought it best to have more of a presence there over the summer. Lida also spent most of her time at the market and was learning the family business well. Marquise felt confident she would make a good merchant someday, and he told her so. The added benefit of spending regular hours in his father's shop was that Brittia respected his time there and rarely visited. He had managed to avoid her almost entirely since the end of school.

Unfortunately, he was also spending less time with his friends. Almost all of Earek's time was committed to helping in Merchant Yulan's tailor shop learning how to keep the accounts and manage the under-tailors. The leopard also had his household chores to keep up on, and his mother made sure he had very little idle time. At least he had managed to visit his brother Jarek on several occasions at Lady Annabella's estates, and Marquiese had walked with him when he did.

Marilana spent the majority of her summer days at Lady Annabella's estates where she continued her studies, trained the horses, and honed her fighting skills. She also had her servant duties to attend to in the castle and stables. When she wasn't there or at home, Marquiese supposed she was out scouting for bandits. Marquiese missed her when she was gone; that's how much their friendship had grown. He also missed Earek's company and found he was actually looking forward to school starting again, although that was almost two months away.

Like most other creatures of Redsands, Marquiese and his family attended service on what was called the National Day of Worship. The service was held at Mystillion's Chapel of the Goddess. He and Lida dutifully followed their mother and father inside and took seats on a simple wooden pew in the second row. He looked up and smiled as Earek led his mother, father, and Adrek into the pew and sat down next to him.

Marquiese was not sure what to expect from the day's festivities. He did not attend worship regularly, and so had not previously had the chance to see the inside of the chapel. It was a large hall decorated with a simple elegance. The chapel was painted white inside and out. A black marble altar was decorated with a white cloth and four large white bowls containing white flower petals. Bouquets of still more white flowers were strewn around the base of the altar and the black stone dais upon which it stood.

The chapel began to fill, and Marquiese recognized many of the merchant children from the school. Klay and Caton walked down the center aisle and acknowledged his smile with a friendly nod. Brittia followed her father and mother in and batted her lashes at him. He smiled politely and was relieved when the lynx and her parents chose the second row on the opposite side of the aisle.

It took very little time before the room was packed full of all types of creatures, from lions and leopards to gazelles and guanaco. The latecomers stood along the walls and crowded in back.

Storm's familiar whinny heralded Lady Annabella's arrival. Moments later, Marquiese watched as she glided smoothly down the aisle with Marilana and Captain-General Zariff in tow. They took their seats in the front row, and Marquise suppressed a smile as he watched Marilana settle between the elder lions. She was dressed in the white and green livery of Lady Annabella's household servants.

Marquiese glanced around and saw to his surprise that there were no heated or dirty looks directed at Marilana. He realized that because she was there serving as Lady Annabella's maidservant, no one had any cause to object to her position next to her Lady in the front row.

The head priest and under-priests entered and took their seats in the front row opposite Lady Annabella. The head priest, a graying sable antelope, approached the altar and Marquiese tried to focus on the service.

"Welcome one and all to this glorious day of life," the priest orated to the crowd. "We have gathered here today in fellowship to celebrate the Blessings of the Goddess and the creation of our high society. Let us remember the First Blessing of the Goddess.

"It was the beginning; people were mindless beasts roaming the frozen lands and merely surviving. Many took refuge in caves. In one large cold cave, the body of a woman was found. Her form was strange, unlike any creature ever seen, yet fair beyond compare. She was as cold as ice and seemed as frozen as the ground beneath her. Many creatures came and went from the cave, leaving the body untouched. However, some of the creatures looked upon the fair face and chose to lie down next to the woman.

"One by one, more creatures gathered, predator and prey alike, until finally they completely covered the woman's body. They shared their combined warmth with the woman, and her body slowly grew warm and eventually came to life. The creatures cared for the woman, keeping her warm, and finding food for her.

"When the woman had gained her full strength, she thanked the creatures and gave them her blessings. She promised to protect them from evil, and, most importantly, granted them the ability to think. And so, from that moment on, our ancestors were born into a new way of life, free to choose how to live, what to think, and what to feel."

The priest continued his oration, enumerating the many Blessings of the Goddess and speaking on the choices that the creatures before him could make to better live their lives in ways that would best please The Goddess. Marquiese found his attention wavering. He had heard much the same before. He let his eyes drift to the front pew where Marilana sat. He wondered how strong her beliefs were. He could not remember her ever mentioning worship or making any of the signs to guard against evil. She did have a small statue of The Goddess on the mantle in the main room of her house, though they had never talked about it. It was a finely crafted piece—

perhaps a gift from Lady Annabella—and much like statues found in many homes, peasant and noble alike.

Marquiese realized he was still staring at Marilana when the sermon ended, and the ringing of the bells roused him from his mental wanderings. He saw Marilana arise and follow Lady Annabella to the dais. The young lioness arranged Lady Annabella's skirt and then knelt slightly behind her on the steps. Marquiese watched Marilana as she bowed her head and held the flower petals that the priest gave her. When the priest finished his blessing, Lady Annabella stood, turned, and started to glide down the aisle. Marquiese frowned slightly as the priest held out one of the white bouquets to Marilana. She took it with a slight bow and then hurried after Lady Annabella.

When Lady Annabella was gone, Marquiese and his parents approached the dais. He knelt and tried listening to the priest's blessing, but his thoughts returned, as they so often did, to Marilana. He wondered as to the purpose of the flowers. Why had the priest given her a bouquet when no one from their pew had received one?

Marquiese stood and followed his merchant parents out of the chapel. He looked around for Marilana and spotted her in the cemetery across the footpath. He saw that Lady Annabella and Captain-General Zariff waited until she rejoined them, less the bouquet, and then they began walking through town. While Earek's father fell into conversation with Merchant Colbran, Earek fell in step with Marquiese. Marquiese thought about asking Earek about the white bouquets, but decided he would talk with Marilana about it when he got the chance.

As more people left the chapel, the procession through the town grew. Lady Annabella led them on a twisting route that ended in the market square. It was almost noon when they arrived, and Marquiese smiled when he saw the market lined with long tables. Two large cook fires burned high on the east end of the square, both tended by cooks in Lady Annabella's livery. Soldiers patrolled the streets of the town, and guards took up positions around the square.

Lady Annabella took a seat at one of the tables and Marilana hurried to fetch food and drink for her. As he watched Marilana, Marquiese took note of the hilt of a dagger hidden in the pocket of her skirt and the same alert intensity she demonstrated when the two of them were sparring. *So she's not just serving as Lady Annabella's maidservant, but also as her personal bodyguard,* Marquiese thought. Given the hectic nature of the festivities, he also realized that it would be an excellent time for someone to attempt an assassination. Marquiese knew that a maid in livery would be easily overlooked and an assassin would not expect her to be either armed or highly skilled in combat. Anyone who recognized Marilana would know she was a bandit hunter, but that just added to Lady Annabella's security by deterring anyone who might be contemplating an attack. Marquiese decided it would be safer for him to stay close by as well.

He and Earek filled their plates and joined a group of boys from school only two tables from Lady Annabella. As they laughed and talked, Marquiese watched the crowd, his eyes studying each and every creature as if they might have ulterior motives for being at the festival. At first he was pleased to see how easily the young peasant children mingled with the merchant children. His eye caught on one of the oldest peasant girls as she chased a group of younger children through the tables.

The girl was laughing and playing without a care. As she passed one of the tables, an older high-class merchant grabbed her by the arm. Marquiese looked toward Lady Annabella, but she and Zariff were conversing with some other merchants. He looked back at the young peasant. She stood trembling in the grip of the merchant as the man examined her. Marquiese was trying to decide what to do when he saw Jarek in the uniform of the town garrison step up to the table and speak to the merchant. The merchant released the girl and spoke to Jarek for a while. The child took the chance and disappeared into a group of peasants mostly consisting of gnarled grandmothers.

Marquiese looked closer at the peasants in the square. From what he could see, there were no school-aged peasants present, nor any young women. None. He felt a pang of sadness knowing an entire group of peasants were not able to enjoy the festivities on the chance that the higher castes would push their advantage on the lower. He had not realized how much of the peasants' lives were affected by the fear of the possibility of abuse. He had always thought of the privileges of rank as something of minor concern. Something that was abused once in a great while, not something that shaped the structure of whole communities and the foundation of caste relations. Was that what The Goddess had in mind when she granted the animals the ability to think? Or the society Queen Maebala envisioned when she formed Redsands? Marquiese doubted either was so. He did not see the young peasant girl again.

Late in the afternoon, musicians appeared in the middle of the square and started to play, the music lively and inviting. Lady Annabella began the dancing by gracefully stepping a turn with Captain-General Zariff, while Marilana watched the milling crowds with intense scrutiny. After this first dance, Lady Annabella graced Merchant Sleater and Merchant Colbran with a dance each, and pairs of people swarmed the middle of the square. Laughter mingled with the music as the masses danced and swirled across the stone streets. Lady Annabella returned to her seat after three dances and watched the festivities with a pleasant smile. The noble lioness spoke with one creature after the next, always greeting them warmly, with an ever alert Marilana standing silently at her side.

As the dance floor filled with more and more young people, Marquiese suddenly realized the precarious nature of the situation. The other merchant youths would expect him to join the dancing, but it would not be wise for them to see the extent of his skills. That's when he saw Brittia making her way toward him, her smile broad and expectant. As Marquiese looked for a way out, he found Earek studying him with a curious, thoughtful expression that slowly turned into a frown.

When Marquiese turned back, he found Brittia smiling down at him.

"Marquiese, would you like to dance with me?" Brittia asked sweetly.

"Oh, uh, alright. Sure," Marquiese said.

He felt like a mouse in the talons of an owl. He stood up and started to take a step forward, when suddenly something crashed into his chair. The chair slammed into the back of his legs and he was thrown forward. Brittia screamed as he twisted to avoid colliding with her. He landed hard on his shoulder, his chair twisted around his feet.

"Marquiese, are you alright?" Brittia asked bending over him.

He rolled onto his back and groaned just as Earek was climbing to his feet on the other side of the mangled chair. People all around were looking to see what the commotion was, while Klay and Caton laughed uproariously at the charade.

"Marquiese! Sorry! Let me help you up," Earek said pulling the remains of the chair off Marquiese.

"What happened?" Marquiese asked.

"I was on my way to get something to drink, but I seem to have tripped," Earek explained sheepishly. "I didn't mean to knock you down. So sorry. Are you alright?"

"I think I should sit down for a bit," he said slowly. Earek helped him to a chair and sat down next to him. "Brittia, forgive me, but I don't think I will be dancing today."

"Oh, Marquiese, it's alright. We can dance some other time. I'm just glad you're not too badly hurt." Brittia clutched her heart. "Can I get you anything? Anything at all?"

"No, thank you," Marquiese said, shaking his head. Brittia gave him a relieved smile, touched him gently on the shoulder, and moved off into the crowd.

"Well done, Earek," Klay laughed. "Not only did you manage to make a fool of yourself, but you managed to disrupt Marquiese's fun as well."

"Too bad, Marquiese," Caton laughed. "Brittia's been bragging all summer about finally getting to dance with you. She had some big plans for your entertainment later, too. Now, thanks to Earek the leopard klutz, you'll never know what those plans were."

Laughing as if they'd never seen anything so funny, Klay and Caton jumped up and went off to mingle; they had a story to share, and they now had an audience to share it with. Earek hung his head in embarrassment and said, "Sorry, Marquiese. I hope you're not hurt all that bad."

"I'll be fine," Marquiese said, watching as Lady Annabella made her way out of the square with Marilana and Zariff, people cheering as she passed. "My shoulder will probably be sore for a few days, that's all."

"So tell me. Why do you not want anyone to see you dance?" Earek asked slyly. "You are either very good or very bad." Marquiese turned to look his friend in the eyes. Earek patiently met his gaze. "You have never had such a look of panic before," Earek said quietly. "Not even when the bandits nearly caught us."

"You noticed," Marquiese said.

"I notice much," Earek replied. "You avoid certain topics. You talk around the edges of certain subjects. You arm yourself and say you don't trust the merchant guards with your safety. You avoid getting too close to anyone. Even me and Marilana. You never talk about your family. You never talk about your past. You tell lots of stories about other places and other people, but you never talk about what you did at those places or with those people. Everyone has secrets. Yours apparently involve dancing. Is that possible?"

"I can't tell you, my very observant friend," Marquiese said seriously. "You have to promise not to mention your suspicions to anyone. My life may very well depend on your silence."

"That serious, huh? Well then, alright, I promise," Earek replied after a moment. "But tell me this. How long has Marilana been keeping your secret a secret?"

"Since before you were her friend," Marquiese said ruefully.

"I thought as much." Earek laughed. "She notices everything."

"Apparently so do you," Marquiese said, touching his friend's shoulder with an outstretched paw.

Just then, the music changed. The tune caused a chill to run up Marquiese's spine and his fur stood on end. It was the Courtship Dance, and every eye turned to the town square. Three young males—a jaguar, a roe deer, and an elk—led three blushing young maidens of the same species onto the dance floor. Each female held a cotton fan like a shield hiding their face as they took up their positions and began this very familiar dance.

Marquiese watched with a forced smile as the couples moved ever faster with music, their movements graceful and compelling. Finally, the girls lowered the fans that had been keeping them apart from their partners and accepted the proposed courtship. Marquiese clapped along with everyone else, relieved that the dance was now over.

A group of single boys, including Earek's older brother Adrek, fell into chairs next to them, wistful smiles on their face, and the one named Skilt, a gray wolf, said, "Someday I hope to dance the Courtship Dance with a blushing young woman."

"You have someone special in mind?" Adrek said absently.

"Maybe. Though it is none of your concern if I do." Skilt laughed and his friends joined in. "What about you, Adrek? Have you talked to your girl about dancing yet?"

Adrek glanced at Earek before replying. "I still have another year of school. A lot can change over a year, and I haven't yet made a decision."

More laughter followed this remark, though Adrek pretended not to notice. Earek's thoughtful scrutiny seemed to make Adrek uncomfortable, and finally he came to his feet.

"I think I will get something to drink. See you later."

Adrek didn't wait for a response and hurried off. Marquiese watched him go and spent a moment wondering at the wide smile that spread across Earek's face. Now, he decided, was not the time to probe.

The festivities gained momentum, and the hours passed. Earek danced several times with Brittia, and she and several of her friends joined the ever changing group at Marquiese's table. Brittia sat next to Marquiese, batting her blue lynx eyes and making small talk. He, in return, graced her with stories from his time in Maefair and told her about the many festivals he had attended there.

When this got old—and it didn't take long for the novelty to wear off—Marquiese told his merchant father of his desire to return home, citing his aching back. In truth, he was really just tired of pointless chatter and Brittia's incessant flirting.

*

The moment they arrived home, Marquiese retrieved his sword and informed his merchant family that he was going for a walk.

"You're not to go alone," Merchant Colbran insisted.

"I will not go far. Do not worry," Marquiese said, deflecting the directive.

"Your safety is of the utmost importance, do not grow complacent here. You are too important."

"I am not without skills to defend myself. I will be fine."

"Stay in the shadows then and be careful," Merchant Colbran conceded with a sigh.

"I will. See you shortly."

Marquiese didn't wait for a response. He hurried to the main road and slipped into the trees heading east. He had been thinking about Marilana and the bouquet of white flowers all afternoon and wondered if she might have returned home yet. He drew his sword and moved with as much stealth as he could muster, keeping the road in sight so that he didn't get lost. Even so, he nearly missed Marilana's house. No lights were lit in the house, and no one seemed to be moving. He approached the garden wall carefully, slipped around to the gate, and listened intently.

"Marilana, are you there?" he called.

Though he meant only to be whispering, his voice seemed extraordinarily loud in the silence of the night. There was no response. Disappointed, he slid to the ground and slumped in the shadow of the garden wall. He knew he should return to the manor. He knew it was a terrible risk to be sitting alone in the dark by a house frequently watched by bandits. He had spoken with a dozen creatures today about Maefair, and he missed it greatly. He knew he could have gone somewhere with Earek to talk, but he felt Marilana would understand him better.

Then a sharp whisper cut through the air. "What are you doing here, Marquiese?"

Marquiese nearly jumped out of his skin at the soft voice in the darkness. His heart raced, and he gripped the hilt of his sword tightly.

"Who is it?" he spat. "Marilana? Is that you?"

"You're lucky I decided to check the road," said the voice. He heard a slight rustling of fabric, but saw only a shadow closing in on him. "I was not planning on returning home until much later."

The shadow resolved into a cloaked and hooded figure, and the figure knelt down beside him. "Are you alright?" Marilana asked, lowering her hood.

Marquiese breathed a sigh of relief and said. "I'm fine. You just startled me."

"What are you doing here, sitting alone in the dark?" she asked. Then continued without waiting for an answer. "You should not be here. I can't protect you if you take risks when I'm not around. Just because it is the National Day of Worship, it doesn't mean bandits aren't around. If I had not decided to check the road and found your bootprints, you could have disappeared without anyone knowing what happened."

"I can protect myself, Marilana," he replied, the heat rising in his voice. "You wander around all the time by yourself. I know you are the better combatant, but I am not a novice, you know."

"Yes, you are skilled. But even I am wary on a night like this. An arrow in the dark can kill without a hint of warning," she reprimanded. "I know these forests much better than you do. I take risks that may well end with my death. If I die, no one has lost anything; if you die . . . ."

She trailed off and let his thoughts fill in the consequences. He knew she did not know what the full impact of his death would be, but he did. He sighed.

"I know it was a risk to come here. I know I shouldn't have, but I also can't live bottled-up all the time."

She studied him in the dark for a moment. "So, then, why are you here?" she asked once again.

"I just needed some time to think. I thought talking with you might help," he said, letting his head fall back against the wall again.

"Come with me," she said quietly and stood up.

Puzzled, Marquiese came to his feet and followed her deep into the forest. She led him silently through the trees and came at last to a wide meadow at the foot of a small, sloping hillside.

"Where are we?" he asked quietly.

"On the northern edge of Lady Annabella's estates. It's far safer than the road by my house," she said sitting down on the grass. She lay back in the grass with her paws behind her head and looked up at the sky. "This is my favorite place in the whole world to stargaze. I love to sit here on clear, moonless nights like tonight and watch the constellations move across the sky. It helps me clear my thoughts when I feel the need to do some deep thinking. I thought it might help you with what weighty issues are bothering you."

"It is beautiful," Marquiese said, lying down beside her. He took a deep breath of the warm night air and studied the stars spread across the sky above them. It was indeed a lovely sight.

"How much faith do you place in the worship of The Goddess?" he asked after a moment.

"Not nearly as much as the priests would like," she replied with a chuckle. "I prefer to take the moral lessons that are taught through the stories and leave the fanatics to their piety. Lady Annabella insists that I accompany her to the chapel on the National Day of Worship, but she does not feel that I need to hold myself to the priests' standards. I do like the lessons the stories teach, however."

"I feel much the same way," Marquiese said quietly. "However, don't most of the stories go against the ways of a bandit hunter?"

"Some people might believe so," Marilana said sadly. "Many people think a bandit hunter embraces violence and hatred, but they don't know that the oaths of a bandit hunter center on the protection of others."

Marilana pointed skyward. "That constellation is the constellation of the Hunter. As the story goes, there was a town beleaguered by a group of vicious outlaws. The people of the town lived in fear for their families and their lives. The outlaws frequently raided the town and stole food and supplies from the people. Anyone who was caught outside during a raid was executed in the town square, man, woman, or child. One day a stranger came to town. He was a simple peasant, a hunter, who earned his living by using his bow to hunt geese and other fowl. He was furious that the people of the town were forced to live in fear, so he chose to do something about it. He set out to hunt the outlaws down one by one.

"It took him many fifnights, but finally, only the leader of the outlaws remained. In a fit of rage, the outlaw leader raided the town alone. The hunter chased him, and they faced each other in the town square. The town folk were in a panic, trying to get out of the way. One small child could not move fast enough, and the outlaw attacked her with his sword. The hunter jumped in front of the child at the last second and took the blade across his gut. The hunter knew the blow was fatal but continued forward, ramming one of his arrows into the outlaw's throat.

"The hunter had delivered the town from the outlaw threat, but did the people of the town praise him? No, they resented him for the bloodshed he had caused; they shunned him for bringing change to their lives. As he lay in the square dying, away from any family or friends, he could have hated the town folk, but instead he forgave them and wished them a future free of fear.

"It is said that The Goddess took his last breath and cast his image among the stars in her thanks for protecting the innocent."

"What an amazing story," Marquiese said.

"I am a bandit hunter, and I don't care if people like me or not," Marilana said firmly. "I don't care if The Goddess is pleased with me, or even if there is a Goddess. I do care about the lives of the people around me. No one should be made to suffer and die because of greed or lust. I am sworn to protect the innocent. That is my calling."

"That's why you stay in Mystillion, isn't it? You have chosen to protect these people," Marquiese said thoughtfully.

"I will be an outsider no matter where I go," Marilana replied. "This is my home, and I will not abandon it."

They stared at the stars in silence for a while.

"How come you do not take the writings of The Goddess as fact, but do believe in the myths of the Hungdie and old ways of healing?" Marquiese asked curiously.

Marilana sat up and leaned toward him. Instead of answering his question, she said, "Does your shoulder hurt from your fall in the market?"

"Yes, a little. It should be fine in a few days," he replied honestly, puzzled by her response.

"Lie still. Close your eyes, and relax your muscles," she instructed.

Marquiese only hesitated for a moment, then did as she instructed.

"Listen to my voice and do as I say," she said in a slow soothing voice. "Breathe in, breathe out. Breathe in, breathe out. Relax your face, your arms, and your paws. Relax your neck, your back, and your legs. Continue to think about your breathing, feel the air flow deep into your lungs and back out your nose. Breathe in, breathe out. Breathe in, breathe out."

Marquiese did as he was told, focusing on his breathing, one breath at a time. He could feel the tension leave his back and neck as he relaxed to her soothing voice.

"Now, continue to breathe. I'm going to touch your arm, shoulder, neck, and chest. You will feel some pressure, but it should not hurt. Just relax and keep breathing in and out," she crooned softly.

Marquiese did not hesitate or feel any nervousness. He just kept breathing, feeling the pressure along his arm, then his neck and shoulder, and finally on his chest and shoulder. He knew he was feeling the pressure, and he knew he could hear Marilana's voice, but his thoughts seemed slow and sluggish. All he could do was relax and breathe.

Suddenly, his eyes popped open and his thoughts cleared. He was immediately on the alert, tense and poised, a lion ready to respond to any threat.

"What did you do?" he growled, his eyes pinning her with uncertainty. "Why was I unable to think or act?"

"I repositioned your shoulder to help you heal faster and I removed the pain," she said quietly. "In order to do so, I had to put you into a trance. I am sorry for not warning you about the temporary loss of control."

He sat up, rotating his arm and shoulder. His pain was gone. The stiffness that had been growing more pronounced throughout the afternoon was no more.

"How did you do that?" he asked curiously.

"By using the old ways of healing," she said lightly. "I would still recommend you take it easy for a couple of days."

"Then you really do know the old ways," he said, feeling somewhat foolish.

"Yes, I do. And it has nothing to do with superstitions. I believe in facts that can be reproduced and repeated."

He studied her thoughtfully. Her face was hidden in shadows, and the starlight made her outline glow silver. She almost seemed ethereal and ghost-like. That and the bright stars reminded him of the white flowers she had taken to the cemetery.

"You do not have superstitions, but you placed that bouquet of white flowers in the graveyard. You said your parents went beyond the southern border, and you have no other family. What, then, is the purpose of the white flowers?"

Without a word, Marilana turned her back to him and wrapped her arms around her legs. She hugged her knees and stared at the stars. Marquiese sighed deeply. This obviously involved one of her secrets, and she was not going to answer him. So instead of pushing the matter, he settled in the grass and gazed up at the constellation of the Hunter.

After what seemed like many minutes, he heard her say, "I was ten. It was the first time I went on the hunt as a bandit hunter."

She hesitated, and he waited patiently, feeling that this was not an easy memory for her.

"There were two bandit leaders. They worked very well together and had commanded a group of about twenty bandits for eleven years or so. Everyone knew their names and feared them. They controlled a large part of the Southern Tip. Mystillion was the center of their activity range. Lady

Annabella sent her soldiers against them, but could not catch them. Bandit hunters refused to hunt them because any hunter caught was skinned alive and staked along one of the main roads. The main leader, a jaguar named Victon, was intelligent and cruel. He had a lustful hunger that he sated with the blood of females old and young and without regard for their species. He did not just rape them; he cut them up as he played with them. He enjoyed making them scream until they died. As the leader of the bandits, he planned raids and successfully looted many merchants' homes. He killed many people.

"His second in command was a huge brown bear known as 'Brute.' Brute was just as intelligent and was the reason they were successful at ransoming captives. He had no love for anything other than looting and killing, but most of the time he knew how to counter Victon's lust long enough to secure the ransom they sought. Sometimes Victon got his way before the ransom was collected; sometimes Brute figured the ransom wasn't high enough to care if the captives lived. Both of them together made the bandit group successful, and both were well trained in the arts of war. No one knows who they were before making their reputations as bandits.

"I chose to pit my wits against them. I was new to the Bandit Hunter Oaths. Yet I was skilled in ways that many others are not. Most bandit hunters have only basic training and intense passion. They get good at what they do, or they die trying. Zariff wanted me to survive, so he trained me in every type of combat and scouting. I vowed to put a stop to those men and their reign of fear. I went to the border and found their tracks. I followed them north toward Mystillion. I could tell that the tracks were several hours old, and I was very cautious letting them get further ahead. I was not trying to catch them in the open; I wanted to track them back to their encampment. When I arrived at the brick manor, they had been gone for many hours."

Marilana paused and shuddered; she swallowed several times before continuing, her voice hoarse and muted.

"The merchant family who lived in the brick manor before your merchant family was only of middle-class and middle rank. They had only enough wealth to maintain two merchant guards. When I arrived, I was far enough behind the bandits that I chose to search for survivors. The merchant and both guards had been slain just inside the smashed front door. The house was in shambles. What couldn't be looted had been broken or defaced. I found the body of their 14-year-old son at the top of the stairs. He had tried to defend his mother, but the bandits had simply bashed in his head. The merchant's wife had been taken into the bedroom by Victon. He had his fun while the rest of the men looted the house. I searched the rest of the house and finally found the two daughters, ages nine and six, in the attic. They had tried to hide, but Brute found them. He shot them with a single thick-shafted arrow as the older tried to protect the younger.

"When I checked them, I was surprised to find the youngest, Zara, was still alive. The arrow had pierced the older through the heart, but had missed Zara's chest and instead pierced her arm trapping her against the wall. Scared and alone, Zara had remained silent all the long hours until I reached her. It took nearly half an hour for me to whittle through the shaft of the arrow and to lift the dead body of her sister off of her. I took her back to my house and cleaned and bandaged the wound in her arm as best as I could. She clung to me and would not let me leave her even for a moment. I sent word to Lady Annabella about my house guest. Lady Annabella brought Healer Magus to my house, and together he and I tended to Zara. I stayed in my house with the girl for three days, nursing her back to health. On the fourth day, Lady Annabella stayed with her and I took up my bow again.

"I went back to the southern border and found the tracks of a large bandit group heading south into the foothills of the mountains," she continued in a stronger voice. "I followed the tracks cautiously. It was late evening when I found the camp. I slipped silently through the sentry line and spied on the camp. I watched Brute sit and make his thick-shafted arrows by a small fire. I watched Victon saunter through the camp and speak to his men. I watched until I located the tent they were using for their latrine. I climbed a tree and took up a position where I could see the tent flaps. I sat and waited for several hours watching various men come and go. The sentry shift changed and still I waited. Finally my target came.

"Victon went into the latrine tent, and I drew my arrow. When he opened the tent flap to come back out, I shot him in his unprotected throat. I stayed in that tree watching. An hour later he was found and the camp went on high alert. Brute took charge and he and the men methodically searched the surrounding area. When they couldn't find any tracks, they set an extra watch and patrolled the perimeter. Brute examined the latrine tent and his fallen comrade. I watched him analyze the trajectory, and he looked directly at where I was hiding in the tree. Luckily he could not see me in the dark, but he did come to the base of the tree, looking for tracks. When he walked under me, I swung down, hanging by my knees. I reached around and slit his throat with my dagger.

"Those were my first kills. And the first time I was compared to a ghost. The rest of the men couldn't believe what had happened. Victon and Brute both killed silently in the same night. The men still couldn't find any tracks, and they began to fear the vengeful spirits. They packed up camp and left. They didn't even bother to bury the dead men. I climbed down when it got dark again and scouted to make sure the men were really gone. I went back to the bodies and cut off their heads. The magistrate at the Mystillion courthouse was astonished when I placed both heads on the rack. The bounties on those two would have made me rich, but I refused to collect. I just wanted to prove they were dead.

"When I returned home, Lady Annabella and Zara were both relieved to see me. They were amazed when I recounted what I had done. Zara lived with me for three months after that, regaining her strength. She never fully recovered mentally, however. She was plagued by nightmares, and men made her so nervous she would have panic attacks. Her great-aunt eventually came to get her. Zara didn't want to leave, but I convinced her to climb into the carriage. I still remember her screams as the carriage pulled away. Two fifnights later, I received a letter from the great-aunt saying that Zara had run away. The great-aunt didn't want to be associated with a crazy girl and had disowned Zara. She never saw her again."

Marquiese stared at Marilana's back for a long time, thinking about everything she had said. Finally he sat up and turned to face her. She rested her chin on her knees and did not look at him.

"I leave a bouquet of flowers on the graves of the merchant family every year in remembrance," she whispered. "They have no one else to remember them."

Marquiese suspected that there was more to the story, but he could tell she was not going to say more about it tonight. He gently put his paw on her shoulder.

"I don't know if anyone told you this at the time," he said quietly, "but you did good. You carried out a death sentence on two criminals and saved uncountable lives."

"Meaningless words," Marilana said bitterly. "Others have said similar things. It doesn't bother me to have killed them, or any of the others. It bothers me that I was too slow to save that family. They were there, right down the road from my house, and yet I was unable to protect them."

"That's why you try so hard to protect the town," he said quietly. "You live here, you know these people, and you want to protect them from harm."

"I have dedicated my life to it," she stated firmly.

"If you were to die on one of your forays into the forest, you would be greatly missed by many people, Lady Annabella not the least of them."

"When a peasant dies, the community goes on as if nothing happened," she replied flatly.

"You are not just a peasant," he reminded her. "You are so much more. You are Lady Annabella's ward, bandit hunter of the Southern Tip, and friend to Earek and me. Your actions have touched many lives here in Mystillion and throughout the Southern Tip. It would be a sad day indeed if you did not return."

"I don't plan on dying any time soon," she replied with a mirthless laugh. "Thank you for being my friend and caring enough to say so."

Marquiese lay back down and watched Marilana's silhouette for a long while. Finally Marilana joined him. She whispered, "My anger is not directed at you. Those were terrible days in my life, and immensely painful, even now."

"I cannot imagine the strength and determination it took for you to live through such things, let alone recount them for me," he said gently.

"It's not secret," she said. "But I really don't like to talk about it, because it was such a terrible thing to witness. Others know about it. The older merchants and peasants all remember the fear that accompanied those times. The soldiers who helped Mother Kalan move and prepare the dead bodies remember the horrors of the house.

"Rumors ran wild for a while after Zara left, saying that she had come back and was a living haunt at the brick manor. That's what started the superstitions about the house. They were all false rumors of course; Zara never set foot inside the brick walls of that place again. I guess I told you the story so you would understand why I place the flowers, not just that the flowers are a remembrance of the dead."

Marquiese thought the explanation made sense, but still had a nagging suspicion that Marilana had not told him everything. He decided not to press her; she would tell him if she wanted to. He watched the stars a while longer and then another question occurred to him.

"I can understand if you don't want to answer my next question, but I am insufferably curious. It is my nature. Where does Storm fit into your past?"

Marilana laughed softly, and Marquiese was relieved to hear the happy tones come from her.

"Oh, my sweet Storm," Marilana mused. "He is one of the best things in my dark life. I was seven when he was born. I was already training hard to become a bandit hunter and engrossed in learning the old ways of healing. There is a spot in one of Lady Annabella's pastures where three large oak trees grow. It is one of my favorite places to sit and practice the self-trances of the old ways. I used to sit there for hours at a time. The mares and foals would graze around me, leaving me to my practice. Storm was more curious and would come up to me and sniff and nudge me until I responded. It started a game of 'who would give in first' between us. Oh, and how he would sulk if I was not there for him to play with.

"As you can imagine, Lady Annabella noticed my love of the horses and had me start helping in the stables. I would spend hours brushing and combing Storm and his mother, the one called Snow.

"When it came time to begin training Storm, he refused to let anyone control him, even the stable master. He'll let the grooms hook a lead rope to his halter and lead him around. And he'll allow a select few to brush him. Any more than that and he turns into a terror, biting, kicking, bucking, trampling, and breaking anything he can. He is a gorgeous stallion, and Lady Annabella had hoped to ride him herself, but Hosten couldn't do anything with him. Other trainers were brought in, but they had even less success."

"What happened?"

"Lady Annabella decided that Storm was too dangerous to keep. He was to be sent to the tanner, but I begged her to let me try," Marilana said. "Lady Annabella was skeptical, but Hosten convinced her. He knew about my special relationship with the colt. Hosten taught me how to train one of the other colts, and then I used those techniques alone with Storm."

"I have trained many horses since then, but Storm remains unique. I trained him first as a war horse, then as a lady's horse. Lady Annabella was not so pleased that Hosten taught me how to train war horses or that I learned how to joust because of it. But my war horses have garnered considerable honor for their riders, and Lady Annabella has often admitted how pleased she is with Storm."

"So that's the big secret." Marquiese chuckled.

"What do you mean 'the big secret?'" Marilana asked rolling on her side to look at him.

"Storm is quite famous in Maefair," he explained. "Rumors from the Royal Palace stables spread quickly the first time he visited. Grooms and stable staff told of how the horse was specially cued into Lady Annabella, and no one else could touch him. He was so beautiful that the rumors were especially attractive. The very idea of owning a horse that would respond to one and only one person was addictive. All the trainers tried to duplicate the process, but no one has ever succeeded."

"Of course not." Marilana chuckled. "It took me months to get Storm to accept Lady Annabella's touch, let alone follow her commands. That horse is one of a kind."

"So is his trainer." Marquiese laughed lightly. "Both head strong and temperamental."

"I can't argue that." Marilana laughed, rolling back onto her back.

They lay there watching the stars in silence for a long while.

"How long do you stay out here?" Marquiese asked lazily.

"Sometimes all night," Marilana replied. "We should probably get you back home though. Your merchant family will be worried about you."

"Yes. And I wasn't in the best of moods when I left," he said. "I need to get back and apologize. Thank you for bringing me here."

"It was a good chat," Marilana replied, rolling to her feet. "I'm glad you feel better."

15

It was the first day of school and Marquiese spotted Earek leaning against the fence and headed his way.

Marilana walked into the schoolhouse, preparing her weapons as always for confinement in the headmistress' office. Brittia and a group of her friends stared at the lioness with open disgust, and Marquiese grimaced. Brittia had ridden into town on her father's wagon, so Marquiese had walked all the way with Marilana that morning.

"Marilana is in for some bad days, I'm afraid. At least for a while," Marquiese said to Earek quietly. "Lady Annabella has ordered Headmistress Ceta to allow Marilana to attend school with Mistress Rose's class for the next three years. Apparently the headmistress had tried to put Marilana in the class below us on the grounds that Finishing School is only for merchants."

"Brittia and the headmistress have been arguing against Marilana's attendance all summer. They feel Marilana is overstepping her position. Brittia has been rallying to get all the merchant youths to shun Marilana," Earek said quietly. "She was not real happy when I pointed out that she had been doing that since we were five, and it hasn't stopped Marilana yet."

Marquiese smiled appreciatively and looked toward Brittia and her sycophants. He frowned when he saw a young male lynx enter the schoolyard. He was tall and rangy and moved with a strong saunter. Brittia greeted him with a smile and many of the girls began to giggle and talk behind their paws. Several of the older boys gathered around him.

"Who is that? I've never seen him before. Am I the only one?" Marquiese asked curiously.

"Trouble," Earek said darkly. His face drew tight with anger, and he and Marquiese started toward the growing crowd. "That's Brittia's cousin. Demdrake."

They stopped at the edge of the crowd and heard the lynx saying, "No, no. I didn't move back. I'm just visiting my sweet cousin for a while." Demdrake touched Brittia fondly on the cheek. "I thought I would come say hello this morning and tell you the news."

"What news?" one of the older boys asked curiously.

"My father has heard rumors from Maefair that someone has gone missing," Demdrake said leadingly.

"Who? Who is gone missing?" asked many voices.

"The Crown Prince."

The whole crowd gasped and started asking questions. Marquiese frowned and looked around at all the scandalized expressions. Demdrake raised his paws to regain his audience.

"Yes, rumor has it the Prince has been hiding for a year in order to complete his succession preparations. He should have returned this summer, but there has been no sign of him."

Whispers broke out again, but quieted as Demdrake continued.

"But there is more. One of my father's merchant guards heard that some big Lord in Maefair has put a bounty on any information about the Prince's whereabouts. The speculation is that someone wants to assassinate the Prince."

Demdrake gloated in the atmosphere of astonishment he had created. Marquiese stood frowning thoughtfully until Brittia decide to regain the attention of the crowd.

"I'm sure the rumors are false," she said airily. "Royals do not just disappear. Princes do not just go into hiding. I'm sure someone knows where he is and that he is safe."

Many of the crowd looked relieved to hear her words.

"Oh cousin," Demdrake smiled fondly at her, "you are so isolated down here. You are precious."

Brittia looked affronted.

"Demdrake, where are you staying? Are you planning adventures while you're here?" an older boy named Abzak asked.

"Demdrake is staying with us while his father takes care of some trouble in the town of Bram's Fen, two provinces away," Brittia announced beaming again.

"What happened Demdrake?" Earek called out. "Did you pinch the wrong girl?"

"Ah, Earek, so good to see you again," Demdrake said coldly, turning to him. "You never had the taste for conquest, so you wouldn't know how delicate some girls can be. I took some sport with a lower merchant girl, roughed her up wonderfully, and for some reason her father took offense. My father will have the matter sorted out soon enough, but he thought it would be better if I took a vacation until tempers cool. I don't mind really. Gives me a chance to see my pretty cousin and maybe settle a score."

Most of the group laughed with him. Marquiese frowned, matching Earek's scowl. Just then the doors to the schoolhouse opened, and Marilana stepped out. She was surprised to find everyone crowded together just outside the doors. She started to ease her way through, angling toward the grass. Brittia tapped Demdrake on the shoulder and he turned, grinning maliciously. Marquiese thought the smile meant trouble and edged his way closer. Demdrake pushed several boys aside, and when Marilana turned to see what the commotion was, she froze in her tracks.

Demdrake was right in front of her. He raised his paw quickly and forced Marilana to raise her chin with the point of one claw. She glared hatred at him. Most of the crowd edged back and dispersed.

"I have no need to watch your play, Demdrake. I'll see you when you're done," Brittia said lightly.

She and her friends moved out of the group and meandered off a ways. Several of the older boys grinned appreciatively and stayed to watch. Marquiese stayed close enough to reach Marilana if needed and Earek stayed beside him. Demdrake looked Marilana up and down and smiled hungrily.

"You are turning into quite the fine maiden," Demdrake said.

"You know I'm Lady Annabella's ward," Marilana hissed. "So you have to go through her to touch me. You should be thankful for that."

Demdrake chuckled, pressing his claw harder under Marilana's chin forcing her mouth closed. "I did not give you permission to speak, Peasant, and I do not want to court you," he replied snidely. "Lady Annabella doesn't need to know what I do to you or any of the other peasant girls."

"You will not touch them. Not them, nor me," Marilana growled through her teeth. "I stopped you before, and I will stop you again."

"You threatened to stop me before, and because of your reputation, I let you intimidate me," Demdrake growled. "This time I will have my way. I have been training with a Knight of the Realm; I am no longer afraid of you."

"Apparently your lessons have not included those in chivalry," Marquiese said coldly.

Demdrake turned slightly to see who had spoken. He smiled broadly when he met Marquiese's eyes.

"You must be Marquiese," Demdrake said coldly. "Brittia has told me about you. She says you have spent a lot of time with this one over the last year. I hope your time has been worth the effort. I think you've had her to yourself long enough; I want a piece of her too. I want to find out how long her tail is. Not every tail is as glorious as others. After all, that is why they keep their tails tied up. The girls don't want to embarrass each other. Has she let it out of its pouch for you?"

"Your problem is obvious. You are vulgar and rude, and that is unforgivable," Marquiese said with disgust.

"Apparently she has not." Demdrake laughed and turned his gaze on Marilana. "She will let it out for me this time. I know Earek has no stomach for conquest, but you're welcome to join me tonight at the peasant girls' boarding house. I'm planning on having some fun while I'm in Mystillion, and I would not say no if you wanted to partake in the play."

"As I said before, you will not touch those girls," Marilana said jerking her head away from his claw.

Demdrake's eyes glittered maliciously. "By all means come and try to stop me," he purred. "You can be my first conquest of the night. Show the others how good it can be."

"The only things you will get are bruises," Marilana hissed.

Demdrake growled and raised his paw to strike Marilana. She braced herself, but Marquiese reach out and grabbed the lynx by his wrist. Demdrake tried to pull away, but Marquiese was stronger.

"You will leave her alone," Marquiese said dangerously.

"So you will at least defend your territory," Demdrake sneered. "You will have to do more than that to stop me tonight."

"We will see."

The school bell rang loudly beside them. Earek moved toward the school and urged Marilana ahead of him with a paw to her arm. Marquiese released Demdrake and pushed past him toward the schoolhouse. Demdrake's amused laughter followed him.

*

They hurried to Mistress Rose's classroom and entered to find the rest of the class taking seats around two tables with place settings appropriate for a formal banquet, three plates, two goblets and a dozen utensils for each seat. Marilana sighed with resignation as they saw that there were only two empty chairs left. Marquiese and Earek hesitated, but Marilana motioned them forward. Reluctantly, they sat down while

Marilana took her place beside a table holding a variety of covered platters. Marquiese studied her face and recognized the blank mask of a servant. He sighed and turned toward the front of the room. Headmistress Ceta and Mistress Rose entered and stood facing them. Mistress Rose held a look of indifference on her face, but Headmistress Ceta smiled triumphantly at Marilana.

"This year begins your education of etiquette, formal dance, and the ways of merchants," Headmistress Ceta announced to the class. "We have the added benefit of having one of Lady Annabella's servants attending this class, so we shall use her knowledge and skills accordingly. She will not take part in the dancing and will not participate in any activities that are designed for merchants only. I expect all of you to study hard and learn well."

Marquiese forced an emotionless mask, hiding his grimace of understanding. Yes, Headmistress Ceta was being forced to allow Marilana to be in the class, but instead of accepting her as one of the students, Marilana was being relegated to act the servant. He glanced at Brittia, and she smiled broadly at him. He had managed to only see her twice over the past three months, but he held in his cringe and smiled politely in return. He still could not afford to make an enemy of Brittia; her influence was still a matter of concern.

Headmistress Ceta left the room, and Mistress Rose began to lecture on etiquette. "Etiquette is more than good manners. It is more than a way to demonstrate respect. It is also a tool. Learn it well, and it will serve you well."

Marquiese stifled a sigh and listened attentively, even though he already knew more etiquette than the class would learn all year. Ironically, Marilana was in the same boat. The thought should have given him a measure of satisfaction, but it only caused him to sigh once more. It was going to be a long day.

When lunch finally arrived, Marilana served, and did so expertly. She started with Marquiese, placing him above Brittia. This, naturally, caused Brittia to frown darkly. It was not a slight; they were, after all, equal in rank. However, Brittia had placed herself at the head of the table as if she were hosting. Instead, since Mistress Rose had not assigned anyone to act as host, Marilana made the determination herself and placed Brittia second.

Mistress Rose circled the table correcting posture, pointing out the proper usage of cutlery, and commenting on everything from dress codes to small talk. Marquiese slouched and made multiple mistakes like he normally did when eating lunch at school, all for show, of course.

"Pay more attention, Marquiese, for goodness sake," Mistress Rose chided him.

"Yes, ma'am."

He grinned, pleased when Brittia was also corrected on a number of points, although he did not think she was putting on an act like he was. After the merchant students had eaten, Mistress Rose excused them.

Marquiese took his time leaving the classroom and was relieved to see Marilana had two plates reserved for her to share with Mistress Rose. He walked out to the schoolyard and joined Earek, Klay, and Caton in their usual spot against the wall. Brittia and her retinue sat close by and chatted happily about nothing at all.

"Marilana did well," Earek commented.

"You know she could have served that meal in her sleep." Marquiese shook his head.

"I was not talking about her ability to serve lunch," Earek said softly. "Lady Annabella did not send her to school to serve Brittia; but instead of refusing, she calmly accepted Headmistress Ceta's direction. She did well to hold her temper and not rile up Brittia. I almost expected her to dump a bowl of stew in Brittia's lap."

"A bout of embarrassment would do Brittia good, if you ask me," Klay commented.

"I have a feeling Lady Annabella is not going to let it continue this way," Earek said seriously. "Brittia may be in for a surprise when Lady Annabella puts her foot down."

"That is the least of my concerns at the moment," Marquiese said darkly.

"Demdrake." Earek nodded. "He is two years older than us, same as Adrek, and should be in his last year of Finishing School. His family moved here three years ago. His mother and Brittia's mother are sisters. His father is an arrogant gold merchant. Mystillion was not big enough for his trade so they moved on after the school year ended. While they were here, Demdrake used his charm to get many of the lower and middle-class merchant daughters to trust him. Eventually, he got a number of them into his bed. Not all of them were willing to take that last step. He actually prefers girls who put up a bit of a fight, the way I understand it."

"He's an arrogant brute and deserves a good thrashing," Caton growled.

"That's why he wants Marilana," Marquiese surmised. "She will fight him, and he thinks he will enjoy it more."

"Not just that," Earek said, shaking his head slightly. "Last time he made a play for some of the peasant girls, Marilana stopped him cold. That is the score he wants to settle. She opposed him directly and challenged his privileges of rank. You can imagine his embarrassment. This time, he apparently thinks that he can beat her."

"She can protect the girls living at the boarding house in her role as a bandit hunter," Klay said, "but she cannot stop him from doing what he wants with her."

"Only if he catches her," Earek reminded him.

"That is his plan, I think," Marquiese said quietly. "That is why he told Marilana he was going to the boarding house tonight. He wants Marilana to have to choose. She can stand and fight him, preventing him from getting to the girls, or she can run from him. He doesn't know her skills, and I know she can defeat him easily, but I am worried about what he will try and do."

"We could go with Marilana," Earek suggested. "Provide support, witness the events, and, if needed, intervene."

"It's your skins," Klay said darkly. "Sorry. I can't help. It is too much of a risk for me."

"Me neither. Sorry, lads. I cannot risk Brittia taking her anger out on my family," added Caton. "I hope everything turns out well."

Marquiese waited as Klay and Caton walked out of earshot before saying, "That might work if we can convince Marilana to let us accompany her. She's an expert fighter; we would need to stay out of the fight itself unless she needs us to intervene. She will probably insist on it."

"Then we'll try to convince her of our plan after school," Earek said. "My father was pleased with my high scores last year and wants me to continue doing well. He has agreed to let me study with you again. He cannot stop me from going with her to the boarding house. I would be proud to help Marilana after what she has done for me."

"Good." Marquiese nodded. "We will do what we can. One thing is for certain: Demdrake is not going to abuse anyone. Not if I can help it."

"Be careful Marquiese," Earek warned. "Whoever you were in Maefair, you are not that person here. Be careful that you do not make Demdrake suspicious. He is pompous and arrogant, but he will not be staying in Mystillion for long, and Bram's Fen is a lot closer to the capital. He may have heard something about you and whatever your secret is."

"I'll be careful," Marquiese assured Earek. "I do not want to run into trouble. I would rather stay away from Demdrake altogether. However, being Marilana's friend, I have learned that what she does is honorable. She is right to protect those girls. I still do not know why she chose to be a bandit hunter, but she has taught me to see the darker side of society."

"I know what you mean," agreed Earek. "I knew what went on, and while I found it deplorable, I never thought it was such a driving force for caste relations. Marilana has shown me that the lower castes have rights just like the upper castes. She has given me her friendship and helped me when I needed help for no more reason than because I was kind and honorable to her. I will gladly help her protect those girls."

The school bell rang, and they walked back inside the school. Marilana and Mistress Rose were moving the last table against the wall when they entered, clearing the center of the room of any obstructions. Marquiese grimaced; it was time for dance practice. Marilana took no notice of the rest of the students, but walked to a desk in a corner and sat facing the wall. She opened her notebook and started to study. Brittia spun excitedly in the middle of the room and approached Marquiese, smiling broadly.

"Marquiese, you will dance with me, won't you?" Brittia asked sweetly.

Marquiese opened his mouth to respond but stopped when Mistress Rose touched his shoulder with her hoof.

"I'm sorry, Brittia. You will have to choose a different dance partner. Merchant Colbran sent a letter this morning indicating that he did not want Marquiese to dance this fifnight. Something about an injury he sustained recently," Mistress Rose said firmly. "Marquiese, I want you to sit over here and watch carefully. You are still expected to learn to dance, even though you will be sitting out this fifnight."

"I understand, Mistress," Marquiese said.

He walked over to the chair next to Marilana's desk and turned his attention to the rest of the class. Brittia pouted for a moment before turning and seizing Earek's arm. Earek shot Marquiese a disgruntled look as Brittia pulled him out to the middle of the floor. Marquiese shared a wink and an amused smile. Then he glanced at Marilana and realized she was watching him. He raised his eyebrows questioningly at her, but she only smirked and dropped her eyes back to her book. *She knows I'm hiding something,* he thought, and he knew he could not be excused from dancing for the rest of the year. That was not going to happen. He knew he could hide his knowledge of etiquette easily enough, but dancing was different. If practiced with the wrong steps, the dancer would find the correct steps nearly impossible to dance when needed.

It was a dilemma the lion pondered as he watched Brittia and Earek step in time to the rhythm Mistress Rose was tapping out with her hooves. They moved together easily, and Marquiese could see they had danced often.

Marquiese also gave equal attention to the other members of the class. They showed varying degrees of skill, from the low-class children who had clearly never danced before to the high-class children who were bored by the slow pace. They went through the dance several times before Mistress Rose finally called a halt to the session, and everyone let out a relieved cheer.

When they were done, Marilana rose quickly and moved to assist Mistress Rose in repositioning the tables. Marquiese frowned for a moment when he saw this, then motioned to the other boys in the class to help. The high-class boys looked at him incredulously, so he walked over and grabbed one of the tables. When Earek moved to help him, the other boys followed their lead. He was, after all, the highest rank among them, and they knew if he did something and they did not, it would look bad for their honor.

In very little time, they had the room set back to rights. Mistress Rose thanked the boys for their assistance, and Marquiese nodded his approval. The rest of the boys returned his smile, clearly proud of themselves, though he noticed that Brittia was giving him a long-suffering look. Of course, the lynx was not impressed with his interference. After all, the lynx saw Marilana as a servant and the more she had to do, the better.

Mistress Rose began to lecture on the laws governing merchant trade, and Marquiese listened attentively. He had some basic understanding of merchant law, but he wanted to learn about it in much more depth.

When the final bell rang, he gathered his school things together and made his way out to the yard to wait for Marilana. Earek joined him, and the other youths gathered around. Brittia took his arm and simpered at him.

"You'll walk me home today, won't you, Marquiese?" Brittia asked pressing against his arm.

He crooked his elbow and offered his arm politely while taking a step back. Brittia smiled happily, laid her paw on his arm, and they started down the road. "Why don't you stop at my house for a while, Marquiese?" Brittia asked him sweetly. "I could tutor you in etiquette and dance. You have no need to study with Marilana anymore. She is not allowed to study what we are learning. She is, after all, just a peasant."

"That is kind of you to offer, but Earek and I will be studying together. Our parents have already made the arrangements," Marquiese said levelly.

"Earek cannot help with your dancing," Brittia pointed out, batting her lashes. "I can."

"My father has strict rules about dancing. And I am not allowed to dance at the moment, as Mistress Rose pointed out. I am afraid I must decline your generous offer," Marquiese said eloquently.

"Oh, Marquiese, you have such wonderful manners," Brittia giggled. "I'm sure with practice your table etiquette will become just as smooth."

"I think I am going to need a lot of practice," Marquiese said, calmly stopping at her gate and holding it open for her. "I hope you have a good night."

Brittia batted her lashes at him and squeezed his arm before starting toward her house. Marquiese held the polite smile on his face until the last of the youths had reached their homes. Then he and Earek slowed their pace until Marilana caught up.

Marilana managed a knowing smirk even as she continued to scan the forest, and Marquiese grimaced. They walked in silence until they reached the brick manor where Marquiese and Lida lived, and the young lioness bolted toward the house after giving Marilana a quick wave. "See you tomorrow."

"See you tomorrow," Marilana called in reply.

Then the trio disappeared into the forest and didn't stop until they reached a small clearing that Marilana deemed safe. She turned to face them, her expression serious.

"I assume you have discussed Demdrake," Marilana said flatly.

"We have. And we want to come with you to the boarding house tonight," Marquiese said seriously.

"We know we have to stay out of your way when and if you fight, but we want to provide witness that is equal in rank to Demdrake," added Earek.

"My word as a bandit hunter is stronger than both of yours put together in the eyes of Lady Annabella and the Magistrates," Marilana said, shaking her head. "I do not want either of you getting hurt. You also need to stay out of the fight so that charges cannot be placed against you later. You stand equal to Demdrake in the eyes of the law. If you hurt him, his family can get the law involved and you both could well end up in serious trouble. You have to promise me not to engage Demdrake or anyone with him in combat."

"You're not going to try to keep us away?" Marquiese asked surprised.

"It wouldn't do any good, would it?" Marilana replied sarcastically. "You two would just conjure up a different plan and show up anyway."

"I suppose that is a good point," Earek said. "So, we stay out of the fighting because we could get into legal trouble, but let you do the fighting and face worse punishment?"

"No," Marilana said, eyeing them both. "As a bandit hunter, I can legally use non-lethal force to stop him from reaching the girls in the boarding house. He might have gotten some training from a knight, but he has no idea what I am capable of. I'm not going to underestimate him the way he is underestimating me, but I know what I am doing and you need to let me deal with the situation. Agreed?"

"Agreed," Marquiese and Earek said in unison.

"Alright. I need to get a staff. Then I know a place outside the boarding house where we can work on your homework and keep watch at the same time," Marilana said briskly.

"What about Lady Annabella, don't you need to study with her tonight?" Marquiese asked.

"I have already taken care of that, she is no longer expecting me," Marilana said dismissively.

They followed her through the trees, surprised when they turned west away from her house. She had readily agreed to their plan—much too readily, in Marquiese eyes—and he wondered why. He glanced at Earek and could see he was puzzled as well.

"Why are we not going to your house?" Marquiese asked.

Marilana looked back at him for a moment and then placed a claw to her lips. "Shhh."

Marquiese frowned, but he also did as she instructed. They moved farther into the trees. Suddenly, Marilana came to a halt. She scanned the area for a moment and then moved slowly around a large boulder. Beyond the boulder, Marquiese spied a small cave partially hidden by a stand of brush. Marilana motioned them to wait, then approached the cave cautiously. She examined the opening and then stuck her arm inside. A moment later, she pulled a full-length quarterstaff from the hole. Marquiese looked at Earek and smiled with amusement.

Marilana got up and brushed herself off. She picked up her staff and motioned them to follow. It was not long after that they reached the edge of the trees and the girls' boarding house set at the back of a small clearing at the edge of town. Marilana hung her unstrung bow, quiver, and dagger on a tree branch and leaned her staff against a huge boulder. She climbed up the rock and sat down. "Up here," she said. "Bring your books."

The lion and leopard nimbly climbed up and found the flat surface atop the boulder big enough for them and their books. They started in on their homework.

The work was not hard, and they soon finished. After Marquiese gathered his books together, he fixed Marilana with a hard look.

"Why did you not go to your house?" the lion asked her quietly.

"You have become so used to my ways that you have forgotten the danger that I live with every day." Marilana shook her head and smiled ruefully. "I live alone, remember. And I may not stop someone of higher rank from having their way with me if they catch me, but I can take precautions. Demdrake is not stupid, even if he makes poor choices. He knows where I live. He knows that my garden is deadly. He will not step foot inside my walls, but he might wait in ambush outside my walls."

"You saw something."

"Several sets of bootprints on the road that I did not recognize. It may not have been anything, or it could have been Demdrake and a couple of his friends. He is arrogant enough to wander the roads alone, and he may have tried to catch me by surprise outside my house. There would have been no witnesses, and the patrol was an hour out. That would have been plenty of time for him to accomplish his goals."

"Instead, you came here to wait for him."

"And you brought witnesses as a deterrent," added Earek. "Very good."

"You two will not be much of a deterrent for Demdrake, but any boys who come with him will have to make a choice," Marilana said seriously. "If it is just me facing Demdrake and three or so others, he would be the highest rank present and they would feel compelled to follow his lead. With you two as witnesses, they have a way out. They can choose to follow him, or they can choose to follow your lead and stay on the sidelines."

Marquiese chuckled softly and shook his head.

"We thought we would have to convince you to let us come along, and you were worried more about us not agreeing to stay out of the fight. If we get involved, the others will also feel compelled to get involved, and they would take his side," Earek mused. "I don't think I will ever be able to predict the path of your thoughts."

"No," Marilana laughed, "probably not."

They sat in silence for a long time as the sun went down in the west. Light flared in the windows of the boarding house and the clink of cutlery could be heard from the open windows. When it was fully dark, Marquiese noticed several torches coming toward them from the center of town. He turned to say something to Marilana, but she was already gone. Her bow, quiver, and dagger still hung in the tree, but her staff was missing.

Marquiese hopped off the rock and took up a seemingly casual stance, leaning against the boulder in clear view. Earek remained on top of the boulder, but took Marilana's former position lounging against the tree.

The torches got closer, and Demdrake and three others stopped on the grass in front of the boarding house, perching the torches atop six poles and giving the area a somber, yellow glow.

Demdrake smiled when he saw Marquiese and Earek and called to them, saying, "So, you wanted to have some fun after all. Good. Very good."

"We came to watch, although I don't think you will be having much fun," Marquiese said without shifting his position.

"You'll change your mind when you see how much fun can be had from a bevy of peasant girls." Demdrake laughed.

"Yeshib, Grenvit, Abzak, you can join us on the sidelines when you feel like you're in over your heads," Earek called to the three youths with Demdrake.

"They're here to have fun, not to nurse weak stomachs," Demdrake responded.

The three youths laughed when they heard this, but they eyed Marquiese and Earek nervously. Demdrake turned his back on them and took a wide stance in the middle of the grass where he was easily seen in the light from the torches.

"I am Demdrake, first son of high-class Merchant Branish, and nephew of Merchant Sleater. I call for this house to be opened to me and my companions," he called loudly.

The faces of young deer, wolves, jaguars, and many others appeared in the windows throughout the four-story brick building, and their anxiety was apparent in their eyes and their expressions. The recessed door at the front of the house was hidden in deep shadows. An older doe appeared in a window of the first floor. She looked scared as she cracked it open.

"This house is closed to all men, young sir. You and your companions need to go home and not bother this house," she called shakily.

"This house is owned by Merchant Sleater, is it not?" Demdrake asked.

"It is, and I am employed by him to manage this house as a safe place for girls to live while going to school. It is not a place for men to visit," replied the doe.

"I am his nephew, and I will enter this house. Come, woman, open the door for me," Demdrake demanded.

"I cannot let you in. Please go home and leave us alone," the woman pleaded.

"If you will not let me in, then I shall break down the door and enter on my own. Get the girls ready, woman," Demdrake ordered.

"Mistress of the House," called a voice from the shadows of the doorway. "Close and lock the shutters and bar the door. The girls do not need to watch this unpleasantness."

"As you say," the doe said quickly and slammed the shutters of the window closed.

The girls all across the building began to pull the shutters closed and soon all the windows of the house had been closed and sealed.

"Who thinks to bar my passage into my uncle's house? Show yourself!" Demdrake called angrily.

Marilana stepped into the light. She stopped at the edge of the top step and leaned almost casually on her staff.

"I, Marilana, Bandit Hunter of the Southern Tip, hold this house secure from you and all who would harm those inside," Marilana called loudly to the night. There was an icy calm to her voice.

"So there you are, Marilana," Demdrake grinned maliciously. "I waited at your house for a long time this afternoon. When you didn't come, I thought you might be hiding from me. I knew you would be here tonight, though. You boasted that you could stop me, and you never go back on your threats. Now I can give you what you deserve."

He grinned wickedly, but Marilana didn't respond.

"Come on, boys. Let's teach this peasant a lesson. Then we can have some fun with the rest of them."

"Oh, so that's why you brought them," Marilana taunted. "Afraid you can't take me on your own. Afraid I might be more than you can control. Is that it?"

Demdrake stalked slowly forward, but the other three hesitated.

Marquiese took advantage of their nervousness and called, "Yeshib, Grenvit, Abzak! You have a choice. You can fight the bandit hunter or you can stand aside. My recommendation is for you to stand aside. I have only lived here a year, but I know I would not want to face the bandit hunter known as The

Ghost. You have lived here longer; you know her reputation better than I do."

"Stay out of this, Marquiese," Demdrake hissed over his shoulder. "You just want to keep the wench to yourself. I will not be denied the privileges of my rank."

Demdrake halted his advance and turned to glare at his three companions.

"You agreed to stand with me in this. You wanted to come have some fun and now we are at the precipice."

"I'm surprised at you, Grenvit. Didn't Marilana save your dad during a bandit raid several years ago?" Earek interjected. "I think I remember that you witnessed the whole thing and said you would never in a million years want to face her."

"She doesn't have her bow," spat Demdrake. "And she can't use lethal force against us."

"And you, Yeshib," Earek continued. "Didn't The Ghost rescue your mother and sister from the bandits who attacked your mother's wagon train? It's been a few years, but I doubt that event could have slipped your memory."

"Earek! Hold your tongue or I will cut it out," growled Demdrake. "This is not your fight. Stay out of it."

"If that is how you treat your acquaintances, I would hate to be counted among your friends," Marquiese commented.

Yeshib and Grenvit looked at Marilana standing calmly on the step of the house and then looked at each other. Yeshib shook his head slightly and Grenvit nodded. Together they turned without a second glance and walked off into the darkness. Abzak watched the other two go and looked back at Demdrake.

"We were willing to stand with you against peasants and join in the fun you said we could have. You promised that you could get us into the house with little resistance. You failed to get the door opened easily. And what's more, they're right. We know better than to face The Ghost."

Abzak turned and ran after his friends. Demdrake looked at Marquiese and Earek still lounging at their ease, and his face twisted with fury.

"You will both pay for this," he growled at them. "You will regret interfering."

"They have not interfered with your intent," Marilana said quietly.

"No, they haven't. And they won't," he growled spinning to face her. "They know it is perfectly within my rights to do as I please with you and the girls in this house."

He drew his sword and advanced slowly on Marilana. She watched him without flinching. As he placed his foot on the bottom step, Marilana stepped to the side.

"I knew you would not stand in my way." He grinned viciously.

"You will not enter this house," Marilana said, her voice calm.

He stepped cautiously up the next two steps, and Marilana matched his steps with her own sideways movement. He smirked as he reached toward the door latch. In that instance, Marilana's staff whirled and smacked his paw. He jumped back in surprise.

"How dare you harm someone of higher rank!" He spat the words.

"I will use force if need be. And it will not be pleasant."

The lynx growled and took several quick steps toward her. She again matched his steps and backed away from him. The lynx grinned and backed toward the door. She matched his movement with her own advance. He lunged forward, swinging his sword, but Marilana sprang away. He reached quickly for the door, and she swung her staff at full extension—hardly more than a blur—and knocked his sword from his paw. It flew in the air, arcing end over end, and landed on the grass.

The lynx growled and came toward her again. Again the lioness matched his steps, backing away. Demdrake stopped at the top of the steps, unwilling to give up the higher position. He growled and drew his dagger. Marilana waited calmly. He started to turn away from her, and then spun back, and launched the dagger at her. Marilana spun to the side, her staff a blur in the torchlight. She deflected the dagger with her staff and sent it flying off into the darkness. Demdrake did not wait to see what happened. He turned and rushed the door, but Marilana continued her spin. She struck her staff across the back of his knees and caused his legs to buckle. She twisted her staff up and flipped him backward down the stairs. The lynx crashed hard to the ground. He lay on his back gasping for breath.

Marilana calmly climbed the steps again and waited.

Marquiese looked up at Earek, and laughed with amusement. Demdrake got to his feet and shot them a dark look. With a growl, he snatched up his sword and made ready once again to charge.

"Enough!" commanded a voice from the darkness.

Demdrake stopped cold and turned furiously toward the new voice. He froze as Lady Annabella walked into the ring of torchlight, Captain-General Zariff, Captain Branth, Merchant Sleater, Headmistress Ceta, and a whole fist of guardsmen behind her. Marquiese and Earek moved fully into the light and bowed. Lady Annabella acknowledged them with a nod and then focused fully on Demdrake.

"Lady Annabella, how pleasant it is to see you," the lynx said smoothly, a smile fixed to his face.

"Keep your flattery for someone who cares for it," Lady Annabella said curtly.

"Forgive me, Lady Annabella. I am out of sorts," Demdrake said finally honoring her with a bow. "You have caught me in the middle of an argument, I'm afraid. This peasant was forcefully stopping me from checking on the security of the house. I warned her that she could be facing punishment for stepping beyond the bounds of her position."

"Lady Annabella, if I may provide witness to the events of the evening," Marquiese said smoothly. "Marilana, Bandit Hunter of the Southern Tip, proclaimed this house was under her protection and used minimal force to prevent merchant son Demdrake from entering."

"She used force to interfere with my privileges of rank. She harmed me, an individual of higher rank, when I approached her," Demdrake argued.

"Enough," Lady Annabella said again. "First of all, Demdrake, this house is owned by your uncle Merchant Sleater. He swore an oath to me that the girls in this house would be safe from all men. You have violated his oath of security, slandering his honor, and risking my seizure of this property. Instead of losing his holdings, he has agreed to your punishment. You are therefore placed under house arrest for as long as you remain in the Southern Tip. Second, Marilana was well within her rights as Bandit Hunter to protect the security of this house with non-lethal force, as she has done. She is not at fault."

"She rebuffed his advances on her," Headmistress Ceta interjected. "She is by law required to submit to his will."

"Third," Lady Annabella continued without acknowledging the headmistress. "Marilana is my ward, and anyone wanting to lay with her must ask my permission. Since you did not ask my permission, Marilana was fully within her rights to evade your advances. She is again not at fault. You know full well that she is my ward and under my protection. You will no longer visit the Southern Tip without my prior knowledge and agreement. You will be escorted back to Bram's Fen two days from now to face the Magistrates in court for charges placed against you there. Your actions are despicable, and if you ever attempt something like this again while in the Southern Tip, you will be spending time in my stockade."

Lady Annabella flicked her paw, and two guardsmen advanced. They seized Demdrake by the arms and marched him out of the torchlight.

"As for you," Lady Annabella said, turning to face Headmistress Ceta. "You are lucky to still be free of my stockade, as well. Did you not understand the instructions I gave you regarding Marilana's education? Was I unclear in my letter? She is to attend Finishing School as part of Mistress Rose's class. That does not mean that you can shove her in a corner and relegate her to the duties of a servant. She is there to learn the ways of the merchant caste at my request. There is no law against her learning. She will henceforth be treated as part of the class. She will learn the etiquette, dance, and all the rest of the curriculum along with the rest of the class, without exception. If I hear of you purposely leaving her out again, you will lose your position at the school. Have I made my instructions clear?"

"Yes, Lady Annabella," Headmistress Ceta squeaked. She bowed her head and curtseyed rather clumsily.

"Now then, it is late, and we all need to get some rest this night." Lady Annabella turned and walked back into the darkness.

Marquiese looked at Earek and smiled incredulously. They turned to face Marilana and saw that the older doe had opened the front door and stood now on the top step next to the lioness.

They could not hear what Marilana was saying to the matron, but they saw how warmly the woman hugged her in response. Then the doe retreated into the boarding house once again and closed the door.

Marilana jumped from the porch, went to the nearest torch, and smothered the flame in the dirt. Then she, Marquiese, and Earek went torch by torch, extinguishing the flames and allowing their eyes to adjust to the darkness.

"There is one thing I don't understand," Marquiese said as they started across the clearing. "How did Lady Annabella know what was going on here tonight? You were not in a position to speak with her or any guardsmen nor to send a letter."

"Mistress Rose." Marilana chuckled softly. "During lunch, I told her what was going on tonight and she went to Lady Annabella."

"Of course," Marquiese mused. "Most people think of Mistress Rose as Headmistress Ceta's underling. They do not stop to consider where her loyalties actually lie."

"She has been my tutor for many years," Marilana said quietly. "And she did not approve of Headmistress Ceta's instructions for my education this morning."

"So tomorrow you will finally get to show Brittia what real etiquette is," Marquiese said, laughing.

"No," Marilana said firmly. "It took me all summer to convince Lady Annabella and Mistress Rose that I should not insult Brittia so much. I will start out acting like I have only the most basic etiquette. Eventually, I will reveal my skills, but not until the last year. Brittia has always made school unpleasant for me. I do not want to face a daily beating for insulting her."

Marquiese studied her as best as could in the dark. He said, "You are hiding your privileges again."

"I am doing what I think is best," she replied softly.

Marilana retrieved her weapons, strung her bow, and led them into the trees. She didn't stop until they were back at the same cave where she had retrieved her staff earlier. This time, she slid the staff in and then rummaged in the cave retrieving something else. An instant later, a spark of light flared revealing the thing to be a lantern.

"What is this place?" Earek asked quietly.

"Just one of many places where I have emergency supplies stashed," Marilana said, shrugging casually. She studied them briefly. "I want to thank you both for what you did today."

"We are happy to help protect the girls," Earek said. "Always will be."

"You have shown us the importance of protecting the lower castes," Marquiese added.

"I'm glad." Marilana smiled slightly. "But that's not the only thing you did today. You spoke out against Demdrake this morning. You helped Mistress Rose rearrange the classroom this afternoon. And tonight you both had the intention of intervening if Demdrake caught me. I saw that in your eyes. You took my side. You helped me. You were protecting me. No one other than Lady Annabella has ever done that, not voluntarily. For that I want to thank you."

"That's what friends do," Marquiese replied quietly, studying her eyes.

She met his eyes evenly. There was no fear, no ambivalence. She truly trusted them. Marquiese could see that. But her trust seemed deeper than before.

"We are glad to help you, Marilana," Earek assured her. "And we also don't expect anything in return. Friendship is not a tally to be balanced. It is just people doing what they can for each other for no other reason than because they want to."

"Thank you for wanting to be my friends," Marilana said softly. "Now follow me. It's late. Your families will be waiting."

16

Brittia had been furious when Headmistress Ceta informed the class that Lady Annabella wished for Marilana to learn the ways of merchants, and learn them without prejudice. It meant that Brittia could no longer order Marilana around like a servant. It also meant that they all had to take turns serving the class and everyone would have to play host at some point.

Brittia had fumed all morning. But ever since lunch, something had changed, and she had not stopped smiling even for a second. It was Marilana, of course, and her apparent travails with etiquette. She was, as only Marquiese and Earek knew, doing her best to hide her table skills. And between her mistakes and his, Mistress Rose was spending half her time at their end of the tables. They were not actually competing, but it seemed that they were trying to see who could give Mistress Rose a headache first.

Finally Mistress Rose excused the class for break.

"Not you two." She pointed to the clumsy brown bear and the slender eland who had been charged with serving lunch to the class; it had not gone well. "Let us talk about your abysmal performance this morning, shall we?"

Marquiese, Earek, Klay, and Caton went outside and took their usual place by the fence, only to find Brittia and her friends eager to join them. Marquiese covered his grimace with a polite emotionless smile.

"I think, Marquiese, that you would have had a much more pleasurable time last night if you had accepted my offer to tutor you," Brittia said calmly. "And the offer still stands, though I am afraid we will have to study at your house until Demdrake returns to Bram's Fen. He would not tell me what occurred last night, but he has sworn to duel you and Earek if he ever sees you again."

"Did he now?" Marquiese said easily.

Brittia shrugged her slender lynx shoulders. "Personally, I don't care that you opposed him. I think your sense of honor is charming; however your table etiquette is in dire need of practice. And after watching Marilana's lack of skill today, she clearly will not be a suitable mentor."

"Thank you again for the offer, Brittia," Marquiese replied. "But as I told you, Earek and I are studying together."

"Hmm, yes," Brittia mused. "But studying what? From the way you and he went out of your way to protect Marilana yesterday, I think I can guess. I hope your studies are worth the trouble. Someday you will have to make a choice. And when you do, I hope it is the right one."

Brittia ran one of her claws along Marquiese's jaw and smiled before turning away.

"She has grown bolder over the summer," Earek commented. "Are you sure you cannot dance today? I would rather you continue to suffer her attentions than have to endure them myself."

"You are so helpful." Marquiese shook his head sarcastically.

The bell rang just then, and the other boys laughed easily at Marquiese's expense. And by the time they were inside, he was grinning as well. As he entered the hallway, he spotted Marilana leaving the library and wondered at the nervous look on her face. Surely Lady Annabella would have taught her how to dance by now, and he wondered if she would try to hide her ability.

"Marquiese, you can take a seat in the corner," Mistress Rose directed. "As for the rest of you, since there is an uneven pairing today, you will be switching partners throughout today's dance lesson. I will call out when to switch and tap one girl at a time to sit out a turn. Brittia, you will sit out first."

Brittia looked shocked at this unexpected revelation, but covered it with a curt nod of her head. She stood to the side as Mistress Rose made sure everyone was paired and ready. Marquiese watched Marilana closely. She was paired with a leopard named Jeof, one of the low-class merchant sons. Jeof seemed more nervous to be dancing at all than to be paired with Marilana.

Marilana curtseyed easily and took Jeof's proffered paw. Mistress Rose started to tap the rhythm of the waltz that the class had started to learn yesterday. Marilana stepped in time with the tapping, but in the wrong direction. Jeof and she both stumbled. Marilana blushed slightly but continue on. She had excellent timing, Marquiese noticed, but was constantly missing her steps. Mistress Rose encouraged her to follow Jeof's lead, but Jeof was not very familiar with the steps and together they stumbled again.

Brittia caught Marquiese's eye and smiled broadly at what they were seeing on the dance floor. Just then, Mistress Rose called for a switch and spared Marquiese from having to return Brittia's smile.

Her time of sitting out now finished, Brittia swept into the group and seized one of the high-class merchant sons. She flowed through the steps of the dance with an easy expertise.

Marquiese sat forward. He watched Brittia's feet for a moment and then compared her steps with Marilana's. Much to his surprise, he realized that Marilana was not dancing the same dance. Her steps were precise, sure, and timed perfectly, but they were not the steps of the waltz her partner was dancing. The result was comedy of errors. Amazingly, she was carefully practicing her own dance, just not the same one as Jeof. Marquiese stifled a laugh when he realized that Marilana had just given him the solution to his own dilemma. Dance precisely, just not the dance your partner is dancing.

Earek stretched his arms and sat back from Marilana's table. He watched his two friends finish their homework. It still amazed him that his friendship with Marilana came so easily. He had lived his whole life knowing who she was, and yet he had not known her at all. He was glad he had accepted Marquiese's offer to study with them last year. These two were better friends to him than any of Brittia's followers had ever been, and he was proud to know they expected him to be honorable rather than opportunistic. He knew they had secrets that they were not willing to share at the moment, but he didn't care as long as they trusted him enough to be his friends.

He watched Marilana critically as she set down her pen and stood up. He had been studying her movements since their first trip into the forest. She never tripped or faltered. She always moved with grace. So he had been surprised at how poorly she had danced in class. He suspected she was hiding her ability just as she was her knowledge of etiquette. He knew Lady Annabella was visiting her every month for the express purpose of learning higher etiquette, and he suspected Marquiese had been part of those visits.

Earek hated agreeing with Demdrake on anything, but even he could see that Marilana was maturing into a serious beauty. He hoped Lady Annabella was right to insist Marilana continue with Finishing School and that she would be safe doing so.

Earek turned his attention to Marquiese and watched how carefully he moved his pen. He knew Marquiese was hiding his own skills at school and wondered what he would do when he had to start dancing this next fifnight.

"Done," Marquiese announced, leaning back. Then he drew a deep breath and said, "I'm sure glad tomorrow is Restday. I really need a break from school."

"Really?" Earek smirked. "It's only the first fifnight, and you hardly did anything. You didn't dance, you didn't use good etiquette, and you didn't have to spend the break today with Brittia. What exactly do you need a break from?"

"For one thing, Brittia's constant assertions." Marquiese laughed. "Even when she's dancing with someone else she keeps shooting me looks. If I have to force one more polite smile, I think my face will crack open."

"But you do such a good job of it," Marilana teased. "You've become an expert at putting her off without offending her. I wonder when she'll catch on?"

Marquiese glared at her when he heard this, and both Marilana and Earek broke up laughing.

"I have to say I was glad that you served me at lunch today, Earek, instead of Brittia," Marquiese said. "Saved me from some serious flirting."

"I'm glad you served me too," Marilana said, grinning her approval. "Because I really did not want my lunch dumped in my lap. And besides, you're really quite good at it."

"My mother insists that proper etiquette is pivotal for a successful merchant," Earek told them. "She has been training me since I was little, and I've been serving customers and potential trading partners ever since. It's so much more important for me than for Adrek. He will inherit Father's rank and business, but I will have to rely solely on my future wife."

"The skills will help you get a good wife, Earek. They will also allow you to help her succeed in whatever business her family is in," Marilana said seriously. "Your mother is correct though to insist Adrek learn as well. He will have to deal with other high-class merchants as well as nobility. Your father has good etiquette, and he knows how important those skills are. I have seen him deal with Lady Annabella, and he has earned her respect. Adrek will have to work hard to keep her respect when the time comes."

"That is true," added Marquiese. "And if you marry Brittia, you will have to work hard to counterbalance her attitude. Because if her current attitude doesn't change, she could find her rank dropping if she starts offending nobles and foreign merchants. True, she would still be a high-class merchant, but she may lose the head position with the merchant council and she may lose her wealth if she cannot continue the high level of trade that her father maintains."

"I see what you mean." Earek nodded thoughtfully. "Is that what Lady Annabella has been teaching you both during her monthly visits to the house here?"

Marquiese looked at him in surprise, but Marilana only smiled.

"I told you he would notice the change in your attitude and figure it out," Marilana said to Marquiese, chuckling.

"I know. I just did not think it would happen so soon," Marquiese replied with a rueful smile.

"You're very observant, Earek, and very good at surmising what is not being said," Marilana told him. "Just be careful not to voice your suspicions too readily. Some things are best left unmentioned."

"That's something I need to practice." Earek nodded his understanding. Then he jumped to his feet. "Speaking of practice. I have one more bit of homework that I need help with. Marilana, if you would assist me, I would be most grateful."

He held his paw out to her. She gave him a suspicious smirk, but placed her paw in his without hesitation. Earek led her into the main room. He said, "Marquiese, if you would be so kind as to tap the rhythm of the waltz we were learning in class today, I would like Marilana to help me perfect my dancing skills."

"Earek, you saw me in class. Dancing is hardly my strong suit," Marilana said quietly.

"I saw your performance, but I also know you better than the rest of the class," he said, smiling easily. "You have far too much control of your steps and your movements and are far too graceful."

"But you are already a good dancer," Marilana pointed out. "You hardly need my help."

"With a basic waltz, yes, but we will be moving on to more advanced dances, and that is when I think you will be able to help me." Earek bowed to her. "May I have this dance, please?"

By then, Marquiese had retrieved a pair of wooden spoons from the kitchen and was tapping the rhythm at the traditional speed for the basic waltz. Marilana studied them both for a moment, then sighed.

"Alright then," she said.

She lifted her skirt and curtseyed. Marilana flowed through the steps easily, adjusting naturally to the small space, and following Earek's lead. By the end, she was relaxed and smiling, and even enjoying herself some.

"My turn," Marquiese said mischievously, jumping up when the dance finished and thrusting the spoons in Earek's direction. He bowed formally to Marilana.

"Marilana, would you do me the honor of this dance?"

"I will," Marilana said, smiling ruefully and curtsying in return.

Earek started tapping the rhythm on the spoons and nearly dropped them in surprise when he saw the increasingly complex and fascinating steps Marquiese was leading Marilana through. Yes, it was still a waltz and the timing was the same, but the skill level needed was obviously much higher.

When the dance was done and the couple parted, Marilana collapsed into her chair by the fireplace, laughing. Marquiese smiled broadly, breathing hard.

"I thought as much," Earek said, smiling at his friends. "You two have been totally faking it."

"You're right, Earek," Marquiese agreed. "I thought I recognized the steps Marilana was dancing in class and wanted to test my theory." He gazed at her. "I was right, wasn't I?"

"All that time you were dancing a different dance?" Earek looked at her with complete surprise.

"That is exactly right," Marquiese answered. "I didn't dance this fifnight, because I was not sure how to hide my ability. But then I started watching Marilana and realized that I could practice a different dance, even if it made me look silly and I could do it without making mistakes."

"But proper practice is important too," Marilana said, giggling. "Otherwise you will never know more than the first few steps or how to adjust to your partner."

"I suppose that makes sense," Earek said, nodding. "At least I know now that I will have a couple of fine tutors once we get to the higher dances."

"Thank you, both of you," Marilana smiled at them, her mirth a thing of beauty. "I have always enjoyed dancing, but I have never had so much fun with it. Most of the time, Captain-General Zariff serves as my dance partner, but he tends toward seriousness, like he does with everything. I have danced with some of the landed-gentry at various festivities, but only because they were instructed to do so. I have never actually had anyone ask me to dance or had the chance to dance just for the simple pleasure of it. You are both skilled, and that makes it even that much more fun."

"Compared to you two, I'm just a novice." Earek shook his head.

"No, Earek," Marilana smiled gently. "You have the manner and control needed to be a great dancer. I will gladly help you learn the steps of the higher dances. Someday you will be the favored partner for every girl in Mystillion."

"No, I think Marquiese will hold that honor," Earek replied. "And the boys will line up to take a turn with you, Marilana."

"I don't think so," Marilana said softly watching Marquiese. "Marquiese and I will not be showing our skills anytime soon."

"But when you do, you will be envied," Earek said firmly.

"Thank you for the thought," Marilana said, "but the only formal dances I will attend will be done so as a servant, not because I was invited."

"Perhaps. But servants and peasants have their own dances, and you will be the best dancer among them."

"Yes, dancing rustic reels and jigs and laughing at each other's mistakes, I can tell you that skill is hardly a requirement," Marilana replied quietly. "Besides you are forgetting that I'm a bandit hunter. I make the other peasants uneasy, and that is not conducive to dancing."

"Wasn't there dancing at Natly's wedding or at Lady Annabella's staff New Year's festivities? Surely the young men would have loved to have danced with you at those events," Earek persisted.

He grimaced when he saw Marilana looking sadly down at her paws and realized he had gone too far.

"The young serving men try not to catch my attention," Marilana replied quietly, "and Natly's new husband requested I not attend the wedding. He felt the attendance of a bandit hunter was a bad omen."

"Marilana, I'm sorry. I just . . . I wish everyone could see you the way I do."

"Perhaps someday they will," Marquiese mused. "Time will tell."

"At least I can practice with the two of you," Marilana said eventually. "And I will enjoy what small pleasures I can get."

17

Marquiese slopped some red wine sauce on the table next to Brittia, and she squealed in disbelief.

Marquiese grimaced and said, "I'm so sorry. Forgive me, Brittia. It was an accident."

He wiped up the spill as quickly as he could, apologized a second time, and then finished setting the plate down in front of her.

"Marquiese, you do not speak informally when serving food," Mistress Rose chided.

"Oh, right, sorry," Marquiese said quickly turning to retrieve the next plate.

"And Brittia, it is not necessary to squeal every time someone spills something," Mistress Rose said calmly. "It happens."

"But Mistress Rose, look! It dripped on my dress!" Brittia wailed pointing at a small splatter of red drops on her yellow skirt. "It's ruined. I'll never be able to wear it again."

"I'm sorry, Brittia. But accidents happen. You know that. This is a time to practice after all," Mistress Rose replied.

Brittia continued to pout, while Marquiese served the rest of the meal and everyone else held their silence.

Marilana sat at the head of the table, tugging at her napkin and fidgeting. It was her job to act as hostess today, but so far she had hardly lifted her eyes much less greeted her 'guests.'

Mistress Rose was also keenly aware of this and leaned down to whisper in the lioness' ear. "As our hostess, I do believe it is your job to welcome your guests to this very delectable meal."

Marilana blushed and nodded. Chiely, the low-class merchant daughter chosen to serve with Marquiese, was just finishing pouring the last of the drinks, and Marilana chose this moment to rise.

"I welcome you all to my friendly dinner and thank you for coming. Please eat and enjoy," she said very quickly and without an ounce of enthusiasm.

Brittia rolled her eyes when she heard this and picked up her fork. Marilana inched her chair back and started to sit back down. Unfortunately, the chair tugged against the runner and caused Chiely to stumble. Screaming, her arms flew in the air and the pitcher of water she had been carrying flew straight into Brittia's lap. Brittia shrieked, and her shriek turned into a cry of outrage.

"Marilana! You did that on purpose!"

"Oh, no! Brittia, I'm so sorry! Please, Mistress Rose, may I take Brittia to the restroom and help her dry her dress?" Marilana asked, jumping up and looking pleadingly at Mistress Rose.

"Oh, very well," sighed Mistress Rose. "Don't take too long. The rest of you please continue."

Marquiese watched this entire episode with increasing curiosity. *What*, he thought, *is Marilana up to?*

Marilana followed Brittia to the restroom where the lynx immediately turned on her.

"What did you do that for? Now my dress is ruined!"

"Is it one of your favorites?" Marilana asked calmly. She took two towels from the supply cabinet and filled the water basin.

"Yes. In fact, it is. Not that it matters to you," Brittia shot back.

"Then I suggest you hold still so that I can clean it. If I don't get that wine sauce out now, it will be stained for good. And then where would we be?"

Brittia displayed a well-practiced frown, but she also allowed Marilana to tend to the stain, dabbing it as if it were the only dress the lynx owned. It took only a few moments to lift the red spots from the yellow satin and dry the garment. When she was done, Marilana put away the towels and poured the water in to the waste bucket.

"Good as new," Marilana said, inspecting the dress one last time. "Shall we return to class?"

"Why did you do this? Save my dress?" Brittia asked suspiciously. "You don't even like me."

"It's a nice dress." Marilana shrugged and, without waiting, turned and left the restroom.

They returned to the classroom in silence and took their seats again. Marilana finished eating quickly and followed Mistress Rose's instructions to dismiss the class. "Thank you all for coming. I hope you enjoyed it," she recited.

"Chiely, Marquiese, and Marilana, please remain. I wish to speak with you three," Mistress Rose said as the students began to exit for break.

Marilana watched Marquiese from the corner of her eye as he caught up with Brittia before she was able to leave the room.

"Brittia, I'm really sorry. Is your dress ruined?" Marquiese asked, his concern showing on his face.

"Don't be silly," Brittia tittered. "Look! It's perfectly fine."

Brittia batted her lashes, waved, and made her typically pretentious exit.

"Marquiese and Marilana, please finish cleaning up, if you will. I'd like a word with Chiely out into the hall." She pointed at the tawny-colored fawn and walked briskly out of the room.

"You cleaned Brittia's dress. Why?" Marquiese asked Marilana as they picked up the last of the dishes and deposited them on the back table. "Do not tell me you have decided to bury the hatchet."

"There is no hatchet to bury. I cleaned her dress because you nearly ruined it," Marilana replied simply. "Red wine sauce, honestly, Marquiese, what were you thinking?"

"You don't care about your own clothes, let alone Brittia's clothes," he said. "Come on. Out with it. Why did you do it?"

"Because now she's not mad at you," Marilana said hotly. "I didn't want her to blame you and hold a grudge. It's your first day of dancing, and you're going to need to start out on a good note."

Marquiese blinked at her, his surprise completely genuine, but the return of Mistress Rose and Chiely robbed him of any chance to respond.

"Chiely and Marquiese, you two go ahead and eat your lunches," Mistress Rose instructed. Then she turned to Marilana and said in a most stern voice, "Marilana, follow me, please."

Marilana's sigh carried her out into the hallway. When they were alone, Mistress Rose closed the door and crossed her arms.

"What was that all about, young lady?" the slender horse said, obviously angry.

"I'm sorry, Mistress Rose. I apologize for disrupting your lesson," Marilana said quietly. "I just didn't want Brittia's dress to be stained, that's all."

"Why in the name of The Goddess might that be?"

"I didn't want her to spend the rest of the day in a bad mood."

"You have never cared even for a moment whether she was happy or not," her teacher said suspiciously. "In fact, you usually go out of your way to make her mad."

"Maybe I've decided to try a different approach."

Mistress Rose heaved a sigh of frustration. "Marilana, I know you're not telling me something. But whatever you're up to, do not let it disrupt my class ever again. Now go outside for break."

"Yes, Mistress Rose," Marilana replied with a sigh of her own.

Marquiese helped move the tables in the classroom out of the way. Then he waited nervously for the bell to signal the start of afternoon classes. He stared out of the window, but he was not really paying attention to what was going on outside. He was lost in thought. The truth was he had not meant to spill wine sauce on Brittia's dress. It really had been an accident; he was just nervous about dance class. Marilana's reaction, however, struck him as calculated. She had offered to clean Brittia's dress and then claimed she had done so hoping to curb Brittia's anger toward him. That, of course, had not really been necessary. Marquiese could easily have offered to replace the damaged dress. No, there was something else going on.

Marquiese's reverie, however, was interrupted by the bell calling everyone back to class, and the room was soon filled with nervous laughter.

Brittia swayed into the room and approached him with a smile.

"Are you going to be dancing today, Marquiese?" the lynx asked him sweetly.

"Um, yes, I am. But I have to warn you, I'm not a very good dancer," he replied nervously.

"Oh, I'm sure you will get better with practice. Will you be my partner?"

"If you really want me to. Of course, I would be honored," Marquiese replied, disguising a grimace with a nod of his head and a brief smile.

"All right, class. Everyone pair up," Mistress Rose called. "We will be practicing the basic waltz at its normal tempo today, so everyone ready."

She waited until everyone had taken their places, gave a last instruction, and then began clopping the slow beat. "One . . . two . . . three."

Marquiese took his first step, stumbled, and just missed crushing Brittia's toes.

"It is alright," Brittia whispered. "Just try again. You will soon be a master."

Marquiese tried and tried again. Each time, he tripped and stumbled, never getting more than a few steps into his dance. By the time Mistress Rose called for them to stop, Brittia was in a foul mood. She had tried to guide him. She had tried to correct him. Yet, despite all her efforts, he had been persistent with his folly.

"Do not worry everyone. We have lots of time to practice," Mistress Rose said as she guided the tables back into position.

"Lots of time to get my toes smashed and my shoes ruined is what she means," grumbled Brittia.

*

Brittia did not walk home with their group that afternoon.

The other students poked fun at Marquiese for his lack of skill on the dance floor and had a good laugh at his expense, but they all said he would get better with practice. One by one, they dropped off.

Finally, it was just he and Earek. They were well ahead of Marilana and Lida, so they slowed down and allowed the pair to catch up. Marilana was intent on the forest, scowling at the trees, her bow at the ready. She spoke not a word, and no one tried to make conversation with her.

Lida left them at the brick house and hurried toward the entrance, while Marquiese, Earek, and Marilana left the road and entered the forest. The lioness remained silent and distant as she led the way to her house. When the door was closed behind them and her traps had been reset, she walked directly into the kitchen. The lion and leopard may have been frustrated, but they let her be and started in on their homework.

Marilana finished her homework silently, then closed her book, and started in on her chores. When she left the house to retrieve firewood, Earek caught Marquiese's eye.

"What is going on with her?" he hissed. "She acts like we're not even here."

"How should I know?" Marquiese quietly growled back. "All I did at lunch was ask her why she cleaned Brittia's dress. She told me she did it so Brittia would not be mad at me, and now she's acting like this."

"You need to say something to her," Earek insisted.

Marquiese was about to reply that Marilana's bad mood was not his fault when they heard the back door close with a thud.

Marilana entered the kitchen with an armload of wood. Marquiese watched her stack the wood neatly in the wood box beside the fireplace, then brush her arms off. He really did want to say something, but he wasn't sure what. When Marilana left the kitchen again, Earek looked up at him and jerked his head insistently toward the other room. Marquiese sighed. He got up quietly and went into the main room. Marilana wasn't there.

"Marilana?" he called. He saw that that the bedroom door was open and ventured that direction. He found Marilana standing in front of the pine wardrobe with the doors open, staring blankly inside. He stopped in the doorway and watched her curiously. She just stood there for a long moment, and then she closed the doors with a swat of her paw and turned away. When she saw Marquiese hovering in the doorway, she jumped with surprise.

"Marquiese?!"

"Marilana! I . . . uh . . . I am sorry. I didn't mean to startle you," he said quickly. "I was looking for you, and . . . ."

"And now you found me. So now what?" She glared at him, the moment of surprise long past.

"I was hoping we could talk," he said forcefully, his temper suddenly flaring. "You've been acting so strange today. Why? What is bothering you?"

"What does it matter to you if something is bothering me?" Marilana fired back at him. "My behavior is my business."

She looked around the room, growling in frustration, then stomped her foot and turned her back to him.

"I'm sorry. Of course it is. I just wanted to make sure you were alright." He looked around the room, searching for some insight into her frustration. His eyes fell on the pine wardrobe and then moved across to the three carved and locked wardrobes. He knew they held formal gowns on loan from Lady Annabella. Then he remembered their conversation.

"Do you not like wearing the fancy gowns?" he asked gently.

Marilana blushed and hesitated before answering.

"They are both more comfortable and more restricting than my normal dresses," she replied carefully.

"That was not what I asked, but I think your blushing answered my question. You do look nice in that gown and dinner was very good," he said seriously.

Then his own words from earlier that day came slamming back to him.

"You don't care that much about your own clothes, let alone Brittia's."

He closed his eyes with regretful understanding. He had attacked her and hurt her without meaning to.

"Marilana, I'm sorry about what I said earlier today. About the fact that you don't care that much about your own clothes, let alone Brittia's," he said, watching her back. "I spoke without thinking. I didn't mean to hurt you. I still don't understand why you were nice to Brittia, but I do know you care about your clothes. I am sorry. I will go back to the kitchen, and you can escort me home when you're ready."

He had turned away when Marilana called to him. "Marquiese."

He stopped and looked at her. She sat down on her bed and took a deep breath.

"I'm sorry, too," she said quietly. "I shouldn't have snapped at you. You don't know everything about me, and I don't know everything about you. I should not have taken your comment to heart. And you were right anyway. I don't care about my clothes the way Brittia and her followers do. I do try to keep my things clean and neat, and I take very good care of Lady Annabella's clothes." She picked at her dress, shaking her head ever so slightly.

"Truth is I don't really know why I helped Brittia with her dress. I saw that I could do something to make her not be mad at you, and I just did it. I didn't think about it. Later, I was mad at myself for doing it. I know Brittia doesn't care if a dress gets ruined; it just gives her an excuse to have a new one made. What's more, I got into trouble with Mistress Rose for doing it. She was furious. I took a risk, and all for what? I didn't gain anything by it."

"Marilana, it really doesn't matter," Marquiese managed a chuckle. "You did something that caught us all by surprise. Why you did it is not important, now that I think about it. The fact that we are all wondering what you will do next time is much more interesting."

Marilana shook her head. "I'm going to act like it never happened and make sure it never does again."

"I don't know. Being nice to Brittia once in a while might be harder on her than it is on you," Marquiese suggested lightly.

Marilana looked up and smiled. "I'll be out in a moment, okay?" she said quietly.

Marquiese returned her smiled and closed the door behind him. He walked into the main room and found Earek standing within earshot. Marquiese jerked his head toward the kitchen, and Earek followed him.

"That was well done," Earek said mischievously. "I'm just glad I didn't have to try to intervene before she drew a knife on you or something."

"Yeah, right." Marquiese glared at him ruefully and returned his attention to his homework.

18

Fall passed without incident. Marilana and Marquiese were officially marked as the worst in class at etiquette and dancing. Earek was easily the best dancer, superior even to Brittia.

Marquiese finally reached a point in his morning sparring sessions with Marilana where he didn't leave every morning bruised from head to toe. He had not yet managed to disarm Marilana, but that was no disgrace. His bow work had improved considerably, and Zariff had him throwing knives with increasing skill. Even his horsemanship had improved, thanks to a few tips from Marilana. Enough so that he was allowed to practice jousting once a fifnight.

Harbingers of winter were manifesting all over the Southern Tip. The snows had not yet arrived, but this morning the fog hung dark and ominous over the land. Marquiese stood at the gate waiting for Marilana. Everywhere he looked, a dark mist lurked; he glanced over his shoulder and the walls of the manor house were little more than dim shadows. For that matter, it was hard enough just to see his own paws when he held them out from his sides.

"I don't know, lad," said the merchant guard beside him, a furry black bear. He shook his head ominously. "I doubt anyone can find their way in this. My advice is to treat it like a blizzard and stay in."

"You might be right, but I'll wait a while longer anyway," Marquiese replied.

"Suit yourself," the guard said.

Both lion and bear froze when a voice rose up from the fog, saying, "I'm glad you waited."

Marquiese squinted, a paw on his sword hilt, as a dark, cloaked shape slowly emerged from the fog. Marilana lowered her hood, and Marquiese relaxed.

"Good morning," he said.

"Indeed it is," she replied with a smile. "Come on, I want to show you something."

"Are you sure you want to go out in this bloody fog?" the merchant guard asked seriously.

"We'll be fine." Marilana smiled at him. "We aren't going too far."

Marilana raised her hood and blended back into the fog, a murky shadow. Marquiese followed. He stayed as close as possible, but as the ground rose and fell, it became harder to make out her shape. The fog around them darkened even further, and Marquiese assumed they were being consumed by the shadows of the forest.

"Marilana?" he whispered. "Where are you?"

"Right here," she said softly from the darkness close by. "Now we must be as silent as possible."

A blurry paw emerged in front of him, and he reached out and took it, grateful for its solid warmth. Together, they walked on in the darkness. Marquiese knew it must be getting close to dawn, but there was not a hint of light to be seen.

Finally, Marilana stopped. She bent down and examined something on the ground. Satisfied, she sat cross-legged and invited him to join her as well. He did so, facing her so their knees almost touched. Marilana laid her paws on her knees, relaxed but alert. He could see her more clearly now, though he had no idea why they were here or what they were waiting for. When he opened his mouth to say something, Marilana raised a claw to her lips. "Shhh."

Marquiese sat and waited. He grew colder and stiffer. All at once, he noticed the fog growing brighter. He forgot his discomfort and watched in amazement. The dull gray fog turned a lustrous purple, then a soft lavender, and finally a rich pink. It changed from pink to red and then to orange. The orange grew more vivid by the second, evolving into a luminous yellow that eventually became a white so bright it was hard to watch. In an instant, crystals seemed to erupt all around them. It was like being surrounded by a shroud of diamonds all sparkling and shimmering with rainbow colors. Then the intensity of the light dimmed and, just like that, it was gone; only to be replaced by a clear cold blue sky and a brilliant sun cresting over the horizon.

Marquiese smiled with amazement. That was the most incredible sunrise he had ever experienced. He looked around and saw that they were sitting on a high red stone outcrop jutting over a deep ravine. The trees sloped away, giving him a clear view of the forest—miles of it—and, in the distance, the Great Mountains rising snowcapped into the sky. When he looked the other way, a wall of tall conifers marched along the ravine in both directions, thick with underbrush, and everything was covered in sparkling white frost. He looked at Marilana and met her amber eyes. They shared a smile for one, special moment. Then Marilana tensed and looked over her shoulder. They heard voices, then a shout from the trees.

Before Marquiese could react, Marilana sprang forward and tackled him. They fell over the red stone outcrop into open space.

Marquiese braced for a long fall, but what he got was a short drop and a surprisingly soft landing. Without even a moment's pause, the lioness hauled him to his feet, spun him around, and shoved him into a crevice concealed by the stone outcrop they had just vacated.

"Don't make a sound," she whispered.

She pulled a shroud of roots over the opening, turned, and sprang down the ravine as sure footed as a mountain goat. Marquiese held his breath as the voices rang loud over his head.

"There!"

"I see her!"

"She'll have to climb back up at some point. Follow her. If you get a shot, take it," the first voice called.

Marquiese watched as a rain of arrows arced in Marilana's direction, but she ducked under an overhang and paused just long enough to avoid the onslaught. Then she sprinted along the ravine bottom and bounded around the bend. Marquiese remained frozen, listening to the sounds of the men running along the edge of the ravine and crashing through the underbrush. Gradually the sounds died away, leaving him hiding in silence. He stayed crammed in the crevice, making not a sound, and watched the shadows shift as the sun rose higher in the sky.

Marquiese had never learned to tell time by the direction and length of shadows, and doubted that knowing would have helped the waiting pass more quickly. Just when he was thinking it might be safe to stretch his legs, a shadow moved along the top of his field of view, and he froze. A split second later, a sharp crack sounded above him, and he gasped as the body of a large boar fell over the edge and toppled down into the ravine. A second figure alighted on the ledge directly in front of him and looked down after the body. Marquiese held his breath as the cloaked figure examined every inch of ground and every tree, then turned. Marquiese heaved a sigh of relief when he caught sight of Marilana's face inside the hood. She turned in one motion, moved the veil of roots obscuring his hiding place, and helped him climb out. She put a claw to her lips and then motioned him to follow. They scampered up to the edge of the ravine and cautiously looked around.

The frost had melted away in the sunshine, but the ground was covered in scuff marks and boot prints. Marilana nocked an arrow to her bow and motioned him forward. She glided into the cover of trees, and Marquiese stayed close, holding his cloak tight around him. It seemed a much shorter walk back, and abruptly they emerged from the trees and out onto the road opposite Marilana's house. They crossed quickly to her gate.

"Step exactly where I step," she whispered.

Marilana opened the gate, lifted her skirt, and stepped carefully onto the path. Marquiese took a deep breath, then followed, closing the gate carefully behind him. He stepped exactly where Marilana had. Marilana unlatched the door and led him inside. He turned to face her as she closed the door behind him.

"Marquiese, I'm sorry," Marilana said, lowering the hood of her cloak and meeting his eyes. "I knew it was risky to go there this morning, but I wanted you to see the diamond fog. Not the best decision."

"No! Don't say that. That was the most amazing sunrise I have ever witnessed. I will admit that getting knocked off a rock and crammed into a crevice for hours on end was not much fun, but it is still the best start I have ever had for a birthday." He laughed.

"I didn't know it was your birthday," Marilana said. "Happy birthday."

"I try not to let too many people know the actual day of my birth." Marquiese shrugged without explanation. "So why is that place so dangerous, and why are we not on our way to Lady Annabella's estates?"

"That ravine is one of the largest in the province, and the bandits use it because it provides them such good cover. I have caught many of them there, so they are always on the lookout for me. I didn't see anyone around earlier, so I hoped we could be in and out without incident. I was wrong." She shrugged. "As for not going to Lady Annabella's estates, she and Zariff left yesterday for Maefair. We don't have to report for sparring practice until they come back unless we choose to. I will still be going during the fifnight to help Hosten with the horses, but you can take a break if you want."

"Well, it is Restday," Marquiese said lightly. "We can take one day off, I suppose. What time is it anyway?"

"You need more practice reading the shadows, I'm afraid," Marilana said, laughing. "It's barely an hour after dawn. You only hid for half an hour."

"Really?" Marquiese said, pleasantly surprised. "In that case, how do you entertain guests around here other than dance?"

"I have a chess set," Marilana said. "Or a backgammon board, if you like."

"I shouldn't be surprised that Lady Annabella would teach you games of strategy," the lion replied, a smile splitting his face. "Let's start with chess."

Marilana retrieved the game board from her bedroom, while Marquiese added wood to the fire and lit the lantern.

"If you'll set up the board, there's something I need to do in the kitchen," Marilana said with a mischievous smile.

"Sure, I can do that."

Marquiese set the board up on a box and carefully arranged the pieces. He heard the sounds of pots and pans clanging and the opening and closing of cupboard doors and wondered what Marilana was up to.

"Sorry I took so long," she said, coming out of the kitchen and finding Marquiese sitting in her chair watching the fire thoughtfully. "Ready to play?"

"You pick," he said, holding out two closed paws.

Marilana tapped his right paw. Marquiese opened it, revealing the white king.

"Looks like you start," he said, placing the kings on the board and turning the white pieces toward Marilana.

The lioness settled herself on the floor and moved her first pawn. As the game proceeded, Marquiese watched her carefully, not at all surprised at her skill level. After Marilana won the first two games, he pulled out all the stops and managed a slim victory in their third game.

"Well played," Marilana said with a grin. She stood up and headed for the kitchen. "I'll be right back."

The sweet smells of something delightful cooking filled the house, and Marquiese couldn't hide his smile. "What is it?" he said when she returned.

"Can't tell you. Not yet," the lioness said.

"One more game and then I should take you back to your merchant family."

"I have nowhere to be today. Best three out of five," the lion countered.

"Challenge accepted." Marilana laughed with an unexpected ease and settled back down on the floor.

Marquiese won the next game using a daring pawn and knight combination, but the fifth game ended in a stalemate. They both seemed particularly happy with the result, as if a draw was the perfect way to end the morning.

"That was fun," Marquiese admitted. "You play well."

"As do you." Marilana smiled up at him.

"My father started teaching me when I was four. Mother used to love to sit and watch us play," Marquiese reminisced sadly. He paused suddenly, wondered if he had said too much. But Marilana responded with a thoughtful nod and then jumped up.

"I have something for you," she said. "Come."

Marquiese hurried after her. When he entered the kitchen he found a small cake cooling on her table.

"Happy birthday," she said, indicating the cake. "It's a traditional white cake favored here in the Southern Tip."

"For me? Marilana!" Marquiese said, smiling in wonder at her. "That is so sweet. Thank you."

"Sweet?!" Marilana exclaimed. "I shoved you in a hole and left you there for half an hour while I ran around killing bandits! That is not something done by someone best characterized as sweet."

"No, I suppose not," Marquiese chuckled. "If not sweet, then special."

He picked up the cake, broke it in half, and held one portion out to her. "Share it with me."

"I could never. It's supposed to be shared with your family and loved ones," Marilana protested.

"Can I not share some with my friend as well?" Marquiese asked. "You were thoughtful enough to make it for me. Please, share it with me."

Marilana eyed him suspiciously for a moment and then took her half of the cake.

"You know, we have the same tradition in Maefair," he said smiling. "And there is no one I'd rather be sharing this cake with than you, my friend. Thank you for saving my life this morning and for making this birthday one of my best ever."

"You're welcome," Marilana replied, taking a small bite.

"You know if you keep doing nice things for people, you may actually lose some of your reputation for being cold and indifferent," Marquiese teased.

"I'll have to be more careful." Marilana rolled her eyes. "I would hate for people to realize I have a kinder side to my personality."

They ate in silence, and Marquiese savored the sweetness of the cake. Marilana had prepared it perfectly, though she frowned slightly as she ate her portion. Marquiese could not imagine what she was thinking about, but a different thought occurred to him.

"You know, I've been thinking about those bandits," he said when he had finished his cake.

"Oh?" Marilana asked curiously.

"You haven't missed school at all this year. Have you not been out on the hunt? Haven't the bandits tried raiding the town or blocking the trade routes? It seems the perfect time of year for their skullduggery."

"Well, the answer is a bit complex," she replied, cleaning their plates.

"What do you mean?"

"Lady Annabella told me not to tell you about it unless you asked. And now you have," Marilana said simply. She dried her paws. "Let's go sit by the fire."

Marquiese went back into the main room, but stayed standing and indicated the chair for Marilana.

"Thank you," Marilana whispered. She sat on the edge of the chair and studied her paws for a moment. Then she said, "Last spring, Lady Annabella asked me to refrain from going out on the hunt and not to miss any days of school if at all possible."

"Why?"

"Because of you," Marilana replied.

"Me?" His frown deepened.

"She says you are to be protected at all costs. I still do my daily patrols, but I watch over your house and Mystillion more than the rest of the county. School allows me to be close to you in case something were to happen."

"Then bandits have tried to raid the town," he surmised.

"Three times over the summer and twice more this fall. A bandit hunter known as The Phantom has been helping in my stead. Together with Lady Annabella's troops, they have managed to stop the bandit raids before they got too close to the town," Marilana said quietly.

"The Phantom? Who is that? Someone you know?"

"Oh, yes. I trained her," Marilana said simply. "She is nearly as good as I am, but she doesn't attend school, so she has more time to track and hunt."

"I see. And Lady Annabella arranged all this with you." He said the words coldly. "So everything you have done since she and I met last spring has been arranged. Is that what you are saying? Even bringing me here this morning?"

"Of course not. Don't be silly." Marilana shook her head. "Lady Annabella asked me to stay close. Only that. I make my own choices on how to fulfill my duty."

"Did she tell you who I am?" he said aggressively.

"Tell me who you are? No!" Marilana looked at him with surprise. "She would never betray your trust!"

"If she has not told you, then I have to assume that you figured out who I am?"

"You assume incorrectly, Marquiese." Marilana met his eyes calmly. "I know you are in hiding for some reason. I suspect the merchant family you live with is not your real family. I suspect that you are more than a merchant, but I have bigger concerns without spending my time trying to decipher your secret. It is your secret. I promised to help you keep it. That is all."

He studied her for a moment, then sighed. "I'm sorry," he said quietly. "I had to ask. I had to know. I am taking a great risk in trusting you."

"If it is such a great risk, perhaps you should have thought twice about taking it," she said simply.

"No, I did not mean it that way. You have earned my trust. And I yours, I hope."

"I would have told you what was going on, but Lady Annabella ordered me not to," Marilana said without apology.

"No. She was right to do so. I had to come to trust you on my own." Marquiese sat down on the floor, stretching his legs toward the fire. "So what did you do over the summer? You were supposed to be close by, but I hardly saw you."

"Oh, I was close by," Marilana said casually. "I did a lot of patrols around the town, read a lot of books while sitting in trees, and other such things. I'm not always close by; I still have my duties to do and my chores, plus I do sleep."

"So when you're not close by, this Phantom is?" Marquiese asked curiously.

"She keeps an eye on things, although I wouldn't say she is always close by. She ranges where she wants and her goal is to hunt the bandits," Marilana shrugged.

"So who is this Phantom? I am dying to know," Marquiese asked curiously.

"Secrets, Marquiese," Marilana chided gently. "We all have them. And I cannot tell you hers."

"Of course not." He smiled. "So how about some backgammon?"

"Sure," Marilana said, laughing. "Best three out of five?"

"Challenge accepted," Marquiese laughed.

19

The winter snows finally came. Three feet of it fell on the day before the New Year, and everything in the Southern Tip shut down. Even Brittia's year-end party had to be postponed.

A bitter cold settled over the county. Several creatures got caught out in a blizzard and froze to death. Many others contracted serious cases of pneumonia and flu. School remained closed even after the two fifnight New Year break. While it wasn't thought wise for the children to risk the walk through the snows, it was also seen as a way to prevent the spread of sickness. Mother Kalan was as busy as ever traveling to the houses of the sick to dispense her herbs and offer her counsel.

Marquiese had been confined to the brick manor with Lida and her mother, Adealy, for three fifnights, and it was growing wearisome. It was late evening when he heard the door slam. He looked up from the book he was reading and saw Merchant Colbran stamping snow from his boots.

"Sorry I'm late," he said as Adealy helped him out of his heavy wrappings. "I came across Mother Kalan struggling through the snow. She was on her way to one of the low-class merchant homes. I gave her a ride in our wagon and then waited to take her back to town. She greatly appreciated the help. She told me this is one of the worst cold spells she could remember. Even the livestock are getting sick or freezing, and six more peasants have died from disease."

Marquiese sighed. It was so sad. Yes, he was frustrated at being locked up, but he knew he was privileged compared to many.

"I thought Mother Kalan was out of herbs?" Adealy asked, surprised.

"Apparently Lady Annabella brought a resupply back with her from Maefair. However, I also heard that some of the horses in Lady Annabella's stables have taken sick, and a number of her servants have been confined to their beds."

"It is hard all over. We've been lucky so far."

"You know those sudden splintering sounds we have been hearing in the middle of the night?" the merchant said. "It has apparently gotten so cold that the sap is freezing in the trees, and that sound is the trees splitting apart."

"My goodness. I can hardly believe that," Adealy gasped.

"I didn't believe it either until I saw one of the trees for myself," he said, shaking his head. "It looked like it had been smashed to pieces by a giant hammer."

Marquiese had heard of such things, but had never really believed it. Trees cracking from the cold! He shuddered at the thought and prayed to The Goddess that Marilana and his other friends were safe and warm.

"But I think we're past the worst of it now," Colbran said hopefully. "It appears the cold is lessening and that it should warm up over the next few days.

*

Merchant Colbran was right. School reopened the following fifnight. It was still cold, and there had been another blizzard, but the temperature was no longer dangerously low, and many of those who had taken ill were on the mend.

The first day back, Marquiese and Lida rode to school on Merchant Colbran's wagon, well bundled up against the cold. They hurried inside and went to their separate classrooms.

"Marquiese! Good to see you well," Klay called as he entered Mistress Rose's class.

"Klay! Good to see you. You too Caton," Marquiese said, embracing the bear and the fox as if they had been parted for years. "Your families are well I hope?"

"Doing just fine," Caton replied.

"Cannot say the same for Earek though," Klay said with a laugh.

"Why? What happened?"

"See for yourself," Caton smirked.

Marquiese looked to the back of the room where a group of Brittia's fawners had gathered. Earek sat in the middle of them with his leg up on a stool looking completely miserable. Brittia sat next to him holding his paw as if he were dying. Curious, Marquiese strolled their way.

"Oh, Marquiese! I'm so glad to see you are well," Brittia called, smiling brightly. "Did you hear what happened? Poor Earek slipped on some ice last fifnight and twisted his ankle. Mother Kalan advised him to stay off of it for two fifnights to let it heal. Luckily, I was staying in Aunt Ceta's house here in town when it happened, so I volunteered to help take care of Earek." She gave the leopard's paw a squeeze. "And haven't I done just a wonderful job."

"You've done very well," Earek said levelly, though he gave Marquiese a look of pure misery.

"The ice can be very treacherous," Marquiese said, hiding his laughter. "I hope you get better soon, Earek. You look to be in good paws."

Mistress Rose entered the room and clopped her hooves for silence.

"Everyone please take your places. We have a lot to catch up on," she said briskly. "We will begin with our etiquette lessons."

Everyone settled around two long tables and Mistress Rose chose two students to act as the servers for the day. It was only in the rush of students to take their seat that Marquiese realized that Marilana was absent. *But where could she be?* he wondered.

Marquiese tried focusing on Mistress Rose's lecture, but he was far too distracted by the empty seat that Marilana should have been occupying. *What if something happened? What if she's fallen ill?*

Marquiese picked up his spoon when lunch was served and stirred his stew listlessly.

"Very good, Marquiese," said Mistress Rose, tapping her hooves for effect.

"What?" Startled, Marquiese looked down and realized he had picked up the proper spoon and was gripping it exactly as it should have been.

"I did it right?" he asked, feigning surprise.

"Yes. A few more accidents, and we might just be able to break your bad habits after all," said Mistress Rose as she moved on down the table.

Brittia caught his eye and smiled encouragingly at him. He returned her smile, but reminded himself to pay better attention. He could not afford to be distracted. Any hint that he was not the lion son of a high-class merchant he claimed to be could prove disastrous.

*

Marilana did not turn up for class the next day or the next. Now Marquiese was getting seriously worried. He had not seen the lioness for fifnights now, and her absence now that the weather had improved began gnawing at him in earnest. Hadn't Lady Annabella insisted she keep a close eye on him at school? She would never shirk her duty without good cause.

That afternoon, mounted guardsmen escorted the children back home, and Marquiese was told that Lady Annabella's etiquette lessons had been postponed until next month. His instructions were clear: remain at home.

Marquiese tried working on his homework, but was unable to focus. He knew that Marilana would never cause Lady Annabella's etiquette lesson to be cancelled, not without good reason. He began pacing. Minutes later, the drawing room door opened, and Adealy peeked in.

"Marquiese, I'm sorry to disturb you, but some of Lady Annabella's guards are here. Lady Annabella has requested your presence at her estate, and you need to go with them."

Marquiese frowned thoughtfully. "Yes, thank you. I had better find out what is going on," he said calmly.

"Should we be prepared to leave?" she asked quietly.

"No! No, I don't think you need to worry about that." He reached out and touched her shoulder reassuringly. "I will not be long. And if I am detained, I will send a messenger."

"Be safe," she whispered.

"I will." He put on his heavy coat, strapped on his sword, and swung his winter cloak around his shoulders. He stepped out into the cold and approached the guardsmen. All wore Lady Annabella's insignia on their cloaks, but their faces were muffled against the cold making the guardsmen unrecognizable. One dismounted and lowered his face scarf. It was Captain Branth.

"Captain Branth!" This was a surprise. "Is everything alright?"

"That remains to be seen," he replied quietly. He directed him toward an extra horse. "We must hurry."

Marquiese swung into the saddle and they set off, his imagination running wild. They rode hard and soon came to Lady Annabella's estates. They passed through the gates and hurriedly dismounted.

Marquiese had never seen the yard so crowded and every face seemed etched with a look of worry. Captain-General Zariff stood waiting for him at the doors of the stable, and Marquiese jogged in his direction. He went inside and lowered his hood in the comparative warmth of the stable. He nodded respectfully in the direction of Zariff, then spotted Lady Annabella and her attendants at the far end of the building and walked briskly to her.

"Lady Annabella," he said, bowing despite that fact that her attention was fixed on the view beyond the stable's north window.

"Leave us," Lady Annabella commanded her attendants. When they were gone, the beautifully attired noble turned away from the window and said, "Thank you for coming, Marquiese. I didn't know what else to do. I have tried everything I can think of, but it has not changed anything. I am hoping you will have better success."

"Better success with what, My Lady?" Marquiese asked cautiously.

"Marilana. She is . . . she has . . . well, I'm not sure how to say it," Lady Annabella said in frustration. "I suppose the best description is that she is pining, but a more accurate one might be that she is despondent."

"Marilana? Despondent?"

"She will only eat and drink when I order her to and almost nothing even then. She has stopped doing any of her usual activities. She has spent every night in the stables with Storm, and every day she lies in the snow in his pasture. The horse will let no one except me even approach her. I have tried talking to her, but she offers no response. The last time such a thing happened, she was five. I hardly expected her to relapse into such behavior."

"Did something happen? Something that hurt her?" Marquiese questioned cautiously.

"Yes. Much has happened over the last three fifnights. As you know, many have perished. Marilana was trying to do her part until the mare we called Snow died in the night after last Restday," she explained.

"The mare that foaled Storm," Marquiese said. He knew how close Marilana was to the horse.

"Yes. The horse fell ill last fifnight. Marilana had been tending her with her herbs and was with her when she passed away," the noble explained. "She blames herself, of course."

"Yes, that sounds like Marilana."

"When in fact, if it hadn't been for Marilana and her skill with herbs, many more of my staff would have fallen ill and some would have surely died. Marilana spent hundreds of hours helping Healer Magus while the bitter cold was upon the area. However, since Snow passed away, she has done nothing. I am afraid she has lost the will to live. I know she thinks of you as a friend. I am asking you to talk to her. Please," Lady Annabella pleaded.

Marquiese looked thoughtfully out the window and could see Storm in his pasture. It was getting late. He could feel the temperature dropping. The sun was already touching the western horizon. He didn't know how his words could be more effective than Lady Annabella's, but he knew he had to try.

"I will try my best," the lion said firmly.

He didn't wait for a response and hurried out the side door. Long strides took him in minutes to Storm's pasture. He stopped at the fence and watched the beautiful stallion circling a dark shape on the ground. It had to be Marilana.

Marquiese opened the gate and stepped cautiously inside. Instantly, Storm's head rose. He snorted and pawed the ground threateningly.

Marquiese closed the gate and raised his paws. "It's okay, beautiful one. I come as a friend of your friend. I mean no harm." Then he called, "Marilana. It is Marquiese. I miss my friend. I was hoping we could talk."

Marquiese waited. He neither saw nor heard any sign that Marilana had heard his words, but she must have said something because Storm suddenly drew up, standing statue still, his attention fast on Marquiese.

Marquiese counted this as a positive sign and took a tentative step forward. Storm snorted softly, but held fast his position. Another good sign. Good. Marquiese crossed the distance with soundless steps and finally sank down in the snow next to Marilana. Storm stretched his nose across

Marilana and sniffed Marquiese before snorting again and turning away. Marquiese watched the stallion separate himself by two strides before looking down at Marilana. She lay well bundled in the snow, staring listlessly into the sky. Her eyes were red and puffy, most certainly from crying.

The sight startled Marquiese. Except for bouts of anger and the occasional blush of embarrassment, the lioness always kept her emotions well in check. This was a side of her he had never seen.

"Lady Annabella told me about Snow," he finally said as gently as he could. "I know she was very special to you."

Marilana did not move, but Marquiese watched transfixed as tears leaked from her eyes and trickled through her fur. He tried to think of something else to say, but comforting her about Snow seemed inadequate. They sat in silence for a while.

"You know, I have been wondering where you were these past few days," he said eventually. "I worried that you had suffered some hardship during the bitter cold. I know you can take care of yourself; that is not what I'm saying. But after being cooped up for three fifnights, I was looking forward to see you. More than that. I missed seeing you. That is closer to the truth. When you didn't come get me for sparring practice, I thought about setting out on my own. But I knew you would have been mad that I took such a risk. When Captain Branth came for me today, I knew something serious had happened, and feared the worst."

He paused, but Marilana just closed her eyes and continued to cry silently.

"Did you hear about Earek?" he asked, not waiting for an answer. "He slipped on the ice and sprained his ankle. How does a leopard slip on the ice and sprain an ankle? I know he is not clumsy, but . . . Mother Kalan said it will be fine if he stays off it for two fifnights. The bad part is that Brittia volunteered to take care of him while he heals. She is staying at his house and tending to him constantly. Earek looked mortified when I saw him at school the first morning. Klay and Caton teased him so much that he started throwing things at them behind

Mistress Rose's back. She told all three of them off and made them do lines during lunch."

He chuckled softly, but Marilana again did not respond. He waited again. Then changed tactics.

"I had a friend once," he said directly. "That friend was one-of-a-kind. Nothing could stop that friend from fulfilling her duty. That friend worked all day long doing chores, going to school, practicing combat, and protecting people. That friend lived a good life, never letting the challenges of life get in the way, never letting other people's opinions change her purpose. I never would have believed that she would succumb to despair. I lived peacefully knowing that she was protecting my merchant family, my friends, and me. I never thought she would just give up. Never."

He paused, but Marilana still did not respond.

"I guess that friend is gone for good," he said, letting his anger show. "I came out here to help, but now I see that the only thing I can do is say goodbye. Well, then, goodbye, Marilana. I will miss you. And I know Storm will miss you too."

He stood up and started to walk away. He hesitated when he heard a sob, but knew he had to take at least one step toward the gate. And one step he took, hoping against hope.

"Marquiese. Please, don't go," Marilana whispered, her voice thick and raspy from all her crying.

"Why should I stay?" he asked, hating himself for the harshness in his voice. But he could not change courses now, not if he hoped to save her. "You don't care about anyone anymore. Not even yourself."

"You don't understand," she said sadly. "Let me explain, so that you might not remember me so poorly."

"You've given up on life," he said without moving. "That's all I need to know."

"Will you not listen?" she begged.

He turned around and looked down at her. She had drawn herself into a sitting position—a hopeful sign—and was staring up at him, though tears still leaked from her eyes. He turned slowly and sat beside her. Marilana clutched her heavy cloak and pulled her knees up to her chest. She dropped her eyes to her feet and swallowed several times.

"I'm sorry my absence worried you. And I'm sorry to hear about Earek's difficulties," she said at last. "I tried my best to save Snow, but nothing I did could turn back the infection. I could not save her, just as I could not save all of those who died these last fifnights. I tried. I tried my best, and it was not enough."

"Of course you did, Marilana," Marquiese said softly, happy beyond words that she was at least talking.

"I offered my assistance to Mother Kalan, but she refused my help. I offered to share my herbs with her, but she said they were probably contaminated with poisons. I traveled to some of the peasant homes and offered my services, but they were afraid and sent me away."

"Only Healer Magus and Hosten would accept my help. Healer Magus encouraged the staff and the guardsmen to let me tend to their families. He took care of the seriously ill, and I helped with preventing the spread of disease. I helped Hosten take care of the horses, those who had taken sick. Only my Snow didn't recover. I know she was older. One of the oldest in the stables. But she was such a strong horse, and she always gave her best."

Marilana pulled a kerchief from under her cloak. She wiped away her tears and blew her nose.

"I beg your pardon. I am out of sorts," she murmured, tucking the kerchief away.

"Don't worry about decorum," Marquiese said gently. He wanted to touch her, to comfort her, but he restrained himself. "I know Snow was one of your favorites. I did not expect her passing to cause such a change of your behavior. Nor did Lady Annabella."

"I will miss her dearly. But that is not the point." Marilana shook her head. "I could not save her, but at least I got to try. How many of the peasants who died would still be alive if I had been allowed to help them?"

"You can't blame yourself for their deaths, Marilana," Marquiese said, choosing a semi-stern voice. "They made the choice to turn away help. It is their responsibility to choose how to live. That is not your fault."

"I know. But were I not a bandit hunter, they would not have been afraid of me."

"Now it is you, my friend, who is missing the point. If you were not a bandit hunter, they would have died long ago along with many more peasants and merchants in ways much more horrendous than the cold," Marquiese said firmly. "How many more people would have died in raids on the town? How many more bandits would be preying on the people of the Southern Tip? How many more families would have been destroyed like the family that lived in the brick manor before me?"

He knew he had hit upon a painful memory, but he thought it necessary. Marilana turned away, her gaze settling on Storm, tears streaming from her eyes.

"What does it matter?" she asked dejectedly. "I couldn't save them. What kind of a protector am I? Zara's family is gone because I was too slow. Twenty-eight peasants dead from illness because I couldn't convince them to let me help. People don't want me around. They don't need me. Other bandit hunters can take over and do better. I could die and people wouldn't care. I feel so worthless. You can say goodbye and walk away. You will have a better life without me."

"For one, I do care. And you know I do. For another, my life would not in a hundred years be better without you," Marquiese said breathlessly. "It pains me greatly to see you throw away your life like this. If I do say farewell and walk away from you forever, it will only be because you have already shut me out and committed yourself to death. I came out here because you are my friend. I don't care that the rest of the town is full of blind, stubborn fools. They don't matter. You do.

"Earek cares, Zariff cares, Hosten cares, and I know Lady Annabella cares. She is so worried about you that she has been standing in the stable for hours watching you, praying that you would come back to her. She brought me here because she is refusing to give up on you. The stable yard is full of servants and guardsmen worried about you. Yes, they know of the many great deeds you have done. Yes, they know that you have killed more bandits than any other bandit hunter. Yes, they know that you have saved countless lives with your vigilance and skills. But it is you they miss, Marilana. The lioness. The special friend. So many of the people here at Lady Annabella's estates owe you thanks for saving them and their families from illness over the past three fifnights. That doesn't seem to be a worthless life. That sounds to me to be someone who has touched many lives for the better."

"That's not what the people of Mystillion say," Marilana said bitterly.

"The people who respect Brittia and listen to her lies? The people who believe that she will become Lady Annabella's heiress? You would let that skinny little show off dictate how you feel about yourself?" Marquiese hissed angrily. "The Marilana I know would never let such lies stop her or poison her attitude. The Marilana I know is a protector of people. Every life is important to her; every life matters. However, even the best champions of life and the best healers cannot save everyone. Death comes to us all eventually. No one can stop that."

Marilana hid her face against her knees. Her hood hid her from him, but he did not move. He waited a moment in silence to see if she would respond. He sighed when she did not, and then said in a quiet, nurturing voice, "A few years ago, I was given a duty that I did not want. I can't really share the details, but what I had to do involved a group of people I barely knew. I performed my duty well. I did the right thing despite my misgivings. I did my duty and stood my ground. But, you know what? The people I was sent to help hated me for it.

"When all was said and done and the people had gone on their way, I felt like giving up. I felt the weight of my responsibility was too much. And you know what made it worse? I knew, as I got older, I would be given even more responsibilities. More people would find reasons to hate me. I was moody and cross for days. Then someone I respected pulled me aside and told me something I will never forget. He said, 'Life is full of burdens. From the lowest peasant to the highest royal, we all must face the challenges that come to us. Some of those challenges will make us feel helpless or useless, but, no matter what, we must remember the passion that drives us. Remember the qualities that you hold most dear. Remember the qualities that make you smile. Remember the passion that makes you glad to wake up in the morning. When you feel your worst, remember you fight for life.' I realized then that I could not let my duties control my life. It was my life, and I would live it the way I chose."

Marquiese looked at Marilana and could tell she was listening. He said, "I do not know everything there is to know about you, my friend, but I do know you control your own life. It is one of the things I recognized in you from the start, and I admire it greatly."

They sat in silence for a while and Marquiese watched the last rays of the sun color the clouds in the west. Then he stood up and knew this was the moment of truth.

"I'm getting too cold to stay out here any longer," he said and turned to leave.

"May I walk with you?" Marilana asked.

"Of course," Marquiese said gently. He held out his paw and helped her to her feet. "I always welcome the company of a friend."

Marilana didn't meet his eyes, but called to Storm with a wave of her paw. The horse pushed toward them and nuzzled against Marilana. Together they walked back to the stable.

Marquiese was not really surprised to see that the staff and guardsmen had disappeared suddenly. Lady Annabella and Zariff were also nowhere to be seen, but Hosten was whistling softly and grooming one of the horses. He gave Marquiese a slight nod when they entered. At the other end, Marquiese spotted Captain Branth pretending to scan a sheaf of paper, a look of absolute relief on his face.

Marilana led Storm to his stall, removed his blanket, and let him inside. Marquiese watched silently as she carefully brushed the stallion and covered him with a lighter blanket than the one he had worn out in the cold. She scratched his ears and spoke softly to him before she let herself back out of his stall.

"Thank you for coming, Marquiese," Marilana said quietly, meeting his eyes finally. "May I escort you home?"

"Of course," Marquiese said firmly.

Marilana's weapons were waiting for her next to the stall, and she belted on the sword, dagger, and quiver, and strung her bow.

"Captain Branth, I am going to escort Marquiese home," she said quietly to the soldier as they passed him. "Would you please inform Lady Annabella that I will be back tonight when I am done? I know she will want to speak with me."

"Be safe, Marilana," the coyote said to her gently. "And I'm glad to see you among the living again."

"Thank you," Marilana replied with a slight blush.

Marquiese opened the stable door for her, and they were shocked to find the yard filled with guardsmen. They swarmed around Marilana in an unexpected display of gratitude for all she had done during the blizzard to help their families and all the hours she had spent tending the sick. Each took a moment to express their thanks. Many hugged her. Some shed tears of gratitude.

It took a full thirty minutes for Marilana and Marquiese to make their way to the foot gate, and when the gate closed behind them, the lioness paused, her head spinning from the encounter, her eyes sparkling brightly in the moonlight.

"I have acted so foolishly," she said, her gaze falling on the lion beside her. "I had no idea they felt like that. How poorly I have acted. How self-indulgent I have been. You were right. And Lady Annabella was right. I was lost in dark thoughts of death and pain, and you helped me to see the light of life and the right of my actions. Thank you for being my friend."

"Any time you need to talk, I will listen. We all feel despair at times. That is when we need friends we trust to help us through the dark," he said warmly.

She smiled at him in the silvery glow and then turned and pointed toward the riot of stars overhead.

"See there. The constellation of the great horse," she said quietly.

"I see. Yes," Marquiese answered, following her outstretched arm.

"The story goes that there was a great and strong stallion, black as midnight. He roamed wild across the land. He could not be caught or tamed. One stormy spring day two small children, a brother and sister, got lost in the forest. They stumbled into a clearing, and there was the great black horse. He reared and whinnied and seemed to charge the children. They were so scared that they couldn't move. They just clutched each other and cried out in terror. Just then a bolt of lightning struck a nearby tree. The tree split in two and burst into flames. Half the tree fell toward the children and would have crushed them, but the stallion kicked the tree as it fell and moved it just enough to save the children. He then knelt next to the pair and let them climb onto his back. The fire started by the lightning was very hot and was spreading rapidly. The stallion raced away from the fire as fast as he could, yet he was careful not to let the children fall from his back. He carried them safely back to their home and their family. He reared up as they ran to their mother, and that was the last they ever saw of him.

"But after that, any time children found themselves lost in those woods, they would catch a glimpse of the stallion, and he would lead them home. When he died an old, old horse, The Goddess rewarded his courage and kindness by placing his image in the sky to roam wild and free for all time and provide guidance to anyone lost at night."

Marquiese stood silent, watching Marilana while she watched the sky, her story washing over him.

"I feel that way a lot," she said eventually.

"Feel how?" Marquiese replied. "Lost?"

"Alone," she answered, casting her eyes downward. "I am an outcast, and I accept that. I'm different from pretty much everyone I meet, and I understand that. I have seen so much death and so much misery that sometimes it is hard to remember the good things. To be honest, sometimes it can be hard to be nice to people who have things I don't have."

"What kind of things?"

"Family and friends mostly. That's why I fight with Brittia so much. She takes her blessings for granted and treats her friends terribly, ordering them around and harassing anyone who doesn't act the way she wants them too. I know everyone expects her to be named Lady Annabella's heiress, but I also know that Lady Annabella will not do that; Brittia has done nothing to garner Lady Annabella's respect, and that is the quality she values the most," Marilana said. "I don't know who Lady Annabella will choose, but she will not choose someone so self-centered that they will destroy the province. Brittia thinks it is all about rank and power, but Lady Annabella wants the best for her people, and Brittia is not capable of serving the people."

"You would be a good leader for the people of this province," Marquiese interjected quietly.

"No," Marilana stated flatly, facing him now. "I am feared. I am an outsider. And, I am a killer. I have seen too much death to be a leader the people could respect and trust."

Marquiese shook his head. "You have seen the worst in people, but that has also taught you to see the best in people. You are a good person. People would follow you if you gave them the chance. You are not alone in the world. People do like you, and you do have friends and a family, even if it's not exactly official. What is true is that Lady Annabella cares about you a great deal."

"Yes, she does. And I'm grateful for that." Marilana sighed. "You are a good friend, Marquiese, and you have reminded me of all the wonderful, beautiful things in life. For that, I thank you. Now come! I must get you home; Lady Annabella will be waiting for me. I need to present my apology to her."

Marquiese wanted to say more; he didn't feel that Marilana was allowing thoughts of the truth he was trying so hard to convey, but he didn't know what else to say or how to bring down her walls and open her eyes. Maybe if he knew her most closely guarded secrets, but he doubted that would ever happen.

They set out. He watched her slip skillfully though the trees and he followed step for step until they reached the gate to the brick manor.

"Thank you again, Marquiese," she said quietly. "I shall see you in the morning for sparring practice. Goodnight."

"Goodnight, Marilana," he replied simply.

She turned and raced back into the trees, a shadow disappearing into the night. Marquiese turned and walked slowly to the house. He found Adealy and Merchant Colbran waiting for him inside.

"Is everything alright?" Merchant Colbran asked, concern etched across his face.

"Yes, everything is better now. Marilana was in need of a friend, and Lady Annabella asked me to help," Marquiese said by way of explanation.

Adealy smiled, and her relief was obvious. "We were worried that it had something to do with Maefair. We have not heard news from the capital for fifnights."

"I'm sure Lady Annabella will tell me if anything important occurs, but she was too preoccupied with Marilana tonight to discuss anything newsworthy," Marquiese said easily. "Thank you for waiting up for me. Please get some rest now. I will be in my room. I have a lot to think about."

"Of course," Merchant Colbran said.

"Goodnight, Marquiese," Adealy added.

"Goodnight. Rest well"

Marquiese went directly to his bedroom, but sleep was a long time coming and his thoughts were deep and disturbing.

Marilana was equally deep in thought as she walked slowly through the silent forest. She thought about everything Marquiese had said to her. She thought about the things Lady Annabella, Captain Branth, Hosten, Captain-General Zariff, and Healer Magus had shared with her, things she had ignored for the past four fifnights.

It was true that Marilana had few friends, and she had been feeling even lonelier since Elza, Jenra, and Natly had moved away. Even Dera had been distracted of late, what with her duties in the library. The brightest parts of Marilana's day were the hours she spent training the estate's horses, sparring, and studying with Marquiese and Earek. She had done none of those things for almost four fifnights. She had hardly slept while tending to the sick and running errands for Healer Magus during the cold spell, and now she was exhausted.

She had been relieved when Lady Annabella and Captain-General Zariff returned from Maefair—yes, because they had replenished her herb stocks and those of Mother Kalan—but mostly because she was glad to have her family back safely. She had not seen Child since the beginning of winter either, and she missed the camaraderie of the young deer. Child had gone beyond the southern border to check on the conditions of the farmers there, and they had both known she probably would not be back for several months.

When Snow died, Marilana had allowed herself to focus on the fatigue and frustration which had only amplified the feelings of despair. Her world had become dark. She had, for days on end, wanted to give up and let the darkness claim her once and for all. She had wantonly ignored all who had tried to comfort her. She hadn't wanted comforting and empty words. Marquiese instead, had not really tried to comfort her, he had gotten angry. Or, at least, he seemed to. It had jolted her away from the darkness she was courting. In truth, she did not want him to be mad at her.

He had taken her rationalization and turned it around on her. Only then did she hear the wrongness in what she was saying. Admitting she was wrong had been the hardest part, but it had changed her somehow. In a positive way. She suddenly felt more aware of her true self. Yes, she was still determined to protect the people of the Southern Tip, but she realized that her fight with Brittia was not serving her goals. Fighting with the people was not protecting them; it was a distraction and a waste of effort.

Marquiese had spoken the truth—she did fight for life. Going forward, she would live her life the way she chose, making her own decisions, and believing in what she stood for. The sudden realization of this brought her up short and she stood stock still in the snow. It was not only her right to live the way she chose; it was every creature's right. As long as they were not hurting anyone else, no one had the right to force them to change, not even her.

Marilana straightened her back. She breathed deeply of the cold, crisp air. She sprang forward suddenly, ready to face Lady Annabella with a renewed sense of hope and determination.

Lady Annabella watched as Marilana walked quietly into her sitting room. She had spent the better part of the evening staring out the stable window while Marquiese coaxed Marilana from her malaise, her love and concern for the lioness welling up inside of her. At first, Lady Annabella was not sure she had done the right thing. Marquiese had his own problems, and she was not sure how deeply he really cared for Marilana. He acted like her friend—even a good friend—but his secret was a barrier around his heart and thoughts. Marilana, however, cared for him more deeply than any friend she had ever had, although she would not admit it.

After seeing Marilana respond to Marquiese in the pasture, Annabella had retired to her sitting room to wait. She had been too nervous to eat and had paced restlessly until Captain Branth had brought word of Marilana's apparent recovery. Since then, she had sat quietly and read the reports from the Southern Tip nobles, though her concentration may have been somewhat lacking.

Marilana stopped three paces from her and curtseyed deeply.

"Well, Marilana, what have you come to say to me?" Annabella said, doing her best not to show the tremendous relief she was feeling.

"I am sorry, My Lady," Marilana said quietly. "I have acted very foolishly and I have caused you unnecessary worry."

"I do not want your apology," Annabella replied. "I want to hear the truth."

"Yes, My Lady." Marilana curtseyed again. "I let myself fall into despair and almost gave up on life. I was foolish to ignore your words and the words of all those who care about me. Marquiese reminded me that I fight for life, that my life is my own to live how I choose, my decisions my own to make, and that I am not alone in this fight."

"He simply said that and you listened?" Annabella said skeptically.

"No, My Lady. He got rather mad at me for a time when I failed to respond to his kindness. It was his anger as much as the words he spoke that brought me back from my dark thoughts," Marilana said with a blush.

Annabella sat back and contemplated the girl. She knew Marilana had strong feelings for Marquiese, but she had never seen her let those emotions show before. Something had changed.

"How do you feel now?" Annabella asked pointedly.

"Different," Marilana said honestly. "I will need some time to process the way I feel, but I do know that I am right to protect the people of the Southern Tip. I am a highly skilled bandit hunter and Healer; I will use those skills as best as I can to serve you and protect my people. I was wrong to assume I knew what others thought or was right for them. I was wrong to treat them badly for living their own lives. Going forward, I will try to see the choices other creatures make through their eyes and act with compassion."

Annabella smiled slightly as Marilana stood straight and defiant before her.

"The first step, and often the hardest, is admitting when we are wrong. I am proud that you have come to these conclusions. Come then, child, I know you must be hungry. I have a tray of food waiting for us to share," Annabella said, indicating the covered tray sitting on her side table.

Marilana smiled her relief and pleasure, but her posture did not drop. She drew out their chairs and placed the food on the table. Annabella joined her and together they sat and ate a very late meal. When they finished, Annabella placed her paw on Marilana's and shared a warm smile.

"You are fourteen now," she said to the young lioness. "You will find there are times when your emotions are confusing or strange. That is all part of growing up. We all go through it. I am your warden, and I care about you. Care greatly. If you ever feel the need to talk, I am always willing to listen and help if I can."

"Thank you, My Lady." Marilana returned her smile. "You have been the best warden I could ever have wanted. You have given me a home when I had none. I will be forever grateful."

"I know you are tired and need a good night's sleep," Annabella said gently. "I want you to stay here tonight, bathe, sleep, and relax. Tomorrow I would like you to stay with me rather than go to school. I have several issues I want to speak to you about, and you should use Restday to catch up on your studies."

"I promised Marquiese that I would spar with him in the morning," Marilana said simply.

"Very well. In the morning you will patrol, train the horses, and spar as usual," Annabella said with a single nod of her head. "And then we will talk."

Marilana quickly cleaned up from the meal, curtseyed, and left, taking the meal tray to the kitchens on her way to the servant quarters. Annabella smiled as she thought about the maturity Marilana had shown, but her smile faded away when her thoughts turned to Marquiese. Only time would tell what would come of their interactions. She hoped and prayed that the future held happiness and not sorrow.

20

Marquiese noticed a number of subtle changes in Marilana's behavior in the month following the events in the pasture. She always held perfect posture these days. She moved with an unmistakable confidence, as if she was proud of herself, her life, and her choices. She seemed to react less to the teasing and harassments of Brittia and her lackeys. Marquiese knew full well that Brittia had noticed the changes too. Yes, she still harassed the lioness, but she had been much more cautious of late.

"Marquiese!" Brittia simpered as they made their way toward the schoolhouse that morning. She held her paw out to him. "Good morning."

"Brittia, good morning!" He lifted the lynx' dainty paw to his lips and breathed just enough to stir the hair on the back of her paw. Not a kiss, but very close and very polite.

It had snowed again last night, and Marquiese and Marilana had broken trail for the other school children, but Brittia had ridden into town on her father's wagon. "Glad to see you made it to school safely."

"Yes, indeed. And you," Brittia said, ignoring Marilana as she walked calmly through the front entrance. "I wanted to tell you, Father said I could invite you to my next party. It's a fifnight from the next Restday. Lady Annabella will be there, and Father says it is time I show her my hosting skills. Isn't that exciting? Of course, we may have to seat you at the other end of the table so Lady Annabella won't see the deficiency in your etiquette skills."

"A very good idea," Marquiese agreed, a bit facetiously.

Brittia held tight to his paw and led him inside the school house still rambling on about the party, the dress she was having made, and the decorations she was planning.

It was a relief when Mistress Rose clopped her hooves and called the class to order, but Marquiese knew he had not seen the last of the lynx. Brittia sat next to him at lunch and refused to relinquish his paw during their break. She even refused to dance with anyone else that afternoon, even though Marquiese showed less grace than usual and stepped on Brittia's toes at least a dozen times.

The lynx refused to back off, however, and sat next to him while Mistress Rose lectured that afternoon. It was a long day. If Marquiese forced one more polite smile, he was quite sure his face would crack, and Earek got a good laugh out of it now that he was no longer Brittia's patient.

"You look like your face is made of stone. Very brittle stone," the leopard said, as they watched Brittia and her friends walking through the snow toward the markets. Marquiese was bracing himself for some serious kidding when the schoolhouse doors opened and Marilana came out armed with her bow.

"It's about time," the gazelle Estala complained to her. "You do know how cold it is out here, don't you?"

Marilana gave her an amusement smirk and said, "Poor girl."

"What's that supposed to mean?" Estala said hotly.

"It means that you chose to wait out here instead of inside a nice warm schoolhouse," Marilana replied lightly. "I am not responsible for your choices. Next time get a ride with your mother or put your hood up. But don't complain to me."

Estala was left gaping as Marilana led her charges onto the road and toward their various homes. They stayed in the wagon tracks as much as possible. It was too cold for chatting and one by one they peeled off and hurried toward the warmth of their individual abodes. Finally, they came to the brick manor.

"Thank you, Marilana," Lida called to her. "See you tomorrow."

"See you tomorrow," the lioness replied, watching as Lida hurried through the gate and up the walk.

Then she turned and headed into the woods, her pace brisk and purposeful. Marquiese and Earek hurried to keep up. They made it to Marilana's house without incidence. She deactivated her traps briefly, and they went inside.

"Good to be inside. It's cold out there," Marquiese said.

"Not as cold as it was, but still not particularly pleasant," Earek said as he and the lion stoked the fire in Marilana's kitchen fireplace.

"So Earek, are you invited to Brittia's late winter party too, or do I have to suffer all by myself?" Marquiese asked once they were ensconced at Marilana's kitchen table.

"Unfortunately, I have been invited," Earek sighed. "I'm not looking forward to it any more than you are. I had enough personal time with her while my ankle healed. You know, I used to love going to her parties. The grandeur, the pomp, the entertainment, the dancing. But with Brittia getting so possessive and controlling lately, her parties have lost some of their appeal."

"Is that so?" Marquiese said with mock surprise. "You mean to say you do not like having to paint a smile on your face and act polite and try to pry her claws off your arm every time she wants to dance?"

"Thank you for summing that up," Earek said, laughing. "At least you won't have to worry about the dancing. Apparently, Brittia requested that you not dance."

"She did, I am afraid." Marquiese grinned. "Apparently, Lady Annabella has been invited so that Brittia can try to make a good impression and secure her heiress position."

Earek caught the amused smile on Marilana's face and said, "What is that smile about?"

"I was just thinking that at least you two will be having a worse time than I will," Marilana said casually.

"Wait!" Earek said suspiciously. "Brittia invited you to the party?"

"Of course not." Marilana laughed. "Lady Annabella asked me to attend her at the party. Brittia won't like it, I'm sure, but I will be there. The good news is that all I have to do is attend Lady Annabella. I think it's going to take both of you to attend to Brittia."

"I think you may be correct in that assumption." Marquiese laughed.

*

Marquiese did not go to sparring practice the morning of Brittia's party because Marilana said she would be busy helping Lady Annabella prepare. Instead, he paced around his room wondering if his presence at the party would turn out to be a mistake. He dressed in his formal grass-green suit; it was not his favorite color, but he hoped it would discourage people from connecting him with any members of the higher castes.

When Lida was ready, he helped her with her cloak.

"You look terrific," he said, eyeing her pale rose gown with white fur cuffs and hem and matching fur hat. This was not Lida's first formal party, but this was the first time she would be allowed to stay up for the whole party, and she was very excited.

"Oh, Marquiese, do try to have fun," she chided him as he fastened his own cloak. "Just remember to be careful."

"Your job is to have fun and not worry about me," Marquiese said with a fond smile.

Merchant Colbran opened the door for them and said, "The carriage is waiting. We don't want to be late."

The carriage was an enclosed variety lent to them by Merchant Sleater, and Merchant Colbran had only accepted the offer so that the women would not have to ride in the open air.

"Not as nice as the one I had in the city," Merchant Colbran grumbled as the driver started down the road.

"No, it's not, dear," Adealy said, patting his knee. "Someday you can buy a new one."

Marquiese tried not to feel guilty; he knew Merchant Colbran would have demonstrated his wealth differently if not for him. The whole family played down their rank and wealth so they did not attract too much attention. Still, Marquiese knew that it grated on Merchant Colbran at times, especially when he had to accept favors from the other merchants, in particular Brittia's father.

When they arrived, Marquiese helped Adealy and Lida out of the carriage and up the steps to Merchant Sleater's manor house. He had to admit Merchant Sleater's family and staff knew how to host a party. Garlands of winter greenery and shuttered lights decorated the steps, funneling guests to the doors and providing a festive feel. Merchant Sleater, his wife Corlda, and Brittia greeted them in the entry hall.

"Come with me, Marquiese," Brittia said, taking his arm, "I want to show you around before dinner."

Marquiese smiled politely and let Brittia give him a tour of the house. It was larger by far than the brick manor, but not near as grand as Brittia made it sound and did not even compare to some he had seen. It was neat and well kept, however. He caught a glimpse of the busy kitchens and was pleased to see multiple cooks and servants smiling and laughing.

Finally, Brittia led him back to the entrance hall. They had just reached the bottom of the steps when the door opened and three new arrivals stepped in. Marquiese bowed and Brittia curtseyed as Lady Annabella lowered her hood. He watched as Marilana helped remove Lady Annabella's cloak and heavy gloves. She then gave them to a house servant who, in turn, accepted them with a shaky curtsey.

"Ah, Lady Annabella, thank you for coming and gracing our simple gathering with your presence," Merchant Sleater said, stepping forward with another bow.

"Merchant Sleater, thank you for inviting me. It is my pleasure to attend," Lady Annabella replied, holding her paw out to him.

Merchant Sleater bowed over her paw, and then turned and indicated the rest of those waiting in the entrance hall.

"You remember my wife Corlda. And my daughter Brittia," he said as the two lynx curtseyed. "And I believe you have met Merchant Colbran's son, Marquiese."

"Of course, it is a pleasure to see you all again," Lady Annabella said with a slight nod of her head. "Let me introduce Captain-General Zariff and my maidservant, Marilana."

Zariff gave a crisp bow and Marilana curtseyed politely. Brittia's grip tightened painfully on Marquiese's arm when she heard this. Marquiese returned a polite smile and wondered if Lady Annabella knew the reaction Marilana's introduction had caused. Judging by the twinkle in her eyes as she met his look, she did and had done it for the express purpose of getting under Brittia's skin; after all most people don't introduce their servants to the party hosts.

Marilana and Zariff dutifully followed Lady Annabella into the dining room. Brittia loosened her grip on Marquiese's arm, smoothed the slight grimace from her face, and followed. Brittia directed Marquiese to a chair at the end of the table opposite from Lady Annabella. Marquiese shared a smile with the lower ranking merchants seated around him. They returned his smile politely, but pointedly said nothing about the seating arrangement. Brittia snagged Earek and led him up to the chair next to hers.

Marquiese took it all in. From his vantage, he could just see Marilana standing behind Lady Annabella's chair, could see Merchant Sleater engaging Captain-General Zariff in conversation, and assumed from the tilt of her head that Corlda was speaking with Lady Annabella. He sat back and watched Lida speaking politely with the woman next to her, and this, at least, gave him some pleasure.

Brittia performed the duties of a practiced hostess for the elaborate six-course meal while musicians played softly in a corner. Marquiese watched his etiquette carefully. He ate using only the most basic manners, while the merchants around him exchanged pointed looks and the occasional smirk. Etiquette aside, the conversation was lively, and they talked of many topics.

"Young Marquiese, you used to live in Maefair, did you not?"

"Yes, Sir, I did," he said to the well-dressed boar, suddenly alert and on guard.

"Did you ever hear of a Lord Castant? Apparently, he was one of the King's advisors. Lady Annabella told me that he has stepped down from his position and his son has been named his replacement. Do you know anything about them?"

"Lord Castant?" Marquiese mused thoughtfully. "I do remember the name, yes. One of the King's top advisors and Great Lord of Draukshar, I believe. His son, Master Enton Castant, rides with the Knights of the Realm and has received several high awards for bravery. He won the King's annual tournament last year and the year previous. His name was known by almost everyone in Maefair, although I have not had the pleasure of meeting him."

"Oh yes, I remember now," laughed a tall oryx on Marquiese's left. "From everything I heard, none of the combatants at the tournament stood a chance against him. He had a landslide victory. I hope he is as good at advising as he is jousting."

Marquiese smiled politely, but did not join in the laughter.

"Who won the tournament this year?" asked the petite tigress sitting on Marquiese's right.

"Oh, a Master Timral Roana won this year. He competed last year as well, but was unable to defeat Master Castant in the final joust, although it was a much closer match than Master Castant's previous win," answered the oryx. "I heard he is a very skilled competitor. Master Castant did not compete this year otherwise he would have been favored to win.".

"Oh, I see," said the tigress. She turned a subtle gaze toward Marquiese. "Young Marquiese, have you heard of this Roana?"

"Nothing specific," he said, feigning a thoughtful expression. "The Roana Family is the Great Lords of Mira's Plateau. They are well respected, but other than that I have not heard anything more of them."

"You seem to recognize many of the names of the Great Families," the woman said with surprise. "How is that, I wonder?"

"Most creatures in Maefair recognize the names of the Great Families, madam," Marquiese said easily. "Many of them have houses in the city, and all of them visit the King's palace at times throughout the year. My tutor taught me their names, crests, and livery so that I might recognize them if they came into my merchant father's shop. Most of the merchant children in Maefair are taught the same. All of my friends were."

"I suppose that does make sense," the tigress said, nodding.

"Did you ever see the King or the Crown Prince?" asked the oryx thoughtfully.

"Not up close," Marquiese shook his head, "I watched them speak to the public once."

"Too bad. I was hoping you could tell us what the Crown Prince looked like. Apparently he is missing or in hiding. Rumor has it that a Lord Frishka has placed a large bounty on any information regarding the Prince."

"What would you have done with a description? Posted lookouts on the road? Searched travelers and merchants?" laughed the boar.

"Oh! Wouldn't it be exciting to be the one to find the missing Prince," the tigress chimed in. "I even have a daughter

I could introduce him to. What do you think young Marquiese? Do you think the Prince could be hiding near here?"

"I would be hesitant to believe any rumors about the royal family. Their ways are not like the ways of merchants," Marquiese replied thoughtfully.

"How very true," the tigress nodded in agreement. "You are an interesting, and intelligent young man."

"Thank you, madam," Marquiese replied simply.

It was not long after when Lady Annabella rose from the table and accompanied Merchant Sleater into the great room. Brittia followed closely, holding on to Earek's arm, but Marilana held her ground and prevented Brittia from getting too close. Marquiese saw a look of irritation pass across Brittia's face as he arose and followed along with the other guests.

The great room had been lavishly decorated. Couches and chairs were spaced around the room for purposes of easy conversation, and the main area remained clear for dancing. Marquiese joined his family and listened as the musicians struck up a lively tune. Lady Annabella started off the dancing with Captain-General Zariff. They danced a complex waltz with great skill, and everyone applauded them afterwards. Lady Annabella acknowledged the applause with a nod, and then accepted Merchant Sleater's invitation for the next dance. Brittia led Earek onto the floor, and the dance floor was soon filled with merriment.

A young leopard approached the settee where Marquiese and his family gathered and bowed with great decorum in Lida's direction.

"Might I have this dance?" he asked her timidly.

Blushing with surprise, Lida looked to her father, and Merchant Colbran nodded his approval.

"Alright," she said quietly placing her paw in his and letting him lead her out into the dancing.

This prompted Merchant Colbran to lead Adealy out into the dancing as well, and Marquiese was left to his own devices.

He took the opportunity to move well away from the floor and into a group of chairs near the wall. He spent a moment watching Lida, laughing as she danced, and her enjoyment filled him with pleasure. He watched Earek and Brittia for a moment, and then let his eyes wander. He realized then that he was not the only one left on the sidelines. There was Marilana, standing dutifully next to a group of chairs opposite the musicians, calmly observing the dancers. Marquiese realized that while he had been left out of the dancing because of his supposed lack of skill, Marilana did not have the choice. She was there solely to see to Lady Annabella's needs. This actually helped him relax a little. After all, if she could cope without feeling self-pity, then so could he.

Just then, the song ended and the dancers dispersed. Brittia joined the group crowding around Lady Annabella and Merchant Sleater, while a number of Marquiese's friends fell in next to him, Earek among them.

"Looks like Brittia dropped you as easily as she picked you up, Earek," a young buck said with a grin.

"Obviously she invites me just so she can have a really skilled dance partner," Earek joked.

"Well, you are a very good dancer," Chiely said. "Would you dance with me?"

"I'm not sure. Brittia might not like it," Earek said hesitantly.

"Oh, don't worry. I think she has her paws full for now," Chiely said, taking his paw and pulling him up.

"Go on, Earek. Have some fun," another of the merchant boys said as they headed for the dance floor.

"Too bad you're such a poor dancer, Marquiese," a zebra named Diof said with a laugh. "You could be enjoying the party with Brittia and basking in a bit of notice from Lady Annabella to boot."

"That's alright. I would rather be free of the responsibilities than have Brittia's claws permanently attached to my arm," Marquiese replied with a smile.

"Well, yeah, Brittia can be pretty controlling, but the chance to have a casual conversation with Lady Annabella would be worth it," Diof added. "She's going to have to choose an heir sometime, and any of us could be a candidate if we could get past Brittia. You already share Brittia's rank; you would have a significantly better chance than the rest of us."

"I don't think rank will have much sway with Lady Annabella when she finally chooses. I'm willing to bet she's going to be looking a whole lot deeper into personality and manners," Marquiese said sagely.

They all looked toward Lady Annabella and fell silent, their individual thoughts playing out into the future. Marquiese, however, turned his gaze toward Marilana as she stood quietly behind Lady Annabella's chair. He had to admit that she looked very nice in Lady Annabella's livery. Her white dress flowed smoothly across her natural form and the dark green of Annabella's house accentuated her neck and cuffs, creating contrast between the white dress and her golden fur, and the dark green belt emphasized her slender waist. He pushed down the thought of asking her to dance, knowing the untenable position it would put them both in.

"She sure is looking fine, isn't she?" Diof said, his voice low so that only the boys could hear.

"Who? Brittia?" Marquiese asked.

"No! Well, I mean, yes, she's pretty enough. But I meant Marilana. I mean I know she is completely off limits, but she is something to look at. Too bad she has no manners and no skill on the dance floor. She might have made a good wife."

"What would you do? Tie her up at night so she doesn't kill you in your sleep?" another said, laughing.

"Or lock her in the house so she doesn't kill off your customers?"

Marquiese did his very best to maintain a neutral expression as the boys laughed, but inside he was on the verge of losing his temper.

These idiots know nothing of Marilana's true character, he thought furiously. *If I am correct, they will have to bow and scrape before her as Lady Annabella's heiress. Someday I will gladly ram their words back down their throats or remove her from this place altogether, but right now I need to stay calm. Getting into a fight will not help matters.*

"What's the problem, Marquiese?" one of them asked, playing out the joke. "You're not amused? Can't blame you, I suppose. She is your tutor, and you do get some of the highest marks in class. That does not stop the rest of us from wondering if all you're doing at her place is hitting the books. For all we know, you could be studying her fine curves a whole lot closer."

"Maybe he is too focused on his homework to notice her curves," an overly plump boar snickered.

"Maybe he is worried about getting stabbed in the back with a knife or run through with a sword," the buck said, chuckling.

"Maybe you are all a bunch of slack-brained fools with too much time on your paws," Marquiese finally replied. He was dead serious, but he said it with a laugh. "Yeah, I do my homework so that I can keep my marks up. You may not agree, but I believe intelligence is a worthy pursuit, and so does Marilana. However, I dare any leopard, lion, buck, or boar to spend any time at all with her and not notice her other qualities."

The other boys all laughed and nodded their agreement. *Good. That shut them up*, Marquiese thought as the musicians started up a waltz and the girls came back to drag their partners back out onto the dance floor. Marquiese sat back and watched for a while, happy for a moment of solitude. Then suddenly he realized that Brittia had left her place by Lady Annabella and was wandering his way. He smiled politely at her and offered her a chair. "Great party," he said.

"Thank you. I hope you are having fun." Brittia watched the dancers moving gracefully about the floor and eventually said, "How is it that Lida has such appropriate etiquette and can dance so well, but you cannot?"

"I don't like to talk about it much," he said sadly. He did his best to sound miserable, and Brittia looked at him with a small frown. "I can do a lot of things very well, but whenever I try to focus on etiquette I completely blank out. It's like all those little rules get jumbled up in my brain and I forget what is proper and what is not. Dancing is much the same. I try remembering which foot goes where and which moves this way and that, and it all gets confused,"

"Maybe you're just nervous," Brittia said thoughtfully. "You should try to relax and let it come without thinking, the way you did a few fifnights ago. Remember? You were so preoccupied by some thought or another that you actually picked up the correct spoon and used it exactly right. Stop thinking so much and let it flow, Marquiese."

"You might be on to something. But I think it will still take a lot more practice before I get it all to flow without thinking," he replied with a grin.

They watched the dancers a while longer, and then Brittia laid a paw on his knee. She said, "I want to thank you so much for coming, Marquiese. I know it cannot be much fun to sit and watch all the time, but I am really glad I finally got to show you my home. It will be mine someday. Or it will be when I take over Daddy's work." She held his gaze for a moment. "I wonder if you would consider living here with me? We could run our fathers' businesses together. We could wield the power of the Merchant Council. And someday I will be much more than just a merchant and so, perhaps, will you. Imagine the power. Wouldn't you enjoy that?"

"I don't know, Brittia," Marquiese replied softly. "I don't know that my merchant father's ore trade is doing so well. If trade does not pick up, we will probably have to move elsewhere. If that happens, I will not be coming back; I will have to stay where the trade is strongest."

"You have been here a year and a half. How much more time will it take to know if you will be staying or not?" Brittia asked calmly.

"A year and a half is hardly enough time to establish a going ore trade," Marquiese said seriously. "It may take a while yet."

"I understand," Brittia sighed. "I hope you will stay here with me. I would truly like it if you did." Then she grinned. "I could help you with your etiquette and dance, and then you would never have to sit out another dance again."

"That is very kind of you to offer, Brittia. And I do appreciate the thought," Marquiese said politely. "But I will have to wait and see where my path leads. Only time will tell."

Brittia smiled and patted his knee affectionately. The music ended, and their friends gathered once again, much to Marquiese's relief. Brittia stood up and grabbed Earek's arm. They headed first for the refreshment tables and then to the dance floor when the music started up again. Brittia, Marquiese noticed, was much like her mother and father. They were all quick to flaunt their possessions and their positions, and it was not a particularly attractive quality. They seemed to spare no one of their pretense, even Lady Annabella. And that was not a wise decision, Marquiese thought. He even saw Corlda go so far as to insinuate that Lady Annabella's dress fabric was inferior to her own, and judging by Marilana's icy gaze, the woman was lucky not to be dismissed at dagger point.

As it turned out, when the clock struck midnight, and he, Merchant Colbran, Adealy, and Lida were preparing to leave, Merchant Sleater seemed to find one last opportunity to wield his influence.

"I'm afraid my carriage is not back yet, Colbran," Merchant Sleater said in a voice that anyone within earshot could easily hear. "Some of my other guests also required a ride, and you will have to wait here until it arrives back, I'm afraid."

"Well Sleater, we will just have to wait," Merchant Colbran replied gruffly.

"That will not be necessary," said a voice behind Marquiese. "I would be glad to give your family a ride home, Merchant Colbran. I am, after all, going right past your manor."

The voice belonged to Lady Annabella, who, like Marquiese and his family, was collecting her cloak and gloves.

"Lady Annabella, that is so kind of you to offer," Merchant Sleater hastened to say, his bow deep and diffident. "But I am happy to see to the needs of my guests."

"I am sure you are, Merchant Sleater," Lady Annabella said with a polite smile. "However, I see no reason to make this family wait. Young Lida here is nearly asleep on her feet. I shall offer the hospitality of my carriage and see them safely home. Come along now."

Lady Annabella swept out the door with Marilana and Zariff close behind. Merchant Colbran and Marquiese ushered Adealy and Lida down the steps and toward the waiting carriage. When they reached the drive, Marquiese glanced back in time to see the furious look on Merchant Sleater's face. When he turned back, Captain-General Zariff gave him a nod and a wink that told him he had seen the same thing, and that it was exactly what the high merchant deserved.

"Shall we go?" the Captain-General said, after they helped the women inside.

"Indeed," Marquiese replied with a smile. He climbed in behind Merchant Colbran. A lantern hanging from the ceiling lit the interior. Across from him, Lida laid her head contentedly in Marilana's lap. Marilana smiled gently at him and placed her paw protectively on Lida's shoulder. They set off.

"Lady Annabella, I have to say that your dress is just beautiful," Adealy said, breaking a moment of silence.

"Why thank you, Madam Adealy. As is yours."

"You have your own seamstress, I'm sure."

"Yes. And I have to say that I am quite fond of her. She does a wonderful job. I do occasionally acquire the services of Merchant Yulan. He is a very talented tailor as well, but this is one of my seamstress' creations," Lady Annabella replied with a smile. After a moment, she added, "I wanted to tell you how very impressed I am with young Lida. You have trained her well in etiquette and her dancing is beautiful."

"Thank you, My Lady, you are too kind," Adealy said, beaming with pleasure.

"Thank you also for giving us a ride home," Merchant Colbran said politely. "It really was unnecessary."

"On the contrary," Lady Annabella replied, her smile tweaked with mischief. "Sleater does not know the meaning of kindness and was clearly trying to make you uncomfortable. I have no objections to disrupting his plans once in a while; it helps to remind him where his place is."

"Of course, My Lady," Merchant Colbran said, sharing her smile.

The carriage turned in at the gate and stopped at the steps of the brick manor. Zariff opened the door on the opposite side of the carriage and helped Adealy out first.

"Marquiese, would you wait a moment. I wish to speak with you," Lady Annabella said as Merchant Colbran started to get out. He hesitated and met Marquiese's eyes.

Marquiese smiled and gave him a reassuring nod. "I will be along in a moment," he said calmly.

Marilana lifted Lida in her arms and gently passed her out the door to Merchant Colbran. When they were well away from the carriage, Lady Annabella said, "Please pull the door closed, Marilana, and sit with us, if you would."

When Marilana was settled in her seat again, Lady Annabella looked across at them both and said, "I want to congratulate both of you on your performance tonight. Marquiese your etiquette was not horrendous, but no one will be inviting you to any parties again soon, which I think is for the best. Marilana you did well to be polite yet solid in your position beside me. I am proud of you. However, you will both need to show some significant improvement at school over the next few months. Mistress Rose has never yet failed to teach a student proper etiquette and, if you continue to resist, Headmistress Ceta may begin to suspect that you are doing it on purpose. I will expect reports of noticeable improvement by the end of the school year, just do so gradually. Are my instructions understood?"

"Yes, My Lady." Marilana bowed her head.

"Yes, Lady Annabella." Marquiese replied. "Understood."

"Very good." Lady Annabella nodded firmly. "Shall we see you in the morning for sparring practice, Marquiese?"

"Yes, Lady Annabella, bright and early," Marquiese smiled.

"Then I suggest you get some rest," Lady Annabella smiled.

Marilana opened the door, and Marquiese climbed out. They shared a brief smile, and then the carriage was off.

21

They didn't talk about it, and they really didn't plan what they were going to do, but Marquiese and Marilana followed Lady Annabella's instructions in completely different ways. They both understood how extremely important etiquette and dancing were in the fabric of society in the Kingdom of Redsands. They understood that both were part of every major gathering, every holiday, and every important event. They also didn't want their charade to put Mistress Rose in a bad situation.

Marquiese made small steps, improving his etiquette gradually but still struggled with his dancing. Everyone noticed, especially Brittia.

Marilana in contrast waited until the beginning of spring, a full month after Brittia's party, before suddenly mastering things like her grip and demonstrating an ever-improving demeanor. Yet no one seemed to notice, and Mistress Rose obliged Marilana by not pointing it out.

Making strides on the dance floor was easier to hide because Mistress Rose had taken the class from a simple waltz, through the allemande, and into the landler. Marilana and Marquiese were not just a few steps, but whole dances behind the class leaders, however there were other students struggling as well. Mistress Rose indicated that they would also learn the steps of the cotillion and then review everything before the end of the year exam.

Marilana and Marquiese both looked forward to their time after school when no one was able to watch their every move. Today was no different. Marilana had been working with Marquiese and Earek on their tracking skills, and this afternoon they were practicing in the mud after a hard spring rain.

Both the lion and the leopard were picking up the skill, and, though the mud made identifying tracks easy, it also made it more difficult to avoid leaving tracks. Still they moved quickly through the forest, and she was pleased at their progress.

"You're getting better," she said when they reached her house. Then she grinned. "For a couple of spoiled merchant boys, that is."

Marilana checked the road carefully before leading them across the road and through the gate. She was halfway up the walk when she spotted a piece of fabric fluttering in the breeze among her rose garden. She motioned for the boys to stay put, then made her way carefully through the garden to the cloth and picked it up. Then she smiled. It was a gray strip of wool with a small, neatly embroidered green rose. The fabric strip was a marker from Child. She had apparently returned to Mystillion safely, and Marilana was relieved.

She put strip in her belt pouch, disarmed her traps, and led Marquiese and Earek into the house. They looked at her questioningly when she joined them in the kitchen, but she just smiled and set out her homework.

"Marilana, I've noticed that Headmistress Ceta hasn't been calling you into her office quite as much as she used to," Earek commented lazily. "Are you sure you're feeling alright?"

"I'm better than fine, thank you." Marilana laughed. "Things turned around after I cleaned Brittia's dress that one day. Since the New Year, I have been careful to serve Brittia politely when it is my turn and ignore her mistakes when it is her turn. She seems hesitant to make up stories about me of late. I rather like the change. Getting beat every couple of days did keep my skin tough, but I would rather not have to put up with the annoyance."

"I guess being nice has an upside," Marquiese said slyly.

"Yes. Now if only we could beat that lesson into Brittia. We would all be better off," Marilana replied with a laugh.

Marilana finished her homework and got up to work on her chores. She left the boys in the kitchen and was tidying up in the main room when she heard the sounds of horses on the road. She paused and listened, and then she frowned. The horses were trotting from the east, so it wasn't Captain Branth's patrol.

Marilana moved over to the arrow slits next to the door and peered out at the road. Much to her surprise, it was Lady Annabella.

"Is something wrong?" Marquiese asked, coming quickly from the kitchen and moving up next to her. "It is too early for the patrol."

"Lady Annabella is here," Marilana said. "I don't know why."

She unlocked the door and hurried to disarm the path. Storm nickered at her, but Lady Annabella's expression was grim as she swept into the house. Marilana followed and closed the door.

"I need to speak with Marquiese alone," Lady Annabella said without preamble. "Marilana, perhaps it would be best if you escorted Earek home now."

"Yes, My Lady," Marilana replied.

"As you wish, My Lady." Earek bowed smartly and hurried to the kitchen. He returned with his pack and cloak and followed Marilana quickly out the door. Marilana hurried Earek down the road, then paused and peered back around the trees.

"Do you think he will be alright?" Earek asked quietly. "I've never seen Lady Annabella look so troubled."

"I don't know, Earek," Marilana replied. "Whatever is going on, it is not good, and we may never learn the details."

They hurried on. One of Merchant Yulan's guards was lounging at the gate of the brick manor talking with Merchant

Colbran's gate guard when they came around the bend. Both guards came to attention.

"You're done early," the former commented gruffly.

"Where's Colbran's lad?" the other demanded.

"Marquiese is still at my house," Marilana said calmly. "He still has some work he wants help with, but Earek felt he needed to return home."

Earek gave her a nod and started down the road toward town. Marilana watched them go for a moment.

"What's going on?" the gate guard asked suspiciously. "You look troubled. Is the lad alright?"

"Yes, he's fine," Marilana said. "But I should get back."

The man frowned at her, but said nothing as Marilana turned and hurried back up the road. She slowed as she approached Lady Annabella's escorts. Storm tossed his head at her, and she apologized for the less than warm welcome with a good ear scratching and neck rub. After a while, Storm laid his head on her shoulder and closed his eyes as Marilana gently stroked his neck. They waited a long time, and the shadows were long by the time Lady Annabella emerged from the house.

Marilana held Storm still as Lady Annabella approached. The noble paused and placed her paw heavily on Marilana's shoulder.

"He may need some time alone. Be patient with him," she said quietly.

"Yes, My Lady." Marilana bowed her head.

Lady Annabella mounted Storm and her escort formed up around her. They turned back east and trotted off in the twilight. Marilana reset her traps as she made her way back into the house. She found Marquiese standing in front of the fireplace with his back to the room, his feet apart, and his arms crossed. He cut such a commanding figure in the dim light that she almost didn't recognize him. Looking at him made her suddenly nervous. Quietly, she took several steps toward the kitchen.

"Marilana," Marquiese said suddenly.

His tone was not just controlled; it was *in* control. It demanded obedience. Marilana's breath caught. She had heard that tone of voice from nobles before. She swallowed and turned to face his back. He had not moved, but continued to stare into the low fire. She started to address him as Lord, but hesitated and forced herself to calm down.

"Marquiese?" she inquired.

"Stay with me," he said simply. "Please."

Marilana took several steps toward him, wanting to comfort him but resisted the impulse to touch him. Instead, she sank to her knees and tried to relax.

"I am here," she replied softly.

She knelt there a long time, waiting and thinking. She studied Marquiese as he stood, absorbed in his own dark thoughts. He had grown since she first met him. He was as tall as she was now, and his lion's mane had started to grow. It was straggly, but Marilana could tell it would grow in thick and lustrous. She was glad she was kneeling and that he was not looking at her, because she blushed at the sudden urge to run her claws gently through the beginning tufts of his mane. She looked down at her paws in her lap and tried to think of something other than Marquiese, but it was difficult with him standing before her.

"Tell me something from your childhood," Marquiese said suddenly making Marilana jump. "Something you remember of your parents. Would you?"

She thought quietly for a moment.

"I don't remember much of my time with my parents," she said sadly. "I remember mostly a warm happy feeling. I remember the soft tones of my father's voice telling me about the herbs in the garden, but I don't remember his words. I can still recall the smell of the herbs as I watched my mother crush them into the stew pot. I remember the warmth of my mother's embrace, and the tears on her cheeks as she said goodbye. I remember watching them shoulder their packs and walk away down the road, while Lady Annabella held my paw and stopped me from following them."

Marilana's throat thickened and she blinked back tears, but she refused to slump her shoulders. She knelt proudly and remembered that she lived her own life now.

"I'm sorry," Marquiese said, kneeling beside her. "I did not mean to make you sad. I just wanted to hear your voice. I just wanted to think of . . . someone else."

Marilana swallowed her tears and nodded her head. She looked up and met his green eyes. The commanding presence had left him; he was just Marquiese again, her friend. She shared a meek smile and said, "I do not have many happy stories to tell, I'm afraid. I think that is why I like listening to your stories. You tell such wonderful stories. I could listen for hours."

"Yes, well, of that I am not so sure."

"I can only assume Lady Annabella brought you bad news." Marilana sighed and looked down at the floor. "Will you be leaving soon?"

It was the one question that had been plaguing Marilana's thoughts, but Marquiese shook his head and said, "No, not yet. Part of me wants to rush off, but I am not ready to return yet. Part of me wants to stay right here." He met her eyes. "It is a very hard choice."

Marilana felt relieved that Marquiese was not leaving, and then she felt ashamed; it was selfish of her and she knew it. She could tell that Marquiese had put a lot of thought into his decision. She hoped for his sake that he was making the right choice.

"You must do what you think is best," she said softly.

"Argh! Now you sound like Lady Annabella," he growled. He sprang to his feet and began pacing.

"That should not be surprising, since everything I know has come from her." Marilana glanced his way, her smile small and warm. Then she perked up and directed the conversation back to safer waters. She said, "You wish to hear about my childhood. Well, I used to play hide-and-seek with some of the younger scullery maids at the castle. We would race through the halls, laughing and frolicking. Some of the other help would cheer us on and some would chastise us. We didn't care. After all, we were young and rambunctious. Even then I was fast, and I would duck around corners and dash through rooms until I could find the perfect hiding place. The others would race past thinking I was still ahead of them. I would then sneak out and hurry back the way we had come and find even better places to hide. Many times it took them so long to find me, that I would curl up and fall asleep.

"Captain-General Zariff used to laugh that I was like his veteran soldiers; I could sleep anywhere and anytime but was refreshed and ready to go the instant it was time to attack. One of my favorite places to hide was in the cellar, on top of the highest shelves next to where the onions and herbs hung in clumps from the ceiling. Oh, how I loved the smell. Those were fun times."

Marquiese had stopped pacing. He sank slowly down on the floor, and their eyes met.

"It is good to hear a happy memory from you," he said, smiling. She returned his smile, but it faded quickly.

"I was four at the time," she said quietly. "Like all good things in my life, it did not last."

"I would advise you against dwelling on those negative thoughts," he said kindly. "The future always brings change—it is the one thing we can count on—and not all of it is bad."

"No, you're right. I have friends now, and that is a very pleasant change." She smiled again. "You also have friends, Marquiese, and I am here for you, no matter what happens."

"Thank you, Marilana, but you cannot help with my present dilemma," he said sadly. "I wish I could tell you about it, but I cannot."

"I don't have to know anything about it," Marilana replied gently. "I can see you are sad and frustrated. You have already made the decision to remain here, at least for a time, and so I can help with that. I can remind you that you have homework to do, etiquette to foul up, and dancing to hide. I can remind you that you are surrounded by merchants that would love to learn your secret and in danger from bandits who would love to destroy your life."

"And you can remind me that I am surrounded by some of the most beautiful things in life." He laughed. "Not the least of which is your wit."

"Such a nice compliment," Marilana teased in return.

He came to his feet, offered her a paw, and helped her up. He said, "And you are correct. I have made my decision and now I must move on. I must keep my thinking clear. I cannot let down my guard. There is too much at stake."

"And now I should escort you home," Marilana said, happy that they still had a few moments to share. "It is getting late."

"Yes, it is time." Marquiese nodded. He gathered his school things, and Marilana disarmed her traps. They set off together and were soon at the brick manor.

"I will see you in the morning for sparring practice," Marquiese said quietly. "Goodnight, Marilana. Thank you for the company."

"Goodnight," Marilana replied. She watched him walk through the gate, then turned and ran into the forest.

*

Marilana watched Marquiese closely over the next couple of fifnights. In a group, he acted like the Marquiese everyone had come to know, laughing, joking, and telling the most evocative stories. When he was left to his own thoughts, however, she saw a different side, a sad and melancholy side.

Today, she saw both. It was a beautiful spring morning and a Restday. She and Child had finished patrolling the surrounding countryside and found it quiet; most of the would-be bandits were busy tilling fields and planting crops.

Just after dawn, Marilana left Child at her cottage and went to meet Marquiese for their morning session at the castle. As she approached the brick manor, she saw him waiting outside the gate and noticed that he was staring off to the north, lost in what were surely dark thoughts.

"Marquiese. Hello," she said, catching his attention. "Are you ready?"

"Ready and waiting," he called, managing a smile.

"Good. Let's see what Hosten has in store for us," she said cheerfully.

They set off down the road and quickly came to Lady Annabella's estates. The stablemaster was indeed waiting for them, and they set to work. Marilana applied her expertise with one of her five-year-old war horse trainees, a well-balanced dapple, while Marquiese rode a dun, one of the three-year-olds that Hosten was training for Lady Annabella's soldiers.

"Excellent progress," Hosten said when they were done.

"That war horse is coming along nicely," Marquiese commented as they headed for the practice yard and an hour of sparring.

"He is ready for a permanent rider. So are my other two five-year-olds," Marilana replied. "Lady Annabella has sent word out to the Knights of the Realm to find if anyone is interested in them. They're ready to start competing. She'll let me know if she gets any responses."

"That would be something special to have your horses ridden by Knights of the Realm," Marquiese said, smiling in admiration.

"The summer before you came to Mystillion, Lady Annabella sold two of my war horses to Knights of the Realm," she replied proudly. "A large bay went to a Master Roatal, High Lord Roatal of Pandensy's eldest son, and the other, a chestnut, went to a Sir Graduin."

"I hope you get some interest this time, as well," Marquiese said, then added firmly. "I know you will."

They rounded the corner of the castle, and Captain-General Zariff was waiting for them. "I think you're ready to begin shooting at Marilana's targets," he told Marquiese. "And this morning, I want you both shooting at the same time."

Marquiese held his excitement in check as he and the lioness strung their bows.

"Focus on your surroundings and your objective," Marilana said to him. "Let everything else leave your mind. Push out all emotion. Emotions can cause you to make choices that you know are illogical. Efficiency, speed, and accuracy come from clarity and focus. Nothing else matters; the world consists only of you and your target."

Marquiese nodded. He stood with his back to the yard and closed his eyes. He took several deep breaths. Marilana did the same. She pictured the empty yard in her mind and prepared to shoot what should not be there. When Zariff gave them the signal, they spun at the same instant, Marilana already pulling an arrow from the quiver at her hip. She ignored everything else and scanned for the targets. She loosed her arrow and instantly drew the next, loosing each arrow in the same moment she located her next target, never wasting time watching its flight or concerning herself with where it landed.

Moments later, her quiver was empty, and each arrow had struck dead-center of its target.

Marquiese emptied his quiver under the watchful eye of the old lion and his protégé, and all but two struck in the center two rings. Marilana smiled proudly. "Well done, Marquiese," she called happily. "Well done."

"For your first time shooting at such advanced targets, you did very well, Marquiese," Zariff said with approval.

"Thank you. But I still have a lot of room for improvement," he said, frowning at his targets. "I don't know if I will ever be as fast and accurate as Marilana, but I can still get better."

"Yes, indeed," Zariff agreed. "Now take your places for sparring."

The young lion and lioness faced off, their swords at the ready.

Marilana was careful not to meet Marquiese's eyes because she had found that doing so stirred her emotions and made it hard to focus. She cleared her mind and focused on his movements and the position of his body.

He began to circle, and she circled with him, matching his movements. When he did not strike, she feinted a lunge and pulled back, spun to her left and struck high. He blocked her strike and retaliated with a low stab at her legs. She jumped back and parried his back arm swing. She struck back quickly and pressed him hard. She forced him to take several steps back, but she knew strength was his advantage not hers. She was faster, and so she now switched her maneuvers from power swings to fast short strikes. For the moment, Marquiese managed to block her strikes and hold his ground. He stepped out of the way of her third strike and swung at her outstretched sword arm. Marilana stepped back to avoid his strike and he pressed his new opening.

Back and forth, they struggled against each other, focused only on the motions of the other. Kicking up the sand of the practice yard and making a chorus of clacks as they met practice sword to practice sword. After a few minutes, Marilana thought they might have to call a draw. She could tell that Marquiese was beginning to tire and could feel her own muscles weakening as well. They were both panting hard, and neither had been able to gain an advantage.

Exhaustion, however, was as much a tool as jabbing and parrying. So, as tired as she may have been, Marilana renewed her attack, delivering a series of quick jabs that he blocked with difficulty. She swung toward his legs and he parried with a downward block. Then she saw her opening. He made a back arm swing at her midsection; instead of blocking the move or simply stepping back, she spun around the swing, barely avoiding the tip of his blade. She brought her own blade down inside the arc of his swing, holding her hilt with only her right paw. As she continued her spin, she grabbed his hilt with her left paw, twisted her blade down, and wrenched the sword from his grasp. She came to rest with a practice sword in each paw, their blades crossed in front of her at the ready.

Marquiese took a step back, breathing hard and smiling. Marilana met his eyes now and returned his smile.

"Well done, Marilana. You took the opening and struck with skill. Marquiese, you have come far. You almost held on for a draw this morning," Zariff said proudly. "You are both done with your duties for today. I'll see you tomorrow, and we'll see if you can repeat today's success."

They bowed to each other, then to their mentor. They had just finished putting their weapons away when they saw Lady Annabella striding their way. Marilana curtseyed to the noble lioness and Marquiese bowed.

"I am sorry to interrupt, but I need a quick word with Marquiese, if you would," Lady Annabella said quietly.

"Of course, M' Lady," Marilana said. She bowed her head and walked toward the castle steps. From the shadows of the castle wall, she stopped and looked back, seeing at once the serious expression etched across Marquiese's face. Whatever the issue, his interchange with Lady Annabella was short and pointed. Then he gave her a short bow, turned, and came to rejoin his sparring partner and friend.

Together, they walked in silence toward the main gate. The guard at the gate nodded respectfully and let them out.

They went north only briefly before disappearing into the trees, their pace steady, their conversation minimal.

When they reached a dense patch of underbrush, Marquiese stopped and called to her. "Marilana. Wait."

When she turned, he was gazing up at the trees and the crisp blue sky overhead.

"It is such a nice day, I would like to enjoy some time outside. Is there someplace we can go?"

Marilana listened for a moment before answering. She heard a series of soft coos off to her left that made her smile. *Good*, she thought. Child was close by and watching, so she knew the area was clear of any threat for the moment.

"There is," she said. "Follow me."

She led him north and farther into the forest. It was not long before the constant hum of a waterfall filled the air, and their path took them in time to the edge of a large clearing. Before them lay a small deep, clear lake fed by a spectacular waterfall. The sight brought an expression of awe to Marquiese's face and a smile of pure pleasure to Marilana's.

The warm spring sun glinted invitingly off the water, casting dancing lights across the narrow meadow and into the dark shadows of the surrounding forest.

"Welcome to my favorite place," she said, spreading her arms wide. Together, they skirted the lake to the waterfall. Marilana found a patch of green grass and stretched out in the warm sunshine. She closed her eyes happily and listened to the sounds of the water and the voices of the creatures that lived there.

"It's amazing," Marquiese said, kneeling down next to her. "Is it safe?"

"Like much of the forest, it has its dangers to be sure," Marilana admitted. "But The Phantom and I scouted the area extensively this morning and saw no signs of bandit activity. Most of them are still occupied with planting and spring repairs, so I am not too worried today."

"I can see that," he mused. "So would it be safe enough then to take a swim?"

"I suppose it would, but . . . ."

"Good!" Before she knew what was happening, Marquiese scooped her up in his arms, dumped the arrows out of her quiver, and launched her out into the lake.

"Marquiese?!" she cried.

She gasped for air as she came to the surface and stood up. The water was chest-high on her. She shook the water out of her eyes and looked around. Marquiese was bobbing lazily in the water not a few feet away.

"Ah, it feels fantastic, doesn't it?" he said with a mischievous smile.

"You threw me in. Boots, quiver, knives, and all," she said in awe. Then she spied his boots on the shore and realized he had planned it all along. "Why you! You . . . ."

"Yes, I did," he said, his laughter echoing across the water. He raised his paw and brought it down on the surface of water, splashing her as she tossed her boots and weapons belt onto the grass.

"Now you're in for it," she called. She splashed him back, then dove beneath the surface and swam into the deep end of the lake. Marquiese followed.

Together, they swam and splashed and laughed until mid-morning. Finally, they waded back up to the shore. There was a huge boulder protruding out into the water, and they settled onto its warm surface. Marilana twisted the water out of her dress and Marquiese did the same to his shirt and pants. For a brief moment, the lioness turned her attention to the trees. Once again she heard Child's soft cooing, a signal that all was still safe.

She and Marquiese stretched out on the boulder and the heat from the stone and sun warmed them to the bones and began to dry their clothes.

"Thank you for bringing me here," he said brightly. "I needed this kind of distraction."

Marilana hesitated a moment then asked, "More bad news?"

"No. Actually, the news was better. But I just needed to relax a bit. And what better way to spend the morning?"

Marilana returned his smile and studied his eyes. She realized that her wet dress was clinging to her like a second skin. She wondered what Marquiese was thinking, but his eyes met hers easily and did not make her uncomfortable in the least. In fact, she felt more relaxed than she could remember in a very long time.

Finally, Marquiese looked away and gazed off across the lake.

"It's funny. I have often been told I am too hard on myself about my training. But you have never said anything about that to me, even though you have heard how self-critical I can be. Why is that?"

Marilana shrugged as if the answer was obvious. "If you want to get better at something, you have to be critical of your own skills. You are the only one who knows how hard you try, how far you push, how much farther you still want to go. You have the makings of a great swordsman. You have trained with me for a year now, and in that time you have improved dramatically both with sword and bow. I can tell you have had many years of training, but you are not set in your ways and have been willing to learn new ways. You have also evaluated some of the new techniques Zariff and I have shown you against some of your old ways and chosen the way you feel most comfortable with. That is one of the most important skills you have shown. Everyone is different, and you will be most successful when you find the way that works best for you."

"Will you show me that disarming trick that you pulled on me this morning?" he asked.

"Tomorrow, I promise," she said smiling. "For now, I think I would like to get something to eat. Do you wish to join me or would you rather return home? "

"I think it would be best if I return home. They will be worried about me," he said quietly.

"As you wish."

Marilana gathered her weapons, checked her bow carefully, and they put on their boots. Marilana led the way straight south to the brick manor. As she waved goodbye and made her way home alone, she couldn't help but feel a little disappointed that he had declined to extend their time together.

22

Marilana stood at the back of the classroom as the rest of students came back from the lunch break. She was nervous. Headmistress Ceta had spent all morning testing their etiquette. Mistress Rose had served the students a full six-course meal while Headmistress Ceta acted as hostess. She had watched the students with keenly critical eyes. As they ate, she asked them questions about the laws of the merchant caste. She had given Marilana little more than a cursory glance and asked her not a single question. In contrast, she had complimented Marquiese on his table manners, posture, and personal interaction and asked him one question after another. He had answered every question correctly, and she had passed him with only a slight admonition to continue practicing over the summer. The other students all passed with varying degrees of mastery. Brittia and Earek, of course, had been perfect. Now they were going to have to show how well they had learned to dance over the year.

"Let's start with the best dancers and work our way to the bottom, shall we?" Headmistress Ceta said to Mistress Rose once everyone had taken their positions around the dance floor.

"As you wish." Mistress Rose nodded her head. "Brittia and Earek, if you would please take your places. We'll start with a simple waltz and proceed from there."

Marilana watched Brittia and Earek complete each dance easily, and Headmistress Ceta praised them both when they were done. Two by two, the rest of the students were called upon to show their dance abilities. Marilana and Marquiese had been true to Lady Annabella's instructions earlier in the year and had shown noticeable improvement during the dance review the last fifnight, but Marilana had been careful to dance only the simple waltz and nothing else. Marquiese had shown improvement in the simple waltz and the allemande. It had been enough that he was no longer the worst of the boys and so Marilana was sure she would not have to dance with him in front of the class.

"Chiely and Marquiese, please take your positions," Mistress Rose called after an hour and a half of watching the dancing ability of the students slowly erode.

Marquiese took Chiely's hoof and bowed to her. They danced the simple waltz slowly without any special additions and made it through without falling down. Chiely was so nervous that she kept making little mistakes. They danced the allemande with similar success, but the landler and cotillion were complete failures. Marilana knew that it was because Marquiese was not dancing the correct dance, but luckily Headmistress Ceta did not pick up on that fact. Instead, she had Chiely dance with one of the other boys and had better luck showing her true skills.

When they were done, Mistress Rose called Marilana and Jeof onto the dance floor, her voice tight and anxious.

Marilana faced Jeof and curtseyed. They danced the simple waltz and only had to start over twice. Marilana was relieved that Jeof was such a poor dancer that she didn't have to explain why her waltz had gone from none existent to perfect. When they started to dance the allemande, however, Marilana stayed true to form and danced something completely different. She felt bad for Jeof. Neither of them passed the last three dances, even when Headmistress Ceta paired Jeof off with someone else.

"Well, you can all continue in Mistress Rose's class next year, however, I do expect you to practice over the summer. Mistress Rose, you have done your customary good job considering what you had to work with. I will see you all tomorrow for the Exhibition Ball when the graduating class will be performing the Dance of the Seasons," Headmistress Ceta said. She smiled at each of the merchant students in turn and completely ignored Marilana.

On the trek home, Marquiese walked side by side with Brittia. He smiled politely at the lynx and accepted her invitation to watch the Exhibition Ball, as she put it, "in her company."

When they reached Brittia's house, Marquiese bowed and wished her a good night. Then the group continued down the road. Marquiese looked around for someone to talk with. The gazelle, Estala, filled the void, chatting non-stop. He missed Earek. Since they no longer had homework, the black leopard had gone straight from school to the market to work in his father's shop. After Estala finally said her goodbyes and hurried up the path to her house, it was just Marquiese, Marilana, and Lida. Marquiese was eternally relieved.

"Marquiese, would you help me with my homework tonight?" Lida asked as they walked along. "I have a whole page of review questions, and a whole page of math to do before tomorrow."

"I would be glad to help you with your homework. I'll bet Marilana would help too, if you asked her nicely," Marquiese said lightly.

"That's okay," Lida said with a smile. "I think your help will be enough."

"I think you're correct, Lida," Marilana added. "I think Marquiese will be more than enough help for tonight."

When they reached the brick manor, there was an awkward moment when Marquiese and Marilana turned to say goodbye. They had spent so many enjoyable afternoons studying together that he felt lost. He was going to miss her company over the summer and didn't know how to tell her.

Marilana seemed to read his mind and said, "We are sparring together tomorrow, are we not?"

"Most definitely," he said quickly.

"Good. Then I'll see you in the morning," Marilana said quietly. She turned, crossed the road, and disappeared in the trees.

Marquiese drew a deep breath. When Marilana was out of sight, he followed Lida and Adealy into the brick manor, and the door closed behind him.

That evening, Marquiese helped Lida with her homework—something he really did enjoy doing—then bade goodnight to Merchant Colbran and Adealy and retired to his room. He lay on his bed and stared at the ceiling trying to decide what to do now that school was out for the summer. Returning to Maefair was one option, but he didn't think the timing was right, there were too many rumors coming out of Maefair. Keeping a low profile here in Mystillion and focusing on his training was another, and he knew this to be the prudent thing to do, if maybe a bit selfish. Marilana was here, and he couldn't deny how much that relationship meant to him.

He didn't remember closing his eyes, and he didn't remember drifting off to sleep.

When he woke the next morning, he realized that the sun was already coming up. He scrambled out of bed half in a panic, hastily threw on some clothes, and started down the stairs. Merchant Colbran stopped him at the bottom of the stairs with a raised paw.

"I'm sorry we didn't wake you for your sparring practice," he said. "But you need to get ready for the festivities, and we thought you would be better off for the extra bit of sleep. We know you did not sleep much last night. I told the lioness, Marilana, that you would not be available this morning. She understood and said she would inform Lady Annabella."

"I can make my own . . . !" Marquiese felt his temper rising. But then paused and pushed the emotion aside. When looked at logically, Merchant Colbran had made the better choice, and perhaps some gratitude was instead in order. "I'm sorry. You are right. Thank you for the consideration."

Without another word, he returned to his room and made ready for the day's festivities.

Several hours later, he was standing at Brittia's side and trying not to yawn. Brittia squeezed his arm and smiled up at him.

"You are becoming such a handsome young lion," the lynx whispered. "Your mane is growing in quite nicely, and you have gotten so much taller of late."

"You are kind to say so," Marquiese replied.

Brittia squeezed his arm, and they turned their attention to the dance floor—neatly laid out in the market square—and watched as the graduating class came out in their costumes. Earek's brother, Adrek, had been cast for the part of Lord Time, and Marquiese could easily tell that Earek was a better dancer than his brother. He wondered if Earek himself would be dancing the same part in two more years.

Brittia interrupted this thought, saying, "You'll surely be a good enough dancer in two years to dance the part of Lord Time. I know I'll be dancing Lady Season. Aunt Ceta has already promised. Wouldn't it be fun to perform such a romantic dance together?"

Brittia squeezed his arm again and sighed.

Marquiese could think of a number of responses to this, but he held his tongue. Instead, he immersed himself in the music and the movement of the dancers and found himself remembering some of the performances that he had seen in Maefair. Those, of course, featured only professional dancers, but he could not remember two lead dancers who put more romantic emotion into it the dance than Adrek and his partner. Surely, Marquiese thought, this was the merchant daughter Adrek was wanting to court.

When the performance ended, he was not surprised when Headmistress Ceta stepped forward and called to the crowd, "May I have your attention everyone. There has been a request made for a courtship dance. Master Adrek and Merchant Yulan have requested this dance, and Miss Vavinta and Merchant Nartol have accepted."

The crowd cheered wildly as Adrek led the blushing Vavinta back out to the dance area. It was a wonderful performance by the two leopards, even if the dancing was only average; the couple made it easily into the mid-paced rhythm before Vavinta closed her fan and placed it at Adrek's feet. He offered his paw to her and pulled her to her feet. Then he kissed her on the cheek. The crowd erupted into renewed applause. Vavinta was blushing so much she looked as if she might faint.

"She's mortified," Brittia said, laughing with delight. "Maybe she'll faint and then he'll have to carry her home. Wouldn't that be romantic? Come on! Let's go congratulate them."

Marquiese let Brittia steer him through the crowds. She made her way to the new couple in short order, and, given her rank, everyone yielded to her approach.

"Adrek, Vavinta, congratulations. I am so happy for you," Brittia said brightly. "You did such a good job today. The dancing was absolutely beautiful."

"Allow me to add my congratulations as well," Marquiese said, shaking Adrek's paw. "I hope you are happy together and prosper."

Brittia led him away, beaming. "You have such wonderful manners, Marquiese," the lynx simpered.

They strolled along the market, her paw on his arm, and were joined by a number of their classmates, Earek among them. Together, the group strolled the market, talking about the performance, the courtship dance, and, of course, the kiss.

That was when Brittia spotted Marilana standing alone and watching the milling masses in the market square. Brittia hissed and directed her followers that way.

"My, my, my. Where did you get such a horrific dress?" Brittia called to her.

The dress was a pale blue and nicely tailored, and it hardly looked horrific. In fact, Marquiese thought it look extremely nice. "Why would anyone ruin a perfectly good fabric like that? Oh, sorry, it's not the dress, it is the creature trying so unsuccessfully to wear it."

Brittia paused while her followers laughed and tittered. "You know, you should not get all moony-eyed over someone else's courtship, Bandit Hunter. This is as close as you will ever get to a courtship, because you know as well as I that no one will ever ask you to dance let alone want to court you."

Marilana stared at the lynx, her face etched with amusement. Brittia wasn't finished. She said, "Which begs the question. Why are you here? Don't you have somewhere else to be? Chores to do? People to kill? Mud to roll in?"

"Correct me if I'm wrong, but I believe you approached me, Brittia. No one forced you," Marilana said sounding bored. "So if you're done, I'll continue to walk around."

Brittia's mouth dropped as Marilana started away.

"That's right. Walk away. Admit the company is too good for you," Brittia called to her.

Marilana stopped and looked back at Brittia. "You will never get the better of me, Brittia, because you cannot even master yourself. You have chosen how you will live and I have chosen how I will live," Marilana replied. "Fighting with you is a waste of my time and energy. Good day."

Brittia stood glaring angrily after Marilana, breathing heavily. Her companions milled about trying to make small talk and not look at her. Marquiese glanced at Earek as Marilana walked away completely at her ease, and could tell Earek was fighting to hold back his laughter.

23

The first two months of summer passed slowly. Like the previous summer, Marquiese spent most of his time in the market, hiding in the back room of his merchant father's shop. Every morning he still went to sparring practice with Marilana, and it was, inevitably, the highlight of his day.

Marilana was bound and determined to teach him the disarming move she had used against him and he was getting closer to mastering it.

They were very evenly matched now. He still had not disarmed her, but several matches recently had ended in a draw. Marilana and Zariff were tireless in sharing their expertise, and Marquiese was eternally grateful.

The National Day of Worship came and went without incident. He had danced the simple waltz with Brittia, but had not added any of the embellishments or flourishes he normally would have. In the end, she had said it was passable and asked him how he had been able to improve during their summer break. "I've been getting some expert advice from Lida and Earek," he told her with a grin.

In truth, Lida had become a very popular dance partner with the younger merchant sons, and she spent a good number of afternoons over the summer dancing at parties to her heart's content.

Marquiese worried that the last month of summer was going to make up for the easy pace of the first two months, and he was right. He had sought out Marilana at her cottage that morning, but she was nowhere to be found. He was fortunate to run into Captain Branth and his patrol, but the Captain had no knowledge of the lioness' whereabouts. He suggested a visit Lady Annabella's castle, and because Marquiese needed to speak with Lady Annabella as well, he decided to make the trip that afternoon. Merchant Colbran had insisted on an escort of two merchant guards, and by the time all was set, it was late evening when they neared the castle's main gate. The guards on the wall called down to the foot gate as they approached. A guard opened the gate and stepped outside the wall to meet them.

"Young Marquiese," the gate guard inquired. "Is there something I can be of service for?"

"I am looking for Marilana," Marquiese said patiently. "It is important that I speak with her."

"She is studying in the castle this evening and should not be interrupted," the guard said thoughtfully. "Is it urgent enough to risk Lady Annabella's displeasure?"

"It is," Marquiese said, nodding firmly.

"Very well," the guard replied. "Your merchant guards will have to wait in the gate house or return later, but I will allow you to proceed to the castle."

Marquiese turned to his escorts and said, "You may return to Merchant Colbran and tell him I have arrived safely. Tell him also that I will make arrangements for an escort when I'm through here."

The guards turned back toward the road, grumbling under their breath and whispering something about love struck foolery, a comment Marquiese chose to ignore.

"This way," the gate guard said. He ushered Marquiese beyond the castle walls and led him briskly across the stableyard to the castle.

They ascended the steps and entered the castle's main doors. Then Marquiese was introduced to a serving man who led him to the dark doors of the library. The serving man told Marquiese to wait and slipped into the library. It was only a few moments before he came back out accompanied by the librarian and Dera, both of whom gave him disgruntled looks. The serving man ushered him inside and then shut the door behind him. Marquiese looked around the room and finally spotted Marilana and Lady Annabella at a table filled with books and writing paper. He hurried over and bowed to Lady Annabella, then shared a brief nod with Marilana.

"Well, Marquiese what is so important that it could not wait until morning and had to interrupt Marilana's studies?" Lady Annabella asked levelly.

"I'm sorry to interrupt, but I am in need of assistance," Marquiese said getting straight to the point. "A letter arrived for Merchant Colbran today. His cousin has requested the family travel to Draukshar in order to attend to some urgent family matters. They are making plans to leave in two days on Restday."

Lady Annabella frowned deeply. "I see. Well, that does pose a dilemma, does it not?" She looked over at Marilana and nodded. "Perhaps you should fill Marquiese in on our immediate schedule."

"Yes, My Lady." Marilana look across the table at Marquiese and said, "Three days from now, five Knights of the Realm and their delegations will be arriving here at Lady Annabella's estates. We were going to recommend that you stay at home and out of sight while the delegations were here. Obviously that won't work now with your family leaving town."

"I cannot stay there alone. It would not look good staying behind while my merchant family attends to business elsewhere," Marquiese said, nervously pacing the library floor. "And I cannot stay here, not with the knights and their delegation arriving. Hiding in town is not an option either."

"It would seem," Lady Annabella said slowly, "that you need somewhere to hide that would be both secure and not likely to attract visitors."

The lioness turned her gaze expectantly on Marilana and said, "Your cottage, for instance."

"I don't know why it wouldn't work," Marilana said quietly. "Marquiese could be seen leaving with Merchant

Colbran on their way through Mystillion. I could meet up with them on the West Road and lead him back through the forest. No one would know he had not traveled to Draukshar except Merchant Colbran's family and the merchant guards that travel with them."

"There are some among the merchant guards that know I am not part of the family and who would certainly keep the secret," Marquiese added. "I do not completely trust them, though they have been true so far. The others would be left to protect the house while the family is gone."

"Then it is settled," Lady Annabella said simply. "You would have to remain in Marilana's house until your merchant family returned. You could meet up with them on the West Road just as you had left them, travel through town on your return, and no one but the family and the merchant guards would be the wiser."

"I could not do that," Marquiese said, quietly shaking his head. "I could not take advantage of our friendship that way."

"It's not as if you're sleeping with me, Marquiese," Marilana scoffed. "You're just staying at my house. Besides, I don't see any reasonable alternatives. If you stayed at my house, I could be seen to be going about my normal business. I would be able to speak with the knights here at the castle, and no one would suspect you were hiding in my house. I am not after all the type to invite others over for entertaining. How long will Merchant Colbran be away?"

"Two fifnights," Marquiese said.

"We can survive ten days," Marilana said. "The knights will be here for only four days. If I have trouble, I can always leave and you'll be stuck in my house with all the traps armed."

Marquiese had to smile at that. The thought of staying in Marilana's house for two fifnights made him uneasy. He did not want to jeopardize their friendship. Still Marilana was correct—he didn't have a better option.

"Thank you. I am grateful," Marquiese said, looking from Marilana to her ward. "I'll settle everything with Merchant Colbran and stay with you for two fifnights."

"Good," Lady Annabella said briskly. "I expect both of you to be on your best behavior. Marilana, I expect you'll want to escort Marquiese home now and discuss the details of his stay. You are both dismissed."

"Yes, My Lady."

"Thank you, Lady Annabella," Marquiese said, bowing at the waist.

Everything went as planned, though Marilana could tell Marquiese was still not thrilled with the arrangement.

They met along the West Road well away from Mystillion and reached Marilana's house without incident. Marilana also had the added security of knowing that Child was in the area and had promised to keep an eye on things whenever Marilana was away.

Marilana heard a series of soft coos from the nearby trees and smiled as she reset the traps. She entered the house and latched the door. Marquiese laid his pack in the corner of the main room and stood staring thoughtfully into the cold fireplace.

"Have you had anything to eat yet this morning?" Marilana asked.

"Oh yes, I'm fine, thank you," Marquiese said turning to face her.

She waited patiently. Then she grinned and said, "Am I so terrible a housekeeper that you are afraid to stay here?"

Marquiese shook his head. "Not at all. I just do not want to cause any hardship between us."

"Relax, Marquiese." Marilana smiled. "You are still stubbornly honorable, and I am still protected by Lady

Annabella. She trusts you, and so do I. So the question is, do you trust me?"

"Yes, of course." Marquiese smiled. "I do trust you. In fact, I would not be here if I didn't."

"Okay. So we're clear on that. Now if you don't want anything to eat, I have some chores to do," she said briskly. "You can do as you like. Read a book, help with my chores, sleep. Whatever you feel like."

Marquiese smiled and followed her into the kitchen. Marilana started in on her chores and rambled on about why she tended the cook fire the way she did, who taught her how to cook, and what it was like in the kitchen at Lady Annabella's estate when she was growing up. She was just making small talk. She had done the same thing when Child was ill—just talking to hear a voice and break the tension. Her talking had a calming effect on Child and apparently did the same for Marquiese. She could tell, because all of a sudden he was helping with chores and discussing the art of cooking.

"I'm not very good and would love to learn more, but I guess I could survive if I had had to," he said as the last of the cleaning was done.

"Well, then, you can help me with the stew," she said, laying out the vegetables. "Then we can play a game of chess."

So they cooked and ate and wiled away the day. Chess, backgammon, idle conversation. Then, as the afternoon began to wane, Marilana gathered her things together.

"Time for me to go to Lady Annabella's castle," she said. "I have to report for my normal chores. Help yourself to whatever you need. If you want to go to sleep before I get back, you can use my room so I won't disturb you when I come in. Keep the lights low and stay away from the windows. I'll be back after dark."

"I'm sure I'll be fine, Marilana." Marquiese smiled. "You've left me here alone before, if you recall. I know the rules. I'll see you when you get back. And thank you. For having me here."

*

That evening, Marilana worked with Lady Annabella's personal staff getting ready for the arrival of the knights and their delegations the next day. Lady Annabella had ordered a welcoming banquet for the next evening. The kitchens were terribly hot and the cooks were rather short tempered, but the air was full of delicious smells. Marilana worked hard for six hours scrubbing the floors and preparing the guest rooms. When she was done, she was hot and sticky. She decided to clean up in the servant baths before returning to her house.

It was just before midnight when she picked her way through the traps to the garden door of her dark house. She heard a sleepy cooing from the trees, gave a short twitter in return, and went in knowing everything had been quiet while she was gone. She slipped inside and found Marquiese sitting in her chair in the main room. He was reading a book next to a mostly shuttered lantern.

"Welcome home," he said. "Is everything ready for the knights' visit?"

"Just about," she said, sighing and performing her evening chores. "The rooms are clean and stocked, the food is being cooked, and the whole castle has been scrubbed clean. Tomorrow, the gardens and outside spaces will be tidied up and everything will be ready."

"How about you? Are you ready?"

"I am nervous about speaking with the knights, but I know that once I start talking about the horses, I'll be fine," she smiled.

"I know you will do great," Marquiese said, returning her smile.

"Thank you," Marilana said hesitantly. "Well, I'm pretty tired. I should get to bed so I can get up early and patrol. You are my guest. You should sleep on the bed. I'll sleep out here so I don't wake you in the morning."

"No," Marquiese said firmly, shaking his head. "I will be just fine on the floor out here. I will not take your bed from you. Go! Sleep. I'll see you in the morning."

Marilana glanced at his bedroll spread out on the floor in the corner and nodded. She was really too tired to argue.

"Goodnight, Marilana," he said quietly.

"Goodnight, Marquiese." She went into her room and closed the door behind her. She changed her clothes, stretched, climbed into bed, and was asleep in minutes.

*

Marilana woke early. She dressed quietly and slipped out of her room. Marquiese was sleeping soundly, so she slipped into the kitchen and ate some fruit. She slipped back out to the garden door, swung her cloak around her shoulders, strung her bow, and left the house. She met Child in the trees and together they set off to patrol. Side-by-side, lioness and doe ranged far and wide around Mystillion, making a complete search.

The sun was well up by the time Marilana left Child and reported to Captain-General Zariff. He listened carefully to her report and then sent her to the stables to help the staff get ready. Marilana worked the rest of the day in the stables, cleaning stalls and bathing horses.

The first of the knights' delegations arrived early in the afternoon. Marilana helped rub down and care for their horses. She was kept busy throughout the afternoon and into the evening as each delegation arrived and more horses needed to be cared for. It was long after dark when she finally finished her chores and was relieved for the night. She could hear the music in the dining hall as she made her way down to the staff baths and cleaned up again before going home.

The moon was high in the sky when she arrived home and found Marquiese asleep in his bedroll. She checked her crossbows, and discovered Marquiese had tended to her evening chores. She smiled with pleasure and relief and went to bed.

The next morning, Marilana made an abbreviated patrol around her house and Lady Annabella's estates. Then she returned to her home. She slipped in the garden door and was surprised to find Marquiese in the kitchen dishing up a bowl of porridge.

"Good morning," Marquiese greeted her brightly. "Do you have time for a bowl, or are you just passing through?"

"I would like a bowl of porridge, thank you. While you're doing that, I'll bring in some more firewood," she said, smiling.

By the time Marilana returned, Marquiese had dished up a second bowl and placed them both on the table along with a bowl of fresh berries.

"I think you have a future as a chef," Marilana said after tasting the porridge.

"Let's hope it doesn't come to that," Marquiese admitted. "I think I'm better at cleaning up after."

When they were done and the kitchen was spotless, Marilana went into her room and traded her hunter garb for a simple, dark blue riding dress. She went back out to the main room and Marquiese stood up and studied her critically.

"You look terrific," he said, even though he could see how nervous she was. He laid a paw on her shoulder and smiled. "Everything is fine. The horses are ready, the knights are here, and you will do great. You have nothing to worry about."

Marilana relaxed a little and returned his smile. She tried to find something to say. When the words eluded her, she took a deep breath and simply nodded her head. "I'm off then."

She strung her bow and headed for Lady Annabella's estate, her pace brisk, and her attention ever alert.

That morning, Marilana and the stable staff bathed the three horses and brushed them until they shone. They cleaned and polished the tack, and the three grooms assisting her knew exactly what was expected of them.

Marilana took a deep breath and heard Marquiese's words of assurance in her mind as the visitors climbed the ladder up to the platform overlooking the training track. Lady Annabella and Captain-General Zariff gave her encouraging smiles as they lead the five visiting knights and various members of their delegations to the top. Several of the knights glanced at her suspiciously, then looked around as if expecting someone else. The last man to climb on to the platform, however, she had met before. He was a strong jaguar with a ready smile.

"Miss Marilana," he greeted her pleasantly. "It is a pleasure to see you again."

"Welcome, Master Roatal. I hope you have been pleased with your mount these last two years." Marilana forced a smile.

"Very pleased indeed," the jaguar nodded. "I couldn't resist the chance to return. I look forward to seeing what you have to show these worthy knights. May I introduce my younger brother, Sir Orthan? He is most interested in finding a strong charger of his own."

The younger jaguar stepped forward eagerly. He was younger than Marilana, but the obvious family resemblance caused her to smile more easily.

"Thank you for offering us the chance to see your newest mounts." Sir Orthan said eagerly. "I have been quite jealous of my brother's charger and look forward to obtaining one for myself."

"I look forward to it as well."

Lady Annabella stepped to the front of the box and everyone turned their attention to her.

"Knights of the Realm, thank you for responding to my invitation," Lady Annabella smiled. "Please allow me to introduce you to my secondary horse trainer and ward of my house, Marilana. Marilana please welcome Master Clain of Abdshar, Master Suwark of Cormorant Creek in Pavlatach, Sir Orthan of Pandensy in Versith, Sir Tavin of Coal Bend in West Cove, and Sir Fasub of Mantalor in Herinsford."

All eyes turned to Marilana with renewed interest, and she nodded her head in thanks to Lady Annabella.

"Welcome, good Knights, and thank you for coming. Five of you have indicated your interest in my newest war horses. At this time, I have only three to offer. Several more will be ready in two more years. Please step to the rail and allow me to detail the three horses before you," Marilana spoke clearly.

Marilana motioned to the grooms, and they led the three horses forward. She described the attributes of each horse as they were paraded along the track. Marilana presented each of the horses' bloodlines and spoke of the strengths of each. After three passes, the grooms carefully saddled the horses and rode them past the onlookers at a trot, then canter, and finally a gallop while she spoke about the training each had received. When she was done with her presentation, she invited the knights to ask any questions that they might have. She watched the five knights carefully as they studied the horses. All were her age or younger, but each studied the horses with trained eyes. Eventually Master Clain, the eldest of the group and a powerful puma, spoke without taking his eyes from the horses.

"Clearly, these are all fine animals," he said with a deep voice, "but I, for one, would like to see them a bit closer."

"Of course, Master Clain, please follow me." Marilana nodded and led the way down to the track.

Master Clain, his fellow knights, and several of their delegation followed Marilana to the track rail. "Is there one horse in particular you are interested in?" Marilana asked the puma.

"Not yet. I do not believe in judging a horse by looks alone," he replied brusquely.

"Might I suggest you take a look at the dapple first?" she asked and motioned to the first groom.

"Very well." They stepped onto the track and approached the dapple. The horse nuzzled Marilana happily and then flicked his ears suspiciously as Master Clain approached. The knights gave all three horses thorough examinations, and then Marilana gave the dapple's reins to Master Clain.

"Just like that?" he asked suspiciously.

"You need to find out if you and he can work together," Marilana said with an even smile. "Take him around the track and try out his paces."

Master Clain held the reins as Marilana backed away. She was impressed as the puma talked to the horse and scratched his ears before mounting up and starting the horse forward. Marilana then gave the reins of the roan to Sir Orthan and those of the black to Sir Tavin, a quiet, but observant eland.

They were all very good with the horses, and Marilana watched as they made their way around the track. She studied the way the riders controlled their mounts, and how the horses responded. The pairings were well matched. After a couple laps around the track, the riders traded off so that each of the knights had a chance to ride each of the horses. Sir Fasub, the youngest of the knights and a wiry tiger, had trouble controlling all three of the chargers, while Marilana disliked the amount of force Master Suwark used in trying to impose his will.

By the end of the session, Marilana could see that her initial instinct about the pairings had been correct.

It was getting late in the afternoon by the time the knights were satisfied with their evaluation of Marilana's three horses, and Lady Annabella was waiting for them when they were done.

"My good Knights, if you would, dinner will be served in an hour. Please consider what you have seen today, and Marilana and I will hear your thoughts in the morning," she announced.

Marilana watched the knights and their delegations head back to the castle. She then turned her attention to the grooms and the horses. She led them to the stables and helped rub the horses down and made sure they were settled in for the night.

Marilana then slipped into the castle and cleaned up before going home.

When she arrived, Marquiese was again reading by the light of a mostly shuttered lantern and was pleased to join her in the kitchen. Marilana ate a bowl of stew and told Marquiese all about her day. He was a good listener; he was relaxed and seemed content to just have company for a while. Marilana felt bad about leaving him alone all day, but she would have to leave him again tomorrow despite her feelings.

She arose early again the third morning.

She met Child and they patrolled the perimeter around Mystillion. She then went back to her house and changed into a rust-red riding dress. Marquiese was still sleeping, and she tried not to wake him while eating a bowl of fruit and the last of the stew.

She draped a cloak over her shoulder, gathered her weapons, and closed the door silently behind her.

She hurried to Lady Annabella's estates and spent the next hour preparing the war horses for jousting practice. Lady Annabella, Zariff, the knights, and their delegations arrived at the track at mid-morning.

"Good morning, my good Knights," Marilana greeted them. She studied each in turn, seeing, in particular, Sir Fasub's sulky posture. "Have you thought of any further questions you wish to ask me this morning?"

Sir Fasub looked at the older tiger standing next to him and then, somewhat predictably, stepped forward to address Marilana and Lady Annabella.

"My uncle and I have discussed the matter," Sir Fasub said regretfully. "He feels that I am not ready to obtain such a magnificent horse at this time. He feels that I need to work on my strength and horsemanship before making such a commitment. Therefore, I must regretfully withdraw my interest in these mounts."

"Perhaps in a couple of years we will be able to visit again and consider a different set of horses," Marilana said with a slight bow.

"I would like that," Sir Fasub said a bit happier. "Lady Annabella, my uncle says we must take our leave of you this morning and return home today rather than wait for tomorrow. Thank you for your hospitality."

"Thank you for your interest in these horses." Lady Annabella smiled politely. "Safe journey home, Sir Fasub."

After Sir Fasub and his contingent were headed back toward the castle, Master Suwark stepped forward. "Well, I, for one, want a second chance to ride these magnificent mounts," the rangy lion said. "They did not seem to respond to me as well as some others. I would like to try again. They may have just been tired from having multiple riders."

Marilana glanced at Master Clain as Master Suwark took the reins of the dapple, but the puma held his ground and said not a word.

"Master Suwark, if I might suggest, this horse responds best to a slight touch," Marilana advised. "Too much force could well confuse your wishes."

"You may be good at training riding horses, but I am a highly skilled combatant," Master Suwark replied haughtily. "I know how I want a war horse to behave. I do not need tips from a mere lioness."

Marilana bit back a caustic reply as the lion abruptly reined the horse around and galloped out onto the track. She felt Lady Annabella's paw on her shoulder, her touch light and reassuring. "Patience," she whispered.

Marilana drew a calming breath and nodded.

It did not go well. The dapple bucked and tossed his head as Master Suwark tried pointing him toward the start of the practice list. The lion cursed and the horse responded by twisting his head from side to side.

"He's not having much luck with that one, is he," Sir Orthan commented to the group.

"He should have listened to Miss Marilana," Master Roatal replied.

"I know a good horse when I see one, and the dapple responded well to me yesterday," Master Clain said, entering the conversation at last. "Do you really believe this young lioness knows how to train war horses?"

"Oh, indeed. I obtained my mount from her two years ago, and I could not have asked for a better trained charger," Roatal replied. "You came here because you liked the way my mount performed at the last tournament, is that not true, Clain? Listen to Marilana. She knows her horses."

Just then, Master Suwark spurred the dapple and sawed the reins. Marilana started forward as the horse reared angrily and threw his head back. Master Suwark crashed to the ground. The dapple spun in a circle and stomped his hooves down toward his tormentor. Master Suwark rolled out of the way even as Marilana sprang between him and the horse. The dapple tossed his head and tried to get around her.

"Whoa. It's all right." Marilana spread her arms wide and talked to the horse in a soothing tone. Though he was still blowing angrily, his teeth barred as Master Suwark scrabbled away, Marilana carefully reached out and took the reins. She moved closer and gently stroked his neck. The horse lowered his head and pressed against her. Marilana whispered, "Be still, brave one. It's all right."

"That was an impressive display of horsemanship and incredibly brave," Master Clain commented once Marilana led the horse back to the rail. "That horse could have killed you."

"You came to look at war horses, not riding horses," Marilana said hotly. "Do not mistake the horses' manners for a lack of spirit. They are well-trained, and I think it is time for a proper demonstration of their training."

Lady Annabella nodded her approval. Master Roatal smiled in anticipation. Marilana turned and vaulted into the dapple's saddle. She cantered down to the end of the track where a guardsman gave her a lance. She turned and walked the horse toward the start of the practice list, the dapple responding easily to her directions.

Marilana glanced at the watching crowd and Lady Annabella dropped her paw. Marilana nudged the horse to start and released the tension on the reins. The horse jumped forward and charged down the track. Marilana focused on her target, dropped the lance to chest level, and cradled it steadily. The tip of the lance cracked loudly against the quintain. Then she urged the horse on and they sped past as the heavily weighted bag spun, only just missing her.

She raised her lance and reined in the dapple as they reached the end of the list. Then she turned, set the horse at a trot, and returned to the spectators.

"Well done, Miss Marilana. I think you are even better than you were last time I visited," Master Roatal called, applauding her.

"Thank you, Master Roatal," Marilana acknowledged. She looked from one knight to the other. "As I indicated yesterday, the horses are trained in joust, rings, horseback archery, horseback sword fighting, and other knightly competitions. They need permanent riders in order to finish their training, thus allowing horse and rider to grow together as a working unit."

She dismounted and turned to face the group, waiting.

Master Suwark frowned and shook his head. "I'll not purchase one of these horses. They are not trained in a manner I like," he said coldly. "Lady Annabella, I must take my leave of you. Farewell."

"Safe journey, Master Suwark," Lady Annabella replied simply.

"Don't fall off your horse," Master Roatal muttered under his breath.

Lady Annabella shot him a warning glance, and the jaguar smiled ruefully.

"I, in contrast, would like to ride that dapple again, Miss Marilana," Master Clain said calmly.

Marilana bowed her head slightly and gave him the reins. He spoke calmly to the horse for a while and then mounted up and rode out on the track. Marilana motioned for the other two horses to be brought over. Sir Tavin stepped up to the black, and Sir Orthan took the reins of the roan. Marilana watched the three horses and their riders critically for the rest of the morning and into the afternoon. She occasionally called out suggestions to the riders, but was otherwise pleased with what she was seeing.

"You knew from the start that these pairings would work the best," Master Roatal commented quietly. "How?"

"Every horse is unique. As is every rider," Marilana replied. "Not all riders are compatible with all horses, nor are all riders compatible with all training techniques. Some trainers and riders prefer to use brute force to get a horse to do what they want. I believe that the best results come when the rider and horse work together as a single unit. I told you when you obtained your mount to spend time learning how he liked to perform, and that you should try to encourage him to perform with you. You said he has met all your expectations."

"Yes, he and I have formed a, well, a bond I guess you could call it," he said, smiling. "My horse doesn't like to be ridden by anyone else. He'll let the grooms exercise him and groom him, but when it is time to work, it is just me and him. Truthfully, I don't like to ride any other horse. I have my riding horses, of course, but when it comes to combat, he is my favorite. Riding him just feels right."

"I'm glad to hear that," Marilana said, nodding knowingly. "Maybe someday I'll have the chance to see you compete on him. I'd like to see how well you and he work together."

The three knights walked their mounts over to Marilana and dismounted. They were sweating and dirty, but all three smiled and rubbed the horses fondly.

Marilana nodded her approval and said to them, "One last piece of advice. Learn how your mount moves; learn his timing; learn his likes and dislikes. Spend time learning how he likes to perform. Do not try to force him to do something that is uncomfortable for him. Adjust your timing and your own movement to his. The best results come when the rider and horse form a distinctive bond and learn to be a team."

Lady Annabella approached the gathering and smiled when she saw how diligently the knights were listening to Marilana's words. When Marilana was done, Lady Annabella called to them. "My good Knights. I would be pleased to discuss the terms of purchasing these fine horses, if you are satisfied with your evaluations. I will allow you to clean up and speak with your delegations, and then I will meet you in my conference room one at a time. No matter how our business is completed, it would please me if you and your delegations would join me for dinner this evening."

"My delegation and I would be honored," Master Clain replied with a smile.

"As would I," added Sir Orthan and Sir Tavin at the same time.

"Will Miss Marilana be joining us?" asked Master Clain.

Marilana looked at Lady Annabella with a mixture of surprise and alarm. Lady Annabella held a clear expression.

"You can if you wish, Marilana. This is your success, after all," Lady Annabella said simply.

"Please, Miss Marilana, I would like to have a chance to speak with you more about your training philosophies," Master Clain said, his grin broad and his eyes sparkling.

"Oh, well, alright," Marilana agreed nervously. "I'll join you for dinner after I do one last check of the horses and cool them down for the evening."

"Marvelous. We look forward to it."

The knights and their delegations headed toward the castle. Lady Annabella held back a moment and shared a smile with Marilana. "Do not take too long with the horses, and please dress appropriately. You will be dining with nobles, so remember your manners. Don't be nervous, I know you can do it," Lady Annabella said quietly. "I'll send a carriage to pick you up from your house at dusk. Do not tarry."

"Yes, My Lady." Marilana curtseyed. She watched Lady Annabella walk away and then took charge of the horses. She checked each to make sure they were still in good condition and then gave the grooms their instructions for walking and grooming them. Then she hurried to the castle and bathed.

By the time she arrived home, the sun was starting to dip toward the western horizon and she knew she did not have much time to change. Marquiese smiled when she came in and then frowned at her harrowed expression.

"What's going on?" he asked. "Are you alright?"

"Everything is fine," she said. "I'm just nervous. One of the knights asked me to attend Lady Annabella's dinner. Master Clain said he would like to speak with me about the techniques I employ in training my horses. I suppose I should be flattered. I just came back here to change my clothes and tell you that I don't know when I'll be back."

"I see," Marquiese said quietly. "Well, I guess you need to change then. You don't want to be late."

Marilana studied his dark expression before going to her room and pulling the wardrobe key from under her bed. She chose a simple summer gown of Southern Tip green and long white gloves. She pulled down her broad-brimmed green hat and secured it on her head. She then opened the small jewelry box that Lady Annabella had given her and pulled out a simple silver chain with a white stone carved like the rearing horse on the Southern Tip crest. She clasped the necklace on and checked her appearance in the mirror. She took a deep breath to calm the fluttering in her stomach, locked the wardrobe, and put on her soft black leather shoes.

Marquiese was pacing the living room when she came out of her bedroom. He stopped and studied her critically.

"Very appropriate," he said, nodding seriously, and then pointed at her necklace. "I've never seen you wear jewelry before. It is a very nice accent. Very nice indeed."

"Thank you," she said, her stomach fluttering wildly.

"Don't worry, you'll make Lady Annabella proud," Marquiese said.

Marilana heard the sounds of horses and knew the carriage had arrived. "I have to go."

She looked back at Marquiese, and he tried to smile at her again.

*

Marilana was nervous all through dinner. She was careful to use proper etiquette and manners, just as Lady Annabella had taught her.

After dinner, Lady Annabella invited her guests into the parlor, and Master Clain and Master Roatal asked Marilana to join them.

The knights peppered her with questions about her training techniques for both war horses and riding horses, and Marilana answered truthfully. The only thing she kept secret was her training of Storm. She and Lady Annabella had decided that Storm would be her secret, her masterpiece, the one that everyone wanted to duplicate, but no one could. Lady Annabella predicted that the speculation and envy would heighten Marilana's reputation and attract more knights to her mounts.

Marilana did find, as she sat talking, that the attention of all these males was a little unnerving, and having Master Clain sitting on one side of her and Master Roatal on the other kept her stomach fluttering. She did enjoy the conversation however, especially when the knights were sharing some of their own stories of horses and home, and this helped her to relax.

It was close to midnight when the guests finally began to retire for the night. Master Clain offered his arm to Marilana, and she walked with him to the door where Lady Annabella was biding her guests a goodnight.

"Thank you for joining us tonight, Miss Marilana," Master Clain said with a regal bow. "I greatly enjoyed speaking with you, and I am eager to begin training with my new charger. He is a magnificent horse. I hope to get the chance to speak with you again sometime."

"It was my pleasure, Master Clain," Marilana replied with a curtsey. "Safe journey tomorrow, and perhaps we shall see what the future brings."

One by one, the knights bade Marilana good night. Master Roatal was the last to leave. He gave her small bow and smiled mischievously, saying, "I enjoyed talking with you, Marilana. You cleaned up very nicely for the evening. Perhaps Lady Annabella will allow you to attend more social gatherings in the future."

"Perhaps," Marilana replied quietly.

"Master Roatal, you are a shameless flatterer," Lady Annabella said, expertly intervening on her ward's behalf. "I suggest you save it for your betrothed."

"Lady Annabella, thank you for providing such a wonderful meal and such delightful dinner entertainment. You should bring your ward with you next time you visit Pandensy. I do enjoy the company of charming and beautiful ladies."

"Goodnight, Master Roatal," Lady Annabella said with exasperation.

Master Roatal bowed to Lady Annabella, smiled and winked at Marilana once more, then swaggered out of the room.

"Finally," Lady Annabella said with a deep sigh. "You acquitted yourself perfectly tonight, Marilana. If Master Suwark had been staying, I would not have let you attend. He prides himself on being the most charming creature in the room, and I would not have allowed him to ply his skills on you. I know you would not have been fooled, but I am not cruel enough to put you through that unprepared. Master Roatal and Master

Clain are charming enough on their own. They like to make beautiful young women blush, but they are basically harmless. They are both happily betrothed and do not like to see a woman pushed beyond her comfort.

"Earlier today they each insisted that I would not have cause to regret letting you join us for dinner. They wanted you here so that they could speak with you, and they stayed close to you to prevent anyone else thinking they could take advantage of you. I know they both hold true to the Knight's Code of Conduct."

"I am glad to know that," Marilana said. "I enjoyed the dinner, Lady Annabella. Thank you for allowing me to attend."

"I am glad you managed to enjoy yourself." Lady Annabella smiled. "Now it is late. The carriage is waiting to take you home. Goodnight Marilana."

"Goodnight, My Lady."

*

Marilana approached her door quietly, expecting Marquiese to be asleep. She unlatched the door and slipped inside. When she turned, Marquiese was pacing in front of the fireplace.

"I thought you would be asleep. I hope I didn't wake you," she said.

"I couldn't sleep," he said simply.

"It's an hour after midnight," she said. "Have you been pacing for seven hours?"

"At least I'm getting some exercise," he said with a grin.

"Did you at least eat something for dinner?"

"I had a bit of bread and cheese. I wasn't very hungry."

"Marquiese, what's wrong? Tell me."

"I . . . I was just worried. Restless," he said. "So how did it go?"

Marilana smiled and walked to her chair. She sat down and leaned back with a sigh. She told him all about her day. She told him about pairing the knights with her horses. She told him about the conversations during and after dinner. She did not tell him about Master Clain's and Master Roatal's flirtations, but she did tell him about their promise to protect her and that they were both betrothed. Marquiese relaxed as she talked and leaned against the wall opposite her. He chuckled when she finished.

"I was worried about Master Suwark," he admitted. "I know his reputation for charming young women. I agree with Lady Annabella that he cannot be trusted. Master Clain and Master Roatal have much more honorable reputations. I had not heard that they were both betrothed, but it doesn't surprise me. I've heard Sir Orthan would never dream of taking advantage of a woman, and Sir Tavin is still young enough to be afraid of most women. Although it sounds like he controlled your charger just fine for being so young yet."

"As young as he is, Sir Tavin is going to be a good competitor in a couple of years. He is big for his age and strong; with the added benefit of a good charger, he will be moving up in the competitions quickly. Sir Fasub is younger than Sir Tavin and is going to need a lot more training before he is really ready for a charger of his own, let alone competing against the others. Even Sir Graduin was in better control when he obtained his charger from me two years ago, and he was the same age as Sir Tavin."

"I know nothing about Sir Fasub or Sir Graduin. I'll have to watch for them if I return to Maefair."

"If you return? You have always said you would return."

"I don't know. Something may stop me. The future is uncertain," he said, looking evasively at the fireplace.

"What would you do if you didn't return? You're not much of a merchant, sorry to say. And you're definitely not good peasant material," Marilana said, chiding him gently.

Marquiese grinned at her. "And you, instead, have all the makings of an excellent noble."

Marilana blushed and looked down at her paws.

"So there was no dancing at dinner tonight?" Marquiese asked quietly.

"No, no dancing. Just a lot of talk."

Marquiese reached out suddenly and took hold of her paw. She looked up and met his soft gaze.

"Dance with me. One dance before bed," he said quietly. "May I?"

"You may," she whispered.

He pulled her gently to her feet, guiding her into the center of the room. Marilana smiled as he led her through the complex steps of a waltz, following easily. He smiled at her, their eyes level, and she became acutely aware of his paw on her waist. She tried to focus on the dance, but found his green eyes very distracting. All at once, she realized that they had stopped dancing and were standing gazing at each other, Marquiese's strong paw still on her waist. Breathing rather fast, Marilana backed slowly away.

"I should be going to bed," she said carefully. "Thank you for the dance. Thank you also for helping me relax after such a nervous evening. Goodnight, Marquiese."

He did not try to stop her; he just dropped his arms to his side and watched her, his gaze warm and intense. She turned toward her bedroom, breaking eye contact at last. She opened her door, then paused and looked back. Marquiese had turned and was staring thoughtfully at the cold fireplace. Marilana went into her room and locked the door behind her for the first time during his stay. She stared at the lock for a long while wondering if she had locked it to stop him from making a mistake they would both regret, or to stop herself. Either way she knew neither of them could allow their emotions to lead them down the path that had momentarily felt so appealing. Feeling disappointed and yet rather hopeful too, she changed her clothes, stretched as she always did, and went to bed.

24

The next few days passed in quiet routine. The knights and their delegations had left, and Lady Annabella's staff had gone back to their normal duties. Marilana resumed her lengthy dawn patrols. After sparring practice—which wasn't near as enjoyable without Marquiese—she would return home, and she and her guest would breakfast together and then share her daily chores. Neither of them mentioned the late night dance they had shared and managed to act as if nothing had happened between them.

On the seventh day of his confinement, Marilana could tell Marquiese was growing restless.

"Come on," she said after they cleaned up after breakfast. "Let's take a walk."

"I shouldn't leave the house," he said firmly. "It's too risky. If someone saw me, there would be a lot of questions, and the deception would be a failure."

"If you stay closed up in here much longer, you'll go stir crazy," she countered. "Come on. Trust me. Just a walk in the forest on a nice day."

"What about bandits?" he asked skeptically.

"I didn't see any sign of bandits this morning, and we'll be careful, I promise." She smiled easily.

Marquiese reluctantly agreed. They gathered their weapons and ventured out. They walked at their leisure for a while and then Marquiese practiced his tracking for a few hours. It was mid-afternoon when they returned to the house, and the lion seemed much more at ease again.

"Thank you," he said. "I really did need to get out of the house for a while and do something different. I practice my sword forms every morning, but getting out and stretching my legs felt really good."

"You're welcome." Marilana smiled. "I'm afraid I have to leave you again. I have my chores to do at the estate. Do you need anything before I leave?"

"No, I'm just fine," Marquiese said, returning her smile.

It was late when Marilana returned, and she found Marquiese in his bedroll on the floor. Though she did not think he was really asleep, he neither moved nor gave any acknowledgment of her presence, so she quietly went to her room and went to bed. The next morning during breakfast Marilana could tell something was bothering Marquiese.

"What's the matter?" she asked him. "You are very quiet and unusually distracted this morning."

"I thought I saw something last night while you were gone," he said quietly. "It was dark, and I was peering out through the arrow slits. I do that when I think I hear something outside. I thought I saw a shadow move along the back garden wall. I couldn't be sure. Then it seemed to move back up the hill into the underbrush and jump into a nearby tree. It didn't make a sound, but it definitely made my hackles rise."

"Show me where," Marilana said seriously.

Marilana went out alone first and scouted around, and then led Marquiese out to the back garden wall. He pointed first to the place where he'd seen the shadow and then to the trees where the intruder had fled. Marilana examined both closely. She then turned and led him deeper into the forest, following a trail only she could see and listening intently. Marilana froze when the trail was crossed by a more recent partial footprint.

"What is it?" Marquiese whispered nervously.

"Shhh." She hushed him with a look and then carefully scanned their surroundings. Something shifted and a flock of birds burst from a tree several dozen paces to her south. Whoever it was, they were now between them and Marilana's house. Not a good turn of events.

Marilana crouched low and led Marquiese quickly to the west. He mimicked her movements and followed closely. Off to the north, Marilana heard a sharp trill. When they entered a small clearing, the trill sounded four times in quick succession. Marilana crouched down and pulled a veil of plant roots away from a small opening, obviously one of her many hiding places.

She motioned to Marquiese, and he crawled in without hesitation. He saw parcels wrapped in oilcloth and long tubes secured in the walls near the entrance. There was a lantern hanging in niche toward the back.

Marilana followed him inside, covering signs of their hasty entry with fresh dirt and scratch marks.

She motioned for Marquiese to remain silent and then drew her dagger. They heard footsteps and suddenly something rather large blocked the light filtering into the cave. Marilana could just make out the tip of a sword glinting as it touched the freshly disturbed earth.

Marilana let out a low grunting growl, and the sword disappeared quickly.

"A Wild badger den," whispered the deep voice of a bear.

"The earth is freshly disturbed. It could be a trick," whispered a second voice, this also that of a bear.

Marilana growled again, this time more harshly.

"I'm not going to stick my head in to find out; I'm not stupid enough to tangle with a badger. Besides that opening is too small to fit through," the first bear whispered.

"All right, all right. Let's keep moving," the second one grumbled.

The light returned as the two creatures moved off. Marilana relaxed slightly, but maintained her attack stance. An hour passed before they heard a series of soft coos. Carefully,

Marilana pushed aside the covering and peered out. She motioned for Marquiese to stay put and then crawled out. She found Child crouched on the far side of a huge oak tree.

"Are they gone for the night?" Marilana whispered.

"No, Sissy," the doe replied. "They have moved on for now, but not for long, I fear."

"How many?"

"Many. Something is afoot," Child said. "I ran to Zariff, and he has his men riding to block the northern villages. He has asked me to scout for him, so I will not be able to watch your house for a time."

"I understand. We'll return there now and secure my doors. I will send word to Lady Annabella that I will not be visiting the castle tonight," Marilana said to her good friend. "One more thing. Were you at the house last night? Marquiese said he saw something."

"Yes. Keeping a watch. It was careless of me. I didn't mean to upset him," Child said. "I will visit you after the bandits have gone south. Until then, take care."

Child slipped silently away, and Marilana returned to the cave.

"Marquiese," she whispered. "Come! We have to hurry. There are bandits about."

Marquiese climbed out. Marilana fixed the dirt at the base of the hole to hide the marks of their passage again, and then quickly led Marquiese back south through the trees. There were many more tracks leading north through the forest, and Marilana realized that the bandits must have been close on their heels. They had been very lucky.

When they reached Marilana's cottage, Marquiese hurried inside while Marilana checked all the traps in her garden. When she came back in, she checked her crossbows and took inventory of her armory cabinet.

Marquiese paced the main room, but made sure to stay out of her way as she moved quickly about checking the windows and supplies. Finally, she banked the kitchen fire, sighed, and sat down at the table. Marquiese came in and joined her.

"I'm sorry," Marilana said quietly. "I should have been more careful and checked the area more closely. I should not have risked you going out there when you suspected someone had been here."

"So it was a bandit that I saw," Marquiese said darkly.

"No. No. It was The Phantom. She was checking on the house in my absence," Marilana replied. "But I should have consulted with her before leading you out into the forest."

"That cave. It's another one of your emergency shelters, isn't it?" he said.

"I knew we could not get back to my house, and the bandits were closing in all around us, so I led us there."

"What's in the oilcloth and tubes?"

"Blankets. A staff, a dagger, and extra arrows. There's also a hiding place for preserved food and lantern oil. I check the provisions every couple of months to keep them fresh."

"How many places like that do you have?"

"Maybe ten spaced out around Mystillion. More at different places around the Southern Tip." Marilana shrugged easily. "The Phantom also uses them. She travels around a lot more than I do, so she uses them more often and also replaces the stores as needed."

"What about the bandits? Have they moved on?"

"They will probably be passing back this way. Maybe a few, maybe a lot. And I know we left more of a trail than I would have liked. If they take the time to look, they will see we came back here. It may turn into a long night." Marilana paused and looked at the clock. "I need to talk to Captain Branth. He will be along shortly."

She led Marquiese into the main room where the lion took up a position out of sight from the door and windows, gripping the hilt of his sword.

Marilana watched through the arrow slits until the sounds of horses grew louder. "They're coming." She looked back at him and said, "Stay out of sight. I'll be right back in."

Then she slipped out the door and carefully made her way past her many traps to the gate and the road. Captain Branth called a halt when he saw her. She approached him and spoke quickly.

"Captain, The Phantom and I encountered a bandit group this afternoon. She is working with Captain-General Zariff as the bandits make their way north. She suspects some of them may return south along this stretch of forest. I will remain here and watch for them. Please let Lady Annabella know that I will not be coming to the castle tonight or in the morning."

"I will tell her," he replied quietly. "Zariff has ordered more patrols along the road this evening as well. We'll watch the houses, and the town is also on high alert. We'll be by a couple more times if you need anything," he replied quietly.

"Thank you, Captain." She nodded and hurried back to the house.

"So now what?" Marquiese asked seriously.

"So now we stay put and let The Phantom and Zariff take care of the bandit threat." She shuttered the lanterns and dampened the fire. "I sent word with Captain Branth that I would be staying here. Lady Annabella will understand my intentions."

"I'm sorry, Marilana," Marquiese said. "I know you would rather be out there helping to protect the people instead of babysitting. I feel useless. I'm good with a sword. Good with a bow. I could be out there helping you."

"Marquiese, no. Look at me," Marilana said gently stepping in front of him and meeting his eyes. "You are a champion of life. As am I. Just because you do not slay the guilty does not mean you are not protecting the people. You are important; your life is priceless compared to these bandits. I would not choose to risk your life just for the chance to track criminals through the forest. I choose how to live my life, and I choose to be here, protecting you. No one has the right to tell me what choices to make, not even you. I am where I am meant to be."

"You call me a champion of life, and yet it seems like everyone wants to tell me how I'm supposed to live my life," Marquiese said angrily. "Everyone thinks they have the right. Even you. You tell me I have to stay here. You tell me I have to stay hidden. That I have to stay safe."

"Well, there are worse things than people wanting you safe," Marilana said gently. "As for me, I will protect you wherever you choose to go. That is my duty, and I have accepted it. Accepted it gladly. I do not fully know who you are. You have the choice to leave that person behind and live a different life; however, I suspect doing your duty and staying safe is the harder path. One thing I do know about you is that you do not choose your path because it is the easy option. Everyone has an opinion. Everyone thinks they know what is best for everyone else. But in the end, it is your life and your choice.

"You asked me what we should do. I told you my plan of action. There are a lot of bandits out there more than a single group. Something big is going on. Getting caught unaware in the middle of it would be disastrous. Even both of us together could easily get overwhelmed. The Phantom has the advantage of knowledge of the group as she has been tracking it for hours already. Without similar knowledge, my instinct tells me it is safer for us to wait this out here. If you don't like it, then tell me what you think we should do before it's too late."

"No, you're right." Marquiese sighed in frustration. "I don't always like my choices, but I know the choice is mine. I will make the proper one and stay as safe as possible. I guess the decision isn't that hard. You don't even know who I am, yet here you are, ready to fight for me."

"Some choices are straight forward, like this one. Others are much more complex with outcomes as uncertain as the blowing wind." She took his paw. "Now come, let's not talk philosophy anymore tonight. Let's get something to eat while we have a few moments."

Marquiese nodded miserably and followed her to the kitchen. They ate stew and bread using the last light of the sinking sun. Then they set about their watch.

As the light faded, Marilana lit the lantern in the main room but kept it shuttered. She paced from room to room, keeping watch from different vantage points, while Marquiese kept his sword close and brooded darkly.

Several hours after nightfall, Marilana motioned for the lion to join her. "Shhh. They're here," she whispered.

Together they peeked out the arrow slits at the dark road and watched darkened shapes hesitantly crossing the open space between the trees. "I count a dozen," she hissed. "And there will be more crossing the road elsewhere."

"Friend or foe?"

"Friend. Lady Annabella's scouts. They are tracking the bandits fleeing to the south." Marilana knew that Child would be ahead of the scouts and tailing the bandits, and this gave her a measure of relief. "The Phantom will be with them."

Marquiese eased back into the room when he heard this and stifled a yawn.

"Why don't you go lie on my bed and get some sleep. I'll be keeping watch for a while yet," the lioness whispered.

"But . . . !"

"No. Go, sleep," Marilana insisted. She guided him to her room and closed the door behind him.

It was hours later when Marilana heard a soft hoot, followed by a chirp. Child! She went to the garden door and stepped out into the night. She made her way carefully to the back garden wall where the diminutive deer crouched, waiting for her.

"What news?" Marilana whispered.

"The bandits are many miles south and still heading for the border. Lady Annabella's scouts are still following them at a distance. I don't know what they were after. They came in a large group, all spread out, scouting the farms and towns as if they were looking for something. Zariff cut them off at the coal road and chased them back south. They didn't seem too surprised and fled immediately," Child reported seriously. Then she smiled. "It's been a very long night. I need to get some sleep."

"Thank you, my dear friend. You did well," Marilana said, smiling proudly. "Goodnight."

Child rose to her full height, hugged Marilana quickly, and bounded silently into the trees. Marilana hurried back into the house and made one more round of the windows. She saw nothing and sighed in relief.

She sat down in her chair and then froze at the sound of a quiet step. She looked up as Marquiese stepped into the room, his sword in his paw. Marilana's heartbeat quickened and nervous flutters invaded her stomach as she looked up at his strong arms and bare chest. It was a good thing she was sitting in the dark, because she was sure her face was as red as a ripe tomato, even through the thin fur on her cheeks. She forced her eyes up to his face, just as he knelt silently next to her chair.

"I heard voices," he whispered.

"Oh, I'm so sorry. It was The Phantom," Marilana replied apologetically. "She stopped by to give me a report."

"And?"

"And the bandits have left the area and Lady Annabella's scouts are continuing their pursuit."

"That is good to hear." He nodded his head and drew a deep breath. "Will you be patrolling this morning?"

"No. I have not yet slept," Marilana said. "And I sent word to Zariff that I would not be at sparring practice this morning. He will understand."

"Of course. Would you like your room back?"

"No. I will sleep here," Marilana said with a warm smile. She curled her feet up into the chair and laid her head on the arm. "Goodnight, Marquiese," she said lightly.

Marilana closed her eyes and immediately entered a healing trance that would allow her body to recover its energy while her mind stayed fully aware of her surroundings. She knew that the lion was watching her, and she knew the exact moment he retreated across the room and crawled into his bedroll.

The mid-morning light was streaming through the windows when Marquiese opened his eyes again. He looked over and saw that Marilana was still sleeping in the chair. He stretched and smiled and came to his feet. He glanced over at Marilana again and was startled to see her eyes wide open and fully awake.

"Good morning." She smiled at him and then uncurled from the chair. "Did you sleep well?"

"Like a log. Yes. I must have needed it."

Marilana set about her morning chores, and Marquiese went into the washroom to freshen up. When he was done, he retrieved his shirt from where he had left it on her bed the night before. He had been uncomfortable about sleeping in her bed and so he had lain restlessly on the floor. He knew now that it had been the right decision.

He stretched a bit more and wandered into the kitchen. Marilana was setting the porridge pot on to cook and had set out a bowl of fresh apples.

"Help yourself," she said. "I'll only be a minute."

While Marilana made her way to the washroom and her bedroom, Marquiese took a knife from the block on the counter and sat down at the table. He peeled and cut up two of the apples. A few minutes later the porridge was ready. He dished up two bowls full and added the apple pieces. Then he thinly sliced the apple peel and twisted the slices into little curls that he used to decorate the bowls.

Marilana came into the kitchen a few minutes later and smiled when she saw this.

"Marquiese, that looks beautiful," she said with a playful laugh. "You can help me prepare dinner tonight for Lady Annabella's etiquette lesson. You may not be much of a cook, but you sure have an eye for presentation."

"Just something I learned in Maefair," he said, picking up his spoon.

They ate in silence for a time, and then Marquiese looked up at her and said, "Can I ask you something?"

"Of course. Just don't expect me to answer if I don't think it appropriate," she said, laughing easily.

"When you laid down this morning, I was surprised at how fast you were asleep. It almost seemed as if you were not asleep at all. Was it a trick?"

"Not a trick. A trance. Called the healing trance, to be precise. It is one of the methods I perfected from my study of the old ways of healing. It is very useful for several reasons. First, it is very quick to enter and just as quick to end, as you noticed. I can enter it just by closing my eyes and concentrating on my breathing. Second, it can speed healing of minor wounds or help me regain my alertness with minimal amount of rest. Third, it allows me to remain aware of my surroundings even though my body is at rest. I knew where you were the whole time, which is why I woke up when you did. Plus, I was listening to the early morning sounds and would have been ready to respond immediately had anyone or anything approached the house."

"It sounds too good to be true. Do you use it all the time?"

"No, I don't. You can't," Marilana said seriously. "Every change made to the body's normal rhythms has a cost, and if pushed too far, most of those costs can become deadly. In this case, the healing trance is very safe under normal conditions.

When you sleep, your body slows its energy use. The little energy that is used goes to digestion, growth, and healing. The trance allows the muscles to relax and regain energy, but it also allows energy to be used by the mind to stay alert and redirects the energy of digestion toward healing. It will keep the body going longer and heal faster, but impeding digestion can be dangerous, because digestion gives the body energy. I never use the trance soon after eating. And the trance is not a replacement for a good night's rest. The mind needs to rest, and if you don't allow it to rest, it can become over stimulated and easily fatigued.

"The biggest risk comes when you use the trance for too long. Your body has only as much energy as you give it, and it needs to rest regularly to maintain its energy balance. If you use up all of your energy with the trance, you will start using your body's reserves. This is not a good idea. When you have no energy coming in, and no more reserves, you can send your body into energy starvation and you could die without proper help to recover.

"I balance the risks with the benefits. I only use the healing trance if I feel the need to, like last night."

"Could I learn it?" Marquiese asked.

"No. Sorry. You're too old. The healing trance can only be learned as a child when the energies and pathways of the body are still malleable. The older the body gets, the harder it is to change."

"I know one thing. You don't sleep as much as most people do. Does that have something to do with the healing trance?"

"It has to do with training. Training and necessity. Most servants and guardsmen learn how to live comfortably with less sleep. It's just a fact of life. A single guardsman assigned to a post must still sleep, even if it is an all day and night post. Captain-General Zariff taught me that there are times when a guard can sleep at his post, at least if it is a low priority post. A guard wouldn't sleep if he were guarding a dangerous prisoner or someone whose life was in emanate danger. However, if he is guarding someone day and night, the guard could sleep while the subject sleeps as long as he takes precautions, lying across the doorway, training to wake with certain trigger sounds, and other such tricks. He could also sleep when other guards are around and he is just waiting, such as while the subject is dining with others. It is very similar for a maidservant. When in public view, the maidservant must be proper and aware at all times, but if waiting out of sight for several hours, sleeping is alright as long as she can wake and be ready when called for. It takes years of training to get really good at it, but most experienced guards and servants are good at it because they have to be. Same for me."

"Nothing can replace a good, uninterrupted sleep, no matter what you say," Marquiese said, with a grin.

"Well, necessity can be a strong motivator. And speaking of motivation, I need to go out and do some work in the garden so we have something for dinner."

"My kind of motivation," Marquiese said, smiling warmly. "I wish I could help, but I should stay inside."

"Yes, you should," Marilana laughed.

25

A part of Marilana may have been relieved to finally have her house back after Marquiese returned to the brick manor two days later, but she quickly found that she missed his company.

This was new for Marilana. The lioness had always enjoyed her solitude. Growing up in Lady Annabella's castle, she had become accustomed to living in the midst of constant activity. Her room in the servant quarters was one of the only places she could find any time to herself. The library was another. It was quiet. Yes, the librarian and her helpers were almost always close by, but they insisted on quiet to allow their visitors to focus. Marilana had spent many hours of her childhood in Lady Annabella's library. She had spent nearly as much time in the library at school. She read to learn, she read to relax, and she read to hide.

Once she moved into her own house, she learned to love the silence and the solitude. She could study without interruption. She loved spending time alone in the forest, tending to her garden, and listening to the sounds of nature. Even when Child had lived with her, Marilana loved her alone time. She was more focused. She had less stray thoughts to distract her from her duties. She was a better bandit hunter. She had been able to perfect her tracking and stealth abilities. When she felt lonely—which she occasionally did—she sought the company of others, especially her friends at Lady Annabella's castle. She sparred everyday and trained her horses. She attended school. Those activities were usually stimulating enough, and at the end of the day, she was happy to retreat back into her own world.

Then Marquiese came into her life. His company was different somehow. She had worried that his stay at her house would only allow them the chance to find out just how long they could tolerate each other, and that they would be pleased when things went back to normal. Instead, she wanted more time. The visit had been filled with extremes: the hectic and the stressful, the dull and the boring. But she would not have given back any of the time they had spent together. Now when she entered her house it seemed empty and lifeless without Marquiese there. She continued to see him every morning for sparring practice and cherished every moment, but it was not enough.

Now, for once in her life, she was looking forward to the start of the new school year so that she could spend more time with him. Her thoughts returned again and again to the late night dance and she could feel in her heart that something had changed in what she felt toward Marquiese.

This was a thought she kept close to her heart as classes resumed for their second year of finishing school. It didn't begin much differently than the previous year had ended. Mistress Rose's focus was once again on etiquette, dance, and the laws of the merchant caste, three important keys to life and society in the Southern Tip.

As classes started, Marilana and Marquiese resumed as they had before, showing slow but steady improvement. Marquiese responded well to their teacher's suggestion that he take one piece of etiquette at a time until he could fit all the pieces together. This gave Mistress Rose a reason to feel encouraged, while still giving Brittia plenty of reason to gloat. Marilana responded to the lynx's barrage of negative comments by simply ignoring her. This, of course, made Brittia even angrier; after all, she had not forgotten Marilana's comment that Brittia could never beat her down.

Marilana's after school routine with Marquiese and Earek renewed as if it had never ended, and she felt as happy as she ever had.

The first day of the second fifnight of school arrived under a blue sky and a brilliant sun. Everyone had taken their midday break outside because the weather had produced a perfect fall day. Marilana sat in an alcove with a book in her paws, though she seemed more interested in watching Marquiese and Earek play wall ball with Klay and Caton than the page opened before her. She was about to give up any pretense of reading when a shadow peeked around the corner and waved. It was Lida, smiling nervously as she came and sat down next to the lioness.

"Lida! Hello! What are you doing?" Marilana asked quietly.

"I hope I am not interrupting," the tawny furred lioness said.

"Not at all. But you do know that Brittia will be furious if she sees you talking to me."

"I don't care," Lida said firmly. "I have a problem, and I wanted to see if you might be able to help me."

"What kind of problem?"

"Well, I'm struggling with my history marks. Marquiese helps sometimes, but he's really not much help. I was wondering if you might be able to tutor me during the lunch sometimes?"

"Well, I'm honored that you would think of me, but you should not dismiss Brittia's warnings," Marilana said truthfully. "She can make life difficult for you and your family if she chooses to."

"That's right, I can," Brittia said stepping suddenly into the alcove with her sycophants in tow. "You should listen to Marilana, little one. It's bad enough that your brother spends so much of his time with her and that he has taken Earek down that path with him. I have let it go too far. I must draw the line with you, I'm afraid."

"I can do as I like," Lida said, jumping to her feet and facing Brittia with her paws in fists at her sides. "You are not the boss of me, Brittia."

"Are you challenging my rank, girl?" the lynx hissed coldly.

"What's the matter Brittia?" Marilana asked haughtily. "Afraid Lida might start getting better marks than you?"

"When your marks are the highest in the school, that is hardly one's worry."

"Then you must be afraid she'll begin to recognize all the less-than-brilliant things you say every day." Marilana leaned against the wall and smiled lazily up at the lynx.

"Tutor the whole school, if you like, Marilana. I hold the highest rank at this school, and nothing you do can ever change that."

"So I can tutor anyone who comes to me, and you won't have a problem with it? Is that what you're saying? Aren't you afraid they might plot against you?"

"Plot against me? What ridiculous nonsense." Brittia forced a laugh, and her followers laughed uneasily. "I don't care what you do, Marilana. Like I said, tutor the whole school. See if I care."

Brittia turned and flounced away, her followers exchanging confused looks and muttering behind their paws.

"Wow! How did you do that?" Lida asked with awe. "I thought for sure I was going to end up in the headmistress' office."

"Lida, what you did was very dangerous," Marilana said quietly. "I redirected Brittia's anger and used it to twist her words against her. However, she will not forget that you put her in this position. You stood up to her as an equal."

"I am her equal," Lida said hotly.

"I know," Marilana said soothingly. "But you are putting Marquiese and your family at risk if you act that way. You must remember that you are a second child here in Mystillion. You have less rank. I know it is hard for you. But it is dangerous, possibly deadly, to forget. You must be in control at all times."

"Yes, Marilana." Lida sighed with resignation. "I won't forget."

"Good. Now come and tell me what you are studying," Marilana said lightly.

Lida opened her book and told Marilana about her history studies and the difficulties she was having. It wasn't long before several of her classmates joined them, as hesitant as they may have been, and the entire group poured over their history books until the bell rang.

Marilana watched as Lida and her classmates made their way inside and felt good about helping them. She had always loved learning and helping others learn. It just felt right. She knew this was part of why her parents had loved being scholars.

She walked confidently into Mistress Rose's classroom and tried not to cringe when she found Headmistress Ceta waiting for the class. The headmistress glared at her for a moment and then did what she always did; she turned away and ignored her.

"I have an important announcement to make, and you will all pay close attention," Headmistress Ceta said when the class had settled down. "This year, as some of you may know, is the year of the Winter Masquerade."

Whispers of delight and curiosity broke out around the room and the headmistress waited until the excitement had subsided and everyone was paying attention again.

"Most of you know what the Winter Masquerade entails, but for those who don't, I will explain," the headmistress continued. "Once every three years, the schools of the province come together for a dance. It is only for the students in Finishing School. It gives all the smaller schools a chance to bring their students together with others students of the same age and similar ability. It is a chance to practice etiquette and dance, meet new people, and make new acquaintances. The dance will be held here in Mystillion, since we are the largest school in the province, on the last day of the first month after the New Year. You have lots of time to perfect the dances that you know. I expect each and every one of you to perform your best, and to hold yourselves to the highest standards of behavior. I will personally punish anyone who brings dishonor on our school.

"Lady Annabella has informed me that she has a number of surprises in store for us this year. She would not tell me what she is planning, and a number of details are still in negotiation, but she did say that I could hint at visits from some high ranking individuals."

Excited whispers broke out once again. This time Headmistress Ceta smiled indulgently. She turned to leave and spotted Marilana standing near the door.

"Marilana, you will not be attending the dance," she said firmly. "We don't need to embarrass our school by allowing a peasant to dance with high ranking individuals."

"Yes, Headmistress," Marilana said, acknowledging this with a small curtsey.

The headmistress left and Mistress Rose called the class to attention again. "So let us get to work. Everyone in your lines."

Mistress Rose had started the new school year with review of the four dances they had learned last year, which were the simple waltz, the allemande, the landler, and the cotillion. Marilana and Marquiese had both shown that they could perform the steps of each dance, claiming lots of practice, but they were careful to do only the steps, and leave out all the flourishes that would have made the dances complete. Now Mistress Rose was teaching them the next new dance, the high reel. Marilana performed the simple peasant reel instead. It allowed her to keep pace during the promenade, which due to the similar sequences in the landler she should be able to perform, but she tripped and stumbled through the more complex paired parts of the dance. When she and Marquiese took their turn together, she found that Marquiese was dancing a different reel entirely and so they still tripped and stumbled, and nearly bumped the line hard enough to knock the rest of the class off balance.

Marquiese feigned a shameful grimace, and Marilana managed to blush with embarrassment. "Sorry, Mistress Rose."

"It could have been worse," Mistress Rose said to them, nodding her encouragement. "The point is that you are trying and effort leads to improvement."

*

Marilana was glad when the final bell rang and signaled the end of the day.

She retrieved her weapons from the headmistress and made her way outside. She spotted Marquiese and Brittia locked in a serious conversation and realized it most certainly had to do with her encounter with the lynx during lunch.

When Marilana and her student charges started down the East Road, Marquiese broke away from Brittia and joined his sister Lida for the walk home. Marilana could not hear what Marquiese was saying, but Lida kept shaking her head, a definite show of defiance, and she refused to meet Marquiese's eyes. Surely he was warning her against challenging Brittia's rank, much as Marilana had earlier. Moreover, Brittia's smile as she walked toward her house confirmed this; the smirk that the lynx shared with Marilana as she entered the gate out front of her house said even more. Rank was a powerful thing in the Southern Tip. Challenging it could have serious consequences.

When they reached the brick manor, Marquiese walked Lida to the front gate where Adealy was waiting for them. The three of them had a whispered conversation that clearly made Earek fidget. He said, "What's going on, Marilana? Did Lida step out of line or something?"

"I am sure that Marquiese will explain it, assuming he chooses to," Marilana said.

A few minutes later, Marquiese rejoined them, and Marilana led them through the forest to her house. No one said a word. Neither did Earek question the lion once they entered the cottage and settled in. They worked at their own pace on their homework and Marilana did her chores. When their books were closed and her work was done, Marquiese finally broke the silence that had ruled over the cottage for the last hour.

"Thank you for letting me brood," the lion said to them. "I am lucky to have such patient friends."

"So what's the story?" Earek asked. "Did something happen with Lida?"

Marilana gave the leopard her account of the encounter with Lida and Brittia at lunch. Then she looked at Marquiese and said, "So what did Brittia have to say to you this afternoon?"

"She warned me that Lida may need a lesson to remind her of her proper place."

"I'm surprised that Lida didn't end up in the headmistress' office or face six lashes with the cane," Earek said. "Brittia must be slipping."

"I convinced her to let the situation be," the lioness said.

"What? How?"

"It was a simple trick of redirection." Marilana shrugged. "I drew Brittia's anger away from Lida and onto me. Then I twisted it back at Brittia. She walked right into my trap. She couldn't back out without looking foolish. I'm sure she'll find a way to get back at me, but I'm more concerned about her getting back at Lida."

"I heard what Headmistress Ceta said to you on her way out of class this afternoon, about not being allowed to attend the Winter Masquerade." Earek sighed. "As if that was some sort of punishment."

"Definitely not a punishment." Marilana shrugged again. "Honestly, with the amount of attention Lady Annabella is giving to the Masquerade, I won't know if I'll be attending or not until I hear it from her. She has the final say."

"Thank you for protecting Lida," Marquiese said. "I can understand why Brittia was so mad. If you hadn't redirected her thoughts, she would have dragged Lida to the headmistress right then and there. Lida took a terrible risk for little gain. I wish she had spoken to me before she approached you."

"It's alright," Marilana said to him calmly. "Lida's a good girl. She'll make an excellent merchant someday. She is in a difficult position. It is taking all her will power to maintain the appearance of being the second child in your 'family.' That is very difficult at her age. She should be learning to take command and reach for what she wants, yet she has to hold back for your sake."

"What is Lida now, eight or nine? At that age, I was frustrated being the second child too," Earek added. "I wanted to be able to do the things Adrek was doing. I wanted to be able to act as Brittia's equal rather than licking her boots all the time. It must be even harder for Lida."

"I try to help her," Marquiese said dejectedly. "She gets fairly good marks on most of her work. Her math is excellent. It is history she struggles with. Neither Merchant Colbran nor Adealy are very helpful when it comes to history, I'm afraid. I sit down with her some times, but . . . ."

"But you feel guilty whenever you do," Marilana said, finishing his thought.

"Merchant Colbran would have hired a tutor for her in Maefair," Marquiese said, sighing. "They play their part to help me, but they chafe sometimes when they cannot get the things they normally would were they still in Maefair. And Lida feels the effects too."

"Like I said, I have no problem tutoring Lida if it helps ease her stress and keeps her focused."

"Thank you, my friend." Marquiese smiled at her. "I just hope we can avoid any unpleasantness."

"Don't worry about Brittia," Earek said lightly. "I have a plan to distract her for the next few months."

"Oh?" Marilana said. "And would this plan have anything to do with costume designs for a certain Masquerade Ball?"

"You know me too well, Marilana." Earek winked. "Or at least you know Brittia's greatest passion. In either case, I think Brittia is going to be spending many an hour looking through books of patterns and bolts of cloth. Never fear."

26

It was Restday, and Marilana led Marquiese into the forest after sparring practice. They had done well that morning, working effectively with the horses and calling a draw when they sparred. Marilana felt good physically, but she had several things on her mind that needed sorting out.

"Marilana? Do you think we can go to the lake for an hour or so?" Marquiese called to her.

Before answering, Marilana studied the late fall sky and the nearly bare trees. She listened to the sounds of the forest. Everything seemed calm and quiet.

"I don't see why not. But we will have to be careful. No swimming this time."

She led him carefully through the trees and scouted thoroughly before coming to the meadow that was home to the small waterfall and the crystal clear lake. Marquiese sighed with contentment as he stretched out in the dying grass and watched the clouds rolling across the bright blue sky. Marilana sat beside him, but kept a paw on her bow and listened intently to the sounds of the forest.

"Why did you want to come here?" she asked quietly.

"Just to relax and spend some time in the fresh air. Everyone has been so busy lately with all the Winter Masquerade preparations, I just wanted some time to enjoy the last days of this fantastic weather."

Marilana smiled when she heard this, but the smile was short-lived. She turned her gaze to the shimmering water and her brow furrowed.

"What's the matter?" he asked quietly. "You've been on edge for days now. What's going on? "

"You're still planning to be sick for the Masquerade Ball, is that right?" she asked softly.

"Yes. I think it would be better if I did not go. I could, of course, slip out before the reveal. But it would still be risky, and somebody would probably figure out which costume was mine in any case," he said lightly. "Of course I had to have a costume and a mask made. It is a shame they will not be worn. Merchant Yulan's wife is a wonderful masker. It is a fantastic grasshopper with two arms connected to the belt. The arms attach to a pair of gloves and follow the movements of my real arms. Then there is a cape embroidered to look like wings. You would have liked it."

"You'll have to show it to me sometime."

"Why do you ask?"

"I'm not supposed to tell anyone, but there is something I think you should know ahead of time," Marilana said seriously. "Later this fifnight, before Lady Annabella leaves for the annual tournament in Maefair, she is going to announce that she has invited some noble children from around the province to come to the Masquerade. Most are from various noble families of the Southern Tip, and a dozen or so are our age. However, she also received a letter of acceptance yesterday from Master Fredrick Arndt and Master Warhaim Arndt."

Marquiese sat up and frowned when he heard this.

"Why did she invite them?" he asked gruffly.

"It's supposed to be a surprise," Marilana said honestly. "But I thought it might be better for you to avoid the alarm and the suspicion. You and she discussed your plan to be sick, so she knows you will not be attending the dance, and you can skip sparring practice while they're here. They will not see you. When I asked why she had invited them, she said she had her reasons. End of story."

"So she is hiding something from you," he said darkly.

"She hides many things from me." Marilana laughed. "Peasant wards are not included in the planning of affairs of state."

"That's true, but I wish I knew her intent," he replied with a sigh. "Why did she tell you ahead of time?"

"Because she wants me to attend the dance." Marilana fidgeted with the hem of her dress and looked down at her feet. "I insisted that I will not attend the dinner and won't stay for the reveal. She agreed, but she insisted that I dance properly. I have an appointment with her seamstress later today to begin working on my costume."

"I'm sure you will do fine," Marquiese said evenly.

Marilana detected a trace of harshness in his voice, but she chose not to ask him what he was thinking. A moment later, he changed the subject and said, "But there's something else bothering you. I can tell. What is it?"

Marilana didn't answer right away. She hadn't planned on telling Marquiese about the increase in bandit activity in the area, but now she thought it better to do so. "According to The Phantom, a number of bandit groups have been very active lately. This fits with what I've seen as well. That raid that we avoided last summer—the one when they seemed to be looking for something and we weren't sure what it was—well, they have been making similar raids all over the Southern Tip. Usually this late in the year, the bandit activity should be lessening, but it is not."

Marquiese frowned. "Why do you think? Was it a bad harvest?"

"No, it was a good harvest, in fact," Marilana replied.

"You want to be out there tracking them, don't you?" he said levelly.

"I'll be honest. I do want to know what they're up to. I want to know what they're looking for," Marilana said darkly. "The raids are following a distinct pattern, one we haven't seen before. It could just be that a new bandit leader is trying out a new idea. But if it is, he has not made any profit given the amount of personnel they're using. It makes me uneasy."

"And?"

"And I have an uneasy suspicion about who they're looking for."

Marilana turned and studied Marquiese worriedly. He refused to meet her eyes. Instead, he sat stiffly looking out at the water as if all the pleasure of their outing had been stripped away.

"You've been here for over two years, Marquiese," she persisted. "Every day the chance increases that someone has shared your description with an interested party. Maybe the bandits are just shooting blind and trying to make you jump. But whatever their plan is, whoever is after you has not given up."

Marilana was afraid to push him too far, but she had to be honest.

"You've been lucky so far," she said softly. "I don't know how much longer you'll be safe here."

Marquiese stared off into the trees, lost in his own dark thoughts. "Are you telling me to leave the Southern Tip?" he asked.

"I want you to be aware of the situation," she said as her stomach froze into a ball of ice. "I don't know why you are hiding here, but I think that whoever is looking for you is paying a lot to find you and I doubt seriously that they are your friend. I want you to think about your options carefully before you do anything."

"Could you hide me?" he asked, his voice still cold.

"I could teach you to be a ghost in the forest," she replied honestly. "I could find you a house deep in the forest. I could make it a fortress that the bandits wouldn't touch. You would have to hide constantly. I would bring you your supplies and try my best to make sure you survived, but it would not be good for you. You are a social creature. Just think about the two fifnights you stayed at my house; you nearly went stir crazy. And besides, even a fortress can be besieged or overrun with enough manpower. I am not invincible, they would eventually stop me and get to you.

"Another option is for you to continue what you are doing now. Move to a new place with new names, new faces, new stories to tell, and new lies to live. But again, I don't know how long it would take for someone to figure it out.

"The only other option that I can see is for you to return home to Maefair and face your past. It is the option you have always spoken of. The one you wanted to take before. I know you are strong enough to face whatever consequences that might bring."

"That option involves taking the fight to my pursuer and facing my duty," Marquiese said.

"You would never need to hide again," Marilana added gently.

"Do you want me to leave?" he asked firmly.

"This is not about what I want," Marilana replied looking down at her paws.

"Marilana, do you want me to leave?" he asked again.

"No, Marquiese, I don't want you to leave," she whispered nervously. "You are the best friend I have ever had. I don't know what will happen when you leave."

"You'll still have Earek," Marquiese said gently.

"Earek defied Brittia and went against his mother's wishes to study with me. The only reason they tolerate his continued contact with me is because of you. When you leave, he will have to face them and make some choices. I don't begrudge him that."

"What is the point of being high ranking if it means turning your back on your best friends?" Marquiese asked softly.

"Are you speaking of Earek or yourself?" the lioness asked honestly.

The lion turned his eyes on her. "You are the best friend I've ever had too," he said. Then he looked away. "The snows will be coming soon. The bandit activity will decrease. I'll not make my decision yet. We are just speculating; they could well be looking for something or someone else. We'll just have to see what the spring brings."

Marilana said nothing. They sat in silence for a long while, she with an eye on the forest even as she studied his stern posture. Marilana would have liked nothing more than to stay right where they were, talking and enjoying their mutual company, but she knew how unwise that was. So she gathered her bow and stood.

"We've been out in the open too long," she said quietly. "We need to move."

Marquiese eyed the trees warily, nodded, and came to his feet. "Yes, and you need to report to Lady Annabella. You have your duty to fulfill."

Marilana said nothing in response to this. She led him quickly into the cover of the trees, and they moved in near silence back to the brick manor.

She wondered as she left him if duty was the only thing she could count on in her future.

*

The last four fifnights before the Winter Masquerade were extremely hectic. Merchant Yulan had so much work that Earek spent every minute outside of school at the tailor's shop. Everyone was getting the last fittings done to their costumes.

Lady Annabella returned early from Maefair, just after the New Year, and she insisted that Marilana practice her dancing every evening rather than doing her normal studies and chores at the castle. Few could match her skill and her grace.

At school, Mistress Rose had her class practicing their etiquette and reviewing their dances under the strictest of criticism. Headmistress Ceta visited all three of the finishing classes every day. The stress at school was high; even the lower classes were feeling the tension.

The last fifnight was, of course, the worst. Merchant families in town had offered to house the students coming from the schools around the province and Lady Annabella was housing the nobles at her castle. Everyone was scrubbing and cleaning as if their lives depended upon it. Lady Annabella sent a contingent of castle staff to scrub the school to meet her high standard. She even had a contingent of servants assigned to decorate the school and another to serve the dinner and refreshments the night of the dance. Marilana overheard some of the staff complaining about the extra work, but most laughed and said they couldn't wait to see all the pomp and glitter.

27

On the day of the Masquerade, Marilana waited nervously in her room in the servant quarters after eating a light meal. All the guests had arrived the day before, and school had been cancelled for the day so that the schoolhouse could be decorated and the food properly prepared. Marilana's attendance at the Masquerade had been kept secret from the other students; it had also been kept from the noble guests. So here she was, pacing in her room and listening to the bustle of activity as the nobles were attired and pampered. Nervous, she was also excited.

That's when she heard a soft tapping on the door. A moment later, Lady Annabella and her seamstress entered. On their heels were two of the seamstress' assistants carrying Marilana's costume. Carefully yet quickly the women arrayed the young lioness in the garment. When they were done, Marilana studied the effect in her mirror. The pale gold gown was covered with strips of darker golden lace that simulated the rise and fall of feathers when she moved. The long sleeves ended in bunches of golden lace that obscured her paws. She wore long white gloves underneath the sleeves. White hose with white slippers encased her legs under the gown. A pale gold cloth wrapped around her neck and covered her head so that no part of her fur could be seen. The beautifully crafted bird of prey mask fit closely over her face, draping golden lace feathers over her head and leaving only her eyes visible. Marilana had practiced wearing the elaborate mask so she knew how to hold her head and move without knocking it off.

Looking back from the mirror her eyes showed a trace of fear that she controlled with a deep breath.

"Ready," she whispered.

The seamstress beamed at her and covered the costume with a voluminous dark cloak. Lady Annabella pulled up the hood and rested her paws on Marilana's shoulders. "Yes, you are. And I want you to enjoy the dancing," the noble lioness said calmly to her ward. "I know you are nervous, and slightly afraid of what the night will bring, but I want you to relax. You are my firebird. Let me worry about the future while you enjoy showing off for a change."

"Yes, My Lady," Marilana whispered, meeting Lady Annabella's smile.

Marilana hurried out to the unmarked black carriage that was waiting in the stableyard. A small escort of guardsmen were dressed in black with no insignia. Earek's younger brother Jarek opened the door and helped her climb in. He climbed in behind her and knocked to the driver.

"We're with you all evening," he said, smiling at her. "If you need to get away from a pursuer, give us a circle signal, and we'll make sure to give your pursuer a proper run around."

"You're just hoping for some excitement," Marilana said, laughing. "I know escort duty is bad enough, but to have to sit and wait for me to return is even worse."

"At least we get to escort the mysterious, unknown dancer of the evening instead of those snobby lordlings." Jarek smiled. "We didn't even know we were going to be on duty until an hour ago when Zariff personally picked us from the barracks. Surely you'll provide us with a little excitement for our troubles."

"Personally, I'm hoping to be in and out without any excitement at all," Marilana replied.

"You'll do fine." He laughed lightly. "You can tell me all about Earek's performance on the ride back, and I'll regale you with soldier gossip. Deal?"

"Deal." Marilana nodded with a laugh.

They arrived shortly and Jarek helped Marilana down. The lioness took a deep breath and hurried into the schoolhouse. The hallway was dimly lit, and she could hear the murmur of voices coming from the eating hall. A servant in Lady Annabella's livery stepped out of a shadowy doorway and hurried to meet her. Marilana glided forward as Lady Annabella had taught her, but kept to the shadowy side of the hall.

"Good, you're right on time," Taslin said quietly. "Dinner is ended, and they are just finishing rearranging the room for the dancing. If you slip in now, no one will notice your arrival."

Just then the door to the ladies room opened, and a group of girls flounced down the hall toward the eating hall. Taslin took Marilana's cloak and gave her an encouraging smile. Marilana caught up with the girls and entered the hall as if she were one of them. Hopefully no one would readily notice.

The eating hall was brightly lit and wonderfully decorated. White and green and red ribbons festooned the walls and crisscrossed the ceiling. White and red flowers, imported from the north just for this occasion, decorated the refreshment tables and hung in bunches around the room. Green winter foliage hung over the doors and accented the candelabras. Marilana took it all in and found herself in deep appreciation of the subtle details in Lady Annabella's planning.

With a hidden grin, the lioness turned her attention to the growing crowd and realized that her sudden appearance was clearly attracting a certain amount of attention. She pushed down her discomfort and scanned the crowd until she spotted Earek's black and white magpie costume. Next to him was a girl in a glittery blue bird of paradise costume. The feathery mask did not cover the lower part of her face, making Brittia instantly recognizable. They were talking to a pair of tall young jaguars; the taller of the two had his face and head covered by an elaborate cobra mask, and the other portrayed a majestic golden eagle. Judging by the descriptions Lady Annabella had given Marilana, she identified the taller as Master Arndt and the other as his brother Master Warhaim. As her eyes continued their tour of the room, Marilana identified a number of the Southern Tip nobles and most of her classmates. She spied Klay and Caton, wondered briefly if they would invite her for a dance, and felt certain they would, along with many others.

Not a minute later the musicians began to strum their instruments. Servants dimmed the oil lanterns placed strategically around the room, and the effect created a ring of shadows around the dance floor. Marilana took a calming breath and began a slow tour around the edge of the dance floor. One by one, the other youths stepped back, giving her fair berth, and drawing further attention to her. In wake of this disturbance, Master Arndt glanced her way. His surprise was clearly evident as he turned his full attention to her, and stepped away from Brittia. Master Warhaim did the same, his eyes filled with anticipation.

Marilana was glad for the mask as heat flooded her cheeks in a deep blush. Master Arndt crossed the open dance floor and placed himself in front of her. Marilana gave him a proper curtsey. He bowed in return and offered his paw. "May I?"

"You may," Marilana said in a soft, singsong-like voice. She placed her paw in his, and he led her out onto the dance floor. As they waltzed, Marilana glanced past the jaguar's shoulder and saw Master Warhaim waltzing with Brittia and Earek waltzing with a girl in a fanciful butterfly costume. When the dance ended, Master Arndt relinquished her paw to Master Warhaim for a second waltz, this one slightly more complex and beautifully played.

As the music continued and the dance floor grew more crowded, Marilana found herself being drawn from one dance into the next; every male wanted his chance, even, as she had predicted, Klay and Caton. Marilana did her best to avoid their eyes, but both the bear and fox watched her suspiciously. Several dances later, she saw the pair talking with Earek and clearly his explanation left the two smiling and nodding.

So far, the only disappointment of the night was that Earek had not yet asked her to dance, and when Marilana tried to track him down, he was nowhere to be found. Perhaps he was enjoying a breath of fresh air, she thought. Hard to imagine that her co-conspirator would not want at least one dance.

Marilana danced another waltz with Master Arndt, and then a high reel with his brother Master Warhaim. When the dance ended, she turned to find Earek waiting for her, his paw held out to her. He spoke not a word, bowing politely instead.

As the musicians crafted another perfectly played waltz, she curtseyed and took her place in front of him. She looked into his eyes. Green. And not just green, but a sparkling green. Earek's eyes, she knew, were brown, not green.

Then she felt her partner's strong paw on her waist, and she faltered slightly at the touch. That was not the paw of a leopard, Marilana knew, recognizing the touch.

Then suddenly the boy in the magpie outfit began to lead her in a more complex set of steps. He led her around the floor, and Marilana fell into the steps as easily and fluidly as if she had been dancing them her entire life. Neither spoke, but his green eyes sparkled mischievously as she gazed at him.

The music ended. He bowed to her wordlessly. Marilana curtseyed. The boy in the magpie costume turned and walked away. Just then, a young eland in the costume of a blue jay stepped up to Marilana and bowed. She curtseyed politely even though the energy of the last dance was still flowing through her veins. She and her new partner took the first steps of a landler, and when Marilana glanced back, the green-eyed boy in the magpie costume was gone. It was several dances later when she spotted the magpie dancing with Brittia. When the couples passed, he winked a brown eye at her. Marilana was so relieved that she took no notice of the vitriol look on Brittia's face.

The night ended with Master Arndt leading her through the most complex waltz she had danced all evening, and they performed it so flawlessly that they were greeted with applause when the song ended. Marilana curtseyed to him and started to pull away when he stopped her with his paw.

"You will stand with me for the reveal, won't you?" he asked gently, holding her paw to his chest.

"Oh, yes," Marilana said in her singsong voice. "But first I must freshen up."

"As you wish," Master Arndt said, allowing her to join the girls flooding toward the ladies room. Marilana bypassed the ladies room and walked confidently to the last classroom. She glanced back at the eating hall as she turned the corner, and saw Earek drawing Master Arndt and Master Warhaim back toward the eating hall. Taslin was waiting nervously, clutching her paws, in the dark doorway. She helped Marilana don her dark cloak. Marilana pulled the hood up over her head as Taslin peeked cautiously around the corner.

"Now! Go quickly," Taslin whispered. "I think someone is watching."

Marilana kept her cloak closed tightly around her as she hurried to the door. She glanced down the hallway and saw Master Warhaim emerge from the shadows and start after her.

Marilana wrenched the door open and sprang down the steps. Jarek saw her coming. She circled her paw as she ran toward him. He opened the carriage door, and Marilana leapt inside. The carriage started moving even as Jarek climbed in and closed the door. She leaned back and sighed.

"A certain Master Warhaim didn't look very pleased at our quick departure," Jarek said with a grin. "Good thing his costume wings can't make him fly, and he doesn't have his horse, or he'd surely be chasing you. You must have made an impression. And I think there are going to be a lot of very livid people when they see you got away before the reveal."

"Then livid they will have to be," Marilana said grinning to herself.

"So did you enjoy the dancing at least?" Jarek asked with a smile.

"I did. Very much so." Marilana laughed. "The most fun I've had in a very long time. And you should have seen Earek. He was dancing up a storm and making a real impression on some of the noble girls."

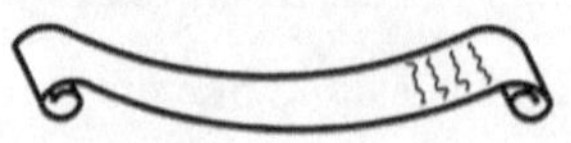

Earek grinned behind his mask as Master Warhaim stormed back into the eating hall. He watched as the two noble brothers conferred quietly. Master Arndt squeezed his paws into fists and then forced them to relax again. The two of them turned and strode in Earek's direction.

"Earek, do you happen to know who the girl in gold was? She seems to have disappeared," Master Arndt asked lightly.

"I have no idea," Earek replied, the lie coming easily.

"I didn't think you would, though she seemed rather interested in you. That said, so did half the other girls in the room," Master Arndt grumbled. "You dance well for a merchant. And your dance with her was particularly masterful."

"Thank you for being so kind, but compared to your last dance, I am just a beginner," Earek countered.

They watched as the girls began to filter back into the room. Brittia swayed toward them smiling.

"Brittia, my dear, do you know who that girl in gold was? She slipped out and ran away," Master Arndt said, offering his paw to her.

Brittia beamed back at him and placed her paw in his. She batted her lashes at him and sighed as he pulled her closer.

"No, Master Arndt," she said breathily. "I have no idea who she was, although I would love to know who her seamstress is. Her costume was amazing. Earek, did your father make it?"

"No, this was the first I'd seen of it," he said truthfully. "I think my father would love to get his paws on the design, however."

Just then, Headmistress Ceta walked grandly on to the dance floor in her green and blue peacock costume and removed her mask. She raised her paws, calling for everyone's attention. She called the roll, starting with the lowest ranking students and ending with Brittia. As each name was called, the student stepped out onto the dance floor and removed his or her mask, bowing or curtseying as was appropriate.

After the students from all the schools had been called, the headmistress read out the names of the noble guests. The crowd applauded politely for each of them. Master Warhaim and Master Arndt removed their masks with a flourish, but did not bow. They, naturally, received the loudest applause.

When the applause died down, Headmistress Ceta called for the last dance of the evening. Master Arndt waltzed with Brittia, Master Warhaim waltzed with one of the noble girls, and Earek asked the noble girl in the butterfly costume for a second dance. She smiled boldly and accepted. The dance was quickly done, and Master Arndt led the nobles out the door well ahead of the rest.

Earek and his merchant friends followed, making their way slowly through the town, laughing and joking and enjoying the last moments of an evening that, as Earek saw it, could not have gone better.

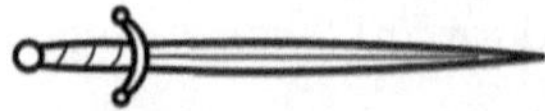

Marquiese was waiting for Marilana when she returned to her cottage the next morning. Earek had joined her on her trek back from the castle since he had spent the morning there visiting his brother Jarek.

Neither seemed surprised to find the lion there. Earek winked at him, but Marilana was far less pleased.

"What were you thinking?" Marilana put her paws on her hips and shook her head as if neither of them had a brain between them. She flashed a look of disbelief at Marquiese. "You took a terrible risk trading out costumes at the dance like that. And for what, a single dance? If someone had figured it out, there would have been no end of trouble."

"Us?" Marquiese replied. "What about you? You were having so much fun you forgot how easily you could have been dragged off. What would have happened if Master Arndt and Master Warhaim hadn't let you go at the end of the night?"

"I had my protection well managed, thank you very much," Marilana retorted in outrage. "Jarek and five other guardsmen were there solely to escort me, and all of Lady

Annabella's servants were told to watch for anyone attempting foul play."

"Servants would not have stopped Master Arndt," Marquiese said hotly.

"Even Master Arndt would have respected Lady Annabella's protection, not to mention the protection I afford myself," Marilana countered. "You had no protection at all. Did you even have the merchant guards escort you to and from town or were you out on the road at night alone?"

"For your information, I was at my merchant father's shop. I walked from the market, and Earek let me into one of the classrooms. There was no risk. We traded clothes, I danced with you, and then slipped out the same way. I rode home in my father's wagon. No one in town even saw me," Marquiese said stubbornly. "My protection was secrecy and it worked just fine."

"Hey, both of you, cool your tempers or I'll have to separate you," Earek said calmly.

Marquiese glared at Marilana for a moment more. She returned his glare, gripping her skirt tightly with both paws, before huffing indignantly and turning away from him. Marquiese dropped his eyes to the floor, anger still pounding in his head.

"Now if you're done venting your worry and concern for each other, might I just say we pulled off a set of perfect ruses, successful in a large part due to my own quick thinking," Earek said proudly. "Master Arndt suspected from the start that you were going to try to slip out before the reveal, Marilana, and I distracted him most effectively. And adding adjustable straps inside my costume made my swap with you a thing of beauty, Marquiese. Since you are slightly shorter than I, the costume would have looked sloppy without adjusting the length. That, quite obviously, would have been a definite clue to those watching."

"So that's why you never danced with me," Marilana said to the leopard calmly. "Tall for one dance and shorter for another. It might well have made people wonder. You also spoke to Klay and Caton and told them not to be so suspicious."

"Yes, they figured it out as soon as they danced with you and saw your eyes," Earek said. "I told them that if you wanted everyone to know, then it was up to you. They thought it was a great jest."

Earek went on talking. He told them all the gossip from the previous night, which seemed to help both Marilana and Marquiese relax, though neither seemed ready to join the conversation. Finally, Earek looked at the clock and sprang to his feet.

"I need to get to the shop," he announced. "It's been an interesting morning. Thanks for the company. It's always a pleasure to pass gossip with friends, even if those friends are not speaking to each other."

"I'll escort you home," Marilana said quietly. "Thank you for your company this morning, and thank you for all your help last night. I could not have done it without you."

"My pleasure." Earek smiled and laid his paw gently on her arm. Marquiese smiled slightly as he watched them, only to fade quickly away as he remembered his duty.

"I should be going too," Marquiese said quietly. "I promised Lida I would describe as many of the costumes as I could from last night. At the very least, I'll be able to describe the Lady in Gold in great detail."

Then he looked at Marilana, his eyes apologizing even before he spoke.

"Marilana, I'm sorry. Earek's right. I was just venting my worries. You don't deserve to have my anger directed at you, not when it's better directed elsewhere."

"I'm sorry too. I was just worried about you," Marilana replied. "Especially when I found out that a group of bandits had made another raid last night along the west coast."

"Bandits raiding in the winter?" Earek asked surprised.

"The winter has been too mild to slow them down very much." Marilana sighed. "They've been making raids whenever and wherever the weather has allowed since the end of summer. It's taking its toll on bandit hunters all over the province. The constant watching and tracking. The Phantom has spent every night patrolling the border trying to figure out what the bandits are up to. And me? I feel like I abandoned my duty last night."

"No, Marilana," Marquiese said firmly. "You were fulfilling your duty to Lady Annabella."

"Duty? I was having fun." Marilana shook her head bitterly. "I was even having fun when I was running from Master Warhaim."

Earek glanced at Marquiese and then gently squeezed Marilana's arm.

"No, Marilana. Lady Annabella was right to have you attend the dance. You were the belle of the ball and had every right to be there. There is nothing about that for you to feel guilty about. You can't just protect life; you need to live life."

"You're nice to say so. But now we should get you on your way. Your father may not mind that you visit Jarek, but he will mind if you're late returning."

Marilana was quiet as she led them through the forest and down the road, and she left them at the brick manor without another word.

Marquiese watched her disappear into the forest and then drew a deep sigh. He had wanted more than anything to spend more time with Marilana, and he could tell she needed comforting. But he wasn't sure he could stop himself when it came to his feelings for her. He had almost lost control once; he couldn't risk doing so again.

28

The month after the Winter Masquerade was full of gossip and most of it was about the Lady in Gold. Marquiese hid his smiles behind looks of curiosity any time the subject was broached. He wished that he had been able to attend the event, he told everyone, if only to have gotten a glimpse of this mysterious lady.

The rumors claimed she was the best dancer of anyone at the party.

Earek had been right; Marilana had been the belle of the ball. Everyone said so. One rumor even claimed that Master Arndt wanted to court her. Of course she had to be a noble; no one of lesser stature could possibly demonstrate such fluid grace, such proud bearing, and such a fabulous costume.

Marilana simply ignored the endless chatter.

Instead she focused on tutoring the younger students during lunch and pretended to try to perfect her etiquette. Marquiese was amazed at how the younger children happily surrounded her. They brought their books and homework and asked endless questions. Marilana didn't care whether the subject in question was history, math, or grammar; she simply offered directions and explanations in ways the children understood. It made Marquiese smile to see her sitting amidst so many children, her manner so much gentler than the bandit hunter he had first met.

Brittia in contrast growled and scowled almost constantly as spring approached. She still flirted with Marquiese and Earek and the other boys. She still ordered her followers around and harassed the other girls. For some reason though, she had begun to avoid Marilana. Brittia scowled at the kids when they were sitting outside with Marilana in nice weather or gathering around a table in the library when it was stormy outside. Brittia gave haughty sniffs whenever Marilana walked by or stood too close, but then she would turn her back and ignore the lioness altogether.

What's more, Marilana had not been called to the headmistress' office in months. She seemed to be maturing and expressing a more gentle side while Brittia seemed to be withdrawing in anger from her larger social circles. The lynx, of course, still held the spotlight and was not about to relinquish it, but she seemed less at ease in her position and more closemouthed, gossiping less and talking only enough to get her point across.

Marquiese's puzzlement at Brittia's behavior formed into worry when the youths from Mistress Rose's class were enjoying a pleasant afternoon and anticipating a well earned Restday the following day. The conversation turned to a new dance they were all learning called a mazurka, a fast, intricate, and difficult dance.

Brittia had not added a single word to the conversation when Estala, the quirky young gazelle, looked over at the lynx and said, "Brittia, I know you'll have no problem learning the steps. You had the complex waltz down in only a few days. Didn't the nobles and the third year students dance a mazurka at the Winter Masquerade? I think that was one of the dances that was most amazing to watch. That Lady in Gold was like a blur across the floor with all the turns and fast steps. It will be fun to learn. What do you think, Brittia? Will you try for that feathered look for your costume when you dance the part of Lady Season in the Dance of the Seasons next year?"

"Why don't you just shut up?!" Brittia growled at Estala.

Marquiese was as surprised as everyone else when he heard this. Brittia never lashed out that way. She always used her wit to twist conversations or mock others into silence. She might dismissively tell someone to shut up and insult them, but a straight out attack was never her style. Marquiese realized that something was seriously bothering Brittia.

"All you do is talk!" Brittia shrieked at the gazelle. "It's enough to drive anyone crazy. Blah, blah, blah! Lady in Gold this, Lady in Gold that. Don't you think I can stand on my own? I'm tired of being compared to that lofty scamp! She shows up just for the dancing and then runs away like she's afraid to show her face. How do you know she is beautiful? Maybe she ran away because her face is horribly disfigured? Why should I want to be like her?"

Everyone took a step back. Estala looked close to tears. Marquiese had never particularly liked Britta, but this was very unusual and he was worried about her. He recognized the jealousy that edged Brittia's anger and realized now why she had been pulling away from the social scene this past month. She had come in second to someone she could never beat, someone she didn't even know, and it had happened at her own school dance. She was avoiding Marilana because she could see clearly for the first time that Marilana had never been affected by their rivalry. Marilana went on doing what she wanted, living her life, while Brittia was consumed with her envy and hatred, her every action compared to that of someone better.

"I'm going home," Brittia spat bitterly and stormed off down the street toward the East Road.

"Brittia, no!" Marquiese called after her, but she did not stop.

Marquiese met Earek's worried look and turned to hurry back into the school to find Marilana. Just as he started up the steps, the schoolhouse door opened and Marilana stepped out. She frowned at the panic on his face. She saw the worried looks on the faces of the rest of the youths and hurried down the steps.

"What is it?" she asked quickly.

"Brittia got mad and stormed off," Marquiese said. "She's headed for the East Road. No escort, no friends, no one."

"Quick now! All of you follow me," Marilana called to her charges. "There may be nothing to worry about, but we should try to catch up to Brittia. Hurry now!"

Once they reached the road, Marilana bent down and traced a footprint with her claw. She looked over her shoulder and motioned them to hurry. The younger children saw the sudden change in attitude of the older students and were clearly worried. Marquiese took Lida by the paw and gave her a smile. "Everything is alright."

"But why did Brittia go off on her own like that?" Lida asked, frowning. "She knows how dangerous the road can be."

"I cannot answer for Brittia's actions," Marquiese said quietly. "But you are right. The road is dangerous, and something bad could happen if we don't catch up to her. So we need to remain quiet and keep up with Marilana."

Marquiese met Earek's eyes and saw the same determination he was feeling. They both scanned the road and the trees as Marilana had taught them. When each student reached his or her house, they hurried up the walk, and Marilana waited only until the door was shut tight behind them.

They only had a few more houses to go before they reached Brittia's house, and Marquiese was hoping they would find her safe and sound there, but for some reason, he didn't feel confident about that.

Once again, Marilana crouched down to examine a track on the road. This time Marquiese could see the deadly focus on her face and knew whatever she was seeing was not good. They were nearing one of the sharper bends in the road and could not see through the trees. Marilana glanced toward the bend and then sprinted back toward them. She motioned everyone toward the side of the road, saying quietly, "Hide. Quickly. Under the bushes. Stay still and don't make a sound. Wait for me to return."

She tossed Marquiese her dagger and said, "Guard them."

"I'm coming with you," he said firmly.

Marilana studied his face, saw the resolve there, and quickly turned to Earek.

"Stay low and silent," she said. She gave the black leopard a knife, then turned and without another word hurried down the road.

Marquiese followed. As they neared the bend, the lioness stayed close to the trees, using the shadows for cover. She motioned Marquiese to keep low. He gripped the dagger tightly, watching for any movement in the trees or underbrush.

Marilana peered around the bend and motioned for him stay. Then she dove out onto into the open road just as a loud crashing sounded up ahead. A scream ripped through the forest. Brittia!

Even before the echo of the scream passed, Marquiese watched as Marilana loosed two arrows, then spun and loosed another. A riderless horse galloped past Marquiese and down the road. A man stumbled out of the trees and fell on the ground. Brittia screamed again. Marilana spun sideways and loosed three more arrows in quick succession. Marquiese saw Brittia stumble from the trees right in front of him; he hooked an arm around her waist and pulled her down. She started to scream again, but he clamped his paw over her mouth.

"Brittia! It's me, Marquiese," he hissed in her ear. "Stay quiet."

She turned and hid her face against his shoulder. Marquiese kept his arm around her and shifted the dagger into his other paw. He saw that Marilana had crossed to the other side of the road. She nocked another arrow and loosed it down the road. He heard a groan as the arrow found its target.

Just then, Marquiese spotted movement in the underbrush just behind the lioness. He was calling out a warning even as the wolf reached over the brush to grab her. Marilana, however, raised a fist above her head and jumped straight into the man. Her fist collided with the man's jaw with an undeniable crunch. The wolf's eyes rolled up in his head and Marilana slit his throat with lightning fast motion that seemed to come out of nowhere. The wolf crashed to the ground and the forest grew quiet again. Marilana scanned the carnage and then moved further down the road. Marquiese urged Brittia to her feet and they followed carefully. When they emerged from the shadows, they saw Marilana crouching over the body of an older otter. Marquiese realized the otter was still alive although he had a crude arrow protruding from his chest.

"Tell me what you know, and I will end the pain," the lioness said soothingly.

"We were told to look for high-class merchant children between the ages of thirteen and sixteen," the otter whispered. "Our leader knew you would be escorting children along this road about this time of day, and he wanted to get in and out quickly. He'd tried the same tactic before but with no luck. This time he got lucky, and that silly lynx wandered into our ambush."

The old otter coughed wetly and then struggled to continue. "Our leader wanted to question the girl about some target or another, to find out if we even needed to continue to look in the area. It was against our instructions. We were supposed to observe the houses to locate possible targets. We weren't supposed to take hostages or give our intentions away."

"Where are these instructions coming from? Who is giving them?" Marilana asked quietly.

"I never saw him or heard a name, but all the bandit leaders are willing to work with him. He is deadly dangerous, and determined," the man coughed again, his strength fading fast.

"I'll do what I can for your family," Marilana said softly. "You were always an honest tracker. Thank you for telling me what you could. Rest now. Be at peace."

Marquiese saw Marilana dribble the liquid from a small vile into the otter's mouth. The otter swallowed and soon became still. Marilana laid his head back down on the ground and turned away.

"We have to move. Now!" she said, ushering Marquiese and Brittia back down the road. They found the other children still under Earek's watchful eye and gathered them together.

"Back to town everyone," Marilana said. "Quickly."

Marilana drove them at an urgent pace back down the road, instructing everyone she saw to stay inside and bar their doors and windows.

She only paused once at the East Road guardhouse and spoke quickly with the officer manning the post. "Get your guards out of the barracks and on the alert. There are bandits about," she said to him.

"Right away," the guard said as Marilana hurried Marquiese and the children through town to the market. Merchant Colbran and Merchant Sleater were talking outside Merchant Colbran's shop when they saw them.

"Brittia?" Merchant Sleater called when his daughter emerged from the group. "What's going on here?"

"Protect them until I return," Marilana ordered the two merchants.

Then, without another word, she turned and ran back the way they had come.

"In here, quickly," Merchant Colbran said, ushering everyone inside the shop. When all were inside and the door was locked, the merchant's eyes fell on Marquiese. "Adealy! She will be waiting. She will be worried. I have to get word to her."

"Don't worry," Marquiese said to him calmly. "Marilana the Ghost is on the hunt. She will take care of Adealy."

"Marquiese, what happened?" Merchant Sleater demanded once everyone had settled in the shop.

Marquiese told them. Earek added bits and pieces. Both kept a wary eye on the door and windows even as they spoke. Most of the children sat around on the floor looking shaken but seemed to be recovering as well as could be expected. Marquiese was worried about Lida though. She sat in the corner shaking and crying silently.

When they were done, Brittia blurted, "Marquiese saved me, Father. I was so upset I left without waiting for escort. I knew it was wrong, but I couldn't stand it anymore. I hurried down the road; I thought if I was fast I would make it home safely. I was almost there when I heard something rustling in the trees. I froze; I didn't know what to do I was so scared I just stood there on the road. Then a jackal stepped out of the trees and I screamed. A horse charged down the road at me and I turned and ran. The horse was next to me and a paw grabbed my arm. Then just as quickly he let go, the horse galloped on down the road. Several more bandits stepped out of the trees, all of them were leering at me. I screamed again and tripped as I tried to keep running. Arrows were flying through the air. I didn't stop to look behind me; I just stumbled on around the bend in the road. Then Marquiese was there, he caught me and protected me. He told me it would be alright and to be quiet. He saved me." The lynx turned and beamed brightly at Marquiese, tear streaks glistening on her cheeks. "You saved me."

"Marilana saved you, Brittia," the lion said shaking his head.

"Nonsense. Marilana is a bandit hunter. She only did what she is supposed to do," Merchant Sleater said firmly. "You were a hero today; you protected my daughter armed only with a dagger."

"Marilana risked her life. Not just for Brittia, but for all of us. And now she's is out there making sure Mystillion is safe. She is the real hero," Marquiese insisted.

"You could have stayed back with the other children, but you went forward and rescued Brittia, risking your own life."

"Earek protected the rest of us," Estala chimed in. "He told us to stay still and silent. He comforted us and sheltered us. He is a hero too."

"Yes, that was very brave, Earek. Well done," Merchant Sleater smiled at Earek.

"I just did what Marilana told me to do," Earek said, shrugging his shoulders.

"Marquiese, you didn't tell them about the last man Marilana killed," Brittia said, a frown tugging at the corners of her mouth. "What was that about?"

"That was a mercy killing. The otter was dying. Marilana gave him an end to his pain."

"What! But that's horrible," the lynx said, shuddering.

"No. He was dying already and in terrible pain; no amount of healing would have helped him. The arrow had pierced his lungs; he would have lain there in pain slowly dying as blood filled his lungs. I recognized the symptoms. I have heard it described. Marilana knew it also. She promised to ease his passing and to help his family."

"She's the one who shot him in the first place. Why would she care if his death was painless?" Brittia argued.

"No, you have it wrong. It was not her arrow. Her arrows are made by Lady Annabella's fletcher and carry his mark. The arrow that otter took was crudely made; I'd guess he was shot by one of the bandits."

"That makes no sense," the lynx said, shaking her head. "Why would his own conspirators shoot him?"

"He saved your life by taking that arrow," a voice from the doorway said. They all started and looked toward the door. Marilana stepped into the room with fire in her eyes. She had two daggers and a full quiver of arrows hanging around her waist as well as a bandoleer of throwing knives across her chest. She stared at Brittia for a moment and then said, "That otter was an honest tracker, a mercenary who hired out his skills trying to keep his family fed. He told me he had tried to stop the leader of the bandits, a jackal called Trol, from setting the ambush, and that he did not hire on to take hostages. Trol didn't listen. During the fighting, one of the bandits tried to shoot you as you were running away. That tracker jumped out and took the arrow. He saved your life."

"He might have. But that does not change the fact that he hired on with bandits. He deserved to die with dishonor," Brittia spat angrily.

"You know nothing of honor," Marilana hissed. She turned away from Brittia and addressed the others. "I'm here to escort you all home. The town is secure. The remaining bandits fled back to the south. It's safe to travel, but we must hurry."

Then she addressed Merchant Colbran. "Adealy asked me to tell you she and the guards are holding the house secure until you, Marquiese, and Lida arrive. I suggest you get started."

It was late the next day as Marilana finally returned home. Her travels had taken her far and wide across the province. She was exhausted and looking forward to a hot meal and sleeping in her own bed. She washed her face and paws and then went into her bedroom to change. She had no sooner opened the wardrobe than a foreign sound drifting on the wind caused her to freeze. Then she heard someone calling her name. *Marquiese,* she thought. *What is he doing here?*

She hurried to the door and looked out. He was standing outside the gate, a wild, panicked look in his eyes.

"Marquiese? What's wrong?" Marilana hurried to secure her traps and led him inside. "What's happened?"

"Marilana, I don't know what else to do. I don't know who else to turn to." The words tumbled out of his mouth. "Mother Kalan and Healer Magus both say they cannot do anything for her. I thought maybe with your knowledge you might know something they haven't thought of."

"Marquiese, slowdown. Who? Who needs healing?"

"It's Lida. I don't know what's the matter with her. Please help her."

"Lida? But . . . ?" Marilana said no more. She grabbed her herb satchel and her weapons and led him back outside.

"What happened?" she asked as they cut through the forest.

"It began after the bandit attack. She was very shaky," Marquiese said quietly. "She stopped crying, but she was still shaky and jumpy all evening. Adealy thought she should go to bed and get some good sleep. Late in the night, she started screaming but wouldn't wake up. We sent for Mother Kalan right away. She spent hours trying different remedies. She got her to stop screaming, but was not able to wake her. This morning, we sent for Healer Magus. He spent hours treating her, but with no more success than Mother Kalan. I fear for Lida's life."

"Marquiese, I cannot promise that I'll be any more successful than Mother Kalan or Healer Magus," she said as they crossed the road and passed through the gate to the brick manor. "Much of what I know, they taught me."

"But of the old ways," the lion said hopefully.

"We shall see." Marilana took a deep breath at the door and then walked inside. Everyone was gathered in the drawing room. Lida lay on the couch in a deep coma-like state, but Marilana saw at once that her paws were twitching and her eyes were moving rapidly under her eyelids.

Mother Kalan threw up her arms in anger the moment she saw the lioness. "Her?! That is your desperate idea, boy? You think a killer can help heal your sister?"

"She is a talented healer," Healer Magus retorted. "Please, Marilana. Come."

Merchant Colbran, his arms holding Adealy tightly, tears in their eyes, met Marilana's gaze with a hollow, pleading expression. Marilana nodded and knelt at Lida's side, examining her carefully. "What have you determined?" she said to Healer Magus.

"As best I can tell, the girl is in a coma brought on by severe mental shock," the aging cheetah said. "She will waste away and die if we are unable to wake her."

"This is not a coma," Marilana said quietly.

"As I told the family already," Mother Kalan said in a tight voice. "The girl is afraid to wake; she is trapped in her own mind, unable to get away from the nightmares brought on by her terrible fright from yesterday's events. However, Healer Magus is correct. She will die if she does not eat and drink."

"You were unable to give her broth?" Marilana asked. She could see the muscles clinching Lida's jaw shut.

"I managed to get some remedies into her, but she fought terribly," the blue fox said, sighing.

Marilana turned her gaze in the direction of Merchant Colbran and Adealy. She said, "There is something I can try. It is a method I have used only once before, something I learned while studying the old ways."

"The old ways?!" Mother Kalan hissed, her fur bristling. "The old ways are deadly if dabbled in by the untrained. You cannot be serious."

"Marilana is well practiced in the old ways," Healer Magus said calmly. "She has trained in them since she was a cub. She knows what she is talking about. If she thinks she can help, then I trust her judgment."

"And in doing so, you condemn this child to death!" Mother Kalan insisted, her eyes on Lida's parents. "I know the child is precious to you. I say her best chance is to wait. We continue with the path we have chosen, which is to see if she wakes on her own. Then even if she does die at least you still have your son."

"It is not your decision to make, Mother Kalan," Marilana said, her eyes still pinned on the merchant and his wife. "You are a respected and talented herb dealer, but you have done all you can. Healer Magus is a well-learned healer; he has also done all he can to help. I am more skilled in the old ways. I may be able to help, but only if the child's guardians wish to accept my offer of help. I will not tell you it is without risk. I will not kill her, but she may not be any better after I have tried. The choice is up to you."

"I trust her," Marquiese said simply.

Marilana did not glance at him, but his vote of confidence helped calm her nerves. She kept her focus on Merchant

Colbran. He looked down and met Adealy's eyes. They came to some silent agreement, and Merchant Colbran looked back at Marilana.

"Do what you can," he whispered sadly. "Please."

"Very well." Marilana nodded. She started to pull herbs from her satchel.

"Marquiese, I will need your help, but I must ask everyone else to leave the room, please."

"But . . . ," Merchant Colbran started to protest.

"It will be alright," Marquiese said with firm assurance. "I will be with Lida and will report any news. You have my word."

The young lion didn't wait for a reply. He gently herded everyone out of the room, closed the doors, and rejoined Marilana at the table.

"Tell me what you need me to do," he said.

"Pull the curtains closed and leave only the one light here on the table lit," Marilana said, her focus on the herb paste she was mixing. When everything was ready, she positioned Marquiese in a chair by Lida's feet. She knelt in front of him and met his eyes honestly.

"I am going to put Lida into a trance. I need you to understand that it is vital that she voices her thoughts. She may reveal things that you have asked her to keep secret. You will need to trust me."

"That's why you asked me to help you instead of someone else," he said calmly. "And you know I trust you. With my life, in fact. I am asking you to help Lida, even at the cost of my secret."

Marilana nodded and turned her attention back to the young lioness. She took up the paste she had made and began to sing a simple lullaby that Lady Annabella had sung to her when she had nightmares as a little girl. She took the paste on the spoon and smeared the paste across Lida's forehead from temple to temple. Then she placed some under each eye along her cheekbones. The last bit she slid inside Lida's cheek and next to her clenched teeth.

Lida jerked her head away, but Marilana was satisfied she had gotten enough in her mouth to serve its purpose. Instead of fighting the girl, she continued to sing soothingly. She pressed gently along Lida's chest and shoulders, moving her paws outward toward her arms. She did this over and over again. Each time she felt Lida relax a little more.

Marilana then moved her paws around to the top of Lida's head and the back of her neck. She gently pressed along the top of the young lioness' spine and each bone of her neck. Lida relaxed even more as Marilana gently pressed the tension from her muscles. Slowly, her face also began to relax. Her eye movements slowed and her mouth opened slightly.

Marilana lowered her voice and spoke softly, saying, "Lida, child, hear my voice. Trust the sound of it. Trust that you are safe and tell me what you see."

"No! No!" Lida murmured. She shook her head weakly. "Marquiese! They want to kill you. They are coming for you. They are trying to make me tell them about you. Where you are hiding. What you are doing. No! No! I won't do it. I won't tell them."

Marilana glanced up at Marquiese's stricken face. Then she began humming again, the lullaby lilted as a peaceful whisper in the room.

"I can't do it," Lida whispered weakly. "They will hurt me. I feel all alone. So alone. I don't want to tell them. Marquiese is too important; I love him like a brother. I wish he were my brother. I wish he could be free and happy."

"Lida, it's alright, child. You are not alone," Marilana cooed.

"I am surrounded by bandits. They are everywhere," Lida sobbed. "I won't tell them. I won't. No matter what!"

"Lida, these are not bandits you see. They are friends. They have come to rescue you," Marilana continued. "They have come to help Marquiese."

"No! They think they are his friends, but they don't know him. He cannot make friends with them. He is too important. They think he is my brother, but they don't know his secret. I won't tell them," Lida said more firmly.

"Lida, they don't care about his secret," Marilana said softly. "They know he is in hiding, and they want to protect him. They want you to come back with them. To come back with me."

"Marilana? Is that you?" Lida sobbed with relief.

"Yes, my child. It's me. It's Marilana."

"Will you take me home?"

"Yes, Lida. Yes, my child. Come with me," Marilana cooed.

"The bandits are chasing us. We can't get away," Lida sobbed with despair.

"We will get away. We will hide from them. We will save ourselves. Follow me."

"But Marquiese will be caught. You need to protect him, not me," the young lioness cried.

"I will protect you both," Marilana whispered. "Come. We will go to Marquiese and we will be safe."

"I cannot keep this secret alone."

"You are not alone, Lida, in keeping Marquiese's secret. Your mother and father keep it as well. So does Lady Annabella. You are not alone, little one. I will help you keep it too. You have my word."

"I believe you, Marilana. I believe you." Lida sighed and lay still.

Marilana examined Lida's eyes and face; she checked the young lioness' vitals. When Marilana was satisfied, she sat down on the floor and leaned back against the couch. She closed her eyes and softly sang the lullaby again. She felt drained. How much time had passed? She didn't know. Hours perhaps.

She was thinking how completely her adrenaline was spent and how much she needed sleep when she felt Marquiese's gentle touch on her shoulder.

"You're exhausted," she heard him say. He laid a soft cushion on the floor next to her and urged her to lie down. "I will watch over you. Tell me what to do."

"She needs to sleep undisturbed," Marilana whispered. "Wake me if she stirs before I do. Give her parents an update, but ask them to respect her sleep at all cost."

With that, the lioness curled up on the cushion and sleep took her.

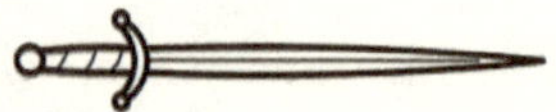

Marquiese watched her for a moment. This, he knew watching the rise and fall of her chest, was true sleep, not one of her trances. He was relieved too that Lida seemed to be sleeping peacefully as well. He walked quietly to the door and slipped out. Merchant Colbran was pacing the hall, and Adealy stood nervously nearby.

"How is she?" Adealy asked tearfully.

"Lida is sleeping peacefully, and Marilana thinks she will wake soon," Marquiese said with a smile. "Marilana is also sleeping, and I told her that I would make sure they were not disturbed."

"She has shown herself to be a true friend," Adealy murmured. "Thank you for bringing her here."

"Have the healers left?"

"Yes, Healer Magus gave Mother Kalan a ride back home," Merchant Colbran said calmly. "She told us to call on her to prepare the body. She was not very polite. She believes we made the wrong choice to trust your Marilana."

"Not surprising," the young lion said. "Mother Kalan does not approve of bandit hunters. Nor soldiers. Despite the peace they bring to the province."

"I am just glad we gave Marilana the chance to prove her skills."

"She need prove herself to no one ever again, in my eyes," Adealy said purposefully. "Now it's getting late. They will be hungry when they wake. I will make a good hearty stew and bake some bread for supper. Please watch over them carefully, Marquiese."

"I will."

Marquiese slipped back into the drawing room. Both Lida and Marilana were still sleeping soundly. He picked up a book, raised the wick on one of the lanterns, and began reading.

Four hours and many pages later, Marilana finally stirred. She sat up and stretched. She spotted Marquiese sitting in the chair and smiled at him. She got to her feet and checked on Lida. Then she came over to him and sat in the chair beside his.

"Thank you for letting me sleep," she said.

"I suspect you have neither slept nor eaten much in some time," he said. "I know you were planning to do both when I arrived at your house, and I will never forget that you hesitated for not even one moment."

"I am just relieved that Lida seems to have come out of it."

"I didn't realize how stressed she was about me and my secret. How worried she was about my well-being," he said sadly. "However, I think I know how to help ease that stress in the future."

"I believe that is all she is asking for."

Together, they watched Lida until she finally began to stir. The moment she did, Marilana went and knelt at her side, stroking her forehead and whispering her name. Marquiese smiled at the gentleness of Marilana's touch and the calm of her voice.

Lida opened her eyes. For a moment, she seemed lost and confused, and the elder lioness stroked her forehead and spoke gently in her ear. Lida's eyes slowly cleared. She smiled weakly and gave Marilana a hug.

"I'll go get your mother," Marilana said standing up and headed for the door. "Marquiese will stay with you."

Marquiese walked over, knelt at Lida's side, and smiled at her.

"How do you feel?" he asked gently.

"I'm sorry I'm so weak-minded, Marquiese," Lida said tearfully.

"No, you are strong, Lida. One of the strongest lions I know. And one of the bravest," he said sincerely. "Listen, I am so sorry I have pushed my burden on you. I promise to help you carry it from now on. I promise to lend both my support and my ear. So any time you feel the need to talk, you can come to me."

"I can?"

"Absolutely. Deal?"

"Deal," Lida agreed. As weak as she was, she smiled at him and Marquiese wrapped her in a warm hug.

"Okay then. Deal," he whispered as Adealy and Merchant Colbran hurried into the room and knelt at their daughter's side. There were tears and hugs and such relief that Marilana smiled broadly as she entered the room with a tray filled with hot stew and fresh bread. She glanced at Marquiese and he returned a small smile. Then he watched as she very quietly set the food on the low table next to Lida's couch and stepped back.

After a time, she said, "I'm sorry to interrupt, but Lida should really eat something. You all should."

"Thank you," Merchant Colbran said, turning to her. "For everything."

"And you will certainly join us," Adealy told her.

When the food was gone and the dishes cleared, Marilana placed a small clear vial in Adealy's paw.

"Three drops in a cup of water will help her sleep without dreams. Three and no more," Marilana said quietly. "Make sure she gets good sleep and keeps eating. She should be back up and around in a few days or so."

Adealy nodded her understanding and murmured her thanks again.

Then Marilana gave Lida a smile and said, "Lida, get your rest. And don't worry about missing school. I'll help you get caught back up."

Lida smiled weakly in return. "I love you, Marilana,"

"I love you too, child."

Marquiese and Merchant Colbran walked the lioness to the door, and the merchant took her paw and said, "Thank you again, Marilana. I am in your debt. If you ever need anything, please don't hesitate to ask."

"Thank you for the offer, but the meal was more than enough to settle our debt. I'm just glad I could help," Marilana said with a slight curtsey.

Marquiese wanted to walk Marilana home but realized she would just have to escort him back again. Foolish. He wanted to say something more to her but couldn't seem to shape his thoughts into coherent sentences. In the end, he just nodded, his eyes filled with appreciation and admiration.

"I'll see you tomorrow for sparring practice," the lioness said to him levelly. Then she turned and walked out the gate and down the road.

29

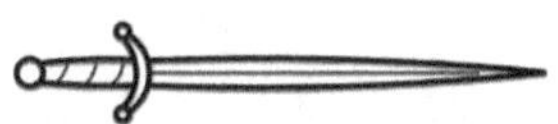

Two years of sparring almost every morning and finally Marquiese managed to disarm Marilana.

It wasn't a thing of beauty, but he managed to use her speed and maneuverability to his advantage, leveraging his strength and all she and Zariff had taught him for one victory in a long series of defeats. He pressed hard, battering at her with quick and powerful jabs. But instead of chasing after her as she stepped back—his normal strategy—he lured her into his reach and forced her to deflect his powerful strikes one after another until fatigue set in. Then he attacked quickly, backing her around the practice yard. Finally, he managed to lock her hilt and, with a quick twist, sent her sword flying across the yard.

He was elated. "Finally," he said, drawing a deep breath.

Captain-General Zariff clapped him on the shoulder. "Excellent job."

As strong and hale as he felt, the lion worried that Marilana would not take even a single defeat well. And indeed when she turned to him, her expression was serious and focused. They exchanged bows, and she said, "You know this means war, don't you? Same time tomorrow. No holds barred."

"I will have to prepare myself for a good thrashing," he said matching her serious tone.

Marilana met his eyes for a long moment, and then cracked a smile.

"You finally did it. You beat me." She beamed at him. "I have nothing left to teach you about sword-to-sword combat.

Starting tomorrow, we will work on stamina and duel wielding, fighting as equals."

"Yes, you both need to work on fighting with shields and secondary weapons like mace and sword-breaker," Zariff added thoughtfully. "I'll see what challenges I can come up with to push your skills farther. Dismissed."

Marilana led the lion quickly to the manor house where he got cleaned up and ready for school. Lida was ready to go by the time he finished. Together they went out to the road and met their escort.

"Good morning, Marilana," Lida said happily.

Marquiese was impressed with how well Lida had been doing since her collapse. Two and a half months had passed, and she was as happy and lively as he could ever remember her being. They talked often of the secret she kept on his behalf, and this sharing had strengthened their bond. He was so grateful.

"Marilana, it's two fifnights until final exams," the young lioness said, taking the escort's paw. "Are you going to be ready?"

"Oh, yes, I'm definitely ready. Both for the exams and for the end of another school year," Marilana said, smiling easily.

As it stood, Marilana was still the worst dancer in the class, though not the complete disaster she had once been. She could now dance all the dances from the first year of finishing school as well as the high reel, however, she still scored terribly low in the more complex waltz and the fast mazurka.

Marquiese had demonstrated more progress. He was now in the middle of the class. Yes, he danced all the dances, but he was careful not to add flourishes that would mark him as the truly gifted dancer that he was. He simply danced the steps.

The pair ranked similarly in etiquette. Marquiese had made steady, dreadfully slow progress, working on one skill at a time. Marilana had made little leaps of progress, showing good form in some areas while continuing to mix up her utensils and glasses.

That, Marquiese thought, was certain to change in the coming year. Lady Annabella was insisting on their continuing improvement, and she would surely not let Marilana continue to hide her skills for much longer. In fact, he suspected the great-noble would begin throwing a whole set of surprises Marilana's way in due course.

This thought caused him to smile as Marilana and a half dozen other students approached Brittia's house. She was waiting for them inside the gate.

"Good morning, Marquiese," she said brightly. "How is my hero today?"

Marquiese smiled politely as Brittia took hold of his arm and walked along with him. The lynx continued to insist that Marquiese and Earek were the heroes of the day and, all these months after the attempted kidnapping, still refused to hear anything else.

Brittia continued to ignore Marilana; however, instead of avoiding her, she simply acted as if the lioness was invisible. Furthermore, she also ignored any conversation about the Lady in Gold. As far as Brittia was concerned, the Winter Masquerade had never happened. Well, unless she was the subject of the conversation, of course.

The rules governing the interaction between the students and their ranks had changed. Brittia no longer demanded that the rest of the students keep their distance from Marilana, though the lioness was far from thrilled when they crowded too close and made it difficult for her to hear the sounds of the forests or scout for tracks along the road.

More importantly, the politics had changed. Marquiese, being of equal rank to Brittia, had unintentionally caused a shift in the balance of power. He had laughed when Marilana had first pointed this out to him, but now he was beginning to see it, and the effects were greater than he could have imagined.

The school day went as expected. Mistress Rose spent the morning reviewing etiquette and protocol. Marilana was chosen to serve the lunch. They had progressed to the point where only one person was chosen each day to serve the lunch.

So far, only Earek came close to matching Marilana's skills. Of course, the lioness could have served three times as many guests and done just as good a job as she had on the very first day of finishing school.

Today, Marquiese was chosen to host. The lion had chosen to use just the minimal hosting skills for class, and since Mistress Rose had never found fault with it, he had never found it necessary to show any improvement in this area. It was a bit embarrassing, however, since he could have done so much better. That, however, would have provided evidence that he was not who he claimed to be, and the attention would have been difficult to deflect.

That afternoon, after reviewing the cotillion for an hour, Mistress Rose turned their attention to the finer details of the Southern Tip's geography. She lectured on the resources found in each of the kingdom's regions. She talked about the transportation involved in moving those resources and what tariffs applied to each.

After the bell rang, they waited outside for their escort and all eyes turned to darkening skies and the heavy gray clouds boiling over the mountains to the south. "Looks like we'll be getting hit with a thunderstorm tonight," Earek said, his eyes on the horizon.

"Oh, just great. Where is that girl?" Brittia said harshly. "The last thing I need is to get rained on."

Just then Marilana emerged with her weapons and followed Earek's eyes to the changing weather.

"Let's get under way," she called to her charges. "That storm will be rolling over us soon enough."

Marilana pushed the pace from dwelling to dwelling, and everyone, Brittia included, was forced to keep up. When they reached Brittia's house, the lynx paused before going inside and turned haughtily in Marilana's direction.

"Oh, Servant," Brittia said loud enough for all to hear. "I have a message for you to convey to your Mistress. Tell Lady

Annabella that I am ready to start my training with her. Tell her I await her command."

"As you wish," Marilana replied with a slight curtsey.

Marquiese gave Brittia a last polite nod, his short mane dancing in the growing breeze. He glanced at the increasingly gray sky and hurried after Marilana and what remained of their group, brooding as he walked.

He finally relaxed when Lida left them at the brick manor and she was safely inside. Then he, Earek, and Marilana entered the forest. The lioness led. The lion and the black leopard spread out and scouted their flanks, increasingly independent of their teacher. Marquiese had been pleasantly surprised when Marilana announced several fifnights before that they were good enough now to track and scout on their own while keeping her in sight. It was a huge milestone, and he took it seriously.

They found the forest free of any signs of bandits and emerged from the trees outside of Marilana's house. She had shown both Marquiese and Earek how to navigate the traps guarding the perimeter of her cottage so she no longer had to disarm them every day, and they followed her through the gate and up the walk.

"Always watch that first step, however," she warned them, "in case I've rearranged things."

Inside, they spread their homework out on the kitchen table and heard the first rumblings of thunder.

"We'll be walking home in the rain tonight, I'm afraid," Earek sighed. "Not that I mind. I would really rather be here."

"Wedding plans are in full swing, I take it?" Marilana smiled. News of Adrek and Vavinta's impending wedding was the talk of the county.

"Yes, the love birds are busy planning for the first day of summer. Father is making all the clothes, of course, even Vavinta's gown. She has been at our house every day for the past fifnight. She and Adrek are cleaning out and redressing the suite of rooms that used to belong to my grandparents on the west side of the house. They will live there while my parents and I stay on the east side of the house." It was understood that Earek's parents would remain in their current suite of rooms until they died, but that the young black leopard would leave the house as soon as possible after finishing school. "Vavinta has it all worked out; she and my mother get along great, plotting and planning. Adrek offered to let me stay in the house if I needed to, but not Vavinta. I see it in her eyes. She'll make sure I'm married and out of the house as fast as possible."

"You sound like you don't like her much," Marquiese mused.

"She's alright actually." Earek shrugged. "She's just under a lot of stress right now, and, as it turns out, she's a lot more like Brittia than I first thought."

"Most of the high-class merchant girls are," Marilana said. "Even the second or third born are trained to be haughty and demanding so that they can marry well and compete with each other on the social scene. The nice ones tend to get pushed aside and forgotten."

"Adealy and Lida aren't that way, I can tell you that," Marquiese argued.

"No, they're not. They seem to have found a balance between power and courtesy, and it's so refreshing, isn't it?"

"Lady Annabella is that way too," Earek said thoughtfully. "The few times I have interacted with her on a social scale, she seems to radiate authority without having to be bossy or pushy about it."

"Yes, but now you are entering the minefield of nobility, where courtesy is wielded as carefully as a razor," Marquiese said, chuckling. "Even so, Lady Annabella is the most honorable of all the nobles I have had the pleasure or displeasure of meeting. You are lucky to have her as your warden, Marilana."

"Yes, I am proud to be her ward and servant." Marilana smiled easily.

"I can't believe that Lady Annabella will start training Brittia soon," Earek said shaking his head.

"Oh, she won't," Marilana said without a second's hesitation.

"Aren't you going to pass on Brittia's message?" Earek asked curiously.

"Of course. It is my duty to carry all messages destined for my warden," Marilana said levelly. "I would never fail in my duty for such a thing like that. However, just because I pass on the message, doesn't mean Lady Annabella has to act on it."

"Lady Annabella will reply with some answer that will remind Brittia that she is just a merchant daughter and not in a position to demand anything of a Great Lady." Marquiese smirked.

"I wish I could see the look on Brittia's face at that exact moment." Earek chuckled. "She deserves nothing less for the disrespect she demonstrated to get her message delivered."

"I completely agree," Marquiese said, glowering. He glanced at Marilana. "Doesn't it make you mad when she acts like that?"

"Why should I be mad?" Marilana sighed. "I have told you before, I am just a peasant. I am blessed to have Lady Annabella's favor, but in the end, I am still just an orphaned peasant."

"You could be so much more if you would let yourself contemplate the opportunities you have around you," Marquiese insisted.

"Yes, you've said that before, and my answer has always been the same."

"You should have at least gotten the recognition you deserved for saving Brittia's life," Earek interjected. "She and Merchant Sleater praise us every day for the little part we played in the event. It's ridiculous."

"In their eyes, you demonstrated the greater bravery," Marilana countered. "You put your lives before others against a foe that outnumbered you and had superior weaponry. That took more courage than Merchant Sleater has in his entire being, and then you were humble about it. Of course you appear like heroes to them. Yes, I slew some bandits. Yes, I hunted the rest of them down. Yes, I secured the county. But I have done so time and time again without praise. Why should I get recognition for something that they have come to expect?"

"You saved Brittia's life," Marquiese said forcefully. "You deserve to be honored and rewarded for that."

Marilana stood up from the table and looked out the kitchen window at the rain that had started to fall. She crossed her arms and turned to face them calmly.

"I do not need them to tell me I have done well. I have saved her from a terrible fate, and that is all the reward I need."

"Despite how you two feel about each other?"

"I dislike Brittia for the way she treats other creatures in general, but I will not leave anyone to be a plaything for bandits. I know what they do to young girls; I know what they do to children. I will stand in their way as long as I can. Her hate is reward enough for me because it means she is alive to hate whomever she wants."

Marquiese shook his head. "Truthfully, I still do not understand why you have chosen the path you have."

"You have seen me in moments of despair," Marilana said quietly. "I have my own emotions to take care of, and, yes, it feels good to be praised for doing good deeds and saving lives. You have also seen me in moments of focus when my entire being is intent on bringing death to those who threaten innocent children. You both have seen more of my heart than almost anyone else. Yet you still do not understand my purpose?"

"You wish to protect lives," Earek said simply. "That is an honorable goal. You do so without prejudice or bias. That is honorable as well. We know the kindness and gentle nature of your heart."

"What is hidden from us is how such a caring spirit can be driven to kill without regard for your own life or future. What we do not understand is what pushed you to dedicate your life to the pursuits of a bandit hunter in the first place?"

Marilana turned her back to them. Marquiese shared a frustrated look with Earek, knowing they were asking Marilana to reveal one of her secrets.

"You are both intelligent and observant," Marilana said, her voice sounding brittle. "I would have thought you had enough clues to guess what happened to me."

Marquiese looked up and realized that Marilana was hugging herself and trembling as she stared out the dark window. He looked at Earek and could see his own concern mirrored in Earek's eyes.

"You were captured by bandits as a child, weren't you," Earek said softly.

Marquiese thought about it and realized Earek had to be right. It made sense, but there was more to it. So he waited. She would either find the words to tell them or she would choose not to.

"I was five," Marilana said eventually, her voice cracking. "I lived at Lady Annabella's castle among the servants. Two of the scullery maids were assigned to be my keepers; one was nine, the other eight. We played together, and they taught me how to live as a servant, how to work. One early summer day they took me to the edge of the forest to pick berries. We were supposed to stay where we could see the walls of the estate and run for help if we needed to. We were having so much fun picking berries, that we didn't pay close enough attention. We got lost in the trees.

"They tried to keep me calm and happy by pointing out different flowers and birds, but I could tell something was wrong. We stumbled into a clearing. I remember the first man stepping out of the trees. He was a huge brown bear with crude leather armor. Two bandoleers crossing his chest were filled with throwing knives. He had a sword and dagger at his waist, and a strong long bow in his paws with a thick-shafted arrow nocked and ready. I stared up at his cruel smile and stood there frozen with fear. I cried out and struggled when a sack dropped over my head and I was picked up. I lost track of how long I cried in that dark sack, carried about like a bag of produce. I would have gladly returned to that sack after what happened when it was removed.

"We had been taken south to an encampment nestled deep in a mountain valley. When the sack was removed, they stood the three of us up in a line for a different man to inspect us. He was a tall lithe jaguar, his fur sleek and shiny. He was immaculately clean, unlike the other men. When he looked at me, I wanted to curl up and hide. He looked us over carefully and questioned the creatures who brought us to the camp. 'How much ransom can we get for three of Lady Annabella's scullery maids?' he asked. We had no answer, and he didn't expect one.

"When he was satisfied, he ordered us chained and staked inside a tent. It was just the three of us in the tent, but we were staked out far enough apart that we could not touch each other. We were left there alone for three days. Once a day a plate of stale bread and a cup of water was brought and left for us. We had to use the plate to carefully push the cup of water to each other across the bare dirt. We were given a bucket to relieve ourselves, but they never bothered to empty the bucket. We were hungry, filthy, and scared.

"On the morning of the fourth day, the jaguar came to see us. He ordered the bucket emptied. He told us that a ransom demand had been sent to Lady Annabella and that we would be remaining his guests until the ransom was met. He sat on the floor with us for a long time. His eyes passed from one to the next, each time examining a different feature, but never lingering on any one of us. Finally the bear stuck his head into the tent. I remember his gravely growl, 'Victon, we have work to do.' 'Brute, what do you think of this little lioness?' Victon replied pointing at me. 'Cute. Now let's go.' Victon smiled at me, got to his feet and left the tent."

Marquiese exchanged an alarmed look with Earek and knew he had recognized the names. The two worst bandits to ever ravage the Southern Tip.

"Two more days passed with barely enough bread and water for each of us to survive. We were weak from hunger and thirst. Then on the evening of the sixth day Victon returned to our tent wearing only pants and carrying a long knife and a cup of something. He smelled strongly of wine. He crouched down next to me and ran a claw along my cheek as he spoke, 'You watch this, cutie. You'll see how much fun we'll have when it's your turn.' He turned his attention to the elder of the maids; she was staked closest to the entry. She cried and tried to back away from him. She begged and pleaded for him to leave her alone, but he simply smiled as he slowly advanced on her. He held the cup to her lips. Trembling, she drank the liquid. She slumped to the ground seconds later. Her eyes were still moving, she was still breathing, but she was limp and could not move. He stretched her out on the floor and took off his pants. He had his way with her, but not just once, and not just rape. He used the long knife to cut off her clothes in bits and pieces, and then he started to remove bits of flesh. He was at it all night. I tried not to watch, but it was so horrifying and the blood would squirt across the tent. There was so much blood. She died sometime in the early morning. He lay there on the floor sleeping in her blood for most of the day. Finally he got up and left the two of us alone with the dead body of our friend.

"We sat there in shock as the body went through the stages after death. The flies came and covered the body in a moving black mass. There were so many of them that we had to cover our faces to keep them out of our eyes and noses. The smell was horrible. Two days passed that way. He came again on the evening of the eighth day. Brute was with him. Victon lit a candle and stuck it on the ground, and then they wrapped the body in a dirty rug and hauled it out. The smoke from the candle made the flies leave and somewhat covered the smell. Victon came back with several lengths of rope. He sat on the floor and tied knots in one length of rope while he basked in our terror and fear. When he was ready, he brought several short pieces of rope to where I was huddled on the ground. 'It's not your turn cutie, but you will watch tonight,' he said to me. He tied my arms and legs so that I was forced to face the other girl.

"She sobbed in fear as she watched and waited in the knowledge that she was next. He took off his pants again and approached her with his knife and knotted rope. He did not drug her; she was weak enough that he didn't have to. She struggled and fought as he stripped her and tied her in disgusting positions. He bit and licked and beat her as he enjoyed her struggles. He tied and retied her in so many ways, each time she strained against the ropes he would laugh and have his way anyway. He kept at her all night and most of the next day. Eventually she went limp from exhaustion. He slit her throat when he was tired of playing with her. As he turned to leave, he smiled at me and drew a heart on my cheek in her blood. He laughed at my renewed tears and left me tied there facing another dead friend.

"I lost track of the days after that. I don't know how much I slept; my dreams were just as bad as the living nightmare I was in. What I remember was waking up in the dark of night. Brute was there; he wrapped me up in a blanket and carried me out of the tent still tied up. He placed me in the back of a wagon, gave me something to drink, and I slept. I have no idea how much time passed. Two days at least. When I woke up again, I was laying on the ground under the trees. Brute was sitting next to me sorting through a small chest filled with gold and silver coins. There was a hole in the ground a little ways away that I assumed the chest had come out of. He gave me some bread and water, and then turned me so that I could see across a clearing. It was getting dark. 'See those three bright stars?' He pointed them out as the sky darkened. 'Follow them and you may just make it home. Thanks for the ransom, cutie.'

"I stood and watched him climb up on his wagon and drive away into the trees. I started to walk toward the stars he had pointed out. I had nothing else to do. I hid in bushes during the days, but at night I followed the stars. On the third night I stumbled out of the trees and walked across a large meadow toward the stars. I didn't realize where I was, but the guards on the walls spotted me and sent help. Half dead and terrorized beyond my understanding, I had returned to Lady Annabella's estates.

"Lady Annabella told me later that I collapsed half way to the walls. The guards gathered me up and carried me to my room. Lady Annabella and Healer Magus cleaned me up and tended to my wounds. It took me a month to come around enough that I knew who was who and where I was. It took two more months before I was healed enough to leave my room and Lady Annabella's estates. When school started, Captain-General Zariff would take me on his horse to school and back again. It was hard for me to be around the other children, but Brittia made me so mad that I fought back. Headmistress Ceta would cane me or try to punish me in other ways. But it meant nothing; what I had already been through was so much worse than anything they could do to me.

"Through the years, I heard stories of other captures and terrors brought on by Victon and Brute. I hated them with every fiber of my being. I vowed to put an end to their reign of terror. With Zariff's help, I began my training to become a bandit hunter. My sole goal in life was to protect others from the same horrors that haunted my dreams. Lady Annabella was not happy about my choice, but she allowed it because it gave me a reason to live.

"When I was ten, I took the Bandit Hunter Oaths. I was not happy, but I was determined. When I tracked down and killed Victon and Brute, I was not proud. I was not satisfied. But it was a promise fulfilled. When word of their deaths spread through the town, the relief was palpable. That feeling of seeing others living with less fear made me feel good for the first time in five years. I continued to hunt bandits; I continued to kill them; I saved as many lives along the way as I could. I did it because I knew that was what I was needed for.

"It has been a hard life. I have seen so much violence. I have so much blood on my paws; I do not want to be praised for causing more deaths. I am a killer. I am feared. I am a peasant that can be pushed aside. But as long as I do my duty, no one else need spill the blood of bandits. Mystillion rests easier now that the worst of the bandits no longer hold sway."

Marilana turned without another word and left the kitchen. Marquiese sat stunned. He looked at Earek and could see the horror and revulsion in his eyes. They sat there in silence for a long time each lost in their own thoughts.

"I remember the years when Victon and Brute held sway," Earek said eventually. "No one went anywhere without five or six companions. Merchant guards and soldiers were everywhere. Fights were frequent, and I was never allowed to be alone outside the house. I never knew what happened to them. But when we found out they were dead, it was as if the world became a brighter place. We could play outside in the yard without fear. There were other bandits, of course, and the forest was still a dangerous place, but nothing seemed as terrifying, because we knew good would win. It was the best thing that ever happened to Mystillion."

"I bet it was." Marquiese nodded his understanding.

"I can hardly believe Marilana told us her story," Earek said. "I can understand why she keeps it secret."

Yes, Marquiese thought, *she would be shunned, treated with revulsion, or pitied. She does not want those things. She wants to live her life with pride and honor. Even without knowing her past terrors, she is treated poorly. People are afraid of her. She was very trusting to tell us. It does not change how I think of her; she is still the same person I have come to trust. She must be wondering what it will do to our friendship.*

Marquiese sprang to his feet. He knew he had to find her and let her know he was still her friend. He looked at Earek and saw the same sudden realization. Together they hurried out of the kitchen and stopped just as quickly. Marilana sat in front of the fireplace in the main room. She hugged her knees to her chest and rested her chin on her knees as she stared into the flames.

"I suppose you would like to leave now," she said calmly. "I'll get my bow."

"Wait! Please," Marquiese said. He sat down next to her. Earek did the same.

"I don't want your pity," she said harshly, misreading their faces.

"We're not here to pity you," Marquiese said gently. "We're here to tell you that we are your friends no matter what. Your story is sad, but it does not change who you are or how we feel about you."

"Actually, I feel I know you better now that I have heard your story," Earek added. "Your experience made you who you are. I have seen your heart and choose to be your friend as long as you will have me. It took a lot of courage to tell us your dark secret. It means a lot to me that you did."

"Yes, thank you for entrusting us with this knowledge." Marquiese smiled. "I now know why you stubbornly protect Mystillion, and why you do not want praise for your success as a bandit hunter. I can see why you take your skills as a fighter and a healer so seriously."

"It means even more that neither of you are withdrawing your friendship," the lioness said. "I was more afraid of losing my friends than I was of telling about those terrible events."

"You cannot get rid of us that easily," the black leopard said with a grin.

"As scared as I was, I had to know how you would treat me after I shared my secret with you. I am truly blessed to have such true friends."

"I can't imagine how much courage it took for you to tell us your story, let alone hunt down those men," Marquiese said.

"It didn't take courage to hunt them down. I never felt courageous or strong. I just did what I had to do. If I didn't, who would?"

"To be honest, I can hardly believe that you stayed sane through it all," the lion said, the short tufts of his mane swaying from side to side.

"Sane? You think anyone could be sane after that?" Marilana looked at him seriously. "I live with the pain and memory of terrible deeds. I lock away beautiful gifts and instead spend my days mixing poisons and devising deadly traps. How many children do you know who spend more time learning weapons and strategy than playing with friends? Other girls played with dolls: I played with knives. I have not lived a sane life."

Marquiese studied her eyes and, for the first time, comprehended the madness of her life. He too had spent his childhood with few friends, spending his days with tutors and armsmasters learning his duty instead of playing.

"Everyone has some madness in their life," Marquiese replied softly. "Some lose their family to illness or accident, some have their family stripped from them, some have duty thrust upon them from an early age, and some live through terrors. Are any of us truly sane?"

"We may not be insane in the same way," Earek added, "but we all choose to live. We can think rationally, and use reason as our guide. You have taught Marquiese and me so much about the larger world around us, and you have done so with strength and logic. You helped me through the madness in my own life, small as it was. I can never thank you enough for that."

Marquiese agreed and said, "You have shown us the depth of your heart, and I am grateful, Marilana. You are not the same person I first met. You don't have to hide the person you have become. In fact, the Southern Tip and Redsands would be greatly enriched if you shared your strength as Lady Annabella's heiress."

"You always come back to that, don't you." Marilana sighed. "My obsession to protect the innocent and hunt bandits has no place in politics."

"You don't have to hide who you are," Marquiese insisted.

"The fact remains that when I turn seventeen, I will lose the protection Lady Annabella has provided for me. I will be a desirable peasant maid alone in the world. Every male I come across will be a potential threat, a threat that by law I can do nothing to stop. I will have to disappear completely."

"Or, you could marry," Earek said calmly.

"It would be better to disappear."

Marquiese didn't know what to say. She was right. Even the other boys at school watched her covetously. If she came of age and lost Lady Annabella's protection, she would be the lowest of peasants, a potential plaything to any lustful male, even if she married. It would only be a matter of time before it happened.

"Hey," he said, touching them both on a shoulder. "The future is not set in stone. There is still a year and a half before any of us come of age and that is a long time to allow for change."

"You're right about that," Marilana said, springing to her feet. "We have to focus on the present and let the future come as it will. At the present, we have finals coming up, and homework that needs to be done. Come my friends, we have work to do."

Together they went back into the kitchen and finished their homework.

30

Marquiese was growing tired of Brittia's attentions. He had stood with her all morning watching the graduating class perform the Dance of the Seasons. Hour after hour of the lynx's suffocating company and less-than-inspiring conversation was trying enough, but listening to her flatterers chatting pointlessly about the performance and endlessly assuring Brittia that she would make a much better Lady Season next year was too much. So when the lynx ask him ever so politely if he might fetch her something to drink, something cold, but not too sweet, Marquiese jumped at the chance. He nodded as if nothing could bring him more pleasure and eased his way away from the giggling girls.

He took his time walking around the edge of the crowd to the drinks table. He had picked up two mugs of punch and was making his way back when he spotted Earek, Klay, and Caton engrossed in some interaction at the entrance to the market. Earek glanced at him and jerked his head in the direction of the street. Marquiese hurried through the crowd and found Brittia and Marilana facing off in the shadows of the buildings. He could not make out what they were saying, but he could see that Marilana's face was expressionless while Brittia was clearly unhappy.

He started toward them. Marilana made some reply to something Brittia said, and the lynx stomped her foot as if what she had heard was completely inadequate. She snapped a quick reply, and Marilana shook her head, clearly defiant. Brittia snarled and drew her paw back, seemingly on the verge of slapping the lioness.

Marilana stared back at her, and did so with utter calm. Brittia hesitated. A moment later, she dropped her paw, huffed in frustration, and turned away. Marquiese slipped around the corner and spotted Marilana walking briskly down a deserted side street toward the edge of town. He glanced back at the crowd. Brittia had her back to him. No one else seemed to be paying him any attention. He set the drinks on a nearby window ledge and hurried down the street. *She couldn't have gotten far, he thought.*

Marquiese was wrong. By the time he made it to the edge of the forest north of town, Marilana had disappeared. He found no sign of her tracks, not that he expected to. He fixed his location at the forest's edge and plotted his course. If the lioness took a fairly straight route, he predicted that she would arrive at the stream that cut through the forest north of Mystillion and formed the waterfall and lake that the two of them were so fond of.

He hesitated a moment wondering at the wisdom of the decision he was about to make and then plunged into the forest. It took him a good portion of the afternoon to make his way to the lake. He moved slowly, listening closely to the sound of the birds, the wind in the trees, and the scampering of creatures much smaller than he.

Marquiese stayed low in the underbrush, wherever possible stepping on solid ground so he wouldn't leave tracks. Finally he could see an opening in front of him and crouched behind a clump of bushes. He peered into the clearing. Before him, the waterfall tumbled into the serene lake, and its magical sound filled the shallow valley. His eyes moved around the clearing, and there on the near bank in the tall grass sat Marilana.

Marquiese sighed with relief. It had been a huge risk following her here. She would not be happy. He shifted his feet slightly, and a startled bird burst out of the bush directly in front of him.

Marilana reacted so fast that the lion barely had time to avoid her arrow with a lightning quick dive roll. He rolled again, this time out of the underbrush and onto his back. He froze, staring up at a drawn arrow.

"Marquiese?" Marilana hissed. "What are you doing here? Are you crazy? I could have killed you!"

"I'm sorry," he said quickly. "I didn't mean to startle you. I tried following you. I wanted to make sure you were all right. But I fell behind. I'm sorry."

Marilana scanned the surrounding trees and slowly released the tension on her bow.

"Foolish boy!" She scowled at him. "I didn't teach you how to track so that you could get yourself killed by sneaking up on your teacher."

"I wasn't sneaking up on you," he replied, coming to his feet. "I just wanted to spend some time with you."

"You mean instead of suffering the rest of the afternoon with Brittia." Marilana shook her head, sighed, and walked back down to the lake. Marquiese followed, taking his place beside her in the grass.

"The forest is dangerous, Marquiese," Marilana chided. "I can't protect you if I don't know you're in the forest. Bandits have been seen all over the Southern Tip. They have been conducting raids almost indiscriminately."

"I saw no trace of them," Marquiese noted.

"No. It has been quiet so far today, but we shouldn't risk staying here too long."

"Okay," Marquiese said. But then he changed subject. "Listen, I saw you and Brittia arguing. What did she want?"

Marilana shook her head in exasperation.

"She wanted Lady Annabella's answer about when she would be starting her training," Marilana said after a moment. "I told her I delivered her message. I also told her that Lady Annabella had not yet made her reply. Brittia got mad and demanded that I insist on a reply immediately. Silly lynx. I refused, of course, and told her she had no right to order Lady Annabella's servants around that way."

"She wanted to strike you."

"She thought better of it," the lioness said simply.

"What was Lady Annabella's reaction when you gave her the message?" Marquiese asked curiously.

"She seemed as unconcerned as she was unsurprised." Marilana smiled slightly.

Marquiese smiled too. He turned his attention toward the lake for a time and sat watching the sunlight sparkle on the water.

"You know there are some people who want to dance with you," Marquiese said out of nowhere.

"Yes, Master Arndt and Master Warhaim have made that quite clear." Marilana sighed.

"Really? Did something else happen after the Masquerade?" Marquiese asked shrewdly.

"They demanded Lady Annabella tell them who the Lady in Gold was. Lady Annabella told them that she would not reveal the young lady's identity until she chose, but that they would learn of it at some point in the future. Then they sent a message yesterday asking if she was ready to make the reveal since it was now the end of the school year."

"Very interesting. And how did she reply?" Marquiese sat up, his eyes taking in her face.

"That they would learn nothing by pestering her."

Marquiese let out a low breath. After a stretch of uncomfortable silence, he said, "They are not the only ones who are excited to dance with you at some point. Earek cannot wait to see what happens when you finally outdance Brittia, and Klay and Caton have both said that they would be more than willing to dance with you again. Probably the understatement of the year. They were both amazed with how well you danced at the Masquerade."

"I'm just glad they're both keeping it a secret," Marilana mused.

"I will say that Earek and I have been rather disappointed that you have not been willing to practice with us. You keep saying that the main room of your house is too small, but I wonder if there might be another reason as well."

He watched her, but she refused to look at him.

"You enjoy dancing," he said quietly. "You enjoyed dancing at the Winter Masquerade. From what others have said, your last dance with Master Arndt was the best dance of the night."

"I won't deny that I had fun dancing that night," Marilana replied quietly. "And I won't deny that I was tempted to reveal my identity just to prove that I was the best dancer. However, the last dance with Master Arndt was not the best dance of the night."

"Why didn't you reveal your identity if you were enjoying it so much?" he asked curiously.

"Because Master Arndt's eyes were full of lust. He would have been thrilled to find out he was of a higher caste, and I knew if he wanted to push the issue with Lady Annabella, I wouldn't have much choice."

Marilana glanced at him and then looked quickly at her feet.

"You were right to be worried about my safety that night," the lioness said softly. "I was just too worried about *your* safety to admit it at the time."

"You're still worried about Master Arndt, aren't you?" Marquiese insisted.

"He wants to meet me." Marilana sighed sadly. "Lady Annabella said that she would tell him someday. I just don't know if his continued interest will be satisfied with just my name and face. I don't know if his interest is just curiosity or if his lust is driving him. I can't out maneuver a great-noble the way I can a merchant, he has too many resources."

"Don't worry too much about the future, Marilana. Arndt doesn't hold his interest in one place too long."

"You sound like you know him well," Marilana commented.

"Better than some, but not as well as Lady Annabella," Marquiese said evenly. "Trust in her judgment. She has your best interest in mind."

They sat in silence for a moment.

"If the dance with Master Arndt wasn't the best dance of the night, which dance was?" Marquiese asked hopefully.

"You know which dance." She held his eye. Marquiese breathed a sigh of relief and then stood up. He offered his paw to her.

"What?" she said.

"Dance with me," he said smiling happily. "Two dances, right here, right now, just you and me with no witnesses. I need the practice."

"Which two dances?" she asked suspiciously. She still had not taken his paw.

"For the second, a more complex waltz than anything you'll learn in finishing school," he said, his paw still extended. "And the first, well, the courtship dance."

Marilana gaped at him. "Marquiese, what? Are you crazy? I can't dance the courtship dance without Lady Annabella's approval, even if it is just for fun."

"It's not for real," he said still smiling. "This is just practice. No witnesses to make it official. Just you and me together having fun dancing. I assume Lady Annabella taught you high style?"

"You want to practice high style?" Marilana blinked in surprise.

"If you'll join me," he replied.

"Alright," Marilana said accepting his paw, "but only for fun, and only because you've made me curious. I want to see your skills."

Marquiese pulled Marilana to her feet and led her to an open patch of ground. He made a grand flourish, bowing with one arm behind his back and one crossing his chest. Marilana held a make-believe fan at arm's length, pretending to hide her face, drew her skirt out on one side, and curtseyed deeply.

The lion's first steps cut a small, well-defined circle, his eyes fixed on his partner's pretend fan. The lioness followed his pace exactly, creating a circle of her own.

Marquiese picked up his pace. He stepped and dipped and hopped, to and fro, round and round, circling and coming face-to-face with her again. Marilana kept pace easily. With each pass, they stepped ever faster and faster. Soon they were both breathing hard and flying through a series of complicated, beautifully choreographed steps. It was almost like sparring, each pushing to stay in step and outlast the other, neither faltering nor breaking form, neither blinking nor looking aside.

Finally the lion could go no more and brought the dance to a smooth, seamless halt; he faced his partner and bowed low. To his surprise, the lioness followed the last of his steps perfectly and stopped at the same moment; she dropped to a deep curtsey, her breathing just as hard as his. He met her amber eyes and broke into a playful laugh. Marilana smiled broadly.

"Now that was fun," Marquiese said, straightening at last.

"Yes. And I think our sparring matches have equalized our endurance." She made a quick scan of the surrounding forest, looking for any sign of threats. Nothing in the forest seemed out of place.

"Do you never stop?" Marquiese said, his voice teasing. "It seems quiet."

"Yes. I'm sorry, but my duty calls for me to be wary, even after such an amazing dance," she said, smiling brightly.

"I did say two dances," he reminded her.

"And I have no intention of letting you forget," she laughed.

"Are you ready then?"

Marquiese held out his paw and bowed. She drew a deep breath and placed her paw in his. She matched his bow with a curtsey. He closed the distance between them and laid his other paw on her thin waist. She laid hers on his shoulder. He hummed the notes of a simple waltz and led her around the clearing. Marilana followed easily. As the beat increased, so did the complexity of the steps and the elegance of the spins. He twirled her around and they moved with spectacular grace across the meadow.

Marquiese watched her the whole time, smiling for the sheer joy of dancing with her. As the imaginary song ended, he spun her around and caught her free paw in his, holding her paws at arm's length, and holding her gaze for a long and powerful moment. Her smile was as warm and compelling as the afternoon sun and far more beautiful.

Finally Marquiese bowed; she curtseyed.

"Thank you for dancing with me," he said softly. "It has been a long time since I have had a partner worthy of such dances, nor one so beautiful."

"You are very welcome," Marilana replied, rosy cheeked. "Thank you for asking me. I enjoyed it. And I must say you are definitely the best dancer I have ever had the pleasure of dancing with. And yes, perhaps the most handsome."

They stood there for a moment more before Marilana looked away. She frowned at the sky and then looked back at him. He had yet to release her paws.

"It is getting late," she said quietly. "Your merchant family is probably getting worried, and I need to report to Lady Annabella."

Reluctantly, he released her paws then, and she retrieved her bow and quiver.

"I must say that was the first time I ever danced with someone armed with a dagger on her belt and a bandoleer of throwing knives across her chest," he said, chuckling as they entered the trees.

Marilana paused and looked back at him with a mischievous smile. She met his eyes for a moment and then turned and led him on. Marquiese stifled a sigh. It had been as good a day as he had spent in long time, and he didn't want it to end. He knew he had to let her go, though. He couldn't risk spending the evening with her; he worried that he would go too far; he worried that he wanted to. He knew his duty did not allow it.

31

Marquiese needed to make a decision. He knew he should not be staying in the Southern Tip any longer. He had been in hiding here for nearly three years.

Lady Annabella took every opportunity to try to convince him to return to Maefair. He knew returning was the right thing to do. He knew it was his duty. He knew it was the only way he would be able to truly live his life, fully and without secrets, but part of him didn't want to give up the easy life in Mystillion. He attended school. He had friends. He had Marilana. He sparred with her every morning and worked on his jousting every day. He was happy. He didn't want to leave.

Marilana, however, was growing increasingly uneasy. She had made him promise not to go anywhere without her, and she was nervous whenever they were together. She rarely spent any free time with him outside their sparring practice. He knew there was something going on that had her on edge, but she wouldn't talk to him about it.

He rarely saw Earek. His brother Adrek's wedding had gone well, and the newlywed couple had spent the entire month thereafter in their suite of rooms. Earek's mother delivered all their food to them, as was traditional.

Because Adrek was missing his regularly scheduled workload at Merchant Yulan's shop, his younger brother agreed to be there on a full time basis. Earek didn't really mind because it kept him busy; the downside was that he had been unable to visit Jarek at Lady Annabella's estate or spend any time with Marquiese or Marilana.

The National Day of Worship gave Earek and Marquiese a day just to relax, dance, and have fun. Not Marilana though.

The lioness was ultra alert and on edge the whole day, and Marquiese had noticed that Lady Annabella had more guards on duty than in previous years. Something was definitely up, Marquiese knew that, but he also knew better than to press Marilana for an explanation.

Two days later, when Marilana was escorting Marquiese home after an hour of strenuous sparring practice, she stopped him short of the manor gate, her nervous gaze taking in the surrounding trees.

"What is it?" he asked her, ignoring the suspicious stare of the manor guard.

"Bandits all over the province are getting bolder," she said earnestly. "This past month they have been raiding almost non-stop."

"Yes, I saw all the extra guards stationed in town on the National Day of Worship," he replied, "but there didn't seem to be any trouble."

"That was only because The Phantom stopped them from reaching Mystillion," Marilana replied. "They made six different raids that we know of that day. Groups of four men wearing feast day clothes and trying to sneak into different worship services across the Southern Tip."

"That is bold," the lion commented. "Dangerously so."

"Three of those groups were discovered before they reached their designated towns, including the group The Phantom caught south of Mystillion. The other three were caught as they headed back to the border. I'm sure there were other groups that made successful incursions, but I don't have any evidence yet. The one thing we do know is that they are looking for something very specific."

"How do you know that?"

"Because none had any loot. No spoils," she answered. "And the bandits who were captured have refused to say anything."

"Marilana, to be truthful, I'm not all that worried about bandits," Marquiese said, trying to sooth her.

"But I am," the lioness said emphatically, her eyes ever busy. "And I think you should be too. The raids are happening too fast. This isn't business as usual. The Phantom has asked for my help. She's heard a rumor of a meeting between all the bandit leaders in the area. I need to do this, and Lady Annabella agrees, even though it is extremely dangerous."

She fixed the lion with a serious look.

"Promise me you won't leave the house for three days."

He looked at her for a long moment. "Alright," he said calmly. "I promise."

Despite a lack of evidence, Marilana felt something very big was in the wind. She and Child had been chasing leads for six days. They had spied on dozens of known bandits and tracked many more. She was tired and frustrated. She had not been home. She had not been to Lady Annabella's castle, and she had neither seen nor communicated with Marquiese. He had promised her three days of seclusion, not six. She knew he would be out and about somewhere—he was not a lion who did well with confinement—and she prayed to The Goddess that he was not out looking for her.

Marilana felt like someone was playing a game with her, the rules of which she was not privy to. She felt like someone was moving pieces on a board she could not see. However, this morning appeared to be en route to their best chance to catch the bandit leaders in one place. She and Child had split up and followed two of the raiding groups. They were converging in the meadow beside the small lake. She and Child had chirped and whistled a quick plan. Child had climbed a nearby tree within earshot while Marilana was concealed in a small cave behind the waterfall. She was their eyes; Child was their ears. They had used a similar scheme when they had chanced upon a meeting of bandit groups almost two fifnights ago.

Marilana crouched low and peered through the mist stirred up by the waterfall as a bear and two jackals, armed to the teeth, walked cautiously out of the trees on the north side of the lake. She watched them move quickly to the narrow end of the lake and cross to the southern shore. They stopped in the exact place where she and Marquiese had danced what seemed now like an eternity ago.

The bandits crouched low and the jackals raised their bows. Suddenly, another bear and a huge boar emerged from the trees on the south, dragging a third creature between them, clearly a captive. When the bandits got to the clearing, they turned their prisoner so the bear, obviously their leader, could get a good look.

"Oh, Goddess above!" Marilana gasped when she saw Marquiese's face. His paws were tied behind his back, and a gag covered his mouth. Marilana swallowed back a sob, then gritted her teeth as Marquiese was forced to his knees.

He was bleeding from a cut over his eye and nasty gash on his arm; his scabbard was empty. The leader smiled cruelly down at Marquiese and said something Marilana could not hear. Marquiese struggled against his bonds, glaring hatred at the bear.

Suddenly, all five of the bandits turned toward an unseen disturbance coming from the west. When the leader turned back to the men holding Marquiese, he was scowling. He gave them an order and waved them back to the south.

Marilana did not wait to see more; she hurried to the back of the cave, squeezed through a small opening, and then disappeared into the long, winding tunnel she and Child had dug many years before.

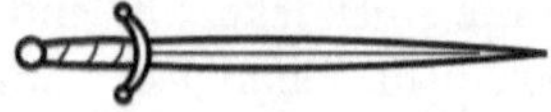

Marquiese's troubles had begun that morning on his way home after sparring practice.

It had been days since he had heard from Marilana, and he was worried. He mentioned his concern to Zariff, but the

Captain-General had no more knowledge of her whereabouts than he did.

The bandits had ambushed him and his merchant guards when they were returning along the road to the brick manor and taken him captive, the very thing Marilana was trying to prevent.

He had at least made a better showing of his swordsmanship than the merchant guards who were escorting him and who now lay dead on the road somewhere between the manor and Lady Annabella's estates. Marquiese had killed two of the bandits before getting hit on the forehead with a well-aimed rock and tackled. He had struggled mightily as the bandits tied his paws behind his back and grunted as one of the men kicked him in the side.

Marquiese growled a curse into his gag as he was hauled to his feet and pushed into the forest. He tripped and stumbled through the trees trying to make as noticeable a trail as possible as the men pushed and dragged him along.

Marquiese snarled as his captors pulled him into the meadow around the little lake and he felt a moment of regret thinking of the quiet times he and Marilana had shared here. They forced him to kneel in front of a huge, badly scarred brown bear who was clearly their leader. The bear looked down at him and a bone chilling smile spread across his face.

"So you are the answer to the riddle we have been chasing for months," he sneered. Marquiese's gut filled with ice when he realized he had been recognized. "He will pay me very well when I turn you over to him."

A group of birds burst from a tree just west of the lake. All five bandits turned to look.

"Quickly! Our associates are coming," the bear snapped, turning back to his men. "We don't have to share the bounty if they don't know we have the prize. Take him back south across the road and then angle west. Stay close to the Lady's estates, but not too close. The others won't follow you there. Wait in the trees west of the estates until I join you. Whatever you do, don't lose him. We need him alive."

His captors forced Marquiese to his feet and hurried him back south into the forest. He stumbled along as slowly as he could, but the men prodded him with their daggers and forced him to keep pace. Then, suddenly, a shrill whistle pierced the stillness of the forest. Birds erupted from trees all around them, hundreds of them.

The bear and boar holding Marquiese froze in their tracks and looked around in sudden alarm, holding their diggers tightly. Marquiese dropped to one knee as he heard the slight twang of a bow. The first man fell, followed quickly by the second. Behind him, Marquiese heard shouts and creatures crashing through the underbrush. He rose to his feet and started to run south. A puma burst out of the bushes on his left only to fall to an arrow. Suddenly, Marilana sprang out of the forest on his right and grabbed his arm.

"Keep moving," the lioness hissed. "You stop, you die."

She darted into the tress, and Marquiese ran as hard as he could, trying with all his strength to keep up with her. Crashing sounds and urgent shouting rose up on all sides of them. Four bandits emerged from the trees on their left, running as fast as their feet would carry them, one fell causing the others to dive for cover.

Marilana pushed Marquiese left through the break in the underbrush the bandits had been trying to block. A heavily armed cheetah appeared out of nowhere, sprinting out of the forest on their right. With a dagger in each paw, he leapt at them, but an arrow caught him in the chest mid-leap. Marquiese had no time to wonder where the arrow had come from as Marilana pulled him on through the trees. He heard an odd trill behind them and saw Marilana raise her bow over her head as if using it to brush away a fly. She kept running.

A sudden hail of arrows fell through the trees around them. Hissing sharply, Marilana jumped sideways and shoved him under dense cover. Marquiese looked at his friend in surprise and fear. An arrow protruded from her thigh, blood was beginning to soak her skirt around the arrow shaft. Seeming unconcerned for her wound, Marilana pulled a knife. She sliced away the gag and the ropes tying his paws together.

"My house is straight south," she growled giving him the knife. "Run there, get inside, and defend yourself until help arrives. Ride fast to Lady Annabella's. Whatever you do, don't stop, and don't look back."

"Marilana? I can't leave—!"

"I can't run with you. I'll slow them down," she said forcefully as the second hail of arrows fell. "Now go!"

She hauled him out and shoved him. He ran as fast as he could. The knife was sticky in his paw. Behind him he heard the clashing of steel blades in furious combat. Fear gripped his heart. Off to his right something smashed through the underbrush. Just ahead he recognized the ridge of trees behind Marilana's house. He dove forward and rolled down the ridge. He came up against the garden wall and looked around.

Nothing was moving yet.

He carefully hopped over the wall and made his way into the house. No sooner had he closed the door, when he heard angry shouts outside. Something thunked against the door behind his back, and one of the crossbows released its bolt. Some creature screamed. Marquiese hurried to the armory cabinet and pulled out a spare bow. He set the knife down but paused in confusion as he realized the stickiness on the knife was blood. A voice rang out startling Marquiese back to action. He strung the bow and grabbed a quiver of arrows.

"I know you're in there, Highness. We will not leave without you. Our employer has placed a substantial sum on your head. He wants you alive so that he can make you and your father suffer horrendously."

Marquiese peered out the arrow slits around the door. Bandits stood shoulder to shoulder just outside the garden wall. He was surrounded and trapped. Marilana had been right; any fortress hidden in the woods could be overrun if there were enough enemies. For the first time in nearly three years, Marilana's house felt more like a death trap than a place of safety.

When Marquiese made no answer, the bandit leader gave the order to attack. Most of the bandits hesitated. One charged up the path from the gate, and got a crossbow bolt in his chest. A rock shattered one of the kitchen windows. Marquiese hurried to the kitchen wondering briefly if Marilana would ever know it had gotten broken.

Marquiese nocked an arrow and peeked out the broken window. A lanky weasel saw him and jumped over the wall only to let out an anguished cry of pain. Marquiese watched the weasel grab at his leg and then start convulsing. Spittle flew from his lips as he fell to the ground. The other bandits looked away in fear, and Marquiese now knew the effectiveness of the poison traps positioned throughout the garden. An angry shout from the leader brought the bandits back to their tasks.

A large wolf climbed on to the wall, but Marquiese drew his arrow and released. The wolf crumpled and toppled back off the wall. Something large hit the back door. Marquiese hurried into the main room. The doors both still held. The sound of harsh breathing brought his attention back to the broken window. A large boar was heaving himself through the window. Marquiese drew another arrow and loosed. The boar slumped across the sill, blood dripping to join glass shards on Marilana's clean counter.

Angry shouts arose outside. Another loud crash shook the back door. Marquiese had nowhere to go, and no one to help him. The last cross bow released its bolt. The third crash against the back door was accompanied by a slight splintering sound. The door still held, but he knew a couple more hits was all it could take. He glanced at the statue of The Goddess standing on Marilana's mantle and sent up a silent prayer. Then he nocked another arrow and took aim out the front door arrow slits. He killed two more bandits as they approached along the front path.

The fourth crashing sound against the back door echoed through the room. Strangely the echo grew louder. Marquiese recognized the sounds of galloping horses and turned back to the arrow slits. Outside the bandits scrambled for cover as arrows streaked through the air. Marquiese took a welcome breath of relief as a large contingent of horsemen engaged the bandits. Remembering Marilana's last instructions, he tossed aside the bow, belted on a spare short sword, and dashed out into the fray.

Captain Branth didn't hesitate. He grabbed Marquiese by the paw and pulled him up behind him on his horse.

"Ride hard!" Captain Branth shouted to his men and spurred his mount forward.

The horsemen formed up and charged down the road. Looking behind, Marquiese could see dozens of dead surrounding Marilana's cottage and littering her once beautiful garden. A second group of soldiers continued fighting the bandits and preventing pursuit. Marquiese turned back forward and saw a group of bandits gathering on the road directly in front of them.

"Don't slow down!" Captain Branth yelled to his troops.

Marquiese braced for a hard impact or something far worse, but just then a salvo of arrows flew from the nearby trees, and half the awaiting bandits fell to their death. The horses of his rescuers easily burst through the remaining bandits and continued at a gallop down the road. They rounded the last bend and charged toward the castle gates.

The men on the walls called down, and the gates opened. The horses charged through the gates and their riders didn't draw rein until they were inside the stable yard. Marquiese looked back through the closing gates, but saw neither his pursuers nor any sign of the other soldiers or Marilana.

With a sigh, he dismounted and thanked Captain Branth for his assistance.

"With pleasure," the soldier replied.

He stood on the lowest castle step for a few moments to calm his racing heart and watched as the men walked their mounts to cool them before leading them off to the stables. He took one last look at the closed gates and then started up the stairs. Just as he reached the castle doors, he heard a shout from the guardsmen on the wall. He turned back and watched as one of the gate guards opened the foot gate. A loan scout stumbled through and hurried to report to Captain Branth.

Marquiese's heart sank and he looked down at the blood that had dried on his paw. He didn't think he had touched his own wounds. That meant the blood wasn't his. *Marilana, where are you?*

Taslin, Lady Annabella's servant waited nervously for him. He nodded and followed her up the stairs to the upper level and down the halls to a wide door. She knocked, waited just a moment, then opened the door for him to enter the war room. Lady Annabella and Captain-General Zariff were hunched over a long table studying a map of the Southern Tip.

"Thank The Goddess!" Lady Annabella sighed with relief when she saw him.

Marquiese launched into a detailed report of the events that had befallen him. When he was finished, Zariff nodded briskly to him and Lady Annabella, then left quickly.

Marquiese stared at the door as it closed, and then turned to face the Southern Tips' noble leader.

"So?" Lady Annabella asked quietly.

"One of the bandit leaders recognized me," he said quietly. "He confirmed the bounty on my head. If he hadn't been so greedy and tried to conceal me from the other bandit groups, I might not be here now. Marilana pulled a very daring rescue."

"She is talented at such things," Lady Annabella commented.

"Yes, but I am concerned that she is not well. She took an arrow in her leg, and I do not know how blood got on the knife hilt she gave me."

"We must believe she will survive as she has before. What now?" Lady Annabella asked in a strained voice.

"It is time," Marquiese said sadly. "It is long past time."

32

Marquiese spent the next few days attempting to reconcile his emotions. He spent much of the first day sitting at windows that commanded a view of the stableyard and trying to compose a letter. He made little headway on the letter, as every time the gate was opened, he found himself searching for Marilana among the arrivals. Eventually he corked his ink and sanded the finished letter. Lady Annabella arranged for a courier to take the letter to Maefair.

After that, Marquiese paced the upper halls of Lady Annabella's castle restlessly. He watched for anyone making reports, but still had no word. Lady Annabella frequently joined him at the windows overlooking the stableyard. She never said a word, but the worry on her face was all Marquiese need to confirm that they shared a common concern.

On the afternoon of the second day, Captain-General Zariff approached Lady Annabella and Marquiese as they held their silent vigil at the windows. Lady Annabella looked at Zariff hopefully.

"The bandit attacks are continuing. Individual groups have been making forays north. I believe they are attempting to gain positions along the North Road to set ambushes for travelers. We have set a perimeter defense and are holding Mystillion county secure. Merchant Colbran and his family have gathered all their belongings and arrived safely to the estate. They are comfortable in one of the lesser guest rooms to wait for further orders."

Lady Annabella nodded her acknowledgment of the report. Marquiese sighed heavily.

"Additionally," Zariff said grinning mischievously, "both Ghost and Phantom have made contact."

"Oh, thank The Goddess!" Lady Annabella exclaimed.

"The Phantom is unharmed and is heading south to try to stem the flow of bandits coming north. Marilana will be reporting to Healer Magus tomorrow morning."

Marquiese placed his paw on the wall to steady himself. His relief had made him momentarily dizzy. He bade Lady Annabella and Zariff a good night, and stumbled back to his guest room. He was going to sleep well for the first time in three days.

Marilana limped slightly as she approached the door of one of the guest suites in Lady Annabella's castle, her herb satchel hanging from one shoulder.

She had not seen Marquiese since his rescue. She had spent the last three days and nights helping Zariff and his troops disperse the remaining bandits. She had tried to find the bandit leader who had recognized Marquiese, thinking she could prevent him from sharing the information with others, but had been unsuccessful.

Marilana took a deep breath and knocked softly on the door. The door opened a crack and Marilana could see only darkness beyond.

"It's me. Marilana," she said quietly.

"Come in." The door opened only wide enough for her to slip in and she stood for a moment letting her eyes adjust. She heard him say, "I'm sorry. I was washing up."

Marilana followed the silhouette into the next room. She closed the door behind her and let her eyes drink in the sight of Marquiese as he stepped up to the washbasin. He had his shirt off.

She whispered, "I'll wait in the other room, if you like."

"No, please." Marquiese dipped his paws into the water in the basin and proceeded to wash his arms. Marilana realized she was staring at the water as it ran off his muscular frame and shook herself back to the reason for her visit.

"I'm sorry to intrude," she said. "Lady Annabella said you wanted me to check on your wounds."

"Yes, that is what I told her," he said picking up the towel and turning to face her.

Marilana fought to keep her breathing under control. Marquiese stood straight and proper, power and authority radiating from him. From this simple act, Marilana could tell that he was no longer hiding who he was.

She dropped her eyes and moved to a side table. She set her herb satchel down and turned back to Marquiese. "Please sit down," she said formally, directing him to a nearby stool with her lightly bandaged paw.

When the lion was settled on the stool, Marilana examined the cut on his arm, the scrape on his forehead, and finally the bruise on his side. She rotated his arm while feeling his side.

"The cuts are healing nicely, and you don't have any broken ribs. The bruise will probably disappear over the next fifnight or so," she pronounced firmly.

She started to turn away, but he caught her good paw.

"Marilana, the injuries do not bother me," he said gently. "That is not why I requested your presence. I wanted to talk with you, and I wanted to do so privately."

Marilana nodded. She had expected as much.

"I am so glad you're alright," he said softly. "When I learned you had reported to Zariff, I was so relieved. I was worried about your injuries when Zariff said you were going to be reporting to Healer Magus."

"That is kind of you, but I will be fine."

"What happened? Please tell me."

Marilana hesitated before telling him the truth. "I fought several bandits before I reached you. One of them manage to slice my paw before I killed him, and then I took an arrow in my leg from that first volley of arrows. I knew I wouldn't be able to keep up with you to run to my house, so I stayed to slow them down. A large group engaged me at first, hoping to slay me, but the leader was smart. He set five of his best swordsmen to keep me busy and sent the others on after you. I took several more cuts, but managed to kill all five. By the time I hobbled to my house, you had gone. I took some time to care for my wounds and extract the arrow from my leg. Luckily it was just a sharpened tip and not a broadhead. It's going to take some time yet to fix my house, however."

He pulled slightly on her paw. Her heart soared with the hope that he might embrace her, but he did not. He restrained himself and gave her paw a gentle squeeze instead.

"I'm sorry for that, and your injuries. It was never my intention to bring this damage down on you."

"You have nothing to apologize for, Marquiese," she said quietly, shaking her head. "I knew your secret was dangerous, and I knew the bandits were looking for you. I chose to protect you. I am a protector, and that is what I live for. It is not something you can control or apologize for."

"I made the choice to stay, even though I knew the risks were increasing," he insisted. "If it weren't for you, I would not have survived. I cannot thank you enough for that. But tell me, how did you know help was coming to your house?"

"The Phantom."

"Wait, that's who you were signaling, wasn't it? When you waved your bow above your head. She was out there, wasn't she? Risking her life just like you were. You and she used whistles and signals to work together without alerting the bandits to your locations. Who is she?"

"I've already told you, if you listened closely."

Marquiese stopped and thought for a moment. He absently brushed his claw across the back of her paw and sent a thrill up her arm that she had to fight down. "The girl from the brick manor? The one who went crazy after her family was murdered? You said you taught her to live again, and then sent her away. But she ran away from her relation." His face cleared as he realized what the rest of the story was. "She came back to you and you raised her. That's how you knew she had never set foot back into the brick manor. You trained her to be a bandit hunter so she could take revenge?"

"No, not revenge. I had already killed the bandits that caused Zara, and myself, so much pain. I trained her so that she has a purpose, a reason to live. Just as Zariff had trained me."

He sat and contemplated her for a long moment still holding her paw gently. She watched him patiently, but then dropped her eyes.

"What will you do now?" she asked quietly.

"I sent a letter to my father in Maefair. Preparations are under way for me to return home."

"As you say, so shall it be," Marilana replied simply.

"Is that all you have to say?" Marquiese asked, a note of hurt edging his voice, his grip tightening on her paw.

"What else can I say?" Marilana replied calmly, meeting his eyes again. "You must go home, Marquiese. You will never be safe unless you face your pursuer, whoever that might be. I can no longer keep you safe. Maefair is your home. It is where you belong. It is where your father is. That is your world. Your life awaits you there, even if there are dangers to be faced. There is nothing for you here."

"My friends are not nothing."

"Of course not," the lioness said kindly. "And because I am your friend, I must insist that you leave."

Marquiese started to protest, but stopped himself and nodded.

"I know you are right," he said finally. "You have been the best friend I could have asked for. I thank you for that."

He let go of her paw and turned away from her. Trying not to let the hurt consume her, she picked up her satchel and left the room.

*

Two days later Marilana was dressed in Lady Annabella's livery and dusting the entry hall when Zariff entered the main doors. He said, "Marilana, run up to Lady Annabella's rooms and tell her the carriage is waiting please."

Marilana curtseyed quickly and hurried up the stairs. As she rounded the corner, she noticed that the door to Lady Annabella's suites was cracked open. She moved closer and heard voices. She had never been one to eavesdrop, but the words she caught chilled her to the bone and she edged closer to hear more.

"He will kill you as soon as he can," Lady Annabella insisted. "He has been seducing the enemies of your family. You allowed him three years unopposed to strengthen his position."

"I have learned much in my time here," Marquiese replied calmly. "I am not the little cub he remembers. I will give him cause to be wary."

"I am not saying your time here did not have its advantages," Lady Annabella countered. "I have seen the changes in you. Only one of those years was required. Now you must regain your reputation. I have done what I can to keep the loyal nobles faithful to you, but it was very hard to do so without letting them know I knew where you were."

"You have done admirably, Lady Annabella. My father and I are grateful for everything you have done on our behalf. And I admit you are correct, I have delayed too long. I will have to be extra careful not to present an opportunity for him to strike at me directly." Marquiese said soothingly.

"The bandit hunters and my scouts have still not been able to find who was giving the orders for the bandits to search for you. I am sure he was funding and directing the search, but he has not left Maefair. He must have an accomplice working with the bandits."

"Once I leave, the bandits will know of it, and will stop searching the province. It will be business as usual, and since Marilana will not be guarding me, you will be able to send her where you will."

"Marilana has to finish her schooling. I will not be sending her out on hunts if I can avoid it."

"If it were not for her I would have died or been found much sooner."

"Yes. Marilana deserves to know the truth, and it would be best if she heard it from you directly. Will you not reconsider telling her before you leave?" Lady Annabella asked in exasperation.

"Will you tell her your plan?" Marquiese countered firmly.

"She is not ready yet," replied Lady Annabella.

"Then I will tell her my secret when she is ready," Marquiese said calmly. "Promise me you will send her to me when it is time."

"I cannot promise that," Lady Annabella sighed. "I cannot promise she will not find out about your secret by then. It will be a difficult year for her, and I will act as I see best for everyone involved."

"She will have to face many changes, but she is strong. She will survive and flourish," Marquiese said fondly. "Please, Lady Annabella, let me repay her friendship."

"I will try, but the future is not set in stone," Lady Annabella conceded. "The carriage should be ready by now—"

Marilana backed quickly down the hall and out of sight. She took a calming breath. When she heard the door close, she then retraced her steps. Lady Annabella and Marquiese had just turned down the hall and were starting toward her.

"Excuse me, My Lady," Marilana said with a curtsey. "The carriage is ready and waiting."

"Very well, Marilana. Stay safe while I am away," Lady Annabella said firmly.

"I will. Safe journey, My Lady," Marilana replied.

Lady Annabella continued down the hall while Marquiese and Marilana stood within arms distance of one another, Marilana kept her eyes demurely on the floor.

"Safe journey, Marquiese," Marilana said with another curtsey.

"Marilana," Marquiese said hesitantly. "I will write to you. You are my truest friend, and I do not wish to lose your friendship. I promise to write. And to Earek too. I ... I'll never forget you."

Marilana hesitated, and then looked up into his earnest green eyes.

"I do not know what dangers await you in Maefair," she said quietly. "I do know that you are much better trained now than when you first came to the Southern Tip. Please, be vigilant."

"I will be extra watchful since you will not be there to guard my back," he replied with a small smile.

"Farewell, my friend. Until we meet again," Marilana uttered the traditional words solemnly.

"Until we meet again," he echoed.

He strode off down the hall, and Marilana watched him disappear around the corner. She went to the window overlooking the stableyard and watched as Marquiese climbed into Lady Annabella's carriage. She watched the escort form up. Finally the carriage rolled out of the gates and she felt like part of her went with it.

Merchant Colbran's two wagons fell in behind them. Marilana caught sight of Lida riding on the seat between her parents; how she would miss the young lioness. Colbran's wagons would leave Lady Annabella's escort once they got into the northern provinces and the scouts were sure they were free of pursuit. They had left all of their merchant guards behind and would hire new ones once they relocated, guards who knew nothing of the young lion who had lived with them for three years in the Southern Tip.

Merchant Colbran and his family were starting a new life of their own, a life without deception and restriction. She wished them the best of luck.

Marilana's attention returned to Lady Annabella's carriage, and her eyes followed it up the road and around the bend. She remained at the window until long after the sun set, staring north toward Maefair, her world far emptier than it had been just hours before.

Appendix

Note on Time

The world in which Redsands is located varies slightly from our own planet of Earth. In Redsands, they have 24 hours in a day, but as most people cannot afford to own a clock, the daily schedule is based on the position of the sun in the sky. This system works fairly well as the difference in amount of daylight between summer and winter is only two hours. The clocks are therefore calibrated at High Noon when the sun reaches its highest point in the sky, also called its zenith. So the difference between High Noon and the common noon, is only a difference in language. However, how a person uses language can give clues about the individual. Most of the population uses dawn, dusk, and noon as references for the time of day. Those who are accustomed to clocks will measure in hours before or after these references.

When compared to a clock, the exact time of dawn and dusk changes throughout the year, but the daily schedule still uses these points as references since many activities require light. Candles, lanterns, and oil lamps can provide light for some activities, but candles and lamp oil are considered luxuries due to their expense, and are used sparingly by most. Other time-of-day references used to indicate passage of time include mid-morning, mid-afternoon, and midnight. Trackers, scouts, bandits, peasants, and others who spend much of their time in the outdoors can learn to measure the passage of time by watching the change of the length and direction of shadows or the movement of the stars and moon.

Note on Calendar

Redsands has a year consisting of 390 days. The year is broken into 13 months of 30 days each. Each month has 6 fifnights of 5 days, making 78 fifnights per year. The first day of the fifnight is called Restday, and every month starts on a Restday. The rest of the days of the fifnight are indicated by counting from Restday. School is held for the local children four days a fifnight for ten months, excluding three months of summer break and two fifnights for the New Year. Children attending school may also indicate the day of fifnight by indicating the day of the school fifnight. So the third day of the fifnight could also be indicated as the second day after Restday, or the second day of the school fifnight. Calendars, like clocks are a luxury not found in most homes. Months are indicated in reference to important annual events and the changing of the seasons. Each season is three months plus seven days with an equinox day at the beginning of spring and fall. Specific events are indicated by telling what day of the fifnight and how many fifnights or months before or after a reference day.

List of Important Days

*All days referenced by month from New Year for consistency of this list.

New Year—1st day of 1st month (start of 2nd month of winter)

School resumes after New Year break—2nd day of 3rd fifnight after New Year

Spring Equinox—8th day of 3rd month

First day of Spring—day after Spring Equinox

Last day of school year (Exhibition Dance)—last day of 5th month

First day of Summer—Restday of 4th fifnight of 6th month

National Day of Worship—Restday of 2nd fifnight of 7th month

First day of school year—2nd day of 1st fifnight of 9th month

Fall Equinox—3rd day of 5th fifnight of 9th month

First day of Fall—day after Fall Equinox

Annual Tournament in Maefair—4th day of 6th fifnight of 12th month

Tournament Ball—day after tournament, last day of 12th month

First day of Winter—1st day of 13th month

Winter Council in Maefair—last day of year, last day of 13th month

Last day of school for New Year break—last day of year

Note on Rank

Rank in Redsands is determined by birth and by merit. Birth determines caste: peasant, low-class merchant, mid-class merchant, high-class merchant, landed-gentry, noble, high-noble, great-noble, royal. Adoption and marriage are the primary ways to gain a higher caste. Disowning from family and abdication of duty will result in a drop in caste. When a non-heir child comes of age, they drop in caste unless they marry an heir to a caste title. Marriage grants the rights of the higher caste heir; these rights remain if widowed, but are lost in cases of divorce.

Rank within caste is determined by merit. Respect and common consensus are the currency of rank. In the peasant caste there is very little change in rank from orphans at the lowest to upper servants at the highest. Peasant rank is determined by wealth and hired position; these can be very fluid, causing drastic shifts in very short time. Successful farmers who own lots of land and upper servants who oversee other servants garnering the highest wages are granted the highest rank. With the merchant caste, the rank is a reflection of wealth and position on the Merchant Council. Possession of a Family name is a token of respect from the royal family and grants higher rank. The ability to maintain financial wealth influences the respect of the community and can grant higher rank as well. With the noble castes, from landed-gentry to great-noble, rank is granted by size of land governed and by respect from other nobles and the royal family.

The soldier class works within and outside the caste system. Soldiers are treated with respect according to rank, but are not granted the rights of the castes. For example, an officer (Lieutenant, Major, Captain, etc.) may speak up in public and attend gatherings as an equal to the merchant caste. However, an officer is only granted the rights of land ownership equal to a peasant and are not able to speak to the Merchant Council regarding laws or leadership. All of the children of soldiers of any rank are considered peasants.

Rank among soldiers is granted by merit alone. All soldier recruits start out as simple guardsmen. As they prove themselves worthy, they can be promoted. Officers are treated with the respect granted to the merchant castes. Knights of the Realm are treated with the respect granted to the noble castes. Soldiers must have a liege to whom they owe allegiance and from whom they take orders. Knights of the Realm can be soldiers or can be individuals of any caste, but they must accept the leadership and regulations of the Brotherhood of Knights to claim the title of Knight. Those who have proven themselves through competition of arms are granted the highest ranks. For example, Zariff is a Knight of the Realm who won many competitions and who has proven himself a very capable officer by gaining the position of Captain-General, he is therefore treated with respect equal to a great-noble, but is only granted the rights of property ownership equal to a peasant.

Characters Around Mystillion

Marilana—mair-ih-lain-ah—[lioness] bandit hunter known as The Ghost and ward of Lady Annabella Ranat. Rank: noble ward, equal to landed-gentry noble, but this is ignored, treated as orphan, lowest of peasant caste.

Annabella Ranat—ann-ah-bell-ah ra-nat—[lioness] The province of the Southern Tip is ruled by the Great-Noble Family Ranat. Lady Annabella Ranat is the only member of the family. Rank: great-noble, highest of noble caste.

Zariff—zär-əf—[lion] commander of all Southern Tip troops in service to Lady Annabella, and a Knight of the Realm. Also Marilana's trainer and mentor. Rank: Captain-General in soldier class, equal to great-noble.

Branth—branth—[coyote] commander of the Home Guard, protecting Lady Annabella's estates and the county and town of Mystillion (mis-til-yən), over which Lady Annabella rules directly. Rank: Captain in soldier class, equal to high-noble.

Dera—də-rah—[coyote] daughter of Captain Branth and Marilana's friend. Training to become Lady Annabella's librarian. Rank: peasant.

Bila—bil-ah—[puma] Lady Annabella's aged librarian. Rank: peasant.

Magus—ma-gəs—[cheetah] Lady Annabella's Head Healer. Rank: mid-class merchant.

Hosten—hōs-ten—[cheetah] Lady Annabella's Head Horse Trainer. Rank: mid-class merchant.

Vikal—vī-kal—[antelope] Lady Annabella's Chamberlain. Rank: high ranking high-class merchant.

Marquiese—mär-kwēs—[lion] posing as first son to Colbran. Rank: high ranking high-class merchant heir.

Colbran—kōl-bran—[lion] high-class merchant attempting to establish precious ore trade in Mystillion. Rank: high ranking high-class merchant.

Adealy—ä-də-lē—[lioness] wife of Colbran, mother of Lida. Rank: high ranking high-class merchant.

Lida—lī-dah—[lioness] daughter of Colbran. Rank: high ranking high-class merchant daughter.

Brittia—brit-tē-ah—[lynx] daughter of Sleater. Rank: highest ranking high-class merchant heir in Mystillion.

Sleater—slē-tər—[lynx] established textile merchant, leader of Mystillion Merchant Council. Rank: highest ranking high-class merchant in Mystillion.

Corlda—còrl-dah—[lynx] wife of Sleater, mother of Brittia. Rank: high ranking high-class merchant.

Ceta—sē-tah—[lynx] sister of Sleater, Mystillion school headmistress. Rank: mid ranking high-class merchant.

Demdrake—dem-drāke—[lynx] first son of high-class Merchant Branish, also Corlda's nephew. Rank: high ranking high-class merchant heir of Bram's Fen.

Earek—air-ik—[rare black leopard] second son of Yulan. Rank: high ranking high-class merchant son.

Yulan—ū-lan—[leopard] established tailor. Rank: second highest high-class merchant in Mystillion.

Xyta—zī-tah—[leopard] wife of Yulan, mother to Adrek, Earek, and Jarek. Rank: high ranking high-class merchant.

Adrek—ā-drik—[leopard] first son of Yulan. Rank: high ranking high-class merchant heir.

Jarek—jər-ik—[leopard] third son of Yulan. Rank: high ranking high-class merchant son.

Kalan—ka-lan—[blue fox] Mystillion town herb dealer, aids all sick and injured creatures. Rank: mid-class merchant.

Rose—rōz—[horse] teacher at Mystillion school, tutor to Marilana. Rank: peasant.

Caton—ka-tän—[silver fox] first son of a high ranking mid-class glass blower. Rank: high ranking mid-class merchant heir.

Klay—klā—[black bear] first son of a low ranking high-class blacksmith. Rank: low ranking high-class merchant heir.

Zara—zar-ah—[deer] also called Child and Phantom, orphan trained to become a bandit hunter by Marilana. Rank: orphan peasant.

Other School Children: Vavinta—[leopard] mid ranking high-class daughter of Merchant Nartol, Estala—[gazelle] low ranking high-class merchant, Chiely—[deer] low-class merchant, Wahlan—[deer] mid-class merchant spinster, Enib—[grey wolf] low-class merchant, Jasmine—[horse] mid-class merchant, Jeof—[leopard] low-class merchant, Diof—[zebra] low ranking high-class merchant, Skilt—[grey wolf] mid ranking high-class merchant, Yeshib—high ranking high-class merchant, Grenvit—mid ranking high-class merchant, Abzak—mid ranking high-class merchant, Natly—[jaguarundi] peasant, Jenra—peasant, Elza—peasant.

Others Around Lady Annabella's Estates: Taslin—[tigress] peasant servant, Shaub—[grey wolf] guardsman in solder class, equal to peasant.

Arndt Family: [jaguars all] The province of Grudent (grü-dent) is ruled by the Great-Noble Family Arndt (ärnt). The Arndt Family includes Lord Armen (är-men) Arndt, Lady Frena (frē-nah), family heir Frederick (fre-drik), non-heir son Warhaim (wòr-hām), and non-heir daughter Graita (gra-ē-tah). Master Arndt and Master Warhaim ride with the Knights of the Realm.

Knights of the Realm: Master Clain—[puma] great-noble heir of Abdshar province, Master Suwark—[lion] high-noble heir of Cormorant Creek county in Pavlatach province, Master Roatal—[jaguar] high-noble heir of Pandensy county in Versith province, Sir Orthan—[jaguar] high-noble non-heir son of Roatal Family of Pandensy county in Versith province, Sir Tavin—[eland] high-noble heir of Breltic Family of Coal Bend county in West Cove province, Sir Fasub—[tiger] nephew of Noble Family Dredgan of Mantalor town in Herinsford province, Sir Graduin—[red wolf] former merchant son from Glancenar province.

Named Bandits: Vax [badger], Nort [weasel], Victon [jaguar], Brute [grizzly bear], Trol [jackal]

Working Animals: Storm—Lady Annabella's white stallion war horse trained by Marilana, only accepts Annabella and Marilana as riders. Snow—Lady Annabella's elderly white mare riding horse, dame of Storm, one of Marilana's favorites.

Acknowledgments

This book would not have been possible without the help and support of so many people. First I must mention my wonderful husband who has supported and encouraged me and has been my most solid sounding board. Next I must mention my sons for always reminding me that there is more life to live. And my family for loving me no matter what comes of my endeavors.

I am thankful for my editor, Mark, for encouraging me to make my story my own while still changing it to make it better. Thanks to Deanna for being detail oriented enough to bring this book to a fine polish, and Kathy for capturing some of those details in color.

I cannot leave out the most important helpers, David, Jaydine, and Zachary, my wonderful beta readers. Without whose help I could not have seen this book from a readers perspective. Thank You all for all you have done to make this endeavor what it is.

About IA Mullin

IA Mullin grew up on a farm in rural Colorado. She helped raise crops and cattle. She learned the value of hard work and fostered a love of animals. She went to Colorado State University to further her interests in animals and science. She graduated with a Bachelor's degree in Zoology. Next, she attended Front Range Community College and attained the status of Certified Veterinary Technician with an Associate's degree in Veterinary Technology. She has worked as a kennel cleaner, vet assistant, and vet tech, with various veterinary offices, the Larimer Humane Society, and volunteered with the Rocky Mountain Raptor Program, a rehabilitation center. She has raised cattle and pygmy goats. She loves all kinds of pets as well as nature and the outdoors.

In 2010, she chose to leave the veterinary field in order to raise her family. She began to write in earnest at that time. She had started her first manuscript as a freshman in high school, but had only written in her spare time as a hobby. Now as a mother of two active boys, she has founded Avio Publishing, LLC and is very excited about being included in the ranks of independent publishers and authors.

"It's been a long journey to this point, but I don't regret any step of it. It has lead me to understand that imagination is the substance of creation. If I can imagine it, I can create it, at least on paper." ~IA Mullin

Forthcoming Titles

Maefair

Marquiese survived his stay in Mystillion only by the skill of his friend Marilana. He left the Southern Tip to return home to his true life in the royal city, Maefair. He must confront the dangerous people responsible for sending bandits to hunt him, however his enemies are also laying their own carefully hidden plans. By the time Marquiese contacts his friends, Marilana's reputation and Earek's social standing have taken some drastic turns.

Can Marilana and Earek come to terms with Marquise's secret identity?

Can they overcome Marquiese's enemies with their friendships intact?

The story continues in Maefair, Redsands Book2.

Redsands

The Kingdom of Redsands stands on the precipice of disaster. Outside forces are aiming to eliminate the royal family and throw the kingdom into chaos. Marilana, intelligent and deadly, has chosen the path to defend her homeland, her family, and her friends. Unfortunately her enemies are aware of her intentions and plan to render her skills useless. In order to survive, Marilana will need Marquiese and Earek more than ever before. Marquiese, however, is entangled in his own feelings of betrayal and loss. If the friends are to save the kingdom and themselves, they will have to push the bounds of skill, compassion, patience, and trust.

Can Marquiese sort out his feelings before all is lost?

Can the friends overcome the greatest threats they have yet faced?

Will they face the future together or fail in the last steps?

Find out how the story ends in Redsands, Redsands Book 3.

Learn More

The world of the Redsands and other worlds yet to be explored are waiting to interact with visitors at magewood.com the internet home of IA Mullin. Come learn more about IA Mullin, her worlds, and upcoming projects. See color maps, read short stories, and join other fans on the Mages of Magewood forum. Sign up for the Mages of Magewood email notifications for future releases, events, and special deals.

If you enjoyed this story, please leave a review or comments wherever you purchased your copy, and encourage other readers to join your experience.

You, the readers, make these worlds come to life and sustain them.

Thank You